Praise for *The Keepers of Truth*

"Michael Collins's new novel displays
and intelligence. Collins is one of tho
is consistently provocative and daring, while also managing to
draw the reader hypnotically along. *The Keepers of Truth*
is a bravura performance, headlong and muscular, and
a delightfully tongue-in-cheek look not only at small-town
America but also the intricacies of the human spirit.
—Colum McCann, author of *This Side of Brightness*

"The best book I've read this year. Prose throbbing to the
rhythm of Auden's "Night Mail" script, but with serrated
razor wire as cutting edge. Unputdownable."
—*Time Out London*

"Michael Collins is a fine writer who brilliantly captures
the incestuousness of small-town existence and
the slow death of a community."
—*The London Times*

"Thought provoking and wildly entertaining."
—Justine Ettler, *The Observer* (London)

"With the maturing style of this novel, Michael Collins has
bridled the voice of the malcontent and has produced
something that is rare enough in contemporary Irish fiction:
a well-written and socially conscientious novel."
—*The London Times Literary Supplement*

"Collins creates a gripping picture of slow-moving,
small-time life, and packs it into a treat of a murder mystery."
—*The Guardian* (London)

"*The Keepers of Truth* is an arrestingly mature novel, the work
of a writer who has left rawness behind and is examining an
entire country's mood and mania with an adult sensibility."
—*The Globe and Mail*

"One of the great things about *The Keepers of Truth* is that,
though it is set in early 1980s USA, it is both an historical
novel and a grimly prophetic one about anywhere."
—*Sunday Tribune* (London)

The Keepers of Truth

A Novel

MICHAEL COLLINS

UNIVERSITY OF IOWA PRESS | IOWA CITY

University of Iowa Press, Iowa City 52242
Copyright © 2000 by Michael Collins
First University of Iowa Press edition, 2021
uipress.uiowa.edu
Printed in the United States of America

Cover design by Erin Kirk New
Text design by Colin Joh

Printed on acid-free paper

Library of Congress Cataloging–in–Publication Data
Names: Collins, Michael, 1964– author.
Title: The Keepers of Truth: a novel / Michael Collins.
Description: Iowa City, Iowa: University of Iowa Press, [2021]|
Identifiers: LCCN 2021028017 | ISBN 9781609388041 (paperback)
Classification: LCC PR6053.O4263 K44 2021 | DDC 823/.914—dc23
LC record available at https://lccn.loc.gov/2021028017

Dedicated to my parents and my wife

SPECIAL THANKS TO

Michael Anania

Rich Frantz

William O'Rourke

Dan and Judith Wesley

Richard Napora

(The cats) Spike, Jasper and Wicklow

The Keepers
of Truth

CHAPTER 1

I call this one "Ode to a Trainee Manager."
   When you enter this town of ours, I would want you to read the following, to enlighten you as to how it is here with us at this time in history. It seems only right. Even in medieval times they used to put up signs that said, "Plague! Keep Out."

   This is what I'd say . . .

   We have made nothing in this town in over a decade. It's as though a plague befell our men, as horrible as any of the plagues that fell on Egypt. Our men used to manufacture cars, sheet metal, mobile homes, washers and dryers, frame doors, steel girders for bridges and skyscrapers. Our town had contracts from Sears and Ford and General Motors. Everybody worked in the factories, bending metal into the shape of car fenders, gaskets, engine blocks, distributor caps, sewing vinyl seats for Cadillacs and Continentals. We had hands throbbing to make things. Factories were our cathedrals, pushed up out of the Great Plains.

   The din of sound, the subterranean rumble of machinery, filled our consciousness once upon a time. You would have felt the buffeted sound of hammers in our encasement of snow when winter gripped us, locked away from the world outside, making things as snow fell heavy across the plains, isolating us. Our furnaces bled against the snow, a crucible of fire amid the plains. There was peace, then, and security, all of us moving under the bowls of streetlights on ploughed streets, proceeding slowly home in our cars, exhausted, as the machines of our existence ate the night shift. You'd have seen the slow trundle of trains full of gleaming cars we had built snaking out to the great cities on the East and West Coasts.

If you happened to come upon us in the summer scorch, you would have seen our men in stained yellow T-shirts, dripping sweat, eating down by the river from steel lunch boxes, guzzling ice-cold Coca-Cola or buckets of cold beer. You would have seen the way they used to drag their forearms across their mouths with easy satisfaction, rise and stretch and walk the factory yards, smoking in long, deep pulls. You might have heard the pop of a bat at the lunch break, our men out in the fields behind the factories rounding bases, sending balls over the brownstone perimeter of our existence. There was cheap beer in the dark shade of run-down bars for men who needed it, and an allotment of whores down by the vast labyrinth of viaducts and foundry cooling pools. We had a chocolate factory, too, where our young women in confectionery hats pasted fudge and caramel drops and taffy brittle on wax baking sheets. You would have come across them smoking against the blackened brownstone walls, pale ghosts covered in flour. They had that luxurious odor of cocoa and cinnamon ingrained into their pores.

And on a warm summer's night, you would have found us in the collective destiny of a drive-in movie, us in our machines in the humid air of summer heat; heard the shrill cries of the drive-in mesh speaker filling our heads with the horror of living in the Cold War, as giant ants from a nuclear holocaust attacked New York City.

It had a perpetual motion, this town of ours, compact and inexhaustible, self-sustaining, the eternal stoking of furnaces went night and day with us in splendid isolation, the keepers of industrialism. You would have believed, like us, that the means of production would never stop ticking, but you would have been wrong.

Our factories by the river are abandoned now, windows smashed, sprouting tufts of grass through collapsed roofs. We are at war with ourselves in the greatest calamity our nation has ever faced. We kill each other in deals gone wrong, in a black market of drugs plied in the shadow of our abandoned cathedrals. Our adolescents slink amid these ruins, scale the chain-link fences, rip the copper piping from the factories, sell it. Rusting fire escapes lead to stairways to oblivion and darkness. There are prehistoric-looking machines dragged out into yards, cannibalized of anything of worth, carcasses of industrialism. Our daughters spread their legs on shop floors where once our men pounded steel. We are encircled by cornfields, hemmed in by crops that it doesn't pay to grow anymore. The commodities exchange has gone to hell. There are butter mountains and wheat mountains, rotting stockpiles of food that need to be destroyed because of overproduction and bottoming prices.

We are now a town of trainee managers. Oh, happy are ye that inherit the deep-fat fryer! What we do now is eat. It has become our sole occupation, our idle hands have found something to take hold of. We take hold of burgers, mostly, in a carnivorous display of sublimated longing for our dead machines. We have McDonald's, Burger King, Arby's, Hardee's, Dairy Queen, Shakey's, Big Boy, Ponderosa, Denny's, International House of Pancakes . . .

Not that you'll ever read this on any signpost outside our town. I've been writing that requiem for years. It was a piece I wrote in journalism class. Ever since I joined the *Daily Truth* last year, I've been trying to slide it into an article. I've been polishing that bit of philosophy like my old man used to polish his '62 Olds. I've been trying that philosophy on for size like women change dresses. I kind of sneak it into conversations down at bars, or at career day at the local junior college. It's like looking at the innards of my own consciousness, that philosophy of mine, a hemorrhage of memory, the entrails of feeling, all raw and bloody. Last year I thought, hell, it can go into the town's time capsule, but my editor, Sam Perkins, this fat irascible asshole, took me back into his office and chewed my ass real good. He said, "We got a history that ain't about words in this town." And this from the goddamn editor of our local newspaper . . . " 'A history that ain't about words.' Jeez almighty!" I just had to shake my head. What they put in that time capsule was parts of a washing machine, a sewing machine, fenders and steering wheels, tires, a switching mechanism from the old railway yard, and a baseball hat from the local UAW, among other things. They

buried them in this sealed crate and then covered it over down
near the baseball diamond out on County Road Five. Sam Perkins
says, "Language changes. It ain't worth a damn. But this here is the
immutable architecture of our past, the machines of our age." He
said that to the people gathered there around the pit. Sam's the
editor primarily because he knows words like *immutable*, and
because he presses the flesh like a politician. He is the *Truth* in this
town, at least he was, once upon a time. Sometimes I call him the
Truth behind his back. I'll say things like, "The *Truth* has spoken.
You must accept the *Truth*."

See, we're fighting a losing battle here in our town. Sam's taken
me aside over the last few months. He says, "Circulation ain't
worth a damn." I like that word, *circulation*, the analogy to blood. It
hints at what we once were. "I'll be damned if this folds . . . ," he
says when he's drunk. I already have the final headline in my
head—PAPER FOLDS.

I still mess with that essay of mine when there's nothing to do,
when I'm stuck at my desk waiting for the AP wire to feed some
lifeline into the paper that must now be filled each day. We don't
have a war, so it makes my job hard. I kind of wish we had a war. We
have lots of good kids here who could die beautiful, patriotic
deaths. Shit, you have to miss Vietnam from a journalistic point of
view. But things are more insidious now. It's not hard to find casualties, what's hard is to get people to admit they *are* casualties. It's
hard to get them to admit there's a war going on. I tried that line,
just like I said it there, the "It's not hard to find casualties, what's
hard is to get people to admit they *are* casualties," down at Lakeview Junior College Career Day assembly, and Dean Holton just
about shit his pants. I was shouting into the microphone. "You ever
wonder about Japanese cars, the names they give them—Accord,
Cressida, Corolla. It's like the Japs are only getting into the English
alphabet, like they're just learning the ABCs." Dean Holton got
the school band to start playing right over me there in the audito-
rium. Three cheerleaders flipping across the stage raised an uproarious cheer that I like to think was for me, but it wasn't. You know,

maybe Sam Perkins is right about language not being worth a damn. The Japanese speak a language of equations and numbers. Two plus two will always be goddamn four.

I get away with all this here in the town because nobody wants my job. The *Truth* really serves as a repository for the court systems to file public notices. My grandfather, the ice monster, started the paper, as he started much of the social fabric of this town, years ago when he made his fortune selling ice, hacking out blocks of ice for all the homes in town and out on the farms. Then he got in on the ground floor of refrigeration units. Made a fortune all over again. His legacy still hasn't melted. And there's the house he left behind, a mansion really. It's what brought me back home, the anchor of my heritage.

Television is where it's at these days. The written word is dead. They got this Linda Carter doing *Eyewitness News*. She's got legs that go to the ceiling. She's the new town oracle, with these lips that were made for sucking cock. Hell, even I watch her, the enemy. She's always on location. The town is just a backdrop for her radiance.

Sam's scared shitless we're going under. "I want to retire with dignity," is what he says. He gets all shaky sometimes. He says softly, "You know I'm dying, Bill. I got the cancer inside me," but that's pretty much bullshit. He's lost. He wishes there was something that would kill him. He drinks warm bourbon late into the night behind the bubbled glass of his editor's office. He keeps this banker's lamp burning all night. Down below us is the old foundry works, a scaffold of towers and walkways covered in rusting sheet metal, a labyrinth of massive snaking pipes and chimney stacks that have done no work in ages. Sam's taken me to the window at night, surveyed the nightmare. Down there in the yard is where most of the drug deals go down. It's where you get sucked off at night. "Right under our goddamn noses," is what he says in his shaky voice. He wears this typesetter's leather cap sometimes when he gets all weepy. "We need a scoop!" is what he says, just shaking his head. There aren't any scoops left, not here anyway. His father,

Jasper Perkins, ran the paper for years. I know this story ad nauseam. Blah, blah blah . . . What I'd like to say about him in his obituary is—THE TRUTH IS DEAD.

All I'm left with is creating postscripts to a dead town that I hash out in full-page spreads for the Auxiliary Firemen's Wives' charity bakeoff. The bakeoff is the story we're going to lead with for tomorrow's edition. I was thinking of a headline—AUXILIARY FIREMEN'S WIVES SELL THEIR BUNS FOR CHARITY—but, shit, you can't slide anything by Sam Perkins. Maybe in a hundred years someone's going to read my article on the bakeoff, and they're going to understand just how fucked things got here in our town in the late twentieth century. That's the thing about language, all right, you have to deconstruct its meaning, you have to decode Auxiliary Firemen's Wives' Bakeoff into an almighty fucking roar of despair.

And then comes a call from Pete Morris down at the police station on West Twelfth. We go way back to elementary school. He said, "We got a situation, Bill," which is something he never used to say. It was just something they said on cop shows, "a situation," but now, when Pete calls, it's always about "a situation." I'd been thinking about writing an editorial about that, about the accretion of new words into our subconscious, but I've been having to write up too many goddamn bakeoffs to get any real work of my own done.

Pete said, "You know that Ronny Lawton, that troublemaker out on Pine and Sixteenth?"

I said, "Yeah, what about him, Pete?"

"I'll tell you what about him. He just called in a missing person's on his father," Pete said. "Looks like it might be time to drag the river."

I said, "Pete, jeez almighty, you got anything more definite than that? I'm leading with the Auxiliary Firemen's Wives' Bakeoff for tomorrow's edition. You have to come up with a body to get that off page one."

CHAPTER 2

On the ten o'clock news, Linda Carter was live outside the county courthouse. I was putting finishing touches to the bakeoff article. I worked this lopsided schedule, the long hours into the night, an induced misanthropy. Sometimes I wish I had no past, no inheritance. There's no reason a guy like me should be prostituting his genius to a dump like this.

Ed Hoskin was down in the darkroom developing prints. We had less than an hour lead time to get things to press. I had gambled and lost big on the Ronny Lawton story.

I had the small black-and-white television on my desk and the police dispatch hissing in the background. They were sealing off the Lawton house. The sound bites were coming in all evening. Ronny Lawton was in for questioning. There was footage of him surrounded by three troopers leading him into the courthouse for questioning. He was in a baseball hat and T-shirt. They kept looping that footage into every commercial break. "Linda Carter has the latest on this breaking story at ten o'clock." She was out at the Lawtons' property one minute, she was out at his old high school the next, she was outside the county courthouse live. She was omnipresent, a destiny spliced together.

Sam Perkins called and roared that things were heating up down at the county courthouse. "Forget the goddamn bakeoff. You're not still working on that bakeoff?"

"I'm just about to put it to bed, Sam."

"Forget the goddamn bakeoff." He was really pissed. He went into this speech about how you've got to have a nose for a story. How I didn't have it. How I was a goddamn ass. How my college degree wasn't worth shit. "You don't send a pig to college to snuff out truffles." I just held the phone away from my ear. I was trying to come up with a way to describe the airy lightness of Mrs. Polski's sponge cake delight from the bakeoff. I was looking for that one metaphor to end things. I was like a dog with a meatless bone, gnawing at marrow.

Ed Hoskin already had a grainy blowup of Ronny Lawton in his hands when he came into my office. I put my hand over the phone. "Wasn't Ronny in the Rifle Club? Check the yearbook again, Ed. This is getting bigger all the time."

Sam was still bitching when the ten o'clock news came on, a panoramic shot of the courthouse. I could see Sam there on the television shouting into the phone at me. That was my idea of irony, the story from within the story, but all I said was, "Sam. Sam, listen to me. What do you want me to run? We got less than an hour." I was speaking to his image on the television. Then the camera left him and found Linda Carter on the steps of the courthouse. I had the volume down. They cut to the footage of Ronny Lawton in a T-shirt and baseball cap surrounded by three state troopers. It was the same shit they'd shown all night.

Sam shouted into the phone, "I'm sending a guy over with the transcript of the phone calls from Ronny Lawton about his old man's disappearance. Run that verbatim, you hear that?"

I mean, there was nothing definite yet about any murder, but somehow, Sam was going wild. I guess that's the kind of intuition I never had. I was still thinking bakeoff, but I said, "I got his senior-year shot from the yearbook all ready to go here. We can lead with that."

"Now you're thinking like a newspaper man."

It was the only thing I'd learned in college. You begin with the yearbook, that unequivocal moment of adolescence, and work from there. That's the moment of incarnation for any journalist's story, the shot from which all stories emanate.

I phoned Pete down at the station. He said, "Shit, have we got a developing situation. This ain't released yet, Bill, but the troopers found blood out at the Lawton place. This asshole did it. I seen him down in the interrogation room. He looks like he's going to crack."

"How much blood, Pete?"

"I don't know. I just heard one of them troopers talking is all. Forensics over in Kale County is going to run a test tomorrow morning."

I said, "Pete, we're under the gun here. I don't have shit to print. You think you could drop me over Ronny's rap sheet? We need it like yesterday, Pete. Ten minutes, Pete. That's all the time I got left."

"I already pulled it for you." He was silent for a moment. "Bill?"

"What?"

"This is probably nothing. We don't have access to birth and death certificates until tomorrow morning, but can you check your old papers for a death notice on Ronny's mother? Seems like she passed away round this time last year."

The line went dead in my ear. The crickets in the foundry yard filled the sudden silence. I don't quite get it, but there was this infusion of blood rushing through me. I mean, it was late as hell, a dead time when I usually turned away from the office for a slow night of watching the *Tonight Show* and falling asleep. Maybe it was some subconscious urge to rise out of the shit my life had become. I wasn't beyond becoming some vulture to pull away at some corpse if it came to it. I was shaking there at my desk, sweat running down the inside of my legs. I poured a strong black coffee, tasted the bitter tar. Outside there was a low rumble of thunder. I opened the blinds and let the downward rush of cool air pour into the office.

I went to the steel cabinet of old microfiche, found the spool from last year, pulled it through the feeder, and checked the old death notices. July 8. One year ago to the day. I looked at the date again. I suppose it depended on how you looked at things. It might have meant Ronny Lawton's father was out getting drunk in his wife's memory. It might have been nothing more than that really. If I'd had time, I'd have checked the graveyard. By now, the sky was flickering with lightning. Rain hissed outside the window. I felt myself brace for the onslaught of a storm, stood in the slash of a blue shard of light. The hair on my arms stood on end as a cannon blast of thunder hit.

There was one other interesting thing in Ronny Lawton's mother's obit. I got another roll of microfiche from 1970 to 1973, scanned through the Vietnam War years obits until I found what I was looking for.

A guy pulled up downstairs and came up with the transcript. I read it slowly. What was known was simply that Ronny Lawton filed a missing person's report on his father via telephone at 8 P.M., July 7. Ronny stated he'd left his job as a short-order cook at Denny's at around seven o'clock, went home to find nobody home, called the police, told them he wanted to file a report, then left to go night fishing at around nine o'clock. When he returned home this morning, he found his father's bed hadn't been slept in. That's when he says he got real concerned. He called again at about 9.30 A.M. and said, "My old man, he's missing, been missing since I called yesterday evening. I seen his bed. It wasn't slept in last night. I called yesterday 'bout this. He's gone. You hear me? How long does it take you assholes to realize he's missing?" There was no mention of his mother's anniversary. Maybe year four, five, six, you forget those things, but the first anniversary?

In the darkroom, Ed buzzed over the intercom. "You want to see what we're getting, Bill?"

"Sure."

This felt like work. I was smiling to myself. I was sort of hoping Ronny Lawton had killed his father.

Ed brought the apparition of Ronny Lawton into slow resolution. I was leaning over him in that sanguine light, him hunched over adding chemicals. "What you got there, Ed?" My breath was filled with the odor of coffee. I was jittery. I needed to piss real bad. "We need something quick."

"We're getting something." It was a hundred degrees in there, a small, dark box of trapped heat. Ed seemed to sift through layers of meaning, adding an alchemy of chemicals, bringing Ronny Lawton's face to the fore. I stared at Ronny Lawton, the disembodied head staring up from a tray, the culled yearbook photo. The jaw faded with more chemicals, the lips lost their fullness, the mouth became an austere slit. I said softly, "I just found out Ronny's mother died on this day last year." I was breathing down Ed's neck. I touched his arm, coaxed him, felt the flex of sinews under the skin panning the print for its hidden mystery. I said, "I got the rap sheet on him. Domestic violence. Ronny beat up his father." It triggered something deep in Ed's head, touched his gift, his clairvoyance. I whispered, "They found traces of blood at the scene, Pete was telling me. It's off with forensics in Kale County." Ed instinctively darkened the eyes, imbued an infinite blackness where there were once pupils, until there was nothing but a death mask of grim fatalism staring up at us.

I shouted, "That's it, Ed! Jesus Christ, Ed. That's exactly it!"

Ed put the print on a peg and hung it. We went out into the hallway, under the soft yellow of a hanging bulb, and smoked. His eyes were watering. His balding head shone with a veneer of sweat. We yawned and rubbed our faces. We had Ronny Lawton in there. We were both exhausted. Maybe we were out of touch with what it was like really to work against a deadline, to put something on paper that people just might read. I was shaking somewhat, from the coffee I suppose, and other things, things that it's not always a good idea to start into.

It had turned almost cold with the pull of rain outside. Flies clotted the hanging bulb in the hallway.

"It's like hearing a confession," Ed said. "I go in there, and they tell me stuff." He was pointing at himself, touching his breastbone.

He looked like a scaffold of bones, the skin drawn tight over his thin body. He had on chocolate-colored polyester trousers with a white belt, the sort of clothes older men wore in Florida these days. Somehow they didn't suit the severe look on his face, the grim regard he had for staring into things. I said, "You did good, Ed." I flicked ash onto the bare floor.

I was looking at Ed's hands like they were instruments.

"Before all that out there fell to shit, I was good, Bill. I used to do the features on the new car models. We had beauty queens from Detroit sent down here for photo sessions with executives, for year-end sales parties out on the riverboats. All high-class. People wanted to capture it all on film."

The hall led to a broken window, air sucking a curtain into the night, pulling the tendrils of smoke from our cigarettes. I said, "It's a gift, Ed. What you did in there."

Ed burped under his breath. His mouth got slack-jawed with bile that had come up. He seemed to hold the bile, got out a handkerchief, took it to his mouth, and let the bile out. Then he took out a small bottle of Pepto-Bismol, unscrewed the cap, and drank the pink antacid. I felt uncomfortable watching him, but it had become a ritual over the year I'd worked at the paper. Ed settled after that, stood quietly and let his tongue roam the dark of his mouth, cleaning his teeth. He looked at me again. His hands tried to grasp at something. He said softly, "I heard this once, 'A single death is a tragedy, a million deaths is a statistic.' Maybe that's what we got to do as reporters, find the single death."

Maybe it was something, way back then at the start of all this, that I remember most, the certainty, the knowing that just maybe Ronny Lawton's old man was dead. Sam and Ed had that gut feeling right from the start.

Thunder dimmed the lights for a moment, made us ghosts in the hallway. I felt the distant artillery of exploding rainburst clouds. Around us, the cornfields were drinking the rain. It was one of those storms that lets men breathe easy, a cleansing rain that gives reprieve from the droughts that have beset us over the years. It was a cold damp that made you shudder. Rain pooled on the wooden floor under the open window. And then I got to thinking that, out by the Lawton place, physical evidence was being washed away.

Ed was counting slowly inside his head, waiting for the image to settle. He said, "I wonder what his old man looked like, I mean, when he was a kid?"

I said, "I'll check his yearbook, Ed."

Ed went in again to the sanguine domain of the darkroom, shut me out. I heard the door lock click.

I went down the hall and left him alone, flicked my cigarette out the window into the dark, watched its brief comet flicker and fall away. I felt things unfolding outside, something malevolent, a dark angel opening its heavy wings into flight over the derelict shit of our dead existence. I felt this transfusion of meaning filling the emptiness inside me. The damp fungal grain, rotting in the silos from the old brewery, had a sour stink that filled our old office. If you listened on still nights you could hear the squeak of rats feasting in the abandoned belly of the sagging silos.

In my office, I sketched the page mock-up, copied the death notice from Ronny Lawton's mother's obit, got out a shot of old man Lawton, and just busied myself until Ed came over the intercom and shouted, "Bill, get this motherfucker out of my sight."

I called Pete one last time. There was nothing new. The storm had cut out power along the road going north, out by Ronny Lawton's place. Ronny Lawton was staying the night at the county jail. He'd submitted to a night's sleep, care of the county. Pete said that Ronny said, "Hell, if you're going to throw in breakfast, I might as well spend the night."

Pete said, "That sound like a guy who's grieving to you, Bill?"

I had it all ready for press, the transcripts of the filing of the missing person's and Ronny's police rap along with four shots, the rifle club shot, the yearbook graduation shot we'd manipulated, and the obituary on Ronny's mother, along with a photograph of her from her yearbook. I set Ronny's mother right at the heart of the page. Ronny Lawton's mother's face embodied something, like the innocence of soda fountains and bobby socks. She stared across the psyche of a generation, captured at a time in our history when we ruled the goddamn world. Ronny Lawton, the dark-faced patricidal killer, was her progeny. This is what she had unleashed into the world. I couldn't have envisioned a more tenuous union. Then, down in the bottom right corner I inset the obit of Charlie Lawton, killed in combat in Saigon. I set the missing father on the other side, him staring out through the ages. You know, sometimes you step back from your own creations, and you know you've gone deep into something, you know you are roaming around in the collective nightmare of our existence. Shit, this was what I've been trying to say all my life. The bakeoff disappeared onto page two. I'd done it all in less than an hour, photos, transcription, positioning.

I put a call in to the typesetters that did up our paper. They sent over a guy to take it. It was a downpour outside. There were reports of power outages and downed trees on the police radio now, spreading out across the land. I called over to the typesetters again. They told me they had a backup generator. They had things under control.

We lost power at the office half an hour later. I lit a candle, marooned myself in the smallness of the editorial room, smoking. I was there with the tools of my trade, desk and chair, typewriter, microfiche, a peg for the morning broadsheet, a blackboard and chalk, a coffee machine. I was feeling good, infused with something like self-worth. This was where language was created, where history skulked in the heads of reporters. It's what I liked to think of most, that moment of creation, of mood and fact coalescing into wet print. You see, I had some things I wanted to say all my life. Problem was, I never had a story equal to my ideas.

Ed was watching me. He'd been alive too long, worked too hard. I knew his story. His tongue came out and tasted the air, then withdrew. He was nodding slightly at me, like he wanted something for me, something better than I had.

Then his wife called. When was he coming home? She needed milk and doughnuts. Ed came back and sat in the shifting dark with me. He smelt sour, like something inside him was leaking.

I looked at my watch. The paper should be coming back from the print shop soon. I was anxious to see how it looked. There was a long silence between me and Ed, the sky outside fractured in blue sheet lightning. The phone rang again.

Ed was on a good while. He ended with something said under

his breath. Then he said what he'd said, again, louder. He said, "I love you." Then he said, "I love you with all my heart." Then he said, "Cross my heart and hope to die."

I mean, the guy was pushing sixty and looked every day of it. It was like some amorous interrogation or incantation. I looked away instinctively.

Ed got off the phone. He hid himself in a puff of smoke. He said in his defense, "I go home at night, and she's got a plate of some-thing good to eat."

Things slowed to a crawl in the lateness of the night. I waited for Ed to come around from being all self-conscious.

Ed got to telling me about his life. That's what he did mostly those days. I listened without saying anything. The gist of it was simply that he'd missed out on escaping our town, stayed through the housing slump when all the factories closed, lost all that equity. "Same house, same walls, same roof, nothing different, but it was different in here." He pointed to his head. "It says it there on our money. Trust. In God We Trust. It's all about belief. We stopped believing at some point. Same as your old man, I guess."

I said, "I guess." I ended that line of conversation.

Ed said his wife, Darlene, started a beautician's shop out of their garage when things got bad. "We did prom pictures during the worst years. That was Darlene's idea, seeing as they were already there for their hair. We bought a big wicker chair up in Chicago, sat 'em in that, made 'em something beautiful for a night. We got this wallpaper backdrop of the ocean and palm trees, blue sky. Darlene came up with the idea of making piña coladas with these little trop-ical umbrellas. That's how we survived."

"On the small vanities that keep us sane," I said softly, but Ed was off in his own world.

Ed looked at me, burped again, took up the bile again, winced, and swallowed it. He stopped for hardly a moment, went on talk-ing. "You ever really look at a woman's body when she ain't pre-tending or posing, when she's just herself, being a woman in the dark, the shape of her back slumped forward?"

I nodded my head slowly.

"You got that girl of yours, right? That all working out?" Ed whispered.

I said, "I guess." A siren wandered aimlessly through the dark outside. I watched Ed's Adam's apple move up and down in his throat. He had his head in his hands. What I liked about Ed was that he gave credit to his wife. He recognized she'd saved his ass, saved their house. He didn't build himself into something he wasn't. That took a lot of courage, seeing yourself for what you are and living with it.

Things dissipated to an excruciating stillness after that. I guess things have always had a way of incapacitating me, of overwhelming me. I got this tunnel vision, felt suddenly buried under the debris of our dead industrialism. We were occupying one of those gaps in history that go undocumented, that long silent stupefaction before some other means of survival comes along to save a civilization. I mean, what can you say about a town where the river self-combusted into a slur of floating flame, where tongues of flame ate their way inland? If that isn't prophetic, I don't know what is. I don't give a rat's ass if you think you can explain it with the combustibility of petrochemicals, with the globular fire of our smelting foundry. I say there's something tragic going on here. I say, read between the goddamn lines of our industrial demise. Mankind has formed religions on less eventful happenings than a river bursting into flame. I wanted to say all that to Ed, but the phone rang.

It was Ed's wife. He called her Sugar Lump. It was goddamn excruciating to see a man like that give in to love. I gathered from the conversation there was a coconut cream pie waiting for Ed at the end of the day.

After that, Ed said he was going home. I went down with him to his car, cupping my hand over a candle as we went down the long stairway. Outside he said, "You only get chances like this once in a lifetime." The storm was still over us. "There's a body out there hacked to pieces. I know there is." That's what he'd seen in that darkroom when he shouted for me.

I said quietly, "I know there is," and the candle died on cue, set us both in darkness. Ed's breath was sour from the bile. It made me flinch, that smell of infirmity, but I set myself beside him and didn't move. He touched my back before he left. He said again, "There's a body out there hacked to pieces. I know there is."

I went up the long stairway. I tried not to think of Ronny Lawton, but all I saw was a river of blood pouring out of some nondescript darkness, an effulgence of blood and bits of a human body hacked to pieces. I kept having to shake my head, to empty that thought, but it came surfacing again. My legs burned with fatigue. I extinguished my cigarette in a red fire bucket filled with sand. The lights suddenly flared. The television materialized into a series of gray dots. Ed McMahon, that asshole, was laughing at something Johnny was saying. The Ronny Lawton story was dead for the evening. I felt this hunger stalk me, the kind of feeling men must have after a hard day's work. My head was aching with that low-grade pain of anxious tiredness. I got up and yawned and looked out at the storm. There was a body out there hacked to pieces. Ronny Lawton was sleeping down at the courthouse with the secret of his father's hacked corpse, or that's what everybody believed.

I called my girlfriend, Diane, long distance to Chicago. She was out. I got her voice, this chipper college voice giggling life away. It's one of those voices that belies the idea that there's anything wrong in this world, that negates the fact that we have atom bombs and disease, that people are killing one another. It was near midnight. I left a message on one of those new answering machines. I said, "Hey, precious." Then I lost it and said, "Where the hell are you?" and hung up. Then I called back and said, "Precious, I'm just worried. Sorry." Then I called back and checked her messages with her secret code and erased the first message. All I can say is, thank God some histories can be obliterated with a code.

I made a grilled cheese sandwich in my boss's toaster oven, opened a can of his mushroom soup, and heated it. The soup tasted good, the soft melted cheese stuck to my teeth. I got a soda and washed things down, and then I slept with my head on the desk.

Sam came in late. He'd been drinking heavily, a pint bottle stuffed into his coat pocket. He had a pencil stuck behind his ear.

The guy from the typesetters had dropped off the edition on my desk while I was asleep. Sam took it into his hands. He said, "Let's see what we got, chief." That made me wince, that sardonic "chief" crap. Sam made this whistling sound and patted me on the back. He said, "Now that's a goddamn edition we can be proud of. That's goddamn journalism." He poured me a drink. He pawed at me in the way drunks touch other men. "That's goddamn journalism, chief." That's when I first realized I had hardly written one single original word for the front page, it was all culled transcripts and pictures, all procedural bullshit, rap sheets and phone conversations from Ronny Lawton to the cops.

Sam pawed me again, said the same thing again. He set about making me one of his famous tuna melts, set the toaster on high, and we celebrated with whiskey and tuna melts. In the luxurious aroma of food, we sat and looked at one another. Sam was ripped. He kept eating and drinking and saying, "That's goddamn journalism, Chief." I sat there in the flickering light of the candle and tasted the slow burn of irony and his bourbon in my throat.

CHAPTER 3

O n any other morning after getting no call from Diane, I would have driven up to Chicago to see what the hell was going on. But the police found a small piece of a finger out at the Lawton place. Sam was shouting into the phone, "Our Ronny Lawton picture and the one of his mother have been picked up by the wire services. It's in the *New York Times, Philadelphia Inquirer, Boston Globe, Chicago Tribune*. Jesus Christ. We've hit the big time! Bill, do you hear me? Get your ass over there now, and see this finger they have!"

I was sort of stunned, but you catch the news service on a slow day and, by God, you somehow pull off what you've wished for your whole lifetime. But it was more than that really. It was the lugubrious sadness of the anniversary of the mother's death that triggered something infinitely tragic about all this, and that appended Vietnam history, the dead brother, that prompted the editors of these big-city papers to carry the story. If you looked at all those family faces, they shared the same gaping jawline, a look of having stared too long at something horrible, a physiognomy born out of the landscape. I knew it as that look of men who have stared at the sky too hard and long, praying for rain.

"You get out there and check that goddamn finger out, Bill. I know Ronny hacked his old man to pieces. I just know it! They got the frogmen bobbing for Old Man Lawton right now in the pond in back of Ronny's place. I want you out there now for when they start bringing in the head and torso and legs!"

I already had a headline in my head on the way out to the Lawton house, before I ever saw the finger—FATHER FINGERS SON FROM BEYOND THE GRAVE.

I went out on my porch in the early morning light. A hum of excitement filled my head. I think I was smiling. In fact, I *was* smiling. I caught myself in the sliding glass door in my underwear and T-shirt. I put down a pot of coffee and let the feeling sink into me. Across the backyard I heard the animals from the city zoo crying in the first light of day, awakening from the dark. I went upstairs and got out one of my grayish suits from the closet. It smelled of mothballs. Actually, it was my father's suit, one of those fifties suits that are slightly oversized, with the pants that ride high, cinched almost at the navel. That's what I like about these suits, the depth of the pockets where you can bury your hands almost halfway down your thighs and give that appearance of profundity, like you're thinking hard and complicated things.

By eight-thirty I was out beyond the city. In a sea of corn, I listened to the tale of Ronny Lawton getting bigger and bigger, edging into the rural folklore of the area. He was "hacked up, awright," that's what everybody was thinking, poor old Mr Lawton, bits and pieces of him buried in the cornfields out back of his house, this awful harvest of human flesh. The radio was full of Ronny Lawton, crackling voices from neighbors who didn't want to mention who they were, saying he was no good, worth nothing. I drove by a man on a tractor with a small radio up against his ear. I knew he was listening to the talk about Ronny Lawton. They said over the airwaves that Ronny Lawton used to drink like a skunk and shoot off his hunting rifle on the property, just pump the night full of lead, blaring his goddamn music out in the cornfields. He shot Stop signs full of holes when he took his car out on the road at night. You had to take the long way around his property to avoid him. Ronny Lawton was no good.

"He was drunk as a wheelbarrow most evenings! Don't you know, dropped out of school at fifteen, ain't never looked back on learning again, worked at Arby's, Burger King, stint with the military, discharged without seeing any active duty, then back home to a job at Denny's as a short-order cook. That's what he learned in the army, how to cook and shoot straight. Got himself a wife that just wasn't going to put up with Ronny's bullshit, fought back, but he got the better of her, got her pregnant before it was all over, before she showed up back at her parents' house in Jackson County, who just said to her to get her ass back to the man who'd got her pregnant, and back she went, and shit, the fighting and screaming. Damn near killed her one time. Saw her out on the road with that kid of hers, walking into town just cryin'. Oh, yeah, I been following the Ronny Lawton story all his goddamn life . . . Him and his old man, let me tell you something. They sure as hell got into it every once in a while, especially after his old man lost his job when General Motors pulled out. Sure as hell fought like they wanted to die out there, fighting it out with words and booze, and Ronny firing his gun above his old man's head . . ."

"You never did hear from the old woman, God bless her soul. Heard she wasted away her last years with cancer up in the back bedroom, never saw the light of day, just died up there, all alone, after her son Charlie died over there in Saigon. They didn't bring her to a doctor or nothin'. Both of them animals if you ask me . . ."

"You got to ask yourself, what sort of animal is Ronny Lawton? The cops had been out to arrest him numerous times, took him in for discharging the gun, for threatening his father, but there were never formal charges against him. Ronny slept in the county jail like it was a Motel Six. Just checked out in the morning. His father always went on down and got him out, said there weren't nothing that couldn't be handled between him and his own son. Indignant, his father was, toward the law which saved his sorry ass more than once. I knew it was going to end up like this. I say, he brought it on himself. I ain't saying any man deserved to be carved up by his son, but you can't say it wasn't coming all these years . . ."

I learned all that in the twenty minutes it took to get out to the property to see the finger. It's amazing how the land holds these stories out here on the edge of our plains, how each person holds the mood of his community in a sort of unconscious oral narrative.

Despite the inglorious prospect of going out to see the finger, my mind was preoccupied with Diane through this droning monologue. She'd never called me back last night. She was in law school at Loyola University, second year. We were going to get married after she got out of law school. At least that's how it was last summer when she came down and stayed out at my family mansion. Diane used to love the mansion, the way the sun rose in the master bedroom, that soft yellow morning light that licked up the darkness of night. We spent last summer together, just the two of us in it, a bewildering, romantic solitude. We went down by the chain-link fence, watched the caged animals, had picnics there like we were in some exotic land. I had nobody left except her. I had her trapped, pinned against the lawn at dusk, feeding her grapes with one hand, pouring out champagne. I kept the world at bay, hid the television and the radio, swooned her with classical music from an old turntable up at the house. I tried to impregnate her, to make her mine, pressing myself into her, staying inside her long after the act of ejaculation. I was a creature pressing its prey against the ground, giving it delicate bites to incapacitate it. I felt her struggle in the end. She complained, "Jesus, don't kiss me like a chipmunk." I kept at her, hid the keys to the car, made up excuses why we didn't need to go out. She recoiled from sex. I tried to bring a certain levity to it, borrowing from the words of Queen Victoria to her daughter, paraphrasing them to Diane, "Just close your eyes and think of America . . ." I wanted to retreat into the posterity bequeathed me, wait out this national depression of ours, hunker down with the legacy. Things had to change. But she escaped my cage.

I wanted to call Diane earlier in the morning, tell her to come down for the weekend, but I didn't want to upset her. I restrained myself. I knew she'd say what she always said, "You must get out of there," like I was in danger, like this was *The Amityville Horror* or something. I said to myself, "She pulled an all-nighter for an exam. She was at the library all night. She's in a hall right now getting ready to answer questions on an exam." That's what I said to myself as I made coffee this morning. I didn't dial her number. I was listen-

ing to the Ronny Lawton story. I had the television on. I was looking at Linda Carter, that ubiquitous bitch down at the courthouse.
And then I did dial Diane's number before I left, but all I said was,
"Good luck on the exam, precious. I hope you ace it," into her
answering machine. That's all I said, then I called her back again
and said, "Even though I can't be there with you, I'm thinking
about you. I'm always thinking about you." Then I said, "Have you
seen the front page of the *Chicago Tribune* yet?" I left it at that. In
love, first comes desire, then torment, then the need for revenge. I
see love as a kind of cancer sometimes.

Ronny Lawton surfaced again, gnawed away at me. He had
potential, his situation, I mean there was a summer's work in him. I
could get a name for myself outside this town, make a break for a
real city, disencumber myself of the rapacious glory of my ancestry,
creep away from everything for the anonymity of Chicago. I was
thinking I might look up who else had murdered whom out here,
what terrible tragedies had befallen these people's ancestors
through the years of drought and bad harvests, what must have
happened in the long cold winter's dark when nothing got planted
and people went crazy for company. That's what I was good at,
going to libraries, paging through old books, that is what college
had done for me. There had to be a hell of bewildering insanity,
moments of fury as a baking sun wilted crops. I remember my
grandfather telling stories of how people went wild when they
heard him coming, screaming and hollering, how children ran out
of the fields, abandoned everything, followed his wagon loaded
down with a huge slab of ice. Even the farmers, out in the fields too
long under summers of heat, made their solitary way up to him and
watched the miracle of ice, let their big, coarse, fat tongues stick
out of their mouths. My grandfather was bringing this ice into one-
hundred-plus-degree weather. He scraped ice from the block, colored it with raspberry and strawberry and charged twice as much.
He used to laugh that, in six months' time, all that out there
around him would be buried in snow, rivers and creeks and ponds
frozen hard. Then his ice wasn't worth a penny. "A matter of per-

ception . . . supply and demand." He used to say to me, "There is no greater example of supply and demand than an ice-maker in the Midwest."

I turned off County Line, followed a dirt road that boiled a cloud of brown dust behind me. Already at 9 A.M., the sun blazed overhead in another July scorcher. A haze of pollen and dead insects smeared my windshield. I had to keep using the wipers to cut my way into this heartland. I stuck to the vinyl seating. I breathed shallow breaths. I could run a story each day, run the old article on old murders and deaths in a boxed area on page one, then take it to the pay dirt of ads on page three. It was all history that could be resurrected real easy, history chipped from the past, an accumulation of facts culminating in this murder. All I really needed was for Ronny Lawton to say nothing for a while, to begin pleading his innocence, and for the body to stay missing.

I turned down a long corridor of corn, and then there it was, a house crouching in the tall grass, almost obscured, reclaimed by the land. Inside was the piece of finger, enshrined in the holy terror of Ronny Lawton's house. I killed the engine, and a throb of insect life surfaced from the fields, this low pulse of mating calls.

A yellow police tape cordoned off the area. Some high-school kids were parked on the side of the road whistling and shouting, "Ronny! Ronny! Ronny!" Churchwomen had brought doughnuts and coffee and juice for the volunteers, some of whom were squatting and wiping the sweat from their faces. There were frogmen in rubber suits back from checking the pond on Ronny Lawton's property. I could see the others, the volunteers, out beyond the house in a human chain spread across the land.

I said, "Morning, Larry."

"Finger's inside, down in the basement, Bill. You got to see it. Seems like Ronny hacked his old man up real good."

I saw the finger, down a long, warm passage that led to the basement. It was on a step of the stairs. The piece of finger looked like an etiolated root, with a single thread of red blood attached. The finger was bent in this morbid, accusing manner, almost pointing

down into the basement, leading the way into the sweating darkness of Lawton's unfinished basement, leading to the prospect of
more bits of Ronny Lawton's father.

"It's been snipped off the hand with something like a pruning
shears," Ed Hoskin said to me. I looked at the clean cut, the pearly
seam of bone in the middle, then looked Ed in the eyes.

I went farther into the basement, to the gloom of cellar light,
smelled the years of cold dampness filled with spores of mold, and
took it all into my head. Ed Hoskin took shots of the finger like it
was a celebrity. I just stood there with my back to him, saw the flash
illuminate the brown, mineral-dripping walls of the basement.
There was a mound off in the west corner of the cellar. Two cops
were slowly uncovering the stones, carefully placing them off to the
side. I listened to the bite of a shovel in the dirt.

The cellar seemed filled with the ghostly existence of austere
economy, lined with jars and tools, hooks hanging from the rafters.
I could imagine a man from earlier in our century fixing things
down here because there was no money for new things, his wife
down by his side in the gloomy tallow of a candle, busy in the seasonal packaging of fruits and meats, making preserves, hanging
smoked meats that would see them through the dead of winter.

"We're bringing in bloodhounds," I overheard a cop say behind me.

Off in the corner hung a sheet, and beyond this was a rudimentary gym, a world postered with grimacing giant men. Huge metal
weights, like wheels from trains, dark and heavy, were piled on one
another in descending weight. Ronny Lawton had improvised.
There were paint buckets filled with dried cement. On each of
them was written the weight of the can. There was a cast-iron
bench with a terry-cloth towel laid down on it. A pull-up bar had
been screwed into a support beam for the house. On a small desk
was a huge can of Joe Weider Weight Gain Powder, along with a
food blender and small needles beside tiny vials of liquid. He had
bits of paper everywhere, pasted to the walls, the self-affirmation,
the singular incantation of his whole being: "Get Big!"

I went toward the stairs, sidestepping the finger.

Ed Hoskin had a tripod set up on the stairs, this elaborate old-style contraption he kept moving, shuffling about up there, his head hidden in the camera box. The tripod looked like a giant spider tentatively deciding if it wanted to come down and feast.

I said, "Ed, I want to come up."

The spider scurried to the side and let me up.

Pete was smoking at the back door. He nodded to me. We went out the back into the tall overgrowth of grass. He looked exhausted, a day's growth on his chin. "You made the AP wires, Bill. That's something, makes up for living in this shithole."

I shrugged. "I suppose it does. I need something to keep me here at this stage."

"I hear you." Pete was staring off into the grass. He pulled a pack of Lucky Strikes from his shirt pocket and fingered the plastic wrapping, removed the gold band slowly. "You want one?"

I lit up and watched the swaying tall grass gone to seed long ago. I said, "What's eating you, Pete?"

Pete turned and looked at me. "I hate when someone screws with my head. Crime lab guys got in here this morning, and I've been hearing them talk. They think this finger was left there on purpose." He raised his voice. "So I said to them, 'Why the hell would someone want to do that? It doesn't make any sense. Why the hell would Ronny leave a clue like that?' And this smart-ass says to me, 'You ever think maybe Ronny didn't do it?' But I said, 'What the hell do you think we're dealing with here? Kidnapping? Ransoms?' I say, shit on all that, Bill. There isn't any money to be had out of this hole. All you got to do is look around you here, and you know that Ronny Lawton chopped up his old man plain and simple. All that finger tells me is that Ronny's old man is dead."

I watched a hovering army of specialists moving in and out of the bedrooms. I stepped back from the spectacle farther out in the yard, looked in on everybody in this grim ordeal of dismantling the house. I saw a cop up in the attic by a window.

"You put me into a room with him for five minutes. Five minutes, and I'd have a confession out of him." Pete held up his hand before me. "Just five minutes. Who the hell needs all this shit here? I call all this just dry humping. The whole goddamn criminal system is bullshit. You know what a jury consists of?"

I shrugged my shoulders. "Tell me."

"I'll tell you. It consists of twelve people chosen to decide who has the better goddamn lawyer. It isn't about justice, that's for sure. Five minutes, just give me five minutes with Ronny, that's all it'd take."

I sort of rolled my eyes: this from the law in our town. But I felt the frustration, the personal inadequacy in the face of all this science, subsumed by men brushing for prints, taking photographs of the basement, even the human chain of volunteers outside had a sense of purpose, although I had to wonder how so many people had so much time on their hands. I was going to take out a small spiral notebook in my shirt pocket, but I just left it there.

Pete said again, "Why the hell would Ronny leave that finger there like that?"

I'd been trying to align this solemn talisman left as a sort of mockery for us, and I said, "Pete, maybe it's them movies they have out now. That *Friday the Thirteenth*, and *Halloween*. What they have going for them is a recognizable element of evil, an immortal figure that rises from a lagoon at a kids' camp. You get caught having sex and some self-incarnation of your own kind kills you. It's not monsters anymore, but ourselves. In *Halloween* they have a guy in a hockey mask who cannot be burned or butchered. He keeps rising up again and again. There's an indignation in this country at what has happened to us. We need to exact a brutalizing punishment, indiscriminate and horrific, upon ourselves. We like to see ourselves mutilated. It's part of our psychosis of dismemberment, deregulation, downsizing, cutting things."

Pete looked at me. "I think you just lost me on that last turn, Bill."

I said, "Pete, that *Halloween* movie had a guy who chopped up his family, right?" I nodded. "*Texas Chain Saw Massacre*, for that matter. All dismemberment. And how about *I Dismember Mama*!"

"Shit awmighty, Bill. That ain't a movie, is it?"

"Yeah. How about *I Spit on Your Grave.* A teenage girl chops this guy's dick off in a bathtub."

Pete just held his cigarette away from his mouth, let the morning air pull at the smoke. He said, "You think that asshole is playing with us, just trying to make himself into some kinda monster?"

"I suppose we got to see how Ronny plays it, but yeah, sure. Why else leave a finger just like that when he knew we'd see it right away?"

Pete gave this bewildered look. "Five minutes, Bill. Just give me five minutes with him."

I said, like they say on those cop shows, "Any other leads, Pete?" because I'd run out of things to say.

"Got a fire-eating wife that hates him. Estranged from Ronny this past year. Got a kid by Ronny, too, three-year-old boy. I was speaking with Ronny's wife this morning. I said, 'I hear you were living with Ronny out at his old man's house up until last year. Did you ever hear Ronny threaten to kill his father?' All she said was, 'I hope they fry his ass. He doesn't pay shit for child support. You suppose I'm entitled to that house if Ronny gets the chair? It's only right and all. He doesn't pay shit for child support.' They were her only words on Ronny. She lives with some guy in a trailer home outside of town. I could hear him in the background, egging her on about inheriting the house."

I went into the house again. The cold stone kept things cooler than outside, everything in a shade of gray. A ring of trees had taken root outside, planted years before to provide shade from the summer heat. The house had that domesticity of a slow rural existence, a honeycomb of small rooms with just the bare essentials lined against plain painted walls. I smelled the wholesome odor of mushroom soup and Hamburger Helper, and a pervading odor of animal lard drippings, which I located in a cast-iron skillet on the range. The kitchen was strung with blackened pots and pans and colanders for shaking flour and draining rice, jars of spices on a fringe of shelf, a scarified cutting block for meat and vegetables.

Above a big porcelain sink hung a crocheted prayer of thanksgiving. A clock ticked away existence above a fat steel range with ornate spreading legs. It was all clean and tidy, despite the mother's death. I was trying to think of where Ronny might have cut his father to pieces, where the fight might have begun. I went into the cramped enclosure of the toilet lined with old bottles of shampoo and Brut aftershave. The rings in the shower curtain weren't broken as I'd hoped, readying myself to shout, "Look at this!"

In the sitting room, there was a patchwork quilt hung over a rocker, a basket of knitting left as a testimonial to a mother's passing, covered with a layer of dust, a book of patterns. Above the fireplace was a picture of Ronny's graduation from boot camp, along with Ronny's father's portrait from the Korean War. Charlie Lawton was there, too, set off to the side with a letter of condolence from the U.S. Army. All of them seemed about the same age in the pictures, sharing the same narrow chin.

Pete was still out there with his pants high on his hips. He was putting the butt of one cigarette to the end of another one. Pete looked at me. "Maybe I'm puttin' all this together now, Bill. All that stuff about cutting things up and all. All them movies about murder. Check out the bedroom. That'll tell you what you need to know." His face was concealed in smoke.

I entered that sullen den of Ronny Lawton's bedroom, off the laundry room, cautioned by a giant poster of nuclear fallout that stated in red lettering *Radioactive! Keep Out.* The tiny square room was plastered from wall to ceiling with a collage of posters of women, musicians, football stars, movie icons, the women in bathing suits, famous stars like Farrah Fawcett, Suzanne Somers, Daisy from *The Dukes of Hazzard,* and Susan Anton, a topography of huge busts and hard nipples. The pictures were pasted in such a way that parts of the bodies of the women were cut up by intersecting posters. The heads of Charlie's Angels had been placed on the androgynous decapitated bodies of the Bee Gees in their white jumpsuits from *Saturday Night Fever.* Roger Staubach's face grimaced through a mask as he obscenely sent a perfect spiral between the splayed legs of a Dallas Cowboys cheerleader who raised two pom-poms in a moment of what must have been excruciating pain. The infamous tongue of the lead singer of Kiss, Gene Simmons, curled into Suzanne Somers's cleavage, and the Rolling Stones' red tongue appeared performing oral sex here and there on the pet of the month from *Hustler* and *Club* magazines. There was also a picture of Rocky in a gym pumping weights. Ronny had two small models of R2-D2 and C-3PO, battery-operated toys. I pressed a red button embedded in the back of C-3PO, and he said in a metallic voice, "May the force be with you."

Pete stood behind me. "My money says anybody who uses scissors the way Ronny does chopped up his old man."

It was a monument compressed into one small space, an imploding nightmare where gravity had become saturated, dense, every inch of the room colonized by a living virus of desire.

Pete picked up a magazine. "Listen to this. He's got this circled. 'Melody, 5'4", 101 lbs. Big brown eyes. Long sexy legs. 36-26-37. Perky hard nipples. My pussy is pink in the middle and very juicy. My small firm ass is waiting for you to kiss it. I like hard, throbbing cock.'" He flicked the pages. "How about this one. 'Kimberly. My clit is wet. I know you want to grab it with your teeth. I want you to lick it. I want you to fuck it. I want you all inside me. I want your hard cock.'"

I said, "At least he's not illiterate."

"I suppose that's one way of looking at it."

After that, things just dragged. Eventually, we saw the finger removed, watched it come up in a transparent plastic lunch bag. It looked for all the world like a bag you'd take a goldfish home in from a county fair.

Then a cop shouted from the cellar. I went down with Pete and Linda Carter and Ed Hoskin and the forensics team in a slow procession, formed a ring around the small unearthed mound. I saw Ed Hoskin shift and bless himself. He stepped away, put his hand to his mouth, and the burn of his innards filled him. I let him pass me.

The mound yielded a small blackened box, like a buried treasure. But it wasn't another piece of Ronny Lawton's father, but the small skeletal remains of an infant wrapped in a half-eaten lace dress. The arms were crossed at the chest, like two little sticks in solemn peace.

"Jesus Christ!" Pete said under his breath.

One of the forensic scientists knelt, like he was in prayer. He used tweezers to extract a piece of lace and bone. "We can carbon-date it."

Ed came back down slowly with the tripod and circled the spidery apparatus, making it crawl to and fro to get a view of the small cocoon infant.

I caught his eyes for a moment. He just averted them, like I was asking him to answer something about himself, like I was challenging him. "I'll see you later, Ed." I touched him on the back. I needed him as an ally in the job.

The cellar would yield nothing else, no more body parts. I went up into the glare of blue daylight, shielding my eyes.

Linda Carter had this bewildered look on her face, some scrap of maternal sadness under the cake of makeup. She excused herself and closed the door of the bathroom behind her and stayed there a long time before she left.

It was a stalemate at the house. I went outside and wandered around the yard. I had to keep focused now, stay with the tangential part of this story, too, with the old news, the old murders, build something out of this. There had to be another story for this evening. I felt that pressure of a deadline. I looked around me, the glare of light beating down with intensity. This was the morning I'd made the AP wires on the vacuity of some yearbook photo. I said, "You got to stay with the basics here." I said that out loud to myself. It became a sort of mantra.

I wandered through the yard, passed the cops raking through the property. The human chain was back from searching, eating sandwiches, and their dogs were lapping up bowls of water. It was hard work out there in the tall fields of corn.

Nothing moved at the Lawton property. It was that sullen

immobility that struck me, that grim metaphor of cars on blocks everywhere with their guts torn out in abandoned efforts at resuscitation, wrenches, cans of oil, hubcaps, starters, batteries, all set out on old rickety tables. It was a prehistoric museum of corn threshers, old tractors, trailers, a rusted canoe, and abandoned cars sprouting in the long, yellowish grass, marbled in bird droppings. I was thinking in terms of sentences, in terms of drama, of these rusting machines as part of a chaos, where a man deconstructed himself by dismantling everything around him until one day he turned and cut his own father into pieces. That's what I wanted to talk about, the sadness of this existence. I didn't know shit about forensic science and fingerprinting, like those scientists, didn't know how to carbon-date a dead infant. I didn't know how to beat a confession out of a prisoner, like Pete. I just stood there and wanted to talk about the sadness of this existence. It was all I could do.

Back at the office I was drinking too much coffee. I was putting the finishing touches to an article that had escaped from me, this long rambling tract of sadness. The small office smelled of burnt toast. Sam had started a small fire in his toaster oven and he was pissed. Now he was cooking an open-faced tuna sandwich, holding a knife and licking it when I looked up. He had some special sauce he used on these sandwiches, which was really just Thousand Island dressing and mustard. I always knew I was to pretend I didn't know his secret. It was part of the job, to taste his creations, to lick my lips with satisfaction. But for the first time in ages, I wasn't hungry. I was scared shitless. Things had escaped me. Sentences were running across the page, a jumble of words.

The small black-and-white television was turned low, a rerun of *The Dick Van Dyke Show*. I looked up and in this tunnel vision of anxiety watched Dick Van Dyke's lean body fall over a sofa. The laugh track reached my ears. That was the sort of thing people in the fifties found hilarious, physical comedy. I just shut my eyes and moaned.

Sam put a call down to Ed. "I'm taking orders here, Ed," is what Sam said. I listened to the static of Ed's reply. I wanted to say, "Jesus

H. Christ! How the hell am I supposed to get a report out with all this bullshit?" but I didn't say anything. Sam caught me thinking it, though. He said, "You nearly ready there?" He eyed his watch. "Deadlines, Bill. Deadlines. That's what the newspaper business is about. It doesn't have to be pretty, just accurate."

The toaster oven was beginning to send up a plume of smoke. I saw the sandwich combust into flame. I shouted, "Sam!" He turned and roared and opened the blackened glass door. I set the article on Sam's desk amid the choking smoke and went out to the bathroom and felt like throwing up. The article went something like this . . .

"How can I speak anymore within a human context without being aware of the universe beyond our own? The yardstick of tribal custom, of kingdom, of country, of empire by which to measure what were once called 'universal laws' has been extended into a dimension beyond the humanities . . ."

I heard Sam shouting outside the bathroom. "What the fuck is this? Are we talking the same language?"

I had my hands to my head in a sort of despair I don't like to admit to. The smell of burnt toast had ingrained itself into my skin. It's all I could smell.

Sam shouted down to Ed Hoskin to get his ass upstairs. I just sat on the toilet seat and listened. My feet scratched the cold porcelain floor.

Ed came up, because I heard him talking. Sam said, "Tell me if you see the connection between this and the Ronny Lawton case, Ed." And then he began reading, "We are in the era of light-years. Our new reference now lies outside any realm of human perception. We know the facts, that $E = mc^2$ (energy equals mass times the velocity of light squared), that light travels at a speed of 185,871 miles per second, that the light from the sun takes nine minutes to reach us. Matter and energy are exchangeable, not distinct. We know protons are positive and electrons are negative. It is our rote cosmic catechism so as not to shame our own planet, committed to memory the same way we learned our times tables, so we wouldn't be swindled on earth . . ." Sam was really shouting at this stage. He had barely got to my discussion of Plato's *Republic* or the specter of Nietzsche's nihilism when he lost it. "What the fuck is this, Ed?"

Ed said, "It's ambitious beyond the scope of journalism as we know it."

"You're fuckin' right it is." He pounded on the toilet door. "Bill. Get your ass out here, now."

I made a theatrical flush of the toilet, like I'd really gone, and came out. My face looked like shit in the mirror, red with effort.

Sam tore the story to shreds on his desk.

I just stood there sort of choking.

"You were out at that goddamn house today, right?" Sam shouted. He tapped on my breastbone. "Did you see anything besides Einstein, Plato, and Nietzsche?"

"Yeah."

"You want to get your ass back in the office and tell the good readers about it?"

Ed handed Sam a grainy image of the finger from the house. Sam swelled his cheeks. He said, "Ronny Lawton chopped his old man up, all right. We're going with that shot right there. Jesus Christ almighty."

I had my mouth half-open, like I was going to lose it.

Sam turned and looked at me. "If you're looking for sympathy, Bill, you'll find it in the dictionary between *shit* and *syphilis*. Now get your ass out of my sight!"

Sam spent the next fifteen minutes cursing while extricating the charred remains of the sandwich from the oven. He had the window open to clear the smoke.

I just slumped at my desk and wrote something that was peppered with the hearsay of neighbors, a testimonial to the monster Ronny Lawton. I told how the cops had found the severed finger, cut with what seemed to be pruning shears. I quoted Pete about the quandary over a lack of blood. I raised the suspicion that the finger was planted on purpose. I reported how the cops were laboriously going through the home, dusting for prints, checking the shed and the property, working late into the night searching for the elusive corpse of Ronny Lawton's father. I got a per day cost of how much it was costing the county, told how many men were working the case. I reported Ronny's estrangement from his wife, mentioned her name and age, the high school she attended, found a picture of her in her yearbook, inset that. I called Ronny Lawton's estranged wife and quoted her, shouting, "I hope they fry his ass." I mentioned that Ronny had a son by this woman, identified the son and gave his age. I reported the fact that Ronny Lawton was honorably discharged from the army, that he had successfully completed his GED while in the army. I finished with the fact that Ronny had requested counsel late last night.

Sam took the story and scanned it, crossed out a line here and there, changed things into the present tense, said, "The present tense holds immediacy, Bill." Then he smiled and said, "Ed, take a look at this."

Ed read it and looked up. "He's got the facts all there sure enough. I like the way you sort of leave it hanging there at the end, Bill," he said. "That's real good writing."

Sam spread his arms wide. "Yeah, kind of like . . . to be continued . . . I like that." He said, "Let's get this to press." He reached across the desk and wanted my hand. "You've been infected by that goddamn college education, Bill, infected by the disease of abstraction."

Ed said quietly, "You're one of us, Bill. We know you got a soul inside of you."

Sam chimed in, "That's right! There's a journalist inside you just waiting to get out, and by God I'm going to drag it out of you. What you got to understand first and foremost in this business is that you got to write for a sixth-grader. That's the level of sophistication out there, Bill. Sixth grade. We call it KISS—Keep It Simple, Stupid."

Ed drank stale coffee, wiped his mouth, and said, "We said when you came here that you were a young man who had the empathy for what has happened to all of us. You would understand. You wouldn't let us down. But Sam's right, Bill. Keep it simple."

Sam ended things abruptly. He said, "Ed!" Then Sam turned and looked at me. "You begin with the facts, is all, Bill . . ."

Ed disengaged his eyes from me and looked at the floor.

Sam said, "I think Bill here deserves one of my famous tuna melts with the special sauce."

Ed smacked his lips and winked at me. "Now you're talking."

I just stood there. My head was spinning. It was maybe the smoke from the toaster oven, the charred odor of a catastrophic fire, that did something to me, the surreal prospect of sitting down to a toaster-oven sandwich and black coffee after what I'd seen that day. This office was a joke, an anachronism in a world of television, a vestige of some old-world ideal of small-town truth and gossip. I said in a shaky voice, "Something is dead out there, something far greater than Ronny Lawton's father." I began shouting. "That's what I wanted to talk about, the flying debris of our industrialism, the something that is dead out there far greater than Ronny Lawton's father."

Sam said, "I hear you loud and clear, Bill." He took my hand and said softly, "But people are only interested in the pieces of Ronny Lawton's father."

CHAPTER 4

The morning sunrise burned away a night of despair, delivered me from the providence of darkness, and still no call on the answering machine. The animals at the zoo were agitated by the heat. I looked out the back porch, saw the rising dampness of cages that had been washed down, smelled the acrid odor of animal feces drifting toward the house. I stood there and inhaled it, one of those memories of childhood, the strange fascination of all those creatures not a quarter of a mile from our house, monkeys and tigers and alligators, things I saw at night in storybooks, but which lived in the glare of morning, creatures that occupied my world. In the first years of my life, I lived amid this strange menagerie, this animal kingdom of the plains. I used to be taken down there by a woman who minded me, to the end of the garden to watch the emus walk the perimeter of the zoo in their long enclosure. I watched it all from my side of the fence.

I went back inside, shut the door. It was another cloudless July morning that would turn to a searing heat by midmorning, making everything sweat and wilt.

I took a long cold shower.

Sam called at 6 A.M. "We made the AP wires again," he shouted.

I guess I'd been waiting on that news all night. I sat there on the edge of the bed with a towel around me. Sam read the abbreviated version, and I fed on the gore of another man's brutal futility. I was a sort of intellectual scavenger. The small litany of facts I'd typed up last night were tucked into various papers across the country.

"Circulation is going through the roof," Sam was shouting into my ear. I could tell he'd been drinking all night. "They're giving

Ronny Lawton a lie-detector test down at the county courthouse. I want you there, Bill." He was silent for a moment. There was a crackling hesitancy. I heard Sam turning spit in his mouth.

I broke the silence. "I'll get on it, Sam."

Sam said, "You're not sore about last night still, are you?"

I hunched my shoulders. "No, Sam, I'm not."

"Good, Bill. You got to trust me on this one. I know what people want to hear. I've been at this business going on thirty years."

"Okay," is all I said.

"You don't have to tell me and Ed there's something else going on here. We lived through it, Bill, this whole town going to shit, everything left in this unmarked grave. Me and Ed and your father are the casualties you're always talking about. I know you don't like to talk about your father's suicide, but he saw things going bad . . ."

I felt the strange clairvoyance of words exchanged across the morning silence. I got up and went to the window, looked off to the dark brownstone fortress of our town's dead industrialism. I could see our office window over by the teetering grain silos from the old brewery along the spine of the old railway.

". . . when his company went bust I saw that look on his face, three hundred men of his out of work, lives ruined . . ."

I said, "Sam, I don't want to talk about it."

"All I'm saying—"

"Sam!" I shouted. "I know I apply philosophy like one applies a dressing to a wound."

Sam said, "Shit, there you go again with that crap."

I said, "Sam, did we make the *New York Times*?"

Sam said, "Yeah. We did. You got it right, Bill." He seemed to hesitate for a moment. "I heard this from a newspaper guy out of Detroit once. He said, 'Speak your latent conviction, and it shall be the universal sense.' I guess what he was saying is, we all understand the world around us if we get told it honest. I don't think I can tell you anything more, Bill."

I said, "I understand, Sam. Thanks." I hung up. I had this eerie feeling being in the master bedroom all of a sudden. My father pulled the trigger on his existence four years ago, right here in the bedroom, took the back of his head off with the force, the meat of his anxiety blown across the room in a pink blossom of gore. My father's girlfriend was in the master bedroom when it happened, right as the pale sun was coming up on a freezing February morning, after a heavy snowfall. He left a simple declarative note, "I must go now," typed and crumpled, as though he'd carried it around with him for a long time.

What I can gather from direct evidence, from the analysis of a smear taken from the inner cheek of my father's girlfriend, sent by her in silent blackmail for a settlement, is that my father had engaged his girlfriend in oral sex less than half an hour prior to killing himself. He must have awakened to Jones, our family dog, barking, slipped from the bedroom, gone down and made peace with the dog, embraced him, for there were dog prints on my father's robe around the chest and shoulders. He whispered some regret in Jones's ears, and then fed Jones a shank of poisoned meat. In the dark of that cold morning, my father had decided his end. He came back into the house, crept back from the cold, and awakened his girlfriend. She said he was freezing cold, shaking, naked standing before her. He assuaged his guilt inside her, took her roughly by her long blond hair, prodded the darkness of her skull with his blunt sadness, filled with the sullen reality of what he had done, and what he was about to do. Jones had stopped licking away at the poison in his little red doghouse, had already gone into convulsions in the cold morning air, hemorrhaging into the snow from his mouth and anus. My father's girlfriend said she heard the dog yelping outside. My father must have heard it all, felt it invade his head, going through the dress rehearsal of his own suicide, roaming the darkness of his girlfriend's skull, imagining the taste of metal, the choking hesitancy, submitting to a last passing of our genetic heritage into the back of his girlfriend's straining throat.

She wanted $20,000 to keep her mouth shut, as it were. I paid it.

They could do nothing with my father's head, a mass of seared meat and gore. It was a closed casket. And poor Jones was unceremoniously taken away to wherever it is that animals are discarded. I never saw either of them again.

I've been told you need to see the face of a dead loved one, the open casket defines death, gives it a definite horror. It's a moment when your brain accepts this final vision. Maybe that was it, the fear that he wasn't in there. He had disappeared so many times in my life. For a time, when the phone rang, I thought it was him calling, like he did in the old days, that voice saying softly, "I am coming home."

I am now the remaining fugitive to this great empire of ice. I've staved off his memory these past years, but there is no real escaping the stigma of a suicide. It betrays a weakness in the family's genetic heritage, a chink in our psychic armor. There is a self-destruct button deep within us that we can get to if we want.

After that, our family name ambushed me. It lurked in homes, in the dorm of the school I attended, the chrome finish of our name on the old refrigerators. It was oppressive. That is what I was attuned to in life, the affront of a simple piece of machinery in the aftermath of his suicide. If our name was there on the refrigerator, I winced and thought of the utter failure, our inability to keep market share, the demise of the company, of my father up in this mansion, taking the gun and putting it deep into the back of his throat. And if I didn't see our name on a refrigerator, I wanted to scream, I wanted to say, "How fuckin' good is this model of yours?" I wanted to open it up, check it out, open and slam the door, check the suctioning mechanism. I wanted to say, "Assholes, does it keep your goddamn college beer cold? Is it so good that you would put three hundred men out of a job? Is it so good that you don't give a goddamn shit that my father blew his head off trying to keep things together? Well, is it, assholes?" In fact, I did say all those things, before I went away and got treatment in a psychiatric hospital late in my sophomore year.

You see, the great horror I and my father shared was the vision of our great progenitor, that asshole, who had himself frozen by the power of cryogenics at death, telling us he'd be back to see what we had done with his hard work, with the great company he had

founded. It was that immortality that haunted us, the interminable
nightmare of accountability, him in some great freezer, this ice
monster waiting to rise again. The ice monster used to speak in
terms of the First Ice Age, and the Second Ice Age, the passage
of his business from selling the blocks of ice to refrigerators, the
great epochs in his own life, and all without a trace of goddamn
irony. He'd start in with this shit, this "In the beginning there was a
man . . ." Jesus Christ! You see, what can you say of a man reincar-
nated across continents, a mercenary who had served in the Russ-
ian army of Tsar Nicholas II, a man who slaughtered his fellowmen
in the uproarious revolutions of Eastern Europe, a deserter who
walked across the freezing wasteland of Russia, stealing chickens
and eggs, sleeping in ditches, a bedraggled figure in military rags, a
marauding pestilence smelling of war and carnage, whispering of
the disaster he'd left behind, longing for a better future. He crossed
to England, a passage spent shoveling coal into a raging furnace
deep in a ship's hull. He had never got past the shoreline pubs
when he was press-ganged into war, blind drunk for going on two
days before he awoke to find himself bound for South Africa, where
he was commissioned into service of war, left to stagger around in
an interminable heat, armed with a bayonet, slashing and burning
out resistance, eventually laid low with sickness before escaping for
the Cape of Good Hope, where he found work on a merchant ship
bound for Liverpool. And from there he continued to Canada and
down to America, along the Great Lakes, down to the convergence
of St. Joseph River, where he at last settled at the age of, get this
shit, twenty-nine . . . That was a history by which we measured ourselves and always found ourselves wanting. No wonder my father
put a gun into his mouth and ended it all. No wonder he had himself committed to fire, to the antithesis of our empire of ice, to the
searing trajectory of a bullet. No wonder my father is hiding six feet
under. He knew the ice monster cometh, that he would be thawed
from the ice ages and roar, "Where is my money!"

I had an hour to spare, so I swam in the early hours of the morning at the local Y, fifty laps back and forth. Swimming was some-

thing I'd done since early childhood and through high school. It had been forced by my grandfather, since, in his memory, the greatest vulnerability he had ever faced was waking up at sea unable to swim on that voyage to South Africa, curled away during the storms, crying to himself. It was some sort of psychological damage, a phobia of total loss of control which he felt compelled to vanquish. It was irrational, but that was the way it was with him. He never went near water, but he kept tabs on my progress, vicariously conquering the only true fear he'd ever endured.

The sudden submersion into the pool eclipsed the immediate present, triggered something deep and primordial in me, what scientists today call a diving instinct, a mammalian adaptation to life underwater, the shunting of blood from the extremities to the heart and lungs to preserve the core body temperature. It was this dull euphoria of buoyed suspension in the cold, chlorinated water that detached me from matters, that let me gain some time truly alone from the world. It was where I escaped my father and grandfather, especially my grandfather. I had found a medium in which to detach myself from him. I had my strokes down, the latent memory of workouts. I swam with a rhythmic ease, closed my eyes, the roll of my body easy and relaxed, my face surfacing, breathing, submerging again, anticipating the wall, tucking and turning, kicking away from the wall, the flagella of my legs kicking, the most elemental of movements. It was where I was most content, like a seed of creation pulsing toward a dark destination.

I stood behind the mirrored glass with an entourage of other people. My hair was still wet. I smelled of chlorine, my skin clean and shiny. They knew I'd been swimming. They were saying, "AP wire again, Bill." I was smiling, taking it in my stride. I had left behind in the pool the night of sweat and fatigue. I was breathing deep, content, recently emerged back into the world of air-breathers. Somehow I felt removed and unafraid in the aftermath of exercise.

Linda Carter hadn't gone national. I don't even think she had looked at me once in her life, but I saw her staring at me, that flustered look of desperation, as people were wishing me well. The murmur of my family fortune, of who and what I was, must have reached her, because I saw her looking at me. I felt the sexual contagion of her long legs and sprayed hair, the way she pushed her hair behind her ear when she spoke. Her perfume enveloped all of us men. It heightened our own self-awareness. Linda smiled at me.

I said, "I love what you've done with the news, Linda. You are a light in the darkness of this town." That unnerved the shit out of her, but she recovered and, showing a fence of white teeth, said, "I like your work too . . ."

I caught the men's eyes and winked and then leaned in an intimacy that wasn't called for, touched Linda's shoulder, and said very softly, "I am just thankful for the rapacious insanity that feeds all of us. I am just thankful that men still feel the need to pick up axes to settle matters." The men thought that was the funniest thing they'd heard in years. We all just laughed, and it was like deflating a giant balloon of tension.

Ronny Lawton looked like shit when he came into the interrogation room. We were invited at the request of his lawyer, a kid in a brown shabby suit with a tie done like a noose.

Ronny stopped our laughter. A small speaker filled our room with what Ronny was saying. He yawned and wiped his face, chewed the inside of his cheek, went up and searched the mirrored glass for a face, went up to the mirror like a zoo animal and pawed at the glass, then turned and said to the man by the lie detector, "How many assholes they got out there?" He wanted a glass of water and a cigarette. He wasn't quite ready for all this yet. He turned and stuck out his tongue, inches away from us on the other side, then rapped the glass with the tips of his fingers. "I ain't done shit, you hear me out there? I called your asses, remember? I called you!" His face gleamed with sweat. He banged the glass. "I haven't done shit! I sure as hell better not lose my goddamn job at Denny's over this shit!" He just kept banging the glass.

A man in a blue blazer, white shirt and tie, and gray pants said matter-of-factly, "Ronny, you break that, you pay for it."

Ronny wheeled around and just stared at the man. He turned again. His hair was cropped, almost shaven in a military style, giving him an atavistic stare, a nose too sharp and long jutting out over the smallness of his lips. He was wearing a tank top that clung to his torso, showing the ripple of muscle beneath the tanned skin. The unnatural tautness of his pecs moved in an elaborate interplay of flexes when he breathed, the veins visible underneath. Two crimson scars revealed massive growth over a short period. Everyone was using steroids these days. It was one of those sublimated reactions to the demise of our town, its insular closure, an almost Darwinian adaptation to survival.

And then Ronny took a deep breath, closed his eyes for a moment, then opened them again. He clenched his fists, crossed his arms, and brought each one to the mirror separately. On the left hand between the knuckles were tattooed letters that spelled the word HERE. He held it there, almost with a presentiment that we were entranced. His eyes stared into the glass. Then he lowered the left fist and raised the right, and the tattooed knuckles revealed the word NOW.

Behind the glass we stayed quiet, whispered the words, felt their immediacy, the physical sense of what they meant. You could imagine each fist raised, the HERE a threat to someone by Ronny, the impending sense of a beating. The NOW on the fist again raised as a swiftness of justice, something lunged into someone's face, a crude philosophy of the street, a sort of HERE and NOW menace.

Then Ronny opened his mouth slow and, uncrossing his arms, brought the two fists together, merged the NOW and HERE into the enigma of NOWHERE. He whispered that word, NOWHERE, to us. With that he went silent, parted the meaning again and turned from us, cleaving apart the abstraction of NOWHERE.

It somehow stunned us, brought a malevolence to his countenance.

The man in the blue blazer said, "We're ready anytime you are, Ronny?"

Ronny inhaled the last of a cigarette, let the smoke pour out his nostrils, then he sat in a chair. Another man, in a white shirt with his sleeves rolled up, put on a series of suction cups along Ronny's tattooed arms and dabbed a swab of Vaseline on either side of Ronny's temples and then attached some electrodes.

And so it began.

"Is your name Ronny Lawton?"

"Yes."

"Are you twenty-two years old?"

"Yes."

"Are you the son of Kyle Lawton?"

"Yes."

It went on that way, Ronny Lawton hooked up to electrodes along the length of tattoos on both arms. He was staring at the whiteness of the interrogation room wall, blinking between answers, the accumulation of facts, the cold, unmodulated voice of the man asking the questions and another sitting at a desk, watching an agitated needle scratch graph paper, adjusting the calibration of the machinery with Ronny's psyche.

"Is your father alive?"

"Shit, was he ever alive?" Ronny Lawton laughed wryly. Then he turned dark and said, "Shit, how do I know!"

The man reading the sheet reset his eyeglasses on the bridge of his nose and hesitated.

The man asking the questions said, "You consented to the test. Do you want to do it right?"

Ronny turned, the tendrils of electrodes emanating from his head, and stared at the mirrored glass. He grew sullen, flexed his arm. "Yeah" was his answer.

The test resumed.

"Is there a body of a child buried down in the basement of your home?"

Ronny jerked.

The man asked the question again. "Is there a body of a child buried down in the basement of your home?"

Ronny nodded his head. "Yes."

"Do you know what happened to that child?"

"Yes."

"Is that child yours?"

"No."

"Do you know whose child that is down in the basement of your house?"

"My mother's." Ronny looked off at us behind the mirror. His eyes took on a severe burning look. Maybe it was the first time he realized that his house was being dismantled, that they were digging up everything.

"Do you know where your father is?" the voice asked.

"No." Ronny touched the bridge of his nose, squeezed moisture from his eyes.

"Did you have a fight on the night your father disappeared?"

"No." He shook his head solemnly.

The man said, "You gotta stay still."

Ronny averted his eyes and then looked straight ahead into the mirrored glass. I felt the undercurrent of calculating cruelty to this line of questioning, the undercurrent of debasement in the slow accretion of detail, each question having its cumulative trenchant effect, wearing the suspect down.

"Did you go fishing the night your father disappeared?"

"Yes."

"Did you have a bad relationship with your father?"

"No." Again the slow movement of the head.

"Did you ever hit your father?"

"No." Ronny jerked and said, "I hit . . . I hit him sometimes." He reset his feet.

The man asking the questions breathed and looked up at a clock on the wall. He said again, "Did you ever hit your father?"

"Yes."

"Did you chop your father up?"

"No!" Ronny's voice broke. "No."

Again, the scratch of needle etched out some cryptic meaning.

"Did you kill your father?"

"No!"

"Do you know where your father is now?"

"NO!"

"Did you have a bad relationship with your father?"

"No!"

"Did you kill your father?"

"No!"

"Do you know where your father's body is?"

"NO!"

It went on that way for another fifteen minutes, the same questions coming slowly, and the solemn incantation of "No" filling the small confines of the room we occupied. It was sweltering in there. I leaned against the glass, stared at the man monitoring the machine, the gleaming sweat under his thinning hair. It was hard to believe people had committed their lives to tracing the metabolic manifestations of a lie, what it does to the alkali in the sweat, the microsecond delay in synapses firing, the slight palpitations in the heart.

"Did you chop your father up?"

"No," delivered now in a monotone voice.

You could tell something had changed, a deadness of effect: the thread of drama, of suspense, had been played out, a law of diminishing returns even in interrogation. The man monitoring the machine knew as much. He said, "We got enough."

Ronny sat still as the man pulled off the electrodes from his head. Ronny said quietly, "Did I pass?" He was visibly shaken.

The man who'd asked the questions didn't answer; the other just rolled away the lie-detector machine out into another room.

In the aftermath of silence, Ronny slumped and put his hand to his temples and rubbed the soft imprints. He went up to the glass. He said quietly, "Miss Carter, you out there? I want to speak with you. I want people to know my side in all this . . . Miss Carter, you out there?" He pointed at the glass, touched it softly. "Hey, you, Mr. Appointed Lawyer, you arrange it with her . . ." He cupped his hands and pressed against the glass. "I know you're out there."

Linda Carter let a smile pass over her. I saw her glance at me for a moment, savor some kind of victory. She put her hand to the mirrored glass where his face was. She spoke, but Ronny heard nothing.

We were led from the room as a fat man entered to interrogate Ronny. We went out into another room, but the speaker was still going in the background. I edged toward it, listened, while a press release was read by a cop in a suit. He just went on about shit we already knew, confirmed the existence of the finger, mentioned that Ronny Lawton's old man's pickup truck was missing. That was something that we had all overlooked. It was something that just couldn't be hid away like that. It's one thing looking for body parts, but try to hide a car. There are only so many rivers and ponds out there.

From the opening in the door, I could see Ronny smoking again, sitting with his arms folded and blowing rings into the fluorescent lighting. He kept at his head, squeezing the temples.

I heard Ronny shout agitatedly, "Did I pass?"

I edged away as the cop kept reading out a long list of things that had been gathered from the house, the trace of blood, some footprints . . .

The microphone caught the fat man's labored breath inside the interrogation room. He spread his mass over the chair, parting his legs for balance and leaning forward with this pendulous fat hanging down from his waist. His bald head had the luster of a polished bowling ball from the effort.

Ronny shouted, "Did I goddamn pass?"

I got bits and pieces of it after that, moved closer to the interrogation room. I heard the fat man say, "Ronny, I heard you used to specialize in deboning chickens in the army. I heard you know how to tease away the skin from the carcass, slip a knife around the cartilage, cut away bone from bone . . . The way I hear it, you can take a skin off a chicken like people take a sock off their foot."

Ronny shook his head. "Jesus H. Christ. I want to know if I goddamn passed. You hear me?" Ronny got up and banged the glass. "I want out, you sons a'bitches!"

I did a desperate thing next, stepped away from the group, went into the viewing room, pulled the door to behind me, and watched things unfold. I took a deep breath and caught the pump of my heart.

The fat man's breath was this bellows of air. He raised his voice. "You want to explain that dirt under your fingernails?"

"I already told them, I was digging for night crawlers out near my place for fishing."

"Ronny, Ronny, Ronny. Don't take me for a goddamn ass. This is how I figure it. You're getting me mad, Ronny, real mad. I got a heart condition, and you pull this shit on me in July, right when I want to be hiding out of this sun. You go and stir up all this trouble. You couldn't have waited for the fall, when at least I could be out looking at the changing of the leaves . . ."

Ronny put his hands to his head and said nothing.

The fat man just shook his head. "This is what I think happened out there at your place. This is what I've put together so far." And the fat man went into a simple outline of a fight that got out of hand, with Ronny killing his old man.

Ronny just stared at the fat man. "I didn't do shit" is all he said.

"I want to tell you, what we do here, Ronny, is fit the crime to the intention, not the act. You understand what I mean by that? Think about that. We fit the crime to the intention, not the act. Extenuating circumstances play into every action. We got to know what someone was thinking when they killed their old man. That's maybe the most important part of all this, knowing what the person was thinking out there when they killed."

"Jesus Christ! Stop saying I killed him!"

"You see, the more I have to work, the more pissed I get. I mean, if someone wants to yank my chain and make me go out there in that heat and drive all over this county looking for evidence, then I'm going to get pissed. I don't like hot weather, Ronny. You only got to look at me to know I can't take this heat."

I just began shaking my head.

Inside, the fat man jiggled as he got going again. He had Ronny light him a Pall Mall, and he smoked and talked, he pointed his finger at Ronny and out to the world beyond them. "What I do for a living is make up stories, probable stories, Ronny. You give me a set of facts, a set of suspects, and I work from there. That's how this game works, Ronny. That's police work right there. Make up a story from a set of facts. So let's just say there was a fight, and things got out of control, and you hit your old man, then we're not talking about first-degree murder, because you weren't planning on killing him. It just happened." The fat man reached out and touched Ronny's hand. "Right now, son, let's look at the facts here. I'm looking at a young man who served his country, a man who got himself his GED while in the army, a young man who was correcting mistakes in his life, and things were looking good for him. He got himself a job as a cook, was earning money for the first time in his life. They're going to hear all that in court, how this young man went about changing his life. 'Course, he had a wife and kid who were busting his ass over money, wanting it all. But he was trying to get on track, and so he lives at home with his old man, so he can save some money . . ."

Ronny shouted, "I don't know what the fuck you're talking about, mister!"

The fat man retracted his hand, but he was insistent, kept going.

Ronny shouted, "This is bullshit!"

"I heard all this from people out where you live, Ronny, people that'll swear you and your old man were like oil and water. You mean you're going to sit there and look me in the face and tell me everybody I talked to is a liar?"

Ronny shook his head. "I fought with my old man. So what? That's not murder!" But it was an admission, and on went the fat man, and Ronny Lawton kept saying, "He went missing is all. I'm telling you the truth. You hear me? You fuckin' hear me?" He turned and began shouting at the mirrored glass again. He shouted, "I don't got to take this, do I, Mr. Lawyer? Mr. Lawyer, you behind that glass? I want you in here, now! Represent me, goddamn it!"

But there was no lawyer. I got an uneasy sense about things. I wanted to get away from there before someone came back.

The fat man spread the starfish of his huge fat fingers over his thighs and licked his lips. Beads of sweat fell from his giant head.

Ronny put his hands to his face and just roared, "Why the fuck are you doing this to me?"

The fat man kept leaning forward. He said, "All right, Ronny. Let's say you didn't chop up your old man, and I never said you did. Let's say you're telling the truth, then you help me prove it."

Ronny stopped abruptly, seemed to pivot on his toes, and looked at the fat man. "I told you what I know."

"Okay then. I got to draw up a list of names of potential suspects. That's how we do things in this business. Suspects, motive, and opportunity. It doesn't get more complicated than that. I want you to help me, Ronny. Who hated your old man, Ronny? Who hated your old man enough to cut him up into pieces?" The fat man took out a small notebook from his breast pocket and leaned into the table. "Okay, Ronny. Start thinking."

Ronny said, "We got a python named Paul that went missing three years back. He got down under the floors, seemingly. At night you can hear him sometimes, moving around the pipes. Who the hell knows how big that mother might be now?"

"Ronny, you goin' to look me in the face and tell me a goddamn snake named Paul ate your old man?"

Ronny said, "I'm just telling you what's out there is all. I read this man went missing in New York, and it ends up these alligators in the sewers had eaten him." Ronny leaned toward the mirrored glass. "That's a true story. I read that somewhere. I swear on a Bible."

"And did the snake have the goddamn evolutionary presence of mind to make that leap from constriction to using a knife and fork to cut your ol' man into pieces, Ronny? Snakes constrict, they swallow their victim whole, Ronny."

Ronny shrugged his shoulders. "I'm just telling you, Paul's out there at the house is all."

"You goin' to cooperate, Ronny?"

"Sure," Ronny said. "Who'd want me out of the way? Is that it?"

"Yeah. For starters."

Ronny was visibly shaking. "Okay, awright then. You want a suspect? I'll give you a suspect. Maybe you want to check with that whore-ass bitch of mine! Yeah, maybe you want to go check her ass out and that asshole she's hitched up with, Karl Rogers."

"You mean your wife?" the fat man said.

"Yeah, that bitch! Check her ass out!" Ronny went up to the window. "Hey, Linda, you want to help prove me innocent?" But she wasn't there. I slipped from the room with at least one piece of information to go on.

CHAPTER 5

Ronny walked after that, went back to his house, though he couldn't leave the county. He resumed his job at Denny's. I was in the office late a few nights later, and things had settled into a stalemate. The AP carried a small piece I'd written about his release, and then things fizzled. Sam was pissed that Linda Carter has an exclusive with Ronny. There was talk that 60 *Minutes* would air her interview in a few weeks if things materialized. That just sent Sam into a tailspin. He drank around the office, kept looking at me and Ed and saying, "I should have got out years ago. I should have seen this all coming. The written word is dead." Our sales had fallen off again.

It was hell for us in the aftermath of Ronny's release, the gloomy depression of having nothing to do again. There was still no call on the answering machine from Diane. I felt that last thread of attachment silently unravel. I called and left long rambling messages late at night.

The days brought no relief, burning with a glaring intensity where all you wanted to do was eat watermelon and hide in shade. A week-old dryness had settled across the plains. It brought a level of alarm in its sudden revelation—a week of no rain. People began to count the days, look to the sky. The mosquitoes were out in force. I spent hours down at the Y in that secret realm of habitual motion, swimming those laps with my eyes closed. It was what made the heat tolerable, what gave me sleep at the end of the long days.

Ed and I spent a morning insetting mesh screens. I kept looking at the AP wire, kept waiting for the phone to ring. Ed caught my eye from time to time and smiled faintly. "We want you and Sam over for dinner a week from Thursday, Bill."

I said, "Sure."

"Ribs all right with you, Bill?"

"Fine, Ed."

"Darlene makes a hell of a sweetbread."

I retreated to the mundane, front-paged a story on bug repellent and citronella candles. We had a home-remedy section, a cure-all on how to treat bites, lifted from *The People's Home Library*, a compendium of natural cures tried and tested by ordinary people. For bites it suggested the following: cold bread, mud or cabbage-leaf poultices, yogurt applications, one part phenol mixed with water from fifty to one hundred parts, table salt, or lamp oil. An onion, cut into rings and placed on a sore, brings relief in minutes, as does catnip. Another cure directs the application of onions boiled in lard to be smeared over the infected area.

Ed drew a sketch of a mosquito and labeled its anatomical parts. We got down an encyclopedia from the shelf, and Ed traced the mosquito while I called the local college and verified a few facts with a biologist on the mating cycle of mosquitoes, average life span, how the mosquito draws blood from its victim, and how much blood they suck up in their life span.

I said, "That looks real good, Ed."

Ed had the discretion not to really say anything, but he said this one thing quietly to me, whispered, "This will come around. I guarantee it."

"How do you know, Ed?"

"I just got a feeling. Give it a while."

It was like an admission about something, or maybe just his way of taking the edge off things. I tried to get at what he meant by things coming around, but it was like he knew he'd said too much or something.

Ed went off to the bathroom in the end, stayed in there for nearly half an hour. I went in. The odor was unreal. I heard Ed's shoes against the floor, saw the black shoes under the door and the pool of his trousers around his ankles. There was just a general silence, the feet waiting pensively, like two cockroaches hiding.

Only a matter of feet separated me from Ed, but I maintained the silence. I shouldn't have come in there. I had invaded his space out of morbid curiosity. It was like watching the beginning of a death unfold, a long, silent suffering that somehow is supposed to enlarge your capacity for human compassion and love. I had not seen that in my father, just that abbreviated end of his brains on the wall. It had left me with nothing. In Ed I saw something that could teach me about humility. I went over to the urinal, but I couldn't go. I turned my head around and kept looking at the floor, at those pensive feet. I heard the lid of the toilet scrape behind the door, something that could only be detected in this quiet. I went to the mirror and washed my hands, stared at the unmoving feet. He was on the squat enamel toilet with the wooden seat, unblinking, holding things inside himself, waiting for me to leave. And so I did. I left without saying a word, because my problems are solely my own. I had no real right to demand that a man with his insides burning become some sort of symbol for me.

Through the long days of silence, I shuffled back and forth from the watercooler, guzzled pints of water, wet the back of my neck with a damp cloth. I stopped sometimes outside Sam's door, hesitated, heard him whispering to Ed. There was something strange in the way Sam and Ed looked at each other when I turned my head. I felt I was catching glimpses of them nodding. At times they seemed locked in clandestine discussion, disengaging themselves when I came into the room. Ed said things like, "Pabst Blue Ribbon it is then, Sam. A twelve-pack should be fine," then he would smile at me. "You have any objections to Blue Ribbon, Bill?"

I said, "No, I don't," when what I really wanted to say was, "What the hell are you saying behind my back?" They went out to lunch and left me alone most days.

I was thinking this paper was going to fold any day now. I had that feeling that this was the end of things for me. I'll let you in on a little secret here. I failed the LSATs big time. I mean, there wasn't a law school anywhere that would have taken me. I even faked illness over spring break of junior year and went for this intensive

week course out in New York that promised dramatic results. I
didn't let on to Diane. She'd said she might take the LSAT test, she
wasn't sure. And I fucked it up big time. That's what has me here
for the most part, and of course the house. I might have forgone the
house if there'd been something out there for me, some law school,
because where the hell are you going to get in this world with a B-
minus average in philosophy from a second-rate college? What
really pisses me off is those asinine questions, those logic games,
feeding fuckin' plants that need this and that much water at this
and that time of the day. I mean, what the fuck has that got to do
with law? I've never seen a geranium testifying in court. Jesus
Christ, it pisses me off. "Gentlemen of the jury, we have here a rose
up on charges of stalking!"

I opened envelopes from the courthouse posting legal notices,
worked the small calculator, and added up words and the price. We
charged 80¢ a word. I copied it all into a small ledger. That's what
we really served as, a blotter of court notices, of who was being
sought in connection with this or that.

All the while I was writing out the notices, I kept thinking there
was something I should have been able to do, to get to Ronny
somehow and make him talk to me, confide in me and not Linda
Carter. I kept saying to myself, "This is a definitive moment in your
career. Goddamn it, go talk to the man. Find out what the hell happened!" I mean, I kept saying that to myself, over and over again.
And then, I called his house and got him on the phone, identified
myself, but all he had to say was "Fuck you! I seen that photo you
done of me, asshole." End of story.

I spent time down at the library, went through old articles from
the county's history, and began what I thought might develop into
a series of articles on the old horrors that had beset us over the
years. In the center of the paper we had the dyed sepia of a bygone
era, dark black ink impressed in an old-fashioned manner. I'd
found a story of Arnold Preston, who, in 1902, in the same week of
our present tragedy, was found hanging from the rafters of his ceil-

ing in his Sunday best, dead some two weeks by all accounts, since that was the last he'd been seen at church services. He hung like a disembodied scarecrow with a Sunday hat tipped back on his forehead, his heavy black boots like two anchors. There was an ungodly pestilence emanating from the house, a swarm of flies that made the air hum when the door was kicked open by concerned neighbors. They went in with rags to their faces, knew what to expect. In the back room were the remains of Arnold Preston's wife and three children, two girls and a boy all under four years of age, with their throats slit.

It was a year of crop failure, when the heat burned the corn to a brown, wilting stalk, when almost everything withered and died. Forty-two days of drought that summer. Arnold Preston had come four years previously to Indiana, an invalid from the Boer War, a man in his forties, escaping the violence and intolerance of Europe. What they said of a man like him, at what he did, was that "He got loneliness."

But somehow, there was a disconnectedness from that past. The story had a wanton forced sadness. We ran it, but as you read it, you asked yourself, why did someone go and dig that up? I knew as much. It made me physically sick just to read through that shit. I wasn't beyond wanting to go out into the county and collect every last edition and burn the shit. "Christ Almighty!" We decided jointly in the editorial room to scrap the project after the first installment. I tell you, my back was up against the wall.

What I did do, to resurrect myself somewhat, was to make up a suggestion sheet, soliciting patrons to list where they thought pieces of Ronny Lawton's old man might be buried. That went down with Sam and Ed. They really liked that. Sam even printed that we'd give a $5,000 reward for the person who predicted rightly where Ronny Lawton's old man was buried. That worked out real well for us. We had a running list of places checked, and in came the new suggestions. Out around the area, the human chains had broken up into small conglomerates of interested and competing parties, divided down church lines. The search for Ronny Lawton's old man became a church social with ice cream and sodas. We ran pictures of the human chains every day. The dragnet of greed stretched out across the land. Sam stared at the shots of the human chains. He said, "That's capitalism at its goddamn best and worst out there."

What the human chains discovered was not the remains of Ronny Lawton's old man but things like old threshers and broken shards of china cups from old dwellings, deep in cornfields long overgrown. And one group found a dumping ground of chemicals in a pond near the St. Joseph River, twenty barrels of chemicals leaching into the water supply. It had to be analyzed, but we as a nation had become used to these exhumations, the silent burial grounds of our industrialism, the great corporations that dumped and spilled with impunity, that poisoned us. The Love Canal phenomenon of silent death, not an Auschwitz of mass graves, but a hidden killer that went airborne and into our water supply, a horror that went into our genes, made us sick with cancer, deformed our children before we ever realized we were casualties of our former industrialism. In the end, the chemicals out in our cornfields were deemed nonhazardous, and even that story died for us at the paper.

We were back to the old schedule, despite the suggestion list, getting the paper off to press by late evening. The inertia of the nightmare hadn't quite waned, but now it was just simmering. The indignation, the fear, had abated. Even my daily checkbox on simply "Guilty" or "Not Guilty" was getting fewer responses. I was now into a long tract on what I called "A Theory of Dismemberment," which I was sending out to the AP wires behind Sam's back each evening. I had this lofty belief that I might still escape, that I had touched something deep in those editors across the country. The gist of my theory was tying Ronny Lawton's old man's being chopped to pieces to the advent of corporate downsizing, to the dismantling of vast infrastructures of power, to the antiunionism that pervaded our nation, to the Republican cry to cut big government, to our sudden abandonment of any collective intelligence

and solidarity. Everything was coming apart. That was the great
metaphor I was working with. What I was doing in between the
goddamn obituaries was writing up this piece about that sense of
"personal growth" we were all being asked to take on, the less-pay-
and-more-hours phenomenon.

Sam was out at the cooler. I got up with a piece I was working on
in my hand. I came toward him and took a drink of water and said,
"Sam, if you could just listen to what I was thinking for a minute,
please?"

I sat in with him. His head blocked out a patch of sunlight, cast
a shadow that cut through me. I was going on about Rocky specifically this day. I said, "Sam, don't you think Rocky is all social commentary, an ironic representation of the megalomaniac sense of
personal growth that has been shoved up our asses in recent times?
Take the gigantism of his physical body. What is it but a new hemisphere into which he has grown, because there is no more land to
discover, no new colony to conquer? He has colonized himself, Ed,
down there in the meatpacking plants of unions, he's sublimated
frustration into the ring. I'll tell you, let's look at Rocky in a few
years, let's see what he turns into. I can see him morph into some
outside creature, alienated, someone who has lost faith in the
American way, shooting up his hometown!"

I crawled away home from the tongue-lashing Sam gave me. I've
never seen a man so irked by genius in all my life. He said I was sick.
I shouted at him, "That's social commentary right there, my friend,
the gospel of our demise. Rocky is a cautionary tale of the horror
we, as individuals, are capable of, when we are cut away from the
collective. This time it ended in the ring, but the fight is going to
spread into the streets."

Sam shouted back at me, "I wish I could buy you for what you're
worth and sell you for what you think you're worth. I'd make a fortune."

Back home, I opened the mahogany liquor cabinet and poured
whiskey into one of those fishbowl brandy glasses. I didn't eat. I
drank until the edge of the day softened into a dull sleep. I slept

from 6 P.M. to midnight. I had a clock set. I rose and got myself ready for the night shift at Denny's, where Ronny worked, though he didn't show for more than a week after his release.

The dead of night had been a world otherwise closed to me, the hours of the insomniac, the silent nightlife of our species. But now I became part of that species, rising at midnight and going down to the diner.

I awoke in bed at that darkish hour, picked out the sound of a mosquito hitting its body against my bedroom window, and pinched it into oblivion. Fireflies lit up the night in twinkling semaphore. I moved around looking for my clothes, poured myself a glass of milk to coat my stomach.

I could feel the vast emptiness of a world devoid of life on the first of those night drives. It was an attenuating compression of detail, of sound devoid of meaning, revealing its component parts, the car lights tracing a solitary trajectory though the night toward the diner, toward the crimson bleed of the strip, the neon of signs hissing at an audible level.

I drove into the lot at Denny's, walked through the doors. It made me queasy, that onerous sadness of yellow brightness, unnatural against the blackness of night. I had entered a domain of male longing. It's hard to fathom the strange instinct that somehow compels men to get in their cars and come down to these joints and drink black coffee, eat stale doughnuts, and smoke. It's a sort of insomnia of disaffection. There's a smell of sleep and booze and mental illness, a sour odor of feet and greased hair.

I sat in a booth and smoked and drank my coffee and just watched things unfold, ate way too much food, grand slams and Coke, and then on to coffee and pecan pie. It was a quiet drama that first night. I watched the kind of men who prey on cashiers at all-night gas stations and at all-night diners, the creeping certitude of their attack, the slow web of words threaded together, "Evenin', howdy, how's everybody this fine night?" or the sullen slump of men who sat and made the counter tremble. I watched them all, the way they leaned like jockeys on their stools, watching the waitresses, looking at legs in white nurse's stockings and shoes, the old-fashioned dresses, pilgrim-brown-and-white-checkered aprons tied at the waist, white bonnet hats, and hair in a bun set with pins. The waitresses, for their part, shared the soft spread of thighs, child-bearing hips, rounded calves, a languid sack of breasts, a supple baby fat, like veal, like things raised away from sunlight. And yes, they lived for the obscurity of dark, left sleeping babies at home, snoring boyfriends, and started their Pintos and Dusters and Chevettes and disappeared.

To stop myself from going really insane, I began studying for the LSATs again. After the first night at the diner, I bought a fat book of questions with big letters, LSAT, written in red ink on the cover, that earmarked me as a loser who was contemplating a life change. So I tore the cover off the book and tore out sections which I fitted in my pocket. I set the sections down in the middle of my paper and began studying each night at the diner. It wasn't long before I was caught up again in the quandary of word problems. I stared with glazed eyes at the double-negative phrases that had to be deciphered. This one was about scarves and hats in a display window, about color coordination, about what combination of hats and scarves could appear in the display according to long criteria of what MUST appear and what MUST NOT appear. I got up and went out to the telephone and said, "Diane. Listen, please. If you're there, pick up!"

I sat through it all for going on a week, kept thinking back to Ed's assurance that things would turn around. But they hadn't. I put my hands to my head and rubbed my temples. I worked on the suggestion list for the next day's edition, but by now even that novelty had begun to fade.

Even in this dark solidarity of losers, there was no escaping myself. I was there in the reflection of the glass, staring back at myself, pencil in hand, mumbling numbers and strings of letters, what could and could not appear in the window display. It was the anxiety of not knowing what to do with my life, feeling each day's separation from the days I'd made the AP wire. I kept at the problems, cheated so much I had to begin leaving the answer code back home. I drank so much coffee I felt it in my sweat, tasted it in everything I ate and smelled. I got up from my booth late in the night and left messages, simple pleas, "Just call me and tell me it's over. You owe me that much." Then, one night, I began reading a question about trains leaving from Nebraska and Chicago traveling and making mandatory stops, with an intersecting section of track that could have posed a potential death trap if speeds weren't calculated. I had the book in one hand and just fed the box dimes and quarters until I was flat out of coins. I had this sickening burn in the pit of my stomach from the acid coffee beans and from the goddamn questions. I sat in the bathroom and stared at graffiti. It's sad what you read in there, the solitary sentences, usually about sex, offers of blow jobs and phone numbers, sketches of cocks and pussy by fledgling psychos. It was like being in a confessional to unspoken desire.

I sat again at my table and watched the silent ambush of longing, a courtship around foodstuffs, stared at a lineup of pies, heard the deep-fat fryer hissing in the background through the late night, things dipped in batter, a griddle with scrambled eggs and rinds of bacon, flapjacks and grits and hashed potatoes and sizzling onions.

I went out into the night air, into the pull of a storm somewhere far off, heard something dislodge way up in the sky, like a boulder, disturbed and sent rolling across the night. But it didn't rain where we were during that week, just heat lightning way out over the Great Lakes.

I got back to the word problems and ended up lost deep in my cranium, at that dead end, at the misfiring synapses that couldn't hold numbers in my head. I got home late in the first week of my vigil, just as the sun was beginning to rise. I was hyped on coffee. The answering machine was blinking. I fell over a chair getting to the machine. The message said simply, "Four hours and eight minutes." It was Diane's voice. It took me a moment to understand what the hell she was talking about. The answer to the problem. I got out the LSAT book and checked the answer key, and it was four hours and eight minutes. I called her back immediately, got the answering machine. I shouted, "Do you think I give a fuck about trains traveling between Chicago and Nebraska? Jesus Christ, Diane, how much fuckin' time have you got on your hands up there? What the hell are you doing up there, Diane? I need to talk to you. I never wanted to be with anybody but you, Diane. Please, why won't you speak to me?" Then I called her back and I said, "Okay, Diane. Just tell me, how the hell did you get four hours and eight minutes?"

I felt the throbbing insomnia of those nights, the slow ingestion of caffeine, seeing black circles ringed with yellow, the strain on the eyes, looking from the light in the ceiling and then into the black outside, the whirl of the ceiling fans turning like we might take off into labored flight at any moment.

I listened to a man tell a waitress called Bee how to take a penknife and cut through a corn on her foot. "You got a potato with an eye in it, Bee?"

She gave him one. He took a knife out of his pocket, flicked the blade before her face, and proceeded to tell her how to soak her feet in a hot bowl of water and Epsom salts for a good five minutes until the skin gave, and then how to pare away at the corn real slow. He cut away at the brown skin and then dug slowly into the eye of the potato and scooped it out.

Bee was smiling at him. She said, "Maybe I just might let you help me." The man held the eye of the potato up so the others could see.

"Order up!" The squeak of the order wheel . . . The smoldering agitation of men wanting to tell her things, men yawning loudly, men whistling to themselves, men drumming the counter, men shuffling their feet, men cracking their knuckles, men rustling the paper, men going "Yep, yep, yep," men letting out long, slow breaths, men going, "I'll be damned," men saying "Shiiiitttt" like they had a slow leak, men making clicking sounds, men dislodging teeth and resetting them in their head . . . It was all a form of a mating call. The unnatural light of existence in that diner, in that test tube, that goddamn incubator of desire, was like a nature special on the sexual antics of spiders and insects, or on those monkeys whose asses turn a violent shade of red that they thrust into other monkeys' faces. It was one of those grotesque *National Geographic* programs where things are rigged so that enemies wander into each other's domain and rip each other's head off in an effort to win the female of the species' favor.

And then came the night when Ronny Lawton arrived in his paper chef's hat with a hairnet showing at his forehead. I tried to speak to him, but he said, "Fuck off! You stay away from me, you son of a bitch!" I stayed through the nights before he became a celebrity, maybe just waiting for him to snap, to want to talk. But he never did. He worked in obscurity until that first Friday night, when some asshole hit upon the idea of going to see old Ronny Lawton, and so came the first of the pilgrims entering Denny's chanting his name.

I stayed through that first weekend. I was deep in a major word problem on that first Friday, a displacement-of-water problem, where some engineers were building a dam. I had line vectors intersecting this way and that, and weights written off to the side on the margin of the page, but it was all shit, and then next thing I heard the procession of noise out of the dark and scrambled to hide everything.

In they poured, filling up the silence of this late hour with their roars.

Ronny Lawton seemed to break out of his sullen manner and cracked a smile like you might crack an egg. "So you've come to see Ronny Lawton?"

A chant went up, "Ronny! Ronny! Ronny!"

The diner just filled with teenagers.

"Hey, Ronny! Don't go putting none of your father in my dinner, you hear me, Ronny Lawton?"

Ronny Lawton slapped his thigh and said, "That's real funny,

assholes." He put on a great act behind the small window in those
first nights. He said things like, "Ronny Lawton knows where you
assholes live." He held up his chopping knife and put it to his
throat and used the dull edge and traced it across his own neck.
"Don't get Ronny Lawton mad!"

"Are you sure this ain't your father's wiener, Ronny?" Someone
held up a link of sausage.

"You want to see Ronny Lawton's wiener?"

Ronny Lawton now spoke of himself in the third person, set
himself up as a spectacle of horror, and enjoyed every minute of it.

"I got a girl here that's dying to meet you, Ronny!" These footballer types held this small blonde by the arms, like she was a sacrifice. She was screaming. The whole place was filled with this
chanting, "Ronny! Ronny! Ronny!"

Outside, the regulars, the sullen men of prey, arrived and then
turned and headed for some other all-nighter, some rock on which
to resume their solitary existence baiting sad females of our species.

Linda Carter had set up a remote feed from Denny's by Saturday
night, went on the air with kids pumping their fists, shouting out
his name. Ronny came out dressed in an apron splattered with
blood and said in an utterly contrite manner, "Linda, I think you
can see here, the people have spoken. They are behind Ronny
Lawton one hundred percent." A huge roar went up behind him.
Ronny Lawton raised his hand slowly, like he was going to show
you a stigma, and said softly, "Ronny Lawton is an innocent man."
Again, the chant, "Ronny! Ronny! Ronny!"

A few days later, I was standing there with the manager, Hank
Rogers, a guy I'd known in junior high school, who was shaking his
head. There was a line of kids snaking around Denny's. This was a
rock concert. Car stereos blared music. Hank motioned me to him
and said, "Bill, this is off the record, but our night profits are up
three hundred and fifty percent the nights Ronny works. I mean,
I've had to go out and hire me another work crew just to keep up
with business. We got him here Wednesday, Thursday, Friday, and
Saturday night, and all the high school kids from here and over in

Carlyle and Cass and Plymouth County just pour in here. Well, I mean, you've seen it, Bill. We could charge admission, and they'd pay. Ronny Lawton is the hottest ticket in town."

Hank took me back into his office and closed the door. "Listen to this, Bill. Ronny came in here the other day, and he demands a big fat raise. I mean triple minimum wage, wants eight bucks an hour. He threatened to go on down to Big Boy. He said he was in negotiations with them. We're talking about a goddamn son of a bitch that chopped up his old man, and he just stands there and says, 'I ain't waitin' all day, Hank. You gonna pay or what?' I mean, what the hell could I do? Three hundred and fifty percent increase in profits on the nights he works."

I said, "You do what you gotta do, Hank."

"He held out for goddamn Employee of the Month, Bill. Jesus H. Christ, I could do nothing about it." Hank just shook his head at me. "You don't think they're anywhere near to busting him, do you, Bill?" I sensed the trepidation in his voice.

I said, "I've heard nothing."

On the door of Hank's office was this sign in big red letters, "If you got time to lean, you got time to clean!" I kept seeing that sign in my head for days. I guess that's the kind of shit that drives me wild, the jingoism of our imprisonment, the secularization of our language to catchphrases.

It was all stalemate still. Three weeks since Ronny Lawton chopped up his old man, and there really wasn't a shred of evidence to nail him. His father's pickup was still missing. There was a finger in some lab somewhere that had been analyzed, and things had been removed from Ronny Lawton's property. But still nothing, just the mania of his recent ghoulish celebrity, a sideshow of late-night entertainment out in the deep Midwest.

Even at the office, Sam and Ed were hardly around. I did the mundane crap as usual, got it done in an hour or so. I spent most of the day at home, holed up from the heat outside, sucking down pink slabs of watermelon, spitting seeds into a bowl. I watched television, cop shows mostly, where the criminals made these blurting

confessions at the end. I watched cartoons as well on the UHF.
Magilla Gorilla, Underdog, Top Cat, Mr. Magoo, Tom and Jerry, the
kaleidoscope of color in the gray of the basement through the midday hours. I was hooked on Scooby Doo and the gang. You gotta
look at the dynamics going on there, how Fred, that blond jock,
always gets that priss, Daphne, alone, sending the brains behind
the outfit, Velma, with her wide-rimmed glasses, off by herself to
solve the crime, and how Shaggy, that inept excuse of gangling
male adolescence, indulges in a sublimated frustration, eating like
a goddamn pig in the company of his bosom buddy, Scooby. I mean,
Shaggy's got a sack of testosterone, he's got to understand that
something ain't right here with Fred and Daphne. There's a volcano of sexual tension in that show, if you just tap into it right. I
was shouting things like, "Let's forget the goddamn ghosts and get
back to Fred and Daphne!" I guess that's the genius of a show like
that, the suggestive quality that lies just beyond the reach of children, that allusive subtext that just screams at a guy like me. You
can deconstruct *Scooby Doo* on so many goddamn levels.

When I was done shouting at the television, which, I admit, I
was doing a hell of a lot, I settled for my evening nap before the
vigil at the diner. I watched the looped reel of Linda's live coverage
from Denny's interspersed throughout the daytime cartoons. Linda
Carter had captured Ronny Lawton.

The Ronny Lawton fiasco had become a politically embarrassing
situation. I'd interviewed the mayor earlier, quoted him for the
morning edition. The mayor was there again on television, saying
he was handing over the stalemate of this investigation to state
authorities. By the time the paper was released tomorrow with my
quote, saying this exact thing, it would be old news. That was the
kind of dilemma I faced. I lived in the slipstream of television's
immediacy. I was like a goddamn baker selling day-old doughnuts.

The mayor was in a white shirt soaked with sweat. He said it was
an abomination, what was happening down at Denny's, but he
could do nothing to stop it. A man was, by all accounts, dead, and
this is what things had come to, a carnival of horror where the strip

was literally backed up a mile, with hot rods and muscle cars and kids in station wagons going wild and shouting out Ronny Lawton's name.

That evening Pete called me, said he had a mandate from the mayor to take care of the situation down on the strip.

I went out with him in the patrol car, and we ate at Fat Bertha's café outside town, and he said, "I ain't equipped for all this crap. The mayor chewed my ass out today, says I'm not worth shit to this investigation, that I let it get out of hand." Pete was digging into an apple cinnamon crumble with ice cream. A pot of coffee steamed in the center of the table.

I just yawned. I was thinking about the LSATs. Ronny Lawton had almost become disengaged from my consciousness. He was all Linda Carter's.

Pete kept eating before me. I wished I'd stayed at home. It was just another night of eating and talking, and, Jesus, if there weren't some of the men from Denny's, the sullen predators, up against the counter talking with the blob Bertha. I'd seen enough of this town.

We went out in the police car. Pete turned into the Howard Johnson's lot and killed the lights, and we watched a requiem of cars and trucks going up and down the strip with windows painted like it was homecoming. Pete said, "All we need is one accident, and the shit's going to fly."

I don't even know why I stayed with Pete through the hours of that night. He sat still most of the time, silent, the pulse of a cigarette bringing him out of the shadows for a moment. Every half hour he called up Larry, who was off down the street in some other lot. I think it was Dairy Queen. Pete'd say shit like, "Let's start this dragnet, Larry." I just rolled my eyes at the dragnet shit, more of that cop talk we all used these days. "Ten-four, Pete." Then Pete started the ignition, flicked his cigarette out the window and hit a switch, and off went the wail of siren and spin of sanguine lights as he floored it out of the lot onto the strip to pull over a car, a beaten-up old station wagon with fake wooden paneling all rusted out. I watched Pete get out and approach the car, the heavy haunch of his ass in a uniform too short for him. He had his hand on his holster. I saw Larry grind to a stop, get out the car with his hand on his holster, and shout, "Everybody freeze, goddamn it!"

They got eight kids out of that car. It was like watching a circus act, one after another, each maybe sixteen years old, their first summer driving, feeling the escape from the monotony of bikes, wanting to be down here where the action was. Pete dragged each one of them out of the car and put them up against the car and frisked them. Cars came by, slow, with the music throbbing, guys whistling and shouting.

Pete used his billy club, knocking the kids' legs wide apart, tapping along the inner thigh, surreptitiously ending by hitting their balls. I saw each one of them slump with the pain, but Pete held them steady, shoved their faces into the roof of the car. He kept shouting, "Assume the position, assholes!" making them lean into the car with their hands behind their heads.

Larry yielded a pipe and a nickel bag of pot along with a case of Little Kings. He said, "Look at what we have here," and grinned at Pete, who had a card deck of IDs in his hand like he was playing poker.

I got out at that stage, and the kid who'd been driving the car looked at me. The kid said, "Hey, you, Bill . . . you that guy from the paper, right? It's me, Ernie Tyler, the kid from swimming over in Cass County. Remember me?" Ernie had a big moon face of youth, pocked with acne, and his hair was cropped short. But his body was tapered in a swimmer's V, a body too mature for his round juvenile head.

I nodded at the kid and said, "How you doing, Ernie?" I'd done a story about the team making the state finals for the first time in a decade, had a picture of them with their heads all shaven like they were poster boys for a cancer treatment program. That was real big then, shaving your head before game day. It was all part of the solidarity.

Pete turned and glared at me. "You know this asshole?"

"I'm like everybody else out here. Right? Why'd they bust me?"

Ernie shouted. He must have thought he had an ally in me right then.

Pete struck him with the billy club in the back, hard enough to take the breath out of the kid and make him drop to his knees.

I said, "Pete," and tried to take him aside, but he wouldn't budge. I said quietly, "Pete, those kids made state finals over in Cass County. They're real big over there. I wouldn't, if I were you."

Pete swiveled his head like an owl and sort of dismissed me, and so I backed off. He hit Ernie again. "What did you say, Mr. Wise Ass?"

Larry chimed in, "Yeah, Mr. Wise Ass."

I just stood there and listened.

Pete dragged Ernie to his feet. Larry had drawn his gun but set it back in the holster.

Ernie had this anguished face on him from the hit. He was holding his guts. "I didn't do nothing. Hey, Bill . . . this is police harassment!"

Pete said, "Asshole, you goin' to tell me about the law? I don't have the goddamn time to take you all in now. So I'll tell you what we're going to do. I got all your IDs here. You get together among yourselves and decide who owns this pot. I got all your names here, and tomorrow morning you get down to the courthouse with your legal guardians and you get your stories straight." He grabbed Ernie again and twisted the kid's strong arm. "You get a record, son, and no goddamn college is going to want to touch your ass. Colleges ain't interested in drug pushers, mister. You hear me, asshole?"

That pretty much quieted Ernie and the others. They stood off to the side of the road while Pete took the keys of the car and drove it into the Howard Johnson's lot and left it there and went in and told the manager about the car.

I looked at the kids. I said, "I'll see you guys in the fall. You think you got a chance at defending the title?"

Ernie had this dour look on his face. He had his hands deep in his pockets. "I guess."

I said, "Pete's just trying to do his job. Maybe I can get things dropped for you kids. Okay, Ernie?"

I actually took the kid's hand and shook it. I mean, shit, kids like them were my bread and butter, the mortar of any small paper. Sports stories were my main item most of the year. That's what kept people buying the paper, parents wanting copies about their sons and daughters.

I got Pete to give the kids back their licenses, but he was pretty much pissed. He kept the beer and pot.

We followed the swim team off the main strip, tailed them until they were heading home. Pete just gave this exasperated sigh and said, "School can't come quick enough. It's gotta end then. It sure as hell better."

I said, "You're a sadist, Pete."

He said, "I don't know what the hell that means, but the world needs—"

"Sadists," I said.

"Yeah, sadists," Pete said.

We reparked the car again, set our ambush. I said, "Pete, can you take me home?" It was like a bad date you couldn't escape from.

We drove out by my place. God, it took forever. Pete said, "One of them kids dies out there, and my ass is in the frying pan. Bill, I seen too many good kids end up hamburger behind the wheel of a car. The whole goddamn city could be sued out of all this shit. That's what it's about, Bill. Saving your own ass, getting assholes to a reasonable age where they might just begin to know right from wrong, where they just might give a shit about others. And so, yeah, there's gotta be guys like me. There's gotta be . . . What is that again you called me?"

I said, "Sadist." Jesus Christ, I wished I hadn't given him a new word. That's all he wanted, new definitions to define himself.

He said, "I got to look that one up." He smiled and extended his hand to me, a junior high school classmate, a man with a billy club, the sadist who could take Ronny Lawton into a room and beat out what nobody else could, a man with the capacity to wrench the secret of Ronny Lawton's father from his son, to do what science had failed, and I took his hand, I took the sadist's hand. I conceded that maybe people needed the shit beaten out of them, and then I changed my mind and left.

He shouted after me, "How do you spell *sadist*, Bill?"

"Like it sounds," I shouted, and locked myself away in the house.

I retreated to my car the next evening, out by Denny's, watched things from there, then took out my LSAT questions, got deep into a problem about scientists trying to bring back a ship from the moon. It was ungodly complicated, angles of entry and speed and forces of gravity, minimum weight requirements. I wrote down the basic facts, extrapolated them, the raw figures, and still I got nowhere. I had the light on in the car, alone in this small grotto of despair, dividing numbers and multiplying this and that, until I went over to the phone box and called Diane and blurted out the question. I said, "What's the proper speed for reentry, Diane?"

The diner was uproarious again. I hung up and went out into the glare of the diner. Everyone was eating banana splits and floats and malted milks. Spoons were flying through the air. Guys were shooting spit balls at one another through straws. The same shit, the chant still going, "Ronny! Ronny! Ronny!" as another sacrificial cheerleader was thrust before Ronny Lawton. She was kicking up her long lean legs, and everybody was staring at her small white underwear. Her shirt was up around her bra. You could see her tan lines, the pale underside of her breasts.

Ronny Lawton had a spatula in his hand, orchestrating things, shouting, "Bring her on up, boys!" He flipped patties in the back. They rose into the air and fell back on the griddle with viscous hisses. Ronny emerged and set a bleeding burger on the counter. The blood pooled on a garnish of lettuce.

The cheerleader type was screaming, her hair like a sea anemone caught in that unnatural yellow light of the diner. It was feeding time in the zoo of our madness.

Ronny was laughing. He banged the table. "Bring her on up!" He did the trick with the HERE and NOW again, brought the enigmatic NOWHERE before the crowd, made them feel his ethereal presence, the kind of thing that comes to kids in their nightmares. He was huge. The crimson scars at his pecs had opened again into sore wounds. He had been thrust into the limelight of suspicion, and he had come through. He was pumping those cement blocks down in his basement again, injecting himself with steroids. He had grown into the magnificence of his own terror, intuited the spectacle he could become. You ask yourself, are there men who would gladly sell their soul to the devil? Ronny Lawton was such a man. He kept roaring, "Bring her on up! Bring her on up!" And then he added out of the blue, "Ronny Lawton's got a ten-inch cock!" and that drove everyone insane. Up went the chant "Ronny Lawton's got a ten-inch cock! Ronny Lawton's got a ten-inch cock!" I mean, things flew through the air, an aggregate of adolescent lust, guys banging the tables, an eruption of malts across tables, the girls shrieking in a sudden hysteria as Ronny Lawton came forward. The footballer types had the cheerleader by the arms and legs, swinging her back and forth. She was hyperventilating, writhing like that girl in *The Exorcist.* Her right breast was totally exposed, the size of a halved grapefruit with that small bud of nipple. The guys were screaming, "Ronny Lawton's got a ten-inch cock!"

Out in the night, I drove home, and I found myself saying over and over again, "Ronny Lawton's got a ten-inch cock!" I turned on the radio real loud and started singing at the top of my voice, but it was still there, that chant, that "Ronny Lawton's got a ten-inch cock!" He was a contagion.

At home, the answering machine was blinking. "Reentry at thirty-two degrees, speed two hundred and thirty miles an hour."

I was losing it. I called her answering machine and said, "Diane, please, I'm begging you." I said, "I know time and distance are the great betrayers of lives. It's not you. There's an invisible physics to our lives." I was still for a moment, then I whispered, "What's the speed for reentry into your life, Diane? Tell me, please."

CHAPTER 6

Dinner at Ed's was something I wasn't looking forward to as I drove out on Lincoln Avenue, along the burnt-out, old red brick warehouses. Hell, yes, I was lit up. Christ, you can't arrive at these cookouts with all your senses intact. I'd ripped into my grandfather's single-malt whiskey, the good shit he'd told us to stay out of until he returned from the dead. Inside the cabinet was this temperance plaque. It said simply, "I don't get headaches. I give them!" That was a credo my grandfather had adopted in business and life. He was forever saying that to junior managers at the foundry: "I don't get headaches. I give them!"

I got some ice from our illustrious freezer, smelled that cold fog in my nostrils, poured the warm whiskey and let it break the ice. Jesus, there's nothing like getting loaded sometimes.

You know, I nearly didn't get all this here, this mansion and the money. I was that close to never having this family name. I was conceived a bastard, in some motel next to this small Midwestern college. Some local girl had been going with my father at the time. She was some nobody, one of six girls in a family that had four sons. My father said she was his only true love, but that might have been just some crap to make me feel better. I don't think I've ever seen a man love women the way he did when he was alive. I think it was maybe about getting away from the grime and dirt of the factory years ago that made him what he was. The way I heard it from my grandfather was that my mother was trash. My father spent years languishing in and around women's colleges, driving onto campuses during football season in his fancy car, tailgating and picking up women. 'Course, that was all before I was born. It's what I heard, and most of it had to be true. My father had an album of himself, out on the

road, shots of him and girls sitting on the hood of his car, an album
of past desire that he kept up in the attic. I found it, early in my
teens. I never said anything to my father, but it was a secret passage
back into the man he once was. It made him more human to me.
My father ended up mostly with townies from the bars. They liked
the flash of his car, the ease he had with money. He disappeared for
upwards of a week or two at times. He was legendary for making
dreams come true, a guy who came into a town, drank with women,
whispered, "What would you want most in the world if you had, say,
a week?" Then he'd lean close and say softly, "I got the time, the
money, and the car. All you got to do is walk out of here . . ." It was
like a dare. That's how he met my mother, at a bar during a game.
He took her up to Chicago to the jazz clubs for a week, the two of
them holed up from the world of industry, drinking away the night
in dark corners, the undercurrent of blues music come up out of
Southern slavery, songs of sadness and longing, eternal lamenta-
tions. He burrowed into the softness of her body, hibernated from
the world beyond, kept himself drunk and content. But it stuck
with her more than all those other women. My grandfather said
there were women only waiting to get pregnant by a guy like my
father. My mother held the family to ransom when she got pregnant. She surfaced into the cold reality of her town some weeks
later, the dry dock of harsh reality, with pains in her stomach or
whatever feeling it is women get when they know they are carrying
a man's baby. "You get a taste of money, and it's worse than any
addiction," that was how my grandfather put it about his life in general, but about my mother specifically. I think he told me all those
things because he feared there was some contagion inside me, that
I needed to be put on guard against the latent past. I have a picture
of my mother in her wedding dress, a picture from up in the attic in
the scrapbook. You can see my mother's pregnant with me, the
swell of her belly, almost five months gone. But she's a beauty, the
high cheekbones of Scandinavian descent, the long finger bones of
her hands holding a bouquet of flowers over her stomach, the delicate neck, the smiling eyes. She's maybe the kind of woman I would

have wanted for myself. It's strange to stare across the years at the person who created you and know literally nothing about her. In the photograph, my mother's in one of those wedding dresses that blossom like a parachute from the waist down. My father had married her in secret. That's what I think about it now, looking at that photograph: she, like some paratrooper, dropping me behind enemy lines. I infiltrated the family name. She died in childbirth at nineteen, in the back room of her home, downstate. My grandfather had refused to let her near our mansion, but I survived.

I went over and stared at the fatal mark of the gunshot that had ended it all for my father. I left it there, because I wanted the ice monster to see what had become of his son, I wanted him to face the reality of what a bullet like that can do to a brain and still leave such a hole in a stone wall. All you had to do was look out from this master bedroom over the foundry yards and old brewery to realize this was no goddamn bedroom, this was a boardroom, an industrialist's wet dream, rising to the roar of machinery, to the smell of sulfur and coke burning. I said, "Why didn't they cut you down in tsarist Russia, you cantankerous asshole? I mean, how the hell did you come from feudalism, and I mean feudalism, to become a giant of industry?" We still have his old gray military coat, tattered and torn, from his time in the tsar's army, in an encasement of glass down in the drawing room. You know, there isn't whiskey strong enough to take the edge off my memory of Grandfather. All through college I kept thinking, here I am studying Voltaire and sloshing around in Proustian evocations of mood and setting, and that asshole of a grandfather, at my age, was either wandering across Europe or already bound for South Africa.

Hell, but coming back to this town after college, slinking back to this inheritance, was the greatest mistake of my goddamn life. I'll tell you, it was like inheriting a world after a nuclear holocaust, nothing worth a damn, roaming the shell of debris, shouting in the silence of a depopulated world. The mansion has gone to hell really, a crumbling brick relic after my father died. Hell, it had always been under siege, a great burden over all of us. I remember, in the sixties, our mansion was hit hard in the saga of our nation's race riots, the houses around us were set on fire, the road torn up and lampposts knocked over and used as battering rams to smash in doors during the worst looting. Our mansion survived, mainly because it's up on this man-made hill my grandfather had built when he got stinking rich. He had that Old World sensibility to understand a house needs to be a fortress. He understood that people are going to want to take what you have away from you. And, hell, yes, he fought against those rioters. We had a hell of a lot of attack dogs brought up from our business during the trouble. So we escaped being burned out of our mansion, and our mansion, in turn, became an island in this wasteland. We became marooned, adrift of the chaos around us. And still, even after what had happened to my father, I was drawn back, because the mansion hinted at a security and a faith. It was the fallen Garden of Eden of my youth. And of course, I came back because of that job bequeathed to me at the *Daily Truth*. I thought, just maybe, I had something to say.

But that's bullshit. I came back because I'd screwed up so bad on those goddamn mind games, those goddamn LSAT brain teasers they have devised to find out if you have the head it takes to make it in the real world.

Okay, so I was loaded, but you might as well know who you're dealing with here. You had to get tanked for the journey I was about to embark upon. So out I went, with a tumbler of whiskey and six bobbing cubes of ice, and it was hotter than hell. It was like being hit with a frying pan. I started up that big-ass car of mine, convertible Buick Electra deuce and a quarter, the last of our great excess, a fortress of the highway. But I took the precaution of putting up the canvas roof. Out I went, headed for the old industrial part of town, because you have to go through it if you're heading out west. There's no other road. I stopped at the end of our drive, picked up the mail from the box, and had a good laugh. There they were, those goddamn offers of credit to my old man. He had achieved a sort of immortality in a circle of mailing lists. He got a lot of shit over the summer. He was more popular than me. He got letters telling him he

might have won ten thousand bucks, that he should respond immediately. Publishers Clearing House was practically knocking down
that door to get him to respond to his newfound fortune. He was
preapproved for a Sears charge card. Craftmatic wanted him to try
a home test of their latest bed for thirty days, risk free. I'd really have
liked to have seen his decapitated corpse on that bed. He got a
coupon book for 50 percent off the Clapper, the light fixture that
turned on and off with a smart clap of your hands. Not exactly what
a dead man needed either. I did sign him up for term life insurance,
since he'd been yet again preapproved. I signed him up for ten
records for a cent from Columbia Record Company and, hell, yes,
the records came to the dead man. I got the Eagles and Led Zeppelin and Electric Light Orchestra out of the deal.

It was going on six forty-five, and the sun hung at an angle of
prophetic gloom out on the road, the burning red and gold lick of
fiery flames blazing through remaining factory windows. I said to
myself, if only all this could be consumed in some great catastrophic fire, if only there were a Mrs. O'Leary's cow of old Chicago
fame to vanquish this era into ash. The vast parking lots were huge
fissures of blistering tar mirage, grass sprouting through wounds
where men once worked swing shifts, a world that churned twenty-
four hours a day. It was that foreground of dissolute emptiness that
set the eye askew, made you understand that this was a place emptied of a great horde of people, good people. I felt that abandonment. There were useless For Sale signs posted on warehouses, as if
anybody would come into this hell and buy anything. This was a
Museum of Industrial Demise enclosed in barbed wire. Your admission was solely to give up your personal safety, to actually dare to
enter. Each broken window was a framed portrait of failure, a
gallery to a defunct industrialism, tool and die machines rusted out.

Down here, I was afraid. I locked my door. I wished I had more
than a canvas roof that could be knifed open. I could be taken out
and literally devoured down here. I would have driven fast, but the
road was littered with glass and debris, and I didn't want to spill my
teeming drink. I had the tumbler between my legs. It felt cold

THE KEEPERS OF TRUTH

against my crotch. It was maybe the only real sensation I was feeling, the only sensation strong enough to equal fear. There was the trepidation of that horror always, being attacked, the sudden immobility of a car that rolls to a dead stop, and the real possibility of a tumultuous horde encircling the car like a shifting microbe and devouring me. Christ, it's what we thought about mostly these days, personal safety from others, and from ourselves, too, internally, I mean like from inside the country, from the gunfire of hopeless men who don't care anymore, men like ourselves who sat in diners and remembered home-cooked meals, men who remembered payday, men who remembered what self-worth meant and couldn't face themselves anymore. It was, plain and simple, a jungle of creeping graffiti down here, a virus stealthily moving outward, along the avenues of the old prairie mansions now abandoned, the virus winding its way around the white pillar coliseums of absentee industrialists who had escaped to Miami Beach. These homes were once sold through the Sears catalogue, assembled in a matter of weeks. I stared at that mitosis of architecture, surveyed the road ahead of me, saw the houses left standing now rented by the room, men mostly hunkered down in small rooms, eating and shitting in the glow of a candle, eating cold beans from a can.

We were self-conscious of our failure. It was there on the nightly news. Someone shot into a crowd from the window of an office building they once worked at, because they didn't like Mondays. They returned, out of habit, but there was no work, and they sobbed about their past, about their self-respect and dignity. Shit, didn't I live this every goddamn night! I poured more of that whiskey into me, felt its coldness invade the internal warmth of my organs. It never said shit about dignity on the television when you saw somebody in a standoff with cops, there wasn't that editorial overtone of political and personal crisis. The political was eclipsed in our America. What you usually saw was the image of a man waving a gun, screaming at police, a bullhorn in the hand of a negotiator behind a squad car, a crack SWAT team angling for a shot, and then the sudden eruption of gunfire, the slumped potato-sack body in a pool of his own blood as the SWAT team, dressed in fatigues and visors, showed themselves from alleyways and doorways and rooftops. What you learned was there was a standing army to pick you off, to gas you out of your house if you put a gun to your wife's head, if you screamed, "I can't see paying this mortgage! You hear me? I lived here fifteen years! I lost my job!" All television told you was that retribution would be exacted from you, you would get your head blown off.

It was all destruction down here, the seasonal fluctuation of temperature in our town. The searing nineties of summer and ice storms of winter cleaved brick from brick, accelerating the momentous decline. We could disappear into absolute obscurity, a lost people, in a postnuclear holocaust, a Pompeii of the twentieth century, buried in a gray ash of fallout, subsumed by the vast rolling prairie cornfields, a wound closed up, *Homo sapiens* circa mid–twentieth century, an archaeological dig site in the distant future, something unearthed way out in an overgrowth of corn. Our history was not secure. It was disappearing before our eyes. I just kept driving and watching, ready to turn and make this car into a weapon if need be. I had my drink tight between my legs. All this was less than a decade's despair and ruination, but each year seemed to add exponentially to inevitable obliteration. You can't overstate any of this. I don't give a shit what you say. You see, we were a decade away from loft living, from urban renewal. The pall of death was everywhere along our Rust Belt, an infestation of poverty, seemingly hopeless. You see, we could not envision ourselves as a people recolonizing this space. It was that awful twilight time before sports bars and cheap eats and discount malls out on the plains, a time before junk bonds, a time before credit financing, a time before we decentralized, a time before we got rid of big government, a time before we busted unions, before we understood the meaning of diversification, before we let women out for good, before the colonization of desire and want, before we fully understood the meaning of pet rocks and Cabbage Patch dolls. I tell you, we were at the dead end of our industrial Darwinism down here. In a matter of months, we would be watching our hostages under siege in Iran, watch the puppet governments of our imperialism fall, watch Islamic fanatics burn our flag and curse us. All we could do was wait for the cowboy Reagan to come and deliver us. But that was all in the future, beyond our scope of understanding. So, for now, I kept my door locked and kept driving to Ed Hoskin's house for dinner.

I arrived at my wit's end, to tell the truth, at the end of a long driveway, far out from the city limits amid the dry, brown farmland. The sun was this huge orange ball in my rearview mirror. It was as if Jupiter had descended into our atmosphere.

Ed lived in a ranch-style house out amid the windblown waves of floating corn. The air was thick with a sticky pollen. I jerked the car to a halt, nearly toppling over a small black jockey figurine in red jodhpurs holding up a lamp. I arrived, blitzed, with a humble offering of a dozen ears of corn and a custard-cream pie in a box. They were all there, out at the side of the house, sitting in lawn chairs, Ed, his wife, Darlene, and Sam. The smell of lighter fuel and charcoal filled the air.

I went up the long drive. The garage had been converted into a beauty parlor, the garage door painted in lipstick-pink curlicue lettering. A small sticker indicated Darlene hocked Mary Kay cosmetics.

This goddamn poodle came out from around the side of the house and got hold of my pant leg. I kicked wildly, and that sent things into a mess.

"Gretchen! Gretchen!" I heard this screaming.

I was trying to shake the goddamn poodle off my leg.

Ed shouted at the dog, and it withdrew and ran around the side of the house again. I heard a woman's voice still screaming the dog's name.

"Shit, keep him away from the flame," Sam said when he saw my eyes, when he smelled that tumbler of booze.

"Oh, jeez!" Ed said. He was in Bermuda shorts, a Hawaiian shirt, and black dress shoes. He was holding up a piña colada with a small floral umbrella. I just looked up and smiled. It was like someone had taken Ed's head and stuck it onto another body.

Then Ed said, "Let me introduce you to Darlene, Bill."

Even my grandfather's single malt couldn't protect me from the excruciating anxiety of it all. Darlene emerged from a camouflage of paisley, disengaging herself from a gaudy plastic chair, the goddamn poodle in her arms, and said, "You didn't kick Gretchen, did you?"

The poodle was pulling this whimpering stunt, like it was injured.

I looked at her, said, "Lady, why the hell have you got a beehive on top of your head?"

Sam said, "That ain't nice, Bill." He sort of grabbed my arm, and down fell the goddamn pie I'd brought, exploded like a cowpat, an ooze of muddy chocolate. "Now look at what you did, Jesus awmighty, Bill." Sam took the tumbler out of my other hand, smelled the whiskey, and made a face.

So they made me lie down on the folding chair in the yard, amid a plastic flock of pink flamingos and fuckin' grinning industrious gnomes pushing barrows of flowers, made me drink a pitcher of water until my bladder was near exploding, and then let me fall back, exhausted.

I heard Sam say, "He's got girlfriend trouble, Darlene."

"That's no excuse to go kicking my baby." Then she said, "What the hell's wrong with my hair? You see anything wrong with my hair, Sam?"

I said, "Darlene, I'm sorry, real sorry."

Just speaking got the dog going into convulsions of barks.

Sam said, "Cool it, Bill."

I said, "Okay, Sam. Whatever you say." It was like I stepped outside my body and was listening to myself there on the chair, that sudden lucidity when you see yourself for what you are, that lugubrious moment of drunken enlightenment, and then I was out cold for a bit, until Ed, that asshole, put a charred piece of meat under my nose. I jumped back into consciousness as Darlene hit the blender switch and began crushing ice for another tropical drink. She had a disemboweled pineapple beside her. It looked like a big grenade.

Ed said, "How 'bout a little something to eat, Bill?"

So I went into contrite mode, and I basted Darlene in compliments like she'd basted the ribs and chickens. I just couldn't say enough about this cookout, how the meat came off the bone. "You gotta gimme that recipe, Darlene. This is some sauce, molasses, honey, something that binds it. And what'd you put on the chicken, Darlene? You seasoned it with something, didn't you? Is that garlic you put in the butter?" Ummm, ahhh, suck, suck, suck, cleaned-off chicken bones and baby back ribs, set down those long gray bones of dismemberment, ate everything down to the carcass, washed it all down with Dracula Kool-Aid the color of blood.

Then I went off toward the cornfields, and up came everything out of my stomach. I came back with this pendant of drool, and Ed gave me a roll of paper towel.

"Raccoons will get all that," Ed said.

I must have gotten it all out of me, because I started feeling normal soon afterward.

The tropical drinks were going around. Darlene had a set of laminated cards with drink recipes on them. "You want salt with the margarita, Sam?"

"Sure."

Ed looked at me and said, "Darlene's got a happy hour out at the beauty parlor. She's always trying to come up with something different."

I said, "Oh."

Ed then went on about Darlene, singing her praises, how she'd saved his ass when things got bad and the town went to hell.

Darlene was some sight, near five feet six inches and well over 230 pounds, though the beehive hairdo extended an extra nine inches out of her head, like an anthill. Ed, sitting beside her, looked like a cricket that had come in out of the corn, all lean and bone, all exoskeleton beside her.

"Darlene," Ed says, "tell Sam about your new idea, 'Car Theft.' This is one of her best yet, Sam, you gotta hear this one."

I got myself up onto one shoulder. The sun was nearly gone. Wind blew the corn in waves, a quiet whispering sound beyond us. Citronella candles glowed around us. The charcoal ash throbbed. We were like a small sect gathered to give thanks.

Darlene just waited to spring her new idea on us. I could see her as this shifting darkness outlined by the candles, rubbing her dog. Her face was obscured. "I suppose Ed told you about us doing the prom photographs, since the gals are out here getting their hair done by me?"

Sam nodded.

Ed interjected, "Darlene has a contract with Mary Kay."

Darlene seemed to turn her girth toward him and admonish him into silence.

Ed said, "You tell it your way, Darlene." He made this ridiculous laughing sound.

Sam raised his arms. "I'm all ears."

"That's all called one-stop shopping, the hair, the pictures, the cosmetics, the happy hour drinks," Darlene continued. "So I got to thinking about things, seeing these gals coming to me all through the year, telling me how things weren't so good for them. Mostly it was man trouble, men not communicating anymore, men all shriveled up and feeling worthless. So I came up with this idea. I said, what is the closest thing to a man's heart?"

There was a moment of silence. The dark had truly settled now. "Well?" said Darlene. "What's the closest thing to a man's heart?" We all seemed to lean into the shift of candlelight.

"His wife," Sam said, and Darlene said, "Hogwash. Don't tell me what you think I want to hear, Sam. Think like a man."

Sam moved his head and emerged in the globular light of a candle. He was shaking his head. "You got me, Darlene."

Darlene didn't even look at me. She whispered, "Your car . . . ," and Sam said, "That's right, my car . . ."

Ed piped up, pointed at Darlene, "A mind reader of the human condition."

Darlene snapped, "You want to put a lid on it, Ed?"

"My car," Sam said again, and touched me. "That's right, isn't it?"

"Yeah, I suppose," I said, but my opinion didn't mean shit.

"Right, so what I decided is to offer a service I call Car Theft. First, we ask you to provide us with your guy's car keys, his license plate number, and the time of day you know he'll be at work. Then, what we do is, go out to his job, steal his car, take it away and wash and polish it and do up the inside, vacuum, empty the ashtrays and spray some cherry air freshener, and then set the car back in the lot all shiny."

Sam said, "Jeez awmighty, that is something." He slapped the side of his thigh. I slapped the back of my neck. Mosquitoes had breached the barrier of smoke, infiltrated our defense of citronella.

Darlene said, "Oh, Lord, you should see the look on a guy's face when he comes out and finds his car looking all new. Their jaws just hang. You see them looking around like it isn't their car. They check the license plate, they try the key in the door, and yeah, it opens, so this is their car, but it gets 'em all mind-boggled. It's like—"

I interjected, "Like *The Twilight Zone*."

Ed repeated what I said, "Like *The Twilight Zone*. You got it right on the money, Bill. Shit, like an episode of *The Twilight Zone*."

Sam looked at Darlene. "How much you charge for that, Darlene, if you don't mind me asking? I mean, that's a hell of a lot of work."

"We got different arrangements. Car Theft and a haircut, Car Theft and a perm, Car Theft and a pedicure, plus cosmetics and the happy hour drinks at fifty cents. You sign up for prom pictures and a mail-order dress, and sometimes we can throw in Car Theft for free. I just couldn't really say, Sam. It all depends. Really, it all depends. We got so many deals."

I sat up in the fold-out chair, absolutely fuckin' bewildered. "Don't the women tell their husbands or boyfriends about this in the end? I mean, this can't go on forever."

"You'd be surprised just how good women keep secrets, Bill. And anyway, we make them sign a contract that they won't tell."

I said, "And nobody's ever been shot out of this?"

Darlene just stared through the shadow of my face. "I got a hell of a lot of testimonials about how Car Theft has brought relationships together. It's a surefire way to get a man to start shaving, to start taking care of himself. Maybe he thinks there's some secret admirer, and he gets his self-confidence back, and maybe, in the end, he might know in his heart that it was his sweetheart all along, but, once the fire is started, it don't go out. I have women inside who've written on the forms that they've been achieving multiple orgasms, and their men can't get enough sex."

I said, "Forms?" incredulously.

Ed said, "Bill, love is a science. It ain't any different from anything else you do. You got to work at it."

"I'll be damned," Sam shouted. He was holding his own grenade of tropical drink.

You could see a strange intimacy developing between Sam and Darlene. He was entranced by her understanding of the human condition. He said, "Ed, how'd you ever find her? She got a sister, Ed?" This just made them snort laughing. Darlene moved under the tent of her paisley dress. She leaned forward, and her hairdo touched Sam's face.

"You never had kids, Darlene?" Sam said.

Darlene seemed to hesitate, to withdraw, but then she said, "There are other destinies beyond having your own babies. I was put here to do a greater good. You see, Sam, all them girls is my babies. They come and tell me all their secrets, and I listen and help them." Darlene started rubbing the poodle under its chin. It gathered his small body up close to her.

Darlene started sniffling. Ed touched her fat arm, and Sam said, "I'm—"

"It's not you, Sam. I'm crying, not for me, but for all the gals who I never get to save. All those gals out there who need a mother."

I just rolled my eyes. I was hungry again, all that food had just jumped out of my stomach before I got to digest any of it.

"You mind if I get a piece of chicken, Ed?"

Darlene said, "Help yourself inside. It's in the refrigerator, all wrapped up."

I moved tentatively along the landing strip of garden lights, up toward the house, and went into the small, compact domesticity of their lives. It was one of our refrigerators, the big old unit with the icebox and crisper and egg holders. It was good just to stand in that margin of cold air, the small bulb casting a rectangle of light across the floor.

I got out the food and put it on a plate. I could hear them all laughing outside. I stepped on a squeezy toy bone on the floor.

I moved silently down a dark corridor, along by the bedrooms. On the wall was a series of shots of Darlene and the dog. The dog was in different costumes, with ribbons tied to its ears in some of the shots. It was weird as hell.

I opened a door to a room at the end of the hall that smelled of chemicals and bleaches. I searched for a light switch, flicked it, and there stretched before me a world of feminine machinery, the pink sinks and showerhead fixtures for washing hair, the space-helmet dryer, the shelving of shampoos and sprays, of glittered nail-polish bottles, those magnifying circular mirrors for staring into the depths of your pores, a tangle of snaking cords connected to hair dryers and curling irons and small bowls of hardened hair-removing wax. I stepped into that cosmetic land, went through hanging bead strands that served as a partition for what can only be described as an enclave of a dream that had seeped from the consciousness of Darlene's psyche and calcified into this small box. It singularly defied any normal ideas about space, a psychological domain of dreams and longings. There was the Mary Kay trademark pink. The irony wasn't lost on me that it was the same pink as Ed's antacid medicine.

There was a rack of pamphlets in pinks and soft yellows beside the dryers, things for the girls to read. I mean, it was a land mine of the psyche. I scanned over the pamphlets: *Turn from a Loser into a Winner, Sell Yourself to Yourself, The Secret to Getting What You Want, Creative Daydreaming, Respect: The Most Coveted but Rarest of Gifts, Ego Nourishment, Practice Asking Others: How Can I Do Better?* and my favorites that just about made me smash up that dump, *Poverty Is Poor People Who Lack Dynamic Dreams* and *Find Part-Time Work—for Your Own Psychological Therapy.*

I found a catalogue of prom and formal dresses, paged through the glossy portraits. In the lower left corner, there was a story associated with each dress, something to help you decide if your personality fitted the dress.

Leah at the Dance—pale blue, lace full-length dress. She had worked very hard. Sometimes giving up parties and games and dances to keep up her grades. Or learn her lines. Or wait tables to earn her tuition. But tonight she'll dance and party and celebrate her graduation—with scholarship honors, class valedictorian.

Fancy at the Dance—ice blue, off-the-shoulder ruffles. Fancy knew instinctively what she'd have to do. She would think of tonight as a challenge—an adventure. Tonight she was going to her first college formal. And tonight she would show her new world just how she got her name, Fancy.

Darlene must have seen the light on in the beauty parlor. I heard her squawk, and they were all on me in a moment, before I could retreat out of the room, pressing down the dark hallway.

I ditched the dress album just in time. Darlene was saying, "So you found it." The poodle started barking, and Darlene said, "Just hush now, we've had enough, Gretchen." The dog showed its teeth, but stayed quiet. You didn't want to upstage Darlene. Even the dog knew that. It just sort of curled into the fat of Darlene's arm.

I was looking at the posters of different landscapes, and Darlene seized on that, went through the merits of girls who might choose the different scenes. There was the Florida Keys, with a palm tree at sunset and the optional blond-haired man in a tuxedo, whom the girl could seemingly be seen walking with through a trick of lights and softening camera effect. "Not all girls will make it to prom," Darlene said softly. "Last-minute disappointments, boys backing out. It is something just in case, an arm to lean on."

Ed went and unrolled a scene from a contraption much like what holds various maps in schools, but much larger, taking up the whole wall. Ed turned a handle, and down descended a tropical island with a pool in the foreground. Darlene angled a light, and the pool had a quicksilver shimmer of moonlight. Sam stepped into the scene, and, Jesus Christ, it looked like he'd been transported in some time machine. "Ed, you want to take a shot of Sam?"

Ed came back and adjusted the light. Darlene gave Sam a paper lei of tropical flowers and a coral bracelet, and when things were set, Ed let a long exposure fill his lens. I got into a night scene in a square in some mystical European city, on the steps of some grand hotel. They had a black evening jacket and pants for me, ill-fitting, but Darlene took me like a tailor's dummy and pinned back the fabric to a pucker behind my back, to that place where the conceit was hidden from the camera's eye, and while standing amid this small brick oasis set deep in cornfields, I became a man of wealth sipping champagne on the steps of an old European hotel. I stood still while they changed different-colored plastic filters to create the ambience of midnight. In the dimension of what had once been Ed's garage, Darlene had resurrected the hidden longings of a generation of the downtrodden. She had somehow glimpsed inside their heads, extracted their dreams from under the alien specter of her hair dryers. She was an illusionist of the highest order, complicit with our dreams, a voice whispering, "You can be anything you want."

The harder you looked, the more you saw in this box. There were testimonials to past proms, a collection of photographs taken by Ed. Over by the cosmetics, there were before and after shots of girls with atrocious acne whose portraits had been shot through a cheesecloth filter, giving them the soft complexion of girls in an Oil of Olay commercial.

The night degenerated into a long discussion of Ronny Lawton after that, about where the body was. Was he really guilty? Sam bellyached about how he was ruined, he couldn't hold out much longer. It soured the mood. He went on about Linda Carter's exclusive with Ronny Lawton; *60 Minutes* had agreed to air it.

Now it was my turn to do the consoling. I put my arm around Sam and stared at the gnarled red paint on Darlene's fat toes showing through her flip-flop sandals. They sort of wriggled with annoyance. She wasn't finished with us yet. We sat amid the candles again among the gnomes and flamingos. Darlene gave Sam something the color of radiator fluid, one of her magical potions, but no matter how much tropical paradise was poured into him, Sam got weepy.

Darlene told us about another of her schemes, not fully realized yet, but coming soon to a head near you. It was called Weekend in Paradise, and in this fantasy, you bought a care package of gluttonous delicacies, small tins of caviar and crackers, red and white wines, ripe cheeses of foreign import, liver pâtés, legs of cold turkey and roast beef, fruit baskets, etc . . . She hadn't decided it all yet.

I said, "Maybe economy and deluxe versions, with costumes."

Darlene said, "We don't ever use that word *economy*, Bill. I got a saying, 'Buying cheap goods to save money is like stopping the clock to save time.'"

I said, "Oh."

"That's right, Bill, we don't use the word *economy*. We envision Grande and Plus Grande." She affected a perfect French accent.

Then she began again about how, of course, you got a choice of a backdrop set of various designs, the interior boudoir of French sensibility in the eighteenth century, a classical Greek setting with complimentary grapes to feed your lover. She went on about getting a toll-free number for orders. Ed said, "Now there's an idea."

I could imagine it, all right, the individualized hemorrhage of our sadness eclipsed for a long weekend where nobody came out, say, a weekend of hard blizzard in February, locked away in an encrustation of ice, our town hidden away as pharaohs and knights and princes and kings, in the kingdom of our own dreams, where all things are entirely possible.

As a parting prize, I got my Polaroid shot on the steps of that stately hotel. I looked magnificent, born for that sort of grandeur. I have a strong aristocratic chin. I said that to Darlene. We were now fast friends. She concurred, that conjurer of desire. She pressed her bigness against me. "Yes, you do, Bill. You have a strong aristocratic chin." As if I'd believe anything she'd say, but, Jesus, I did.

I stood in the hallway with Darlene and her dog, Ed and Sam, all of us shuffling for the door. And above the door was this hand-embroidered plaque, faintly lighted, not for those entering the house, but for those leaving, for Darlene herself no doubt. It said, "When somebody says NO, they really mean MAYBE. And when a person says MAYBE, they really mean YES."

Sam seemed to hesitate. He looked at Ed and shook his head. "What you got there, Ed, is what men only dream of having." He smiled at Darlene. Again, the moment of melancholy.

"Florida, Sam . . . There's women down there, wealthy women, wealthy, widowed women, Sam."

"Has it come to that?" Sam shrugged his shoulders. "Me on a date?"

Darlene engulfed Sam with the hugeness of her fat right arm.

"I want to get the Ronny Lawton story out of the way, real quick, and just get the hell out of here. I'm not going to spend my remaining years chronicling the psychos of this town. No, I'm not." He looked at all of us. "I just want Bill here to get on this story and get it done, end it. Maybe we can go out with a bang, just get us one up on television." Sam looked at me. "That's where Bill comes into the picture. I'm counting on him."

That pretty much came out of nowhere, so I just half smiled in acknowledgment that things were put to me to solve. It was like the booze had turned on something deep inside Sam, unsettled him for a moment, or maybe it was just looking at Darlene that set something off inside him.

I said, "You know they made him Employee of the Month down at Denny's."

Sam just looked sad. He said, "Maybe we should get a picture of that, what do you think, Ed?"

Ed said, "Sure." I think he wanted us gone. It was late. Mosquitoes buzzed the night air.

Darlene just smiled and changed the subject. She said, "I got a book with an accompanying tape inside, Sam. *Sex! Beyond Menopause*. It's a clinical overview of the sex spots deep inside every woman."

Sam was just looking at Darlene, who left and got the goddamn book and tape, even though Sam was looking like he wanted to run for his life.

Darlene presented Ed as a reformed lover, a guy she'd whipped into sexual shape. Ed just shrank from her candor, a lean rake in plastic white shoes and polyester pants.

Sam left like a goddamn schoolkid, with the book under his arm.

Darlene shouted after Sam, "Knowledge is power!"

I left that night thinking Darlene just might be a genius. She might hold the key to another dimension, a form of time travel, a pioneer of the new interior, the vast mind-scape that went far out beyond our plains, a terrain greater than any Montana. I went back through the nightmare of our old industry, kept wanting Darlene to come down here and unfurl one of her facades, make all this disappear, cover it over, dispel the fear. I was ready for make-believe. It was better than the present. There are times when you want to see the emperor's new clothes, when it's better that way.

CHAPTER 7

What the zoo got a few days later was Paul, the constrictor from out of Ronny's old man's place. The snake was huge, over eight feet long. It had somehow survived on mice and rats beneath the floor, though when they found the snake, it was in pretty bad shape, half-molting and inert. It had seemingly gotten so big it was trapped. Ronny came back home from Denny's, and he took Paul from the ripped floor bedding, came out into the daylight with the snake around his neck. It hardly moved, though its forked tongue flitted and read the air. There was a huge crowd out there on the property. I didn't see any of that in person. Linda Carter had been on the scene. It all unfolded on television. It only added to the myth of Ronny Lawton, made him more of a nightmare. Rumors were flying that maybe Ronny had fed the pieces of his old man to the snake. I knew that constrictors only ate living things, but still, that didn't stop people believing what they wanted to believe. There were even rumors that the vets down at the zoo were going to cut it open just to be sure, but Pete told me that was just all bullshit. He said, "They're going to x-ray it is all." Ed had somehow found out about the snake in time to get out there to the house. He got a picture of Ronny with the constrictor, and that made our headline the next day. I also got the X ray of Paul from the zoo. Those two pictures got all the way to the AP again, carried in the human-interest sections of all the big daily papers. We had gained one back on Linda Carter.

Back at the office, we just laughed our asses off, and Sam passed out Dutch Masters cigars, and we puffed away an afternoon. I was just breaking my sides for some reason. I just couldn't get that

name, Paul, out of my head. It kind of showed the simplicity of
Ronny Lawton, naming something like that Paul. I don't know why
I found that so funny. I kept saying the name, "Paul," and Ed and
Sam kept leaning forward and busting a gut. I think it had something to do with the Dutch Masters cigars. Shit, they got a way of
going to your head if you're not used to them. But right under that
haze of smoke and all that laughing, we were real nervous, we were
thinking, what next, how many times can our luck hold on us?

And over the following days, that staleness of the story settled
like the cigar smoke in our clothes, bitter. Linda Carter's special on
Ronny Lawton loomed, and things were hell down at the office. I
got my work done and escaped to the cold tiled Y, stripped to my
swimsuit, and submerged myself from the world for hours until my
fingers withered and my skin turned dry from the chlorine.

Sam and Ed were tight as a knot back in the office. I assumed
they were trying to come to some settlement about how to off-load
the paper. A sprawling news service interest had begun to subsume
our kind of paper. What they wanted was to create a boilerplate of
stories for insets on pages 3 and 4, while on the front page they ran
local-interest stories for each community. There'd nearly been a
deal the previous year, before I joined our paper, but Sam had
scoffed at the offer, hunkered down, and waited.

I really had nothing else to do besides the swimming, so I called
up Ronny Lawton's estranged wife, Teri. I got the same barrage of
flying insults, the "I hope they fry his ass" line, but I said, "Maybe
you can help yourself get that house, Teri. Maybe there's something
you've overlooked." She was working at Osco at 4 P.M., so she said,
"You'd have to get your ass out here by two."

Before I hung up she said, "Hey, you think you could see your
way to bring out a twelve-pack of Old Milwaukee and a box of
Marlboro soft-pack?"

I said, "Sure, Teri."

She had a voice like she'd eaten shards of glass.

What happened next was one of those embarrassing conjunc-
tions of events or circumstances that pushes the envelope of

believability, but then again people's paths cross in our town. We are not a metropolis.

Ronny Lawton's wife was one of those delectables of human wreckage that grow out of the dunghills of our industrial wastelands.

I drove off the main road, through a scar of land cut through wilting corn, and emerged into an opening of dry dirt. Jesus, another day without rain, another ninety-plus day, the sky now taking on a sanguine glow at night with airborne dust.

And then there it was, a solitary trailer that looked for all the world like it had fallen from outer space into this opening.

I killed the engine.

"You that guy from the newspaper?"

"Yeah."

Ronny Lawton's estranged wife was beautiful in a trashy way, dirty-blond hair tied back in a ponytail. She was the sort of vision most men must dream of rescuing, what's referred to as a diamond in the rough. She was squatting by a small plastic pool beside the trailer. A small kid was splashing about. She reached in for her kid, Ronny Lawton's kid, that is. She had her back to me, the tight denim shorts riding the crack of her ass, showing the crease of each crescent cheek. I hesitated and just stared at her. She seemed to hold that pose for just a second too long to make me understand her own self-awareness. She turned, put the kid on her hip, curled her hair behind her ear, and said, "You got beer with you . . . What's your name again?"

"Bill."

"You bring it, Bill?"

"I have it."

She wore a red gingham shirt tied above her waist, showing the soft, distended nub of her belly button like the tie on a balloon. Her skin was brown from the days in the sun out here.

We walked to the trailer door, this dilapidated, rusting box with big plastic flowers that turned in the wind. The hot smell was something oppressive, an odor of urine from the kid, a biscuity smell. A solitary fan creaked and blew the smell and heat around. The windows were all open, and still the metal frame absorbed the day's heat. A small generator puttered outside, a lifeline that kept things just bearable for her and the kid, kept the refrigerator going.

Ronny Lawton's estranged knew what I was thinking. It's something these poor people have, some presentiment of the disgust they instill in ordinary people. I suppose it's a defense mechanism. They need to know what they're up against.

I doled out the beer and cigarettes, set them on the Formica table. She got down two cups.

"You think I'm not worth shit, right? You come here in that fancy-ass car of yours."

I didn't have the experience, as it were, to negotiate hostile witnesses. All I said was, "I'm only trying to find out who killed Ronny Lawton's old man and just maybe help you get that house of his." I said it straight-faced and monotone.

We started drinking after that, put away three bottles each before she began to tell me anything. I learned she never completed high school, got pregnant by some unknown guy in her sophomore year, moved in with Ronny when the kid was less than a year old, then got herself pregnant just before Ronny went into the military. Ronny was pissed about the first kid, kept hitting it, so it went off to her grandmother in Iowa, who had a house and some money. She lived in the Lawtons' house while Ronny was away in boot camp. She worked sometimes at Osco Drug, but mostly stayed home and cooked for Ronny's old man and sat in sometimes with Ronny's mother, but she was out of it in her last months. There was nothing to do but change the sheets, turn Ronny's mother over, and rub down her skin with a sponge. Ronny's father was really down in the dumps after the sheet metal plant he was working in shut down. " 'Price of fuel just shot up, and people got scared of big cars and Winnebagos.' That's what Ronny's old man used to say anyways, when he was alive that is."

Finally, we'd arrived at Ronny Lawton's old man. I poured her bottle of beer into her cup. It had taken that long. But the kid

began to cry, and Ronny Lawton's estranged dipped the kid's paci-
fier in the beer and stuck it into the kid's mouth. It just sucked
away and settled down in a small cage beside the table.

I couldn't really bring things around, so I flat out said, "I want to
ask you this, and I want you to tell me straight. You think Ronny
killed his old man?"

Ronny's estranged put the cup to her lips and drained it, wiped
her small lips, and kind of leaned into me. I smelled her cheap perfume; it cut through the vapid hotness. "Of course he done it, Bill.
Him and his old man hated each other."

She alarmed me: the sudden intimacy, saying my name like that,
though it's a name that begs familiarity. Still, I took back my hand
slowly, reset myself on the worn bench, and said softly, after clearing my throat, "Any particular reason you know Ronny killed his
old man?"

She nodded her head, then drew away and lit a cigarette and
tipped her head back and blew a stream of smoke into the small
confines of the trailer. The smoke rose through a half-open Plexiglas window in the roof.

"Ronny was an asshole, but his father was one better. Let me tell
you how I heard it, then you decide. The way I heard it was,
Ronny's old lady was in real bad shape, pain and bleeding, female
problems, needing some kind of operation. She was in pain all the
time. Ronny's old man just kept insisting there weren't nothing
wrong with her. He was an asshole, Bill. I mean a real asshole." She
leaned forward, set that bewildering beauty of her face in the cradle
of her palms, elbows balanced on the table, and said, "Ronny said
she used to scream at night with the pain. Ronny's old man just
couldn't take it, went out fishing in the dead of night to get away
from her. That was when Ronny's old man lost his job, when they
lost their insurance. Ronny was left there alone with his ma."
Ronny's estranged touched her temples. "Maybe I forgot to mention, Ronny had a brother who died in Vietnam."

"Charlie," I said softly.

"Yeah, that was it. That's maybe how Ronny's ma lost the will to live, her son dying like that." She stopped for a moment. "This making sense?"

"Sure, you're doing fine."

I hesitated, and Ronny's estranged looked at her small kid in the pen. She looked at me. "You got kids?"

"I'm not married."

"You did the smart thing, Bill. It isn't what it's cracked up to be." She poured more drink. I pinched the bridge of my nose, felt the heat around me.

"Well, where was I? Oh, yeah. Ronny came around when his old man was out and started going in to his mother and rubbing cream on her back, bringing her water to wash, changing the sheets, bringing her up slices of apple and orange. The way Ronny tells it, he started working at Dairy Queen when he was fourteen, got a note from school that allowed him to work fifteen hours a week. So he saved up his money and he took his mother into town to see a doctor. This was big shit, 'cause Ronny didn't have a license at the time. His mother was sayin', 'We can't take the car,' but Ronny wasn't listening to her. So they get there, and the doctor sees her for all of five minutes, keeps 'em waiting going on an hour of course in his waiting room, and what he said was, 'She's got six months, maybe a year tops, if she doesn't get her uterus out,' and then he left, and a nurse helped Ronny's old lady get dressed. He gave her a prescription for the pain. Ronny said to me he was cryin' inside hisself, but he didn't let on or nothing. He went and got her medication down at Osco, used the money he'd earned and set it down on the counter. Then Ronny took his ma out for an ice-cream float down by where he worked. He made it himself, put nuts on it and ground up those pills and mixed them in and set down the float with one of them long spoons."

Ronny Lawton's estranged wife took my hand, squeezed it. I could see she was going way back to a better time, roaming around the good memories. She was visibly drunk, a kind of faint smile on her face, and that rasping defensive voice was soft and quiet. I nodded for her to go on, because I wasn't good at steering conversation.

"Shit, look at me . . ." She sniffled and wiped her nose with the back of her hand. "So Ronny takes her out to dinner at the Holiday Inn out on Main Street. They got the best salad bar and steaks any-where around, but they got a dress code out there, too. They said, 'You gotta have a jacket, sonny!' and Ronny took this fat guy aside and he says, 'That's my mother, and she found out today she's going to die.' I mean he didn't hit nobody or nothing. He could be like that back then. So they came up with what the guy called a 'a dead man's jacket' for cases where people don't come dressed proper. They slipped him into this mustard yellow coat, and in he went with his ma on his arm. They ate whatever they wanted. Ronny got up and went to the waiter and he says, 'When you bring them cof-fees, sir, slip these pills into my mother's coffee. She just found out today she's going to die.' They got themselves coffee with cream, and them pills worked real good. Ronny's ma never cried or noth-ing. She was just looking around at all these fancy businessmen with their girls that came down for dinner. They had this guy in a tuxedo playing the piano. Ronny's ma says, 'I wonder if he might just know some Duke Ellington, Ronny. You think he might?' And so Ronny went up to him, and he got some money in his hand, which he put over this fishbowl where these guys take their tips, and he says real softly, 'Maybe you could see your way to doin' a lit-tle Duke Ellington, sir?' And the guy answers him, 'Maybe in a while, kid,' so Ronny leans into him real easy, like he was telling him a secret, and says, 'My mother just found out today she's going to die,' and the guy says, 'Jeez awmighty,' and he announces Ronny and his mother, asks people to stand and give them a round of applause, then he sings 'Tie a Yellow Ribbon Round the Old Oak Tree.' He didn't know any Duke Ellington. They got going after that, but it was night, and out they went to the house, and Ronny's old man was waiting with a belt. To hear Ronny tell it, he got beaten near to death, and I know he ain't lying, 'cause I seen the marks on his back. Ronny's ma was just screaming to leave Ronny alone, but Ronny's old man just kept going at Ronny. He kept say-ing, 'You ain't the man of this house, no you ain't.' He just beat

Ronny so bad, Ronny pissed blood." She shrugged her shoulders. "That's it. That's how come I know Ronny chopped up his old man." She stopped abruptly, said, "What time you got?"

"Three-ten."

"Shit. Maybe just one more. You think you might see yourself to dropping me into town, Bill? I gotta be at work by four."

"Yeah, sure." The sweat just poured out of me in that trailer. I kept wiping the sting of sweat out of my eyes, staring at her soft face, the curious sad longing of the way she told things. She reached down and touched her kid. It was all but naked, in only a diaper, playing with this plastic ball inside its cage.

Jesus, it was a broiler in there. The fan wobbled and clicked with each rotation. I looked through the window out on a searing sun way up in an expanse of blue. I said, "You got any ice?"

Ronny's estranged took out some cubes from a small refrigerator, one of ours, the small portable unit. She took a cube and rubbed it at the nape of her neck, then put the cube in her mouth. She rubbed another over her kid's forehead. It looked up and took the cube in its small, doughy hands. "Don't eat that, Lucas."

I moved my ice cube around my wrist. My grandfather said that's where you needed to put the ice, at that point where the blood was closest to the skin. I said, "I don't get it. It seems like you love Ronny?"

Ronny's estranged crunched the ice in her mouth, pushed the cube to the side of her mouth, and her cheek bulged slightly. She leaned over her cup and let the ice fall into it. She whispered, "Maybe I did. But he became his father's son." Her eyes opened wide. "There may have been love in him, but it all got beaten out of him that night. When we was first going out, he told me that story. I said to myself, 'That's a man I want inside me. That's a man that I want to make my babies,' but it weren't never like that really between us, not really. Maybe he was different before his ma got sick, but he weren't no different than his father afterwards. I seen them in the house together, father and son, going at it like two junkyard dogs."

I shouldn't have said what I said next, but I did. I said, "Why did you let yourself get pregnant then?"

She shook her head, let a smile break across her face. "That is it, all right, isn't it just. You upper-class people is always wanting to know how we go on having babies. You want to know why we survive, right?"

I said, "I was out of line."

"It don't really matter, 'cause you were thinking it, one way or another. You got that car of yours, that convertible, and you come out here, and you see me and think, 'Now, how come she won't fuck me?' You think, what the hell, she's been on her back before. She's been with a murderer and some guy who can't even afford a real house, just a trailer. Isn't that right, Bill?"

"No."

"You're a liar. You know why I stayed with Ronny?"

"Why?"

"'Cause he's got the biggest cock I ever saw. I was mad for his big cock."

I said, "I'm sorry."

"What the hell are you sorry for, needle dick?"

The kid started crying, and that ended that. I was almost faint, my mouth open in a dog pant. I drank more beer. I said, "I thought you were interested in getting that house. That's what I came out here for, to see how things might be, what you might have been able to tell me about Ronny, about where he might have put the pieces of his old man. That's all."

It was 3:45. Ronny's estranged didn't even seem to pay me any attention. She had the kid in her arms, took it over to a pullout bed, and changed its diaper. I watched her hold up the legs like she was cleaning a turkey and paint the kid's pink ass white with cream, sprinkle powder over the kid's privates.

I said, "Listen, I'm sorry. Okay?"

Ronny's estranged turned. "You gotta take me to town." She handed me the kid. "You want to take Lucas outside for a minute?"

I took the kid in my arms, went outside into the brown dirt yard.

The kid pulled at my ear. I went out by the rim of corn, felt it rustle in the stir of wind. Where I stood, you could see each furrowed trail in the corn going far into the field.

I turned and was going back by the trailer when I saw a glint of steel on the ground. I went over and picked up a pair of shears and quickly set them inside my shirt. I got over by the car and put them in the back of the car.

Ronny's estranged called me. "Bring him in." She'd stripped and gotten into jeans and a white shirt and put on a pair of canvas shoes. "Bring him in, Bill."

She took the kid from me, set it in the pen, closed down this wooden gate over the top so the kid was in a cage. The kid started crying, but all Ronny's estranged said was, "Karl is bringing you McDonald's if you quit that crying, Lucas." She pushed his colored ball his way. It was filled with some beads that made a noise. Then she shut the door of the trailer, and we got into the car. I was pulling out when she said, "Maybe we shouldn't have left it like we had a party in there." She gave me the key. "I don't want Lucas crying again, seeing me. You just go on in and get them bottles and cigarettes."

We left in a storm of dust, out along the scar of brown dirt until we hit pavement and headed toward town. On the way in, she gave me a list of places to check, places Ronny had taken her out on the property. There was a tornado shelter out by the overgrown wreckage of a farmhouse Ronny Lawton's grandparents had built when they came out to the Midwest. "I know that's where he used to hide his beer, years ago, away from his father. He had himself a bed down there he used to take me to when we was first dating. I ain't saying there's anything down there, really, but it's a place he went is all. It's real hard to find, maybe a mile away from where they live now. There's a giant grove of trees out where the old house used to be on Kinsey Road. From there you go on in fifty feet, in through the long grass. You got to stomp around, feel for the foundations of the house, then from there, it's maybe another one hundred feet further into the field. Just feel for a hollow sound. I don't know if I could even find it by myself, but it's out there, and if it's there, maybe it's worth checking out, I suppose."

She began applying makeup in the small vanity mirror, took out a Mary Kay lipstick from her purse. She said, "How much does a car like this run, Bill?"

I told her, and she smiled.

"How fast a car like this go, Bill?"

I told her, and she smiled again. She kept applying the makeup. "You don't look like the kind of guy that should be working for a paper."

"What's that mean?"

"You don't look like a regular stiff."

"What do I look like?"

She smiled at me. "You fishing for a compliment, Bill?"

I didn't say anything. I kept driving, then I said, "Where do you get that stuff?"

She turned and looked at me. "You mean this?" Her hair was being blown around in the hot wind.

"Yeah, the cosmetics."

"I get 'em where I get my hair done, out on Birch Road."

"Darlene Hoskin's place?"

She shrugged her shoulders. "Yeah, you got a girlfriend that goes there or something?"

I said, "I know Darlene."

"Darlene's something else! I got a prom dress from her, sophomore year. Her husband took my portrait out at her place. They're real nice people. I don't think I ever paid her all I owed her for my dress. That's the kind of people they are."

We pulled into the Osco lot. Ronny's estranged had transformed herself into something beautiful, the blue eye shadow and light blush on her cheeks. She dabbed some perfume in the smallness of her cleavage. She kissed a tissue and left an imprint, the lips soft and wet, and she said, "How do I look, Bill?" without so much as a hint of self-consciousness, like a child, like we'd known each other for years. She just propped herself against the door and stared at me. "Well?"

"Great, I guess."

"What the hell you mean, you guess?"

"I mean great, just great." I had my hands firmly on the black steering wheel, tensed up.

She took out these gaudy looping earrings and inserted a wire into a hole in each earlobe, saying almost in a distracted way, "Bill, I ain't a snitch. I think people do all sorts of things that is between only them and the bedroom walls. I don't want you thinking me a snitch, but Ronny never paid me no child support or nothing. He even denied it was him that got me pregnant. He said it didn't figure right, how he had it in his head, him going off to boot camp and all, and me ending up pregnant." She was still for a moment. "I mean, it's plain as day. Lucas is the spittin' image of Ronny!"

I said, "Yeah."

Ronny's estranged shrugged her shoulders. "I gotta survive as best I can, is all. What I told you out there was the truth. Ronny wasn't always an animal. I don't think I'd ever have loved an animal. I don't even blame him. It was . . ."

There was maybe something in that ellipse. I hesitated, waited for her to say something more. I didn't want to overstep my mark. In the end, I was left to finish things, "You got a right to something better than that."

She leaned and kissed me on the side of the cheek, a softness that unsettled me. I hit the damn horn on the wheel and jerked and she laughed. I could see the soft white color of her neck since she'd taken her hair and set it back on her head, that delicate trace of her neck, the small feminine bones.

"You're all thumbs, Bill." She just stayed there looking at me. "You're sweet, Bill. I like talking to you. Maybe, if you want, you might come visit me again. I might remember more things. I don't go to work until four each day. You sure could help me out some, if you had the time, that is."

"What about the guy you live with?"

"Karl, what about Karl? All we'd be doin' is talking, right, Bill? I'm helping with an investigation is all. Anyways, he's gone by seven and not back until six. He works way out by Elkhart."

I heard myself giving her my number. She wrote it down with her lipstick on a tissue paper. She smiled at me. "Just in case I think of anything else . . ."

I watched her move across the shimmering asphalt. She shouted, "I really like that car, Bill," and disappeared into Osco.

I felt that lingering suggestiveness, the booze no doubt. The sun beat down on my head. The tissue paper with her kiss was on the seat. It was surreal, all of it, and that kid of hers out in his cage. That was a crime in and of itself, neglect. I should have been repulsed. I should have called the County Department of Child Services is what I should have done. I pulled out of Osco, got going toward the office. There was an edition that had to be done before 10 P.M. I had gone out this afternoon simply to establish motive, and where Ronny Lawton might have hidden the pieces of his father, and I ended up giving her my phone number and sort of establishing something like a date with Ronny's estranged. I mean, Jesus Christ, I should have just hightailed it out of town. I was just fucking things up.

All I had really established in weeks of work on this story was simply that Ronny Lawton probably did have a ten-inch cock. I had some corroborating hearsay from his wife. That was the culmination of my investigative prowess, a banner headline—REPORTER CONFIRMS: RONNY LAWTON HAS TEN-INCH COCK. "Jesus Christ. I'm not cut out for this line of work," I shouted. "She likes the goddamn car is all! She wants Ronny's house is all!" I kept shouting inside my head. "You gave her your goddamn phone number!" I said, "You better get into that LSAT book, asshole. You better get your ass in gear, mister!" I pulled in off Main Street, went in, and had something to eat at Burger King. It was going to be a few hours before I got the legal notices in order down at the office. I was sitting there in the cool air-conditioning, thinking about what the

hell I was doing with my life. I had this lovesick feeling in my stomach like some junior-high kid. I kept trying to fool myself, make
believe it was hunger, but it wasn't. What kind of asshole gets a
hard-on over a suspect's estranged wife?

I shoveled the fries into my mouth, eating mechanically. And
then I remembered those cutting shears. How the hell had I forgotten them? I ran out to the car, opened the back door, and reached
under the seat. I put my hand down into the vinyl seats, opened the
goddamn trunk to see if they had fallen through, but they were
gone. Christ! I'd had them on the seat. I knew I'd put them there.
My heart was pounding. The one piece of physical evidence I might
actually have had was gone. I'd lost it! Was it stolen? I thought
back to what had happened out there, tried to piece things
together. I hit the hood of the car. Dammit! She must have seen
them in the back of the car. That's why she sent me back into the
trailer for the beer and cigarettes. She'd seen them! I checked the
back again, fished under my seat, and then I felt them, way under
my seat. They must have slid under there when I went down the
long dirt road. I said to myself, "Jesus! You've got to be more care-
ful. Come on!" I held the shears, let them catch the glint of sunlight before I realized my prints were all over them. I folded an old
newspaper around them and headed for the office.

CHAPTER 8

I waited almost two days before I did anything about the cutting shears. And so began some of the longest days of my life, a totally mentally exhausting tension, almost that terrible shaking that got me sent away after my father had killed himself. Ronny Lawton's estranged had done something to me, touched a part of me that wanted to retreat from things, that made me think back to Diane and the time we had together, alone. I even thought about getting some depressants to help me sleep. It was the shears that were the problem. I was like a dog with a bone. I hid them back at my house, behind a collection of antique books. I circled the bookcase with animal possession, took them out, looked at them, and then hid them someplace else, down in the basement, near the boiler, then up in the attic. What if the house burned down? I buried them in a Ziploc bag, outside, under the old oak tree on our property. I was out of my mind. I went down the long garden to the compound of animals. I could hear my own heart, the pounding in the dark, but it was not my heart that was pounding. Before me were those long-necked mutes, the emus, watching me through the fence. Their beaks opened and closed in some silent conversation, like they were talking about what I had done. They had a language different from any other animal, a hollow thumping from deep in their long necks, the sound of a heart heard through a stethoscope. It was that sound I kept hearing, a ubiquitous Poe nightmare of the telltale heart, the reverberation of sound in that darkness. It was as though the very darkness was thumping with the anxiety of this buried secret. I stumbled back from the birds. They followed along the fence until I turned and ran back up to the house. My head was split in two with the tension. I wasn't in long before I got all scared a squirrel might have seen me bury the shears and think it was a cache of nuts. I left them there in the end. I took three sleeping pills with milk and got out a Duke Ellington album from my father's collection to tape it onto a portable cassette player I had got when I was trying to master French in college.

I went at the LSAT book again, went down into the cold basement of our mansion and retreated from the world. The heat had infiltrated the upper part of the house, made the wood creak and expand. It was hard opening windows. They stuck from the heat. It was going on two weeks of temperatures in the nineties. Life settled into a sort of torpor of sleeping and lying near fans. This was how it went during the plains summers, sweat and hide. I did my hiding in the basement. I was sifting through the ways to get to Ronny Lawton, to try to get something on him. And then I was thinking about Ronny's estranged, and how she said what she did about Ronny, about how he'd been beaten real bad. I didn't know if I really wanted Ronny to confess. Maybe there are justices that must be meted out outside the law. I was thinking of Ronny and his mother, of that night out on the town, a kid being a man for the first time, coming to terms with illness and death. I was thinking about my own mother. You know, I think I understood how Ronny Lawton felt about his old man. It was the way I felt about my grandfather. It's the way my father felt, the knowing that maybe somebody just might have survived, if they'd been taken care of properly by doctors.

I knew it was the house, the old memories intermingling with the present. But I had nowhere to go. When I shut my eyes, I saw the vision of Ronny Lawton's fists with that enigmatic NOWHERE searing against the dark.

A trembling sensation just ran through me over the next few days. I couldn't eat with the shot of anxiety. I shouted, "Grandfather, you asshole!" I made a fist and shook it at ancestry, down in the bowels of our mansion. I was doing it maybe for my father as well. Of course, we hadn't really ever gotten along, but that was because of my grandfather. He demeaned us, kept us subservient to his whims. He held our inheritance at bay, led us like donkeys after a carrot, always out of reach. The money came trickling in trust funds, in monthly checks that kept us excruciatingly strapped for cash. Even this house, this goddamn house was something that had to be preserved, a provision my grandfather put in his will, the stipulation that all funds were contingent on residency at the mansion. That asshole who'd traveled the globe had anchored us to the plains, isolated us in the pith of industrialism. But, just maybe, I might be able to make a break from all this now if I could just find out where Ronny Lawton had the pieces of his old man hid.

I knew I thought way too much about my grandfather, but, here amid his possessions, he was still alive. The only true gift he might have bestowed on me was my name, Bill, not William, just plain Bill on the birth certificate. He named me, not my father, and of course my mother was dead. I had been seen as destined for industrial relations, for talking with union bosses, for that everyman matter-of-factness, the peace broker. People liked my name. They used it freely. They remembered it. It was all "Hey, Bill" this and "Hey, Bill" that. In this line of news, it was good to have that name. And it had a double entendre that somehow really broke up my grandfather, that old industrialist. Bill meant a form of payment. I was a pun to him. That is what Bill meant first and foremost to him, before he even learned Bill was a name. He used to laugh in the old days, when my father was alive, when we used to meet sometimes down at the factory, saying to his buyers things like, "Have you seen our Bill? Let me show you our Bill," and then he'd introduce me and give that great bear roaring laugh of his, until everybody got the joke and put two and two together. "Oh, Bill and Bill . . . Yes, that is a good one." That was the kind of dry humor we endured. My grandfather had a scheme behind everything. I wasn't beyond acknowledging that. He said naming something was an essential part of its being. Its name set it on a particular path. When he was roaming the Old World, he went by the name Vladimir, but he changed it to Igor when he came to the plains, when he began selling his ice. The name Igor had an edge, a gypsy foreignness needed in a trade of goods where congeniality was detrimental. It was a seller's market, that ice business. Congeniality only brought the price down, it wasted time, it created an uneasiness for the seller, established a common ground. My grandfather was carrying a perishable item into desert heat. I used to think of him as something akin to the Child Catcher in *Chitty Chitty Bang Bang*. Behind a staccato tongue and ill-fitting black clothes flapping in the heat, Igor cast his baleful eyes on his customers, panted and grunted as he chiseled out his ice. He used to take out his dentures and say, almost with a lament, "I was blessed with bad teeth in those days. I had a smile like a rotting forest." He had a horse of bones, a crippled thing that lurched across the horizon of shimmering plains, shackled in a chain harness. My grandfather walked as much as he could beside the horse, in laceless boots with black wagging tongues, aligned with his horse in a mutual forlorn journey into hell, each prisoner of the other, his horse frothing dreadfully at the nostrils. He affected a misery beyond even that of his customers. "That, my young friend, is what kept others from selling ice. They said to themselves, 'Looking at him, the ice man, there must be no money in that business.'"

Who knows if any of that shit was really true. Maybe it was all made up after the fact, part of the fable, but he kept that parsimonious resolve through the rest of his life, so you knew the sentiment was honest. All through my youth, I had to get out there on the weekends in autumn and winter, with my father and grandfather, and collectively we chopped and split wood to feed the woodburning stove my grandfather had insisted we use. It was part of his immigrant tradition, the resolve to stay self-sufficient, to keep the body ready for battle. People used to come by our great gates, the ordinary workers going down to the foundry, and there they would see us all day long at the chopping, the splintering wood crisp in the cold air, the sound carrying out to the gate, its hidden scent released with the cut of ax metal. It was all show and grunting, my grandfather singing songs of revolution, shouting in his native tongue, us in boots and woolen trousers, his descendants, dressed wholly antiquated, like Paul Bunyans in checked shirts, three-generational figures panting with effort, our bodies smoking in the cold air.

But that was so long ago. Now, stowed away in the basement by myself, hiding away, the question was, simply, how long was I going to let this go on? I had the shears outside. Did I have the courage to find out that maybe it wasn't Ronny Lawton at all, that just maybe his estranged and her boyfriend, Karl, had come up with a plan to frame Ronny, so she could get the house for herself? I mean, who the hell knew? I was grasping at straws.

I wanted to get near Ronny Lawton's estranged again. I knew I was out of my mind, but I was thinking maybe she might implicate her boyfriend, Karl. There was no way she'd kill Ronny Lawton's old man. Karl had killed the old man for the house. Maybe she didn't even know about it. Maybe Karl just had enough, just kept hearing about that house and went out and did something about it. But of course, this was all bullshit. You have to have physical evidence to back up any theory.

I went up into the inferno of the sitting room, and the Duke Ellington record had hit a skip halfway through. I stopped the cassette player. It was late, late enough for Ronny Lawton to be at work. The sleeping pills tugged at me. Sleep was coming down right when I needed to get going. I put on a pot of coffee, sat in the kitchen, and waited. I had two strong black measures of coffee, laced them with sugar.

At Denny's, Ronny Lawton was in that twilight of the night when the kids had gone home. He was left with only himself in the brightness of the light. The tables were littered with tall malt glasses and half-eaten plates of burgers and fries. Three extra women hired for the night shift lingered at the end of the counter and smoked, leaning their heads way back and breathing long streams of smoke into the air.

I passed them, and they ignored me. A sign said Seat Yourself.

I felt the war of the sleeping pills and the caffeine fighting it out in my blood, the ebb and flow of jerky alertness, the shortness of breath from tiredness, but also a slight hesitation, a deadness in my right arm as I took out the cassette. One of the waitresses materialized and poured me a coffee, unasked, out of habit I suspect.

I worked on my nerves again for another five long minutes, kept checking my watch. Ronny was on the phone. He was talking quietly.

I turned up the volume on the cassette player and pressed the start button.

People jerked and turned and passed obscenities.

Ronny had his back to me, but he turned slowly with the sound and stared across the brown-carpeted floor at me. He had the phone away from his ear. His mouth was agape.

I let it play for another fifteen seconds or so, then killed it. One of the waitresses said, "What the hell you trying to pull?" but I didn't take my eyes off Ronny Lawton. He came slowly toward me. He was a physical presence, the scars on his face, the smallness of his eyes, like slits, the hanging ancestral Lawton chin, the gape of horror. He slipped in beside me in the crescent-shaped seat. He smelled of marijuana. A cigarette burned in the center of his face.

I said softly, "I got motive, Ronny. I know how your mother suffered. I know how you took her to the doctor . . ."

Ronny's eyes blinked in the glare of light. He took the cigarette away from his mouth. I could see every spot on his face, the blueness of veins around his thick neck. On the upper left of his work shirt was a metal pin that said Employee of the Month. Ronny looked at me. "You been speaking with that cunt, right?"

I said, "Who?"

"That don't mean shit, what she says," he said almost into my ear. "I'm clean."

It was another of those expressions that came from television.

The waitresses looked over at us.

I stayed my ground. I let his body press against mine. He had a net holding back his hair. He smelled also of cooked meat and spice, though the marijuana was almost sweet, intoxicating.

I said, "I heard you used to rub powder on your mother's back during heat like this. I heard how you took your mother to the doctor. I know you were there when she found out she was going to die."

Ronny rolled his eyes. "You call that goddamn evidence? That ain't got nothing to do with anything." Ronny touched his cigarette to his temple.

My voice was pasty. I had my hand over the cassette.

"That cunt's sayin' I did it, right?" His eyes opened wide for a moment before becoming slits again.

"She feels sorry for you, maybe," I answered.

Ronny pinched the bridge of his nose. "That's all bullshit." He leaned into the table. "We got nothing together anymore."

"You telling me that stuff about Duke Ellington never happened?"

"I ain't saying it never happened. What I'm saying is, it don't mean I chopped up my old man."

There was a piece of tobacco on one of his teeth, making it look like it was a brown spot of decay. It made him seem more callous, just that extra touch of ugliness that condemns men in our eyes. His big index finger touched the back of my hand. His face was close to mine. He said, "You don't want to fuck with me, so you don't." He took the tape out of my recorder, put it in his shirt pocket.

It was probably the biggest leap I was ever going to take with Ronny Lawton as he stood and glared at me. It wasn't a punch thrown, or a curse, or a threat, because that's what he craved, violence. It was just mushy emotional shit I decided to whisper in his wake. I said, as he started to turn and walk away, "Maybe you got me wrong, Ronny. When I heard that Duke Ellington, I saw a woman in pain and a son rubbing powder into her back. I saw love."

Ronny Lawton turned and came back and smiled obliquely. His eyes had a watery fatigue. His hand trembled when it came down slowly on my shoulder. "I don't ever want to hear you mention my mother again. You hear me?" I felt the pressure of his hand dig into my shoulder, knead deep down to my bone. He leaned into me. His unshaven cheek touched mine. He blew smoke at me. "I heard you was in the funny farm there for a spell. I heard how your father blew his brains out. I heard how he poisoned your dog. You was in the funny house for a spell, right?"

I said, "Yeah."

Ronny Lawton kept his mouth beside my ear. It was almost obscene, like he was kissing me. He whispered, "You know people say things about you."

I swallowed and averted my eyes. "What's it they say?"

Ronny shook his head. "I ain't getting involved in any of that."

Ronny dropped his cigarette into my coffee, and it hissed and smoked, then died.

I left, and Ronny followed me along Main Street and out along the old industrial part of town. I watched him in the rearview mirror, felt the reverse psychology of his menace, the way he undermined me as a lunatic. I circled down by the river and came around by Main Street again. Ronny was flashing me with his headlights. I went into Denny's lot and waited, and shit, I was scared that maybe I had touched something deep down in him, awakened the latent passion that had made him chop his old man into pieces. I just waited, ready to scream my head off, if need be, as he tapped on the window like a cop looking for a license. I obediently rolled down the window.

Ronny's face was in darkness.

I stayed inert, my hands on the wheel.

Ronny seemed to be speaking to himself. He said, "This is the first time in my goddamn life I got some money in my pocket. I'm Employee of the Month in there." His face was looking in on Denny's, staring at that small galaxy of light. He turned his face to me then. "You understand what that means to a guy like me, having money for the first time, having my name up on a plaque in there?"

I gave a laconic "Yeah."

Ronny told me about the merits of his Ford Mustang, how to pop the clutch and make it do burnouts. He made car noises of engines revving, talked RPMs, cam shafts, shit I didn't know a hell of a lot about. He'd gotten that car on finance from a dealer who was giv-ing him good terms, a dealer who wanted Ronny to give all state-ments to the press or media or the cops from that car. I listened to him tell me that. His hand came into the car, found my shoulder, a tentacle seeking out its prey. He stopped dead and then started again with some thread of an idea. "I had a goddamn brother die for this country. You know what it's like, when you get a letter home telling you that? You know what it's like for people, when they get that letter, and then they stop, and they realize they've been going on normal for days, when in all them days their son was dead some-wheres? Maybe that's the worst part of everything, that time when you was laughing your ass off or doing stupid shit when your brother was dead." His face invaded the car, the hotness of his breath close to my ear. I just stayed still. "You got those pictures of my father and my brother and me, way back when this all began, all of us in service shots, and what you did was make us the enemy. That wasn't right, you hear me? It wasn't right!" His fingers squeezed my shoulder. "We would have all died for this country, all of us. What you were looking at was the faces of men who had given themselves to their country."

I gained some sort of confidence, entered into his sadness. His hand had eased on my shoulder. I said softly, "You know where your father's body is, right, Ronny?"

Ronny whispered, "We're all living in that time of laughing and doing stupid things now, in that time when we don't know for sure if he's dead. It's just like with my brother and how he died. You see that? The not knowing is the hardest part, the waiting game. You see that, right, how the waiting just eats you?"

I didn't, so I said again, "You know where your father's body is, right, Ronny?"

Ronny wasn't looking at me, but he said, "How can I do any-thing that's going to save me from the chair in the end? I tell you where I figure my old man might be buried, and you're going to think I did it. There ain't a way to bury my father's memory, not any way I know anyhow, and not get myself fried in the chair."

I said very softly, "You can tell me."

Ronny Lawton stepped back from the car, turned his head for a moment to that small experiment cage where he eked out a survival, stared at Denny's, the place where he was now getting more money than he'd ever had in all his life. His face caught the errant light. His eyes turned and caught my look. He shook his head, emerging from the transfusion of our secret talk.

I said, "Where, Ronny? Tell me."

Ronny brought the enigma of his tattooed hands together on my window frame, the NOWHERE almost obscured in the dead light, a silent answer to my question.

CHAPTER 9

Somehow I dragged my carcass down to the office late the next day, dutifully went about the old routine. I saw Ed for the first time since Ronny's estranged had mentioned she knew Darlene.

"Ed. A funny thing the other day. I was out checking some facts with Ronny's estranged, and she tells me Darlene's been cutting her hair for years. I'm surprised Darlene didn't mention anything out at the barbecue, when we were talking about the case."

"Darlene's the best hairdresser in town, Bill." He looked at me. "I don't quite get what you're insinuating, Bill." Then came that subterranean bile, up from the volcano of his slow indigestion, up through the dark passage of his esophagus. And out came the handkerchief.

I stopped dead there in the office. I looked at Ed. "What I mean is, we might have been able to get a statement from her sooner, get a piece on how she felt about things, about Ronny and his father."

Ed had this stolid look on his face. "You're saying something I don't quite understand, Bill. What the hell are you insinuating?"

"No, Ed, you got it all wrong. I wasn't 'insinuating' anything. Ronny's estranged lives out your way. Darlene cuts hair. Why wouldn't they know each other? What I was thinking is just how small and interconnected everything is. That's all. I'm just making an observation about towns, that's all."

But Ed wasn't letting go of this. He just called home, turned his back to me, and got Darlene on the phone. He began talking to her.

I went into my office and had started typing when Ed came in and tapped me on the back. He handed me the black receiver. Darlene was on the other end. "Maybe we didn't put two and two

together, Bill, 'cause Teri uses her maiden name. She doesn't go by
Lawton." Ed's bony hand clawed at my back. He was saying over
my shoulder, "Tell him, Darlene. Tell him."

I said, "Darlene. Ed's all bent out of shape, and I didn't mean
anything by it. I was just out with Ronny's estranged and saw her
makeup, and it just came out that you did her hair. That's all. No
big deal. It doesn't mean a damn thing, Darlene. Ed just took me up
wrong." I was looking back at Ed, but he just stood there, eating
that sourness. "Ed?" I said. I put my mouth to the receiver again. "I
gotta go, Darlene. By the way, thanks for the barbecue the other
night."

Ed kept glaring at me. "If you don't have a lead, don't just go
barking up any old tree. You hear me, Bill?"

"Sure . . . Ed, come on. I'm sorry." He walked away from me to
the door. He turned. "When it comes to Darlene, I don't give second chances."

I mean Jesus Christ, I'd never seen a guy get so bent out of shape
like that over nothing.

Sam sat it out in his office, but I knew he was listening. I kept
typing, had my eyes closed, holding things in. "Don't go blaming
me for your failures." Ed muttered things like that.

I got up and went to the cooler, poured a tall glass of ice water.
Ed went off and then came up from the darkroom with a print of
what the drought was beginning to do to the land. He showed me
the picture, a sanguine sunset out by Johnson's Creek that was all
but dried up. Ed looked at me and smiled. "Friends, Bill?" I mean,
just like that, he changed his tune.

I took his hand. I felt like breaking down, but I didn't.

We put the paper to bed in the next hour. Sam came into our
office. The toaster was going in the other room. "I got tuna melts
all round, and chips." But he wasn't smiling or anything. Two dark
patches of sweat emanated from his armpits like phantom gray
wings. He was holding his flask of rye whiskey in one hand, a knife
in the other. He had that melancholy look of an old dog with that
droop of his jaw.

We ate the tuna melts. They tasted good. Hunger sort of reared itself as an afterthought. Sam poured a round of whiskey. You had to drink on his terms. It was part of the job.

We spent most of the evening sitting around down at the River's Bend Tavern doing boilermakers, dropping whiskey shots into tall ice-cold beers, staring at the shadows of men hiding from the heat and themselves. The River's Bend was one of those haunts that had been a granary years before, a turn-of-the-century wooden construction heavily coated in soft resin. Its ceiling ascended into a cathedral darkness of rafters. When there had been work, this place used to be standing room only.

Ed loosened his tie and sat with his back to the old wooden wall. Sam ordered two pitchers of Old Style and a half bottle of Wild Turkey and a small decanter of water, meted out our poison. There were some weeks it seemed like all we did was drink in this town. This was one of them, a drug of boredom administered against the heat, the quiet waiting period when everyone silently prayed for crackling storms to beat across the plains. In fact, above the bar was this sticker that said simply, "A barman is a pharmacist with a limited license."

I paced myself through the drinking, kept myself from talking about Ronny Lawton and what I'd found out at his estranged wife's place. Sam went on about Florida retirement communities. He had a brochure that had come in the mail, a glossy foldout of smartly dressed retirees in plaid pants on golf courses in minicarts. "It's all self-contained, Ed. Right there, you see? That is what I was thinking, that pink building there, right on the eighth hole, has efficiency units for sale." Sam's long finger pointed things out. "It comes with a golf cart, right there. What you get is access to the course between six A.M. and nine A.M. for free. Evenings cost, but not much, maybe eight bucks for eighteen holes. They got a community grocer who will deliver your groceries. See here in the pamphlet? Right here, Ed."

There was a picture of a college kid smiling at a camera holding a brown bag of groceries. An old lady was linked on to his bronzed arm. It was a cloudless day. A small testimonial caption under the college kid read "Todd Chambers. Florida Community College. Degree: Public Health." "My gramps died before I was born, and my grandnanna lived in some home in Nebraska. I grew up without ever seeing them. I always wanted grandparents. That's why I joined the Adopt-a-Grandma program. Emily has kind of become my grandma."

Under the grandmother was an apt, but laconic "Todd's a real sweet kid. I bake him Toll House cookies."

Ed made a whistling sound and leaned into the table as I stared at a convention hall of gray heads playing bridge on another page. His movements wobbled the table and made our beers tremble. "Darlene likes bridge." He looked up at Sam. "I ever tell you about Sunset Living, down near Naples? We get maybe a brochure a week from them people. Darlene filled out some contest, and now they're on to us. They know our intentions, but, hell, you can only be cynical so long. I mean, you got to see this place. It's a community set beside white sand beaches against a blue sky and palm trees, a community of retired professionals who have come together to pool their resources for a quality and dignified retirement. They got probably the best medical services you'll ever find. They got two orthopedic physicians who've done hundreds of hip replacements, one general-medicine doc on call, a nutritionist for private consultation and seminars, and five nurses. There's a home alert system in each unit. You fall down in the shower, and it alerts the medical staff. When you first get there, they give you a med bracelet with all your allergies and medical needs printed up, so they don't have to waste time if something might happen. They got all your vitals right there."

Sam said, "I'm not planning on dying just yet, Ed. That sounds like a goddamn hospital."

"Maybe I'm not quite explaining it like it is in the brochure. It's all unobtrusive, Sam. It's a support network, a safety net just in case."

Sam nodded. "But have they got a golf course, Ed? At my place, they got a function room that can hold two hundred people easy. Friday evening is an all-you-can-eat buffet of breaded shrimp and pasta salad and RC Cola. They got social hours and happy hours for widowers and widows. It's included in the monthly maintenance fee, all of it."

"I gotta ask Darlene about the golf. The way Darlene figures it, we might just open a beauty parlor down there. Old women have nothing but their hair, is what Darlene says."

Sam looked at Ed. "Ed, you landed on your feet when you got that Darlene."

Darlene had become a strange love interest for Sam, something deep inside him wanting the maternal care of a fat, middle-aged woman who could take care of him as he got old, feed him if need be, puree carrots and peas, tuck a bib around his neck. He needed someone to cut out coupons, someone to make sure he took his heart medication.

I laughed. "Maybe I should look into early retirement."

Sam ignored me. "If you do it right, Ed, it can be the best years of your goddamn life."

"Your golden years," Ed chimed in.

Sam poured a round of whiskey, and we dropped them into our beers, added a pinch of salt, and drank. We all sort of leaned back and seemed to take view of where we were. Two pool tables were set far back in the tavern, the haunt of the terminally unemployed, a series of slot machines that flashed in the gray dusk, a beleaguered world of bets, red in the side pocket, three cherries wins, not cash, but more credit on the slot machine. You don't ever come away with money. We listened to the click of balls in the gray heat of the tavern, a useless fan turning hot air. These are men who chew tobacco, men who stare into their spit cups. The cups somehow contain the extent of their profundity, their disgust, cups brimming with brown juice. They read their future like gypsies reveal tea leaves.

"Florida is a hell of a paradise, Ed," Sam blurted, snapping back from somewhere far away. "I ain't making the same mistake twice.

Property values are going up by the week down there. It's like, you get in early or you ain't getting in."

I was still looking around me. I said, "I suppose we have always been a nation of migrants, so why not internal migration of our aged, down to Florida."

Sam rolled his eyes. "Oh, jeez, here he goes again with his crap." We called for new frosted mugs. Our beer was getting warm.

There just didn't seem to be any way of bringing up the shears at this stage. I should have brought it up when I got to the office. Now I just couldn't bring the conversation around.

Ed had a wide grin on his face, slack-jawed from the drink. He said, "Let's hear just what goes on in that head of yours, Bill. What are you thinkin', right now, when you see me and Sam here like this? You're thinking something. I can see it."

So I opened the wound of my consciousness, forgot about the shears, and went on about bullshit. I said, "I call this one 'The Unburdening of History,' or simply 'Garage Sale.' "

Sam's head bobbed in the gray light. "I ain't listening." He put his hands to his ears and started humming.

"Sam," Ed said. "Come on now."

I set the scene. "Garage in Midwest America, Saturday afternoon, glorious day . . . You got that? Also, think of a Florida airport.

"Okay. See them arrive by plane in floral shirts and khaki pants, our aged, refugees from our industrial nightmare North, refugees from harsh winters, men and women suddenly disposed of, all they worked to maintain over a lifetime in one garage sale put on by their middle-aged son.

"Descend with me into the bowels of the Garage Sale. 'Ma, I know you waxed that table for half a century. I know, Ma, but you gotta understand, you can't fit a table like that in an efficiency down in Florida. People don't want antiques anymore, Ma. It's all built-in stuff down there.' So you engage in cruelty. You have to be firm with these parents, stop them dead in their tracks like spoiled kids. So you sell the table for a song, you don't even want to mention the price to Pa, 'cause he'd shit his pants. You got to lock him up inside, getting it done on a Saturday when there's a big baseball game going on, doubleheader. Get a keg of beer to move this shit. You've got to oil the pump. That's the way of business. Give 'em beer when they come sneaking around your stuff. Pa's old push lawn mower is marked ten dollars, but sells eventually for three, a lifetime of *National Geographic* magazines, thirty years, not a single one missing, all sold for five dollars to a man who was turning his back and walking away, a man who felt he was paying too much as he waded through wads of twenties.

"Okay, so you need a little drink to get this ball rolling. You have a set of *World Book Encyclopedias* and *Year in Reviews* that go back to when you were a kid. It's where you found out all your facts through grade school, junior high, and high school, and this guy says, 'Ten bucks!' and you just about lose it. You thumb through a page in this and that book, keep the encyclopedias until last. In fact, you sit your ass on them, in defiance. You kind of take offense when people give you that look, but you persevere. It's a damn nice day. You smile, and you drink, and you loosen up. You say to yourself, 'I am the proprietor of shit!' That's what you have to be thinking all the time. This is your ruse over them. It's pass the shit day.

" 'Marge, get over there.' That's your spreading middle-aged wife with the honeydew tits. 'Honey, can you tell this lady about the wedding dress?' There's a silk skin of a wedding dress on a mannequin's torso that's been watching you fix stuff for years. It's been like your goddamn guardian angel down in the basement. The dress is ivory, aged and smelling of mothballs, authentic turn-of-the-century garment. 'Look, you can see it there in the picture of our great-grandmother in 1897 . . . Yes, it's the same dress!' That's it, Marge. Wind up for the pitch. The sepia image of history stares out into the seventies. God Almighty, you're about to get rid of that piece of shit for once and for all, that dress stored and then taken out over the years, tried on by descendants, each girl writhing like a snake into the translucent satin skin of our distant old matriarch,

'Oh my God, look, Hatty has her grandmother's shape, the wide hips and small torso, the flat chest before Granny got all big with her pregnancy. Just look at the picture! Put your hair up like Granny. Hatty, that's it! Oh, my God!' The girls think it's a gas, they really do, but none of the descendants will wear this up the aisle. It gets shoved back into the basement to watch me fix things. You're about to see it go, and down comes the gavel for seven dollars and fifty cents to a woman who will rip out the seams and make something, she hasn't quite decided what yet, curtains, no doubt, for a small country bathroom. That's what she says to Marge, who is crying. Looks like you might just have to send her ass inside.

"Men dispose of history much better. Hell, we've been doing it for eons. The glass bowls from the turn of the century are marked five dollars each. They were handblown in Tennessee, beautiful cobalt blue. You're pretty firm about that price to this hog in a dress and canvas shoes with monstrous calves who stinks up the garage. You might just let the set of six, with matching plates and bone-handled cutlery, silver-plated, all go for twenty-five dollars. That's where you draw the line. But she snorts and moves away. She wants the tablecloths thrown in as an enticement. She says as much, takes them in her fat hands. You say that is 'hand-embroidered by three generations of industrious Christian women who lived before there was television, who died out before man walked on the moon, who lived through the Depression. You're joking me with that offer, right, lady?' A fat woman in polyester turns up her nose. She complains the linen smells of mildew, 'stored for going on fifty years in the attic.' It all goes for twenty dollars, glass setting, cutlery, and linen, all to be recycled at the annual charity auction in New Carlyle, piecemeal.

"Old black-and-white television. 'Needs an antenna, no doubt, partner. Could I turn it on? Why, I don't have an electrical outlet, but trust me on this one. It works real good.' Didn't you watch the Super Bowl on it in January? That television has got that greenish-colored reception, 'like you're looking back into a time machine, boss. By the way, help yourself to a beer.' Two minutes later, and he still can't decide. 'So stick a wire hanger into that hole right there, buddy, you ain't getting a television for under forty bucks these days.' It sells for a measly seven dollars, and the guy is still bargaining down. You have a good mind to charge him for the goddamn beer, but then you get sense. You see the playing field. To win the game, you got to get rid of everything. That's the primary focus. It's pass-the-shit day. A cathedral radio for a buck fifty needs a vacuum tube. Shit almighty, it's hard just to let it go for that price, even if it doesn't work. It looks big, substantial, but you remember the game. You are the proprietor of shit. It's pass-the-shit day. A dusty mop for ten cents is a bonanza. A nickel for a heavy steel Matchbox racing car.

"'Say, look here, kid. This garage set has a ramp that raises and lowers and two gas station attendants who hold gas nozzles. It's all going for, say, five bucks. Whatta ya say, partner? Make a hell of a Father's Day gift, kid. Take your old man way back. See, this dirt wipes right off. Whatta ya say, kid?' Sold, for five bucks. Just take the cash out of his hot little hand. Cars and attendants included, sure thing. Wouldn't want to separate those guys from the garage—lifers, those guys. Sure, you'll take money from a kid. You bet he's got a real big basement that needs filling. Send the kid out real quick, before he changes his mind, sort of push him on his way to his bicycle, which somebody has bid nine dollars for, and Marge has taken the cash. Shit, Marge! Jeez almighty, you sold the kid's bike. The kid is looking nervous. Hand the money back, get the kid off the property. Oh, God, it's hard work dispensing with our history. Pump that keg again, cold beer against the forehead.

"'Howdy, girls. We have two Spanish-looking dolls with big wide dresses that you use for hiding toilet paper. You never seen that? You're pulling my leg, girls. You ain't lived until you got one of these.' Show them the plastic anatomy of these dolls. You got another set right over here that are lamps. You just screw in a bulb right at their vitals, and you got yourself a hell of a night lamp. 'For you, ladies, eight dollars for all four.' Deal struck at eight bucks even. Jesus Christ, there's a sucker born every day. They buy a flyswatter, unmarked, so you push it and ask for two, settle for one fifty. They don't have fifty cents. A buck even, when you would have sold it for a quarter. Hell, live a little.

"The baptismal vestments of Great-Aunt Clarice, who died of TB, have turned to a delicate cobweb of disintegrated lace. You ain't making a cent on that shit. Marge objects. But you take her hand gently. They are silently put in a black plastic sack, along with pirate teddy bears wielding daggers, without eyes, some with patches, dolls missing limbs, cracked porcelain disembodied heads, an old steel iron you put on a fire. Each item has a jaded history, generations of artifacts jettisoned by you, their middle-aged son, who has been willing them gone for years. Nostalgia is a commodity that needs basements and attics to live. It needs a dimension of space. It's a luxury, this history of ours. Nobody will buy the year-books. It's a grim reality. Box them up and set them out on the sidewalk. 'Sure that's a good couch, but you paid forty bucks in 1952 for it, Pa.' He's broken through the barricade of chairs you put at the front door. The baseball game's over. But that couch stinks to high heaven. Its arms are frayed and shiny with oily dirt from greased hair. You stare at the impression of your old man's bony head there on the couch. You might just relent. That's your old man's head there, the indentation of a lifetime of living, and then you remember, you are the proprietor of shit, and this is pass-the-shit day. So you have to frog-march your old man back into the house. It ain't easy being the asshole, but you've got to lighten the load.

"The encyclopedias go for twenty, and then something gives inside you, a sudden memory. You remember doing that project on the Ottoman Empire, way back in junior high, pasting in all the facts, your pa squeezing that rubber glue onto cardboard for you. Night settles. You have to chop up the old box-spring bed frame. You stare at a cartography of urine, remember the times you got in with your parents at night, when you were afraid of the dark, the remnants of their past love. You keep hacking away at your history. You keep drinking the beer, grill a few dogs, and your old man comes out, and he's shaking. The couch is set out on the sidewalk for the college kids to come and take. Your old man goes out and lies down on it, obstinately. Your ma starts screaming, it's his couch. You have to drag him back, sit his ass down. You inflict a conspiracy of silence. You keep drinking. The college kids are around, all right, you've seen them all day, circling in their station wagon, those predators who need to furnish their dorm rooms. Say, they just might take the old dresses for a fancy costume ball they have up there at the college in late autumn. Pa says Ma wore one of them dresses out on the sidewalk to her first Sadie Hawkins dance. They went on a hayride out by Abe Rosen's barn. You blank it all out. You think, pretty soon, he won't have a mind to remember any of this. It's a genetic mode of survival, this forgetting, this dementia, when it comes. He'll forgive you, because he won't remember any of this. But for now, just set what you can't sell on the sidewalk. People can't resist something that's for nothing, that's one sure thing. Lock your door, and go to sleep. You'll see, in the morning, all gone, a dream.

"Well, looky here at this for a fine return on a lifetime, a hundred and twenty-four dollars and fifteen cents. You must be shitting me! You've been out here all day hocking shit, but that's all there is. And there, look at you, you forgot to subtract the eighteen for the keg, two for ice, four for the ad in the paper, three for the signs that led the scavengers into our street hidden away among other streets. You subtract all that . . . Let's see now . . . twenty-seven from a hundred and twenty-four is ninety-seven. Okay, the revised tally is ninety-seven dollars and fifteen cents. That wouldn't cover going Greyhound to Atlanta."

Ed said, "Holy shit. You didn't just make that up, did you?"

Sam said, "Don't encourage that crap, Ed."

I said, "Yeah, Ed. Don't you know, we got a self-destruct button deep within us in my family."

Sam hid behind his drink.

I wiped my lips, pretty exhausted.

Ed was still going, "You didn't just make that up, Bill, did you?"

We fell silent again. Sam had a way of smacking his lips that brought a finality to things. An old farm bell rang, and the bartender signaled to us that we were getting a free pitcher. At River's Bend, you didn't just drink, you drank to get drunk. They had a clock over the door with a saying, "No drinking until after five!" The numbers on the clock were all fives.

Sam got back to the retirement brochure again. I just kept staring into the reality of retirement, into the retirement my father had never known. The more I kept looking, the more I could see its potential, the vast institution of services. Take even the finality of death, what can be extracted from that pageant after the doctors and medical community have collected their money, once insurance agents have paid up, begrudgingly, once they dispose of the corpse. There are the florists, the crematoriums and cemeteries, the headstone makers, the groundskeepers, the ministers, the morticians, the limousine services, the newspapers that print the obits, the print services that make up the mass cards, the lawyers who make and amend the wills, the receptionists who show you into the law office, the cleaning ladies who come in the night to polish the mahogany wood, the airlines and rental cars used by the bereaved who come to bury their deceased parents, the mechanics who work on those cars, the cleaners who vacuum out the cars, the gas stations that sell the fuel, the hotels and eateries where the bereaved stay and eat while they are making arrangements, the day trips to Sea World and Disney World, because once you're down, hell, the kids are going to insist on seeing Mickey and Goofy, plus the souvenirs, the T-shirts and pins and pens and cups you have to bring back for the neighbors who are minding your dog, Mitch, and your cat, Mindy, and feeding your hamsters, Herbie and Matt, and your goldfish, Priscilla, and your tortoise, Edward.

Ed said, "Look, there's a mail-in card for a recipe book, *One Hundred and One Things to Make in a Toaster Oven.*"

Sam cast his hand out over the gray of the tavern. "You know, the saddest thing I have to reckon with is that I'm worth more dead than alive." Sam just clamped up after that, hunched down into his chair, and sipped his beer. He let smoke out of the side of his mouth.

Ed tried to steer the conversation like you might turn a horse. He was drunk. He leaned into the table. "I want to explain something to you, Bill, about how I acted a while ago."

I said, "It's all forgotten, Ed."

Ed said, "No. I got some explaining to do."

Sam was downing another shot of whiskey, distracted.

"Seems like our dog, Gretchen, had a false miscarriage on us. Darlene's all upset about it. You got me at a bad time, Bill. That was all."

Sam seemed to shake himself from his inebriation. "A what, Ed?"

Ed just looked at us. "What we figure is, Darlene does, anyway, is that Gretchen was trying to pretend she was pregnant, since she knows that all Darlene ever wanted was a baby. Dogs got this uncanny ability. It's a scientific fact, so it is, Darlene says. It's what she calls a 'sympathetic pregnancy.' "

I didn't fully understand what the hell he was saying. "You mean, the dog was acting like some surrogate mother?"

Sam leaned back and went off the goddamn chair, and down came the pitcher, whiskey and all. He was breaking his ass laughing.

We got things cleaned up, and Sam kept at Ed, right through the late hours of the night.

Ed said in his defense, "Gretchen had the signs of a miscarriage, Sam. I saw it with my own two eyes. I'm not saying I fully understand how it all works, but it does, at some chemical level."

The malaise of boredom and inebriation reached a point where it was necessary to call Darlene to come and get us. The joke had been played for all it was worth.

Darlene was wearing a floral-patterned dress, a virus of color, when she arrived at the bar. Gretchen was out in the car, wrapped in a blanket.

Of course, Sam changed his tune when Darlene was around. He said, "My deepest condolences to Gretchen, Darlene. I know it comes as a shock."

Darlene said, "It broke my heart, honest, Sam, it did." But you could see she was pissed Ed had said anything.

Darlene looked stiffly at me. She just sort of changed the discussion, looked out over all the drunk men and said, "Goddamn it, why do men live in the past?" She said it out of the blue like that.

Ed shrugged his shoulders, said, "We were only talking, Darlene."

I said, "I think it was Emerson who once said, 'A man's wife has more power over him than the state has.' "

Darlene gave me this dirty look. She gave us her take on history. She said, "You can't squeeze the toothpaste back into the tube. Not you, Ed, or you, Sam."

Sam looked at Darlene and then at Ed, and he just smiled. You could see the bond there between those three. It was something that you didn't get these days, that closeness between younger people.

I raised my glass and shouted, "Darlene, you're a Nietzsche of suburbia!"

She said flatly, "What the hell's a Nietzsche?"

Outside, I left them standing around looking at Gretchen. It was one hell of an ugly-looking poodle, that tight crop of curly hair like Darlene had given the damn dog a perm. Darlene was going on about biological processes of the female anatomy, about the synchronization of periods when groups of women live in close proximity.

Sam was saying, "I'll be damned." I mean, he was saying it like he really meant it. Darlene had that much of an effect on him.

And there went any chance of mentioning the shears. A goddamn day of silence, of subterfuge. Jesus Christ! Even through the drunkenness, I felt the maddening ineptitude. I was withholding goddamn evidence. Christ! It just surfaced like that, self-debasement and ridicule. I knew what it was though, that sick feeling of being in love, holding off because I was afraid I might just implicate Ronny's estranged.

That goddamn dog and its sympathetic pregnancy and all that shit. Sam said, "Come on over here, Bill."

It just got to me all of a sudden. I went and stood and looked at the dog. Darlene was wiping away that crusty shit poodles get in their eyes. The dog was licking Darlene's hand. Darlene was holding the dog like an infant. It was sick, all of it. How the hell was I back in this shithole? But of course, I knew the answer: those goddamn LSATs!

I drove the few blocks to the Y. The caretaker was closing up, but he let me in anyway. He still had some things to get done. I swam a few laps, then trod water, catching my breath. I went under, let myself sink and stayed still, assumed the fetal position, kept my eyes closed, and held my breath. I waited there in the deep end of the pool, felt the pressure against my ears, the distortion of sound around me, a liquid sound of things impinging. I opened my eyes to the murky light, extended my hand before my face, stared at the disembodied hand, closed my eyes again, and waited in that embryonic stage, wanting the fetal memory of a time long forgotten inside my mother that could never be recovered, never remembered, no matter how hard I tried. I stayed still, eased into a new stillness, went into that anaerobic dimension, into the starkness of fear. I felt the burn in my lungs begin, let out a slow release of breath until there was nothing in my lungs, held on for the euphoria of suffocation, for panicked constriction, fear centering in the cavity of my chest until it was almost too late, then I unfurled my body and pushed from the bottom of the pool, breaking the cold surface, gasping for air. It felt like emerging into another dimension, the floating white blobs of consciousness before my eyes, the rasping dryness of my windpipe, the wheezing, fitful involuntary breaths. By midsummer I did little else at the pool, maybe twenty laps, then I began pretending I was dead, inert at the bottom of the pool, dormant, waiting to surface at the last moment, staying down there away from the world, trying to stare back into a past that had been eclipsed for me. I got so good I could go nearly three minutes, a dark ball hiding at the bottom of the Y.

I went down by the office, sat around, and thought about things. My chest was sore. The chlorine burned my eyes. I went into the toilet and put in some eyedrops, blinked the saline tears, felt the flood of relief. I looked through the obits for the next few days, the succinct notes that encapsulate the lives of loved ones. I edited a few of them. I was afraid of what was at home, the image of the shears buried. I'd made a fatal mistake burying them like that. I had to make it right, get things on track.

I called Pete, even though it was real late. I couldn't get through the night. I said, "How about coming out by my house, Pete? I got something big, real big."

Pete seemed to hesitate. "How come you didn't call me during regular office hours?"

"Pete. I got something that just might break open this Ronny Lawton case."

"Yeah, well, midnight isn't exactly the kind of hours I keep."

I held the receiver to my ear. I heard Pete's wife in the background. Pete said, loud enough so I could hear, "It's just the guy who called me a sadist. Go back to sleep."

"Pete, for Christ's sake, you can't be serious. Pete?" I raised my voice. "Pete! Come on!"

"Yeah, well, I looked it up. Bill, I'm not a sadist, not by the definition they got in my dictionary. How do you define it, Bill?"

I took a deep breath. "I was using it figuratively. Now, come on, Pete. Jeez, we go way back, and when I get something big like this, who do I call? You, Pete. You. Now come on. This can't wait until tomorrow morning."

I heard Pete grunt, rise, and set his feet at the edge of the bed. "You want to tell me what this is all about now?"

"Evidence, Pete. Physical evidence. That's all I can say. I'm down at the office right now, but go on out by my place and I'll meet up with you."

"I just hope you didn't touch anything. Did you, Bill?"

I set the receiver down before he could say anything and left for home.

There was a call from Ronny's estranged when I got home. I answered the first time, heard her voice, and hung up. She called back. I listened as she left a message on my machine. She was down at Osco. She was lonely. She was sad. All that stuff she told me had made her cry. She wanted to know if I would come down and see her. She didn't say why. She said, "I need to talk about this."

I got the phone after a minute. I picked up and let the tape in the answering machine run. "Talk about what?" I said.

"Why did you hang up on me, Bill?"

"I didn't."

"Don't lie to me, Bill. Men is always lying to me. Don't you start, please."

"I got someone coming over right now, Teri. How about I come out by your place tomorrow, during the day?"

"You got a girl there or something, Bill?"

"I'm as single as they come. You don't gotta worry about that."

"Who says I'm worried, Bill?"

I hesitated, felt the transgression. It was better to let things go unsaid, let her lead the discussion.

"Bill?"

"Yeah."

"I was kidding, Bill. You got a girl, big deal. I got a man. We're even."

"Yeah." I kept it simple.

"You mind bringing out beer again, and some cigarettes? I don't get paid until Friday. I'll pay you back."

There was an uneasy silence. I felt her breath in my ear. "Maybe you might bring some chocolate milk for Lucas? I swear I'll pay you back." She waited, then said, "Bill, you still there?"

"Yeah."

"How many girlfriends does a guy like you have?"

"Listen, I gotta go now."

"Bill?"

"Yeah."

"How fast that car of yours go? I mean, if you just floored it and kept it floored?"

"Maybe one thirty-five, I suppose. I never tried it."

"You mean, you got a car like that, and you never took her all the way, you never tried to see how far she'd go?"

I could feel the innuendo across the static on the line. She said, "Sleep tight, Bill." Then she was gone. I got a dial tone in my ear after a moment.

I was starved for attention there in the isolation of my mansion. I replayed her message a few times. I liked the way she kept saying my name, the gentle incantation of my name that echoed inside her head. I knew she was thinking about me. It was a feeling that eclipsed everything else for a few moments. I wanted to go down there to Osco and see her under the sharp incandescence of pharmacy lighting, take her outside and just stare at her. What I was thinking was, how the hell wouldn't she want me? It wasn't bragging or anything, just a fact, when you looked hard into her life and saw it for what it was.

I was still thinking about that when Pete rang at the door. I had the front door wide open, only the screen door closed to stop the invasion of mosquitoes. A current of warm air flowed through the house. "You in there, Bill?"

"Come on in, Pete."

Pete was still pretty sour toward me when he arrived. His hair was all slicked back, like he'd taken a shower. He was wearing shorts and a T-shirt. "So, what the hell you got for me? I just hope the hell you haven't touched anything, that's all I got to say." It was like he knew I'd fucked something up.

"Pete, I said I was sorry." Maybe it was the heat, first Ed and now Pete acting all pissy over nothing. "Just follow me, Pete."

I hadn't even dug the shears up. We went through the library and dining room to the kitchen, past the glass case with my grandfather's old war coat illuminated by a small fluorescent bulb.

I got a shovel and dug up the dirt, withdrew the plastic sack teeming with moisture, and in we went. I set it on the table and in a theatrical flourish said, "Exhibit A."

Pete made a whistling sound. A wing of hair stuck out from the side of his head. "What the hell is it, Bill?"

"Maybe the shears, or the kind of shears, that cut the finger off Ronny Lawton's old man."

"Jesus H. Christ, where the hell did you get 'em?"

"I was out with Ronny's estranged, just checking to see her side of what the hell she thought of Ronny. I was on the property, and there they were, just lying on the ground. I never thought I'd be defending Ronny Lawton, but maybe there's a possibility that Ronny's telling the truth."

Pete pulled at his chin, began shaking his head in utter disbelief. "You've just blown this whole case to shit, Bill. You should have called me. I mean, shit on it, Bill. Any lawyer is going to cry foul. You can't just waltz in and take physical evidence off someone's property. There's procedures, dammit. What you did is kill this case."

I guess I knew that was coming, the truth, that I'd compromised physical evidence.

Pete gave me this look of contempt. "Did you get your prints on it? Tell me you didn't."

I said quietly, "I had to pick them up quick when she wasn't looking."

Pete rolled his eyes. "I was thinking we might have got them back out onto their property, but not if you got prints on them."

"Just wipe 'em off. Can't we just do that?"

"Bill. Use your goddamn head. Shears out there with no prints is going to look like a plant." Pete stared down at the shears. "I can't cover for you, Bill. Not on something this big. I mean, shit, you should have called me on this . . ." He put his hands up in the air. "This is on you, Bill. You've screwed up everything. I'm going to have to make a report on what happened here, Bill. I just can't get involved in bullshit like this . . . This is my goddamn career we're talking about."

I had this giddy sensation, like I was going to pass out. It was hard just breathing. "Pete . . . Pete . . . It doesn't have to go beyond you and me. Just you and me." I grabbed at his arm. "And I'm not talking. Listen, I got an in with Ronny's estranged. I got it on tape inside. She wants to see me again."

Pete shook off my touch. "Bill, this isn't just my goddamn job that's on the line. Complicity in something like this, replanting evidence, is a felony. You understand what that means? They lock your ass up and throw away the key." Pete backed away from the shears. He just kept shaking his head. "No, this is all on you, Bill. I just can't. I got a wife. No." He hiked up his shorts in a sudden halting manner, a final defiance.

I felt the separation. I was, plain and simply, done for. Once this got out, I was finished with the paper, the end of everything. I'd have to get my ass out of town, just leave and hide. Hell, there could even be some charge brought against me. And maybe in the end I was just plain scared of not seeing Ronny's estranged again. In fact, that was it right there.

I said, "Okay, Pete. I fucked up. I'm not denying it. But at least now we know what we're dealing with. Maybe this isn't just a cut-and-dried case against Ronny Lawton. So, shit on the shears I got here. You see, Pete, I've gotten in tight with Ronny's estranged. She called me tonight. She wants to talk."

Pete was staring down at the shears.

I pressed him. "Yeah, that's right. She didn't see me with the shears or nothing. She gave me this sob story of how Ronny was abused. She knows something. She was all for blaming Ronny, but I got a sense there was something else going on. You know what she said to me?"

"What?"

"She wanted to know if she was going to get the house, just like she said to you, way back when all this started. That's motive right there, Pete."

Pete seemed to have settled somewhat. He looked me in the eye. "This was cut-and-dried. We could have got the shears checked out, and that would have either cleared or implicated her . . ." But he was coming around slowly.

"I'm going out by her place tomorrow, Pete. I think I can get something out of her. Maybe I'll intimate something about the shears, see how she reacts?"

Pete sort of shouted, "That's what you can't do! Dammit, Bill, you got to forget about the shears right now. That's the whole damn point. Forget the shears!"

"Forget the shears. Right." I sort of grimaced, pulled a contrite face.

Pete touched the bridge of his nose, pinched the tiredness in his face. He began shaking his head again, the idea roaming his brain. "No, I can't go along with this, Bill. You see, right there, you go mentioning the shears! No! Just plain *no!* I'm going to report what happened tonight. There's nothing I can do. You screwed everything up! End of story!"

I tried another tack. I said, "Okay, make the call. You file your report, you end all this on the grounds of mishandling of information. See how the mayor takes it! Yeah, go on and tell him how you felt obliged to bring to light that an amateur reporter with his head up his ass just waltzed out there to Ronny Lawton's estranged and found a piece of real evidence just lying on the ground. I guess the mayor is going to see it your way, though. I guess he won't be pissed you never even went out there." I was shouting that out, in this voice of ridicule. "They're going to love you, Pete!"

That changed Pete's mind real fast. He got downright conciliatory. He said, "I guess, you lie down with dogs, you get fleas." He was still brooding, but he was trapped. He looked at me. "I got a wife to worry about, Bill. Maybe you could do me a favor and play it my way from now on. All I want in life, I have right now. Don't lose it for me, Bill."

That touched something inside me. I just saw the humanity in him staring back at me. He was scared.

Pete looked at me. "You better play it slow, Bill, I mean real slow, with Ronny's estranged. You just can't go mentioning nothing about the shears. You got to start over again. You got to think before you act."

I said, "I will." I got Pete away from the shears, steered his eyes from the table so he was looking directly at me.

I said, "Maybe Ronny's estranged just got it in her head to get her boyfriend to kill off Ronny's old man. She's living in shit out in a trailer. She's got a kid that she leaves alone in a cage when she goes to work. Or just maybe she didn't plan it at all. Her boyfriend maybe got tired of hearing her going on about getting no child support. Maybe, just maybe, she went on a good deal about how she deserved that house out there, and her boyfriend just went about getting it for her."

Pete nodded. "That's the way you're going to have to sell it to her. Give her an out, different versions."

"Right," I said.

Pete eased and took a long, deep breath. "I'll tell you this for nothing. I don't give a damn who goes down for cutting up Ronny Lawton's old man. Neither does city hall. We just need somebody put away for this, and soon."

"It might be nice to get the real killer, though, right?"

"I suppose." Pete looked at me. "I had my heart set on busting Ronny Lawton. What he's doing down at Denny's is a slap in the face. It's the kind of thing that's disintegrating this country." He let out another long sigh. "Christ. Don't go looking at me like that, Bill. I'll go along with you only so far."

I had no objections.

Pete got all serious then, he'd made up his mind finally. He said, "First thing you have to do is forget about those shears. They gotta go."

"Where?"

"Dispose of them, Bill. Jesus!"

Our eyes fell on the shears, and all of a sudden, it was hard to think of how to get rid of them. I looked up at Pete.

Pete stood in the glare of the kitchen light, his skin a sickly white. He had a habit of biting his nails. He spat out a nail and seemed to nod, playing things out in his head. "Maybe I interview this boyfriend and get something out of him." He looked at me hard. He kept at his nails, gnawing at them and spitting out bits of nail. "Maybe I'm going to regret this. I'm not convinced that Ronny didn't chop up his old man, but I'll give you a chance to prove me wrong."

I said, "Thanks."

Pete went back to looking at the shears. "Well, then, what we got to do now is cover up this mistake, get rid of those shears."

I stayed quiet for a long time, giving that look of contrition.

Pete put his hand on my back. "I'm putting my ass on the line for you, Bill. Don't let me down."

We sat at the table and just continued to stare at the shears. It's pretty hard to figure out how to dispose of something. We considered throwing them off a bridge, going way out in the cornfields and throwing them there, stashing them in a neighbor's trash. In the end, Pete said, "Just bury them back out in your garden, Bill. There ain't no sense going all over the county with them in the car with your prints all over them. Shit, I've seen more ironic things happen than you hitting a tree and having those shears there with you when the fire department drags your ass out from the wreck." He gave one last definitive look. "Just bury them out there."

I went out and buried the shears again, because I had to, but I sure as hell wasn't going to keep them there. I was burying them only because I couldn't get away from the house right then, but I planned on dumping them down in the river. I went out back, sweating bricks that a neighbor might see me, but all the lights were off in the few houses around me. Anyway, we had an expanse of garden and trees that would have made it impossible for anybody to see what I was doing. So I buried the shears again.

I came back in, and Pete had helped himself to some cold cuts and apple juice. He was out on the back porch. I realized I'd not eaten all day. I got some cold meat, and we ate in the light of the moon.

I said, "Pete, thanks."

Pete looked at me. "You got a tomato, or an onion, Bill?"

I went in and got a tomato out of the crisper, cut it into thin slices and salted it, and came back out.

Pete took the plate and looked at me.

I said thanks again.

Pete had the cold cuts on the end of a fork, hovering over his plate. He held them there like he was going to say something, but all he did was take the cold cuts to his mouth and eat.

It was going on one-thirty when the phone rang again. I almost jumped. "That's got to be her, Pete. Come in. Wait'll you hear this." We headed into the front room. I let the answering machine get it, so it was all getting recorded, then I picked up.

"Your girlfriend still in the house with you, Bill?" Her voice played through the speaker.

"How come you're so interested whether I have a girlfriend?"

I looked at Pete. He had his plate of cold cuts in hand. He raised his eyes and grinned.

"I didn't see a ring on your finger, and I was just thinking, 'How come a guy like that isn't married?' I was thinking, 'What's behind those blue eyes?' "

"You remembered the color of my eyes?" I said, and again winked at Pete.

"What color are my eyes, Bill?"

"Pale green."

"Now how the hell did you get that right without even having to think?"

I said, "Someone said once, 'The eyes are the windows to the soul.' "

She breathed deep into the phone. "I like that, Bill. I just might use that line myself. I guess that's what college guys say to girls, right? Quote books and stuff?"

Pete made a face like he was impressed. He had tomato juice running down his chin. He wiped it away with the back of his forearm and waited for me to say something.

Ronny's estranged said, "You probably think I'm not much of a mother, leaving my kid out there in his pen like that. Right?"

"I wasn't thinking that."

"Don't goddamn lie!" Her voice rose, then she lowered it. "Bill, don't lie to me. Men been lying to me all my life. Promise me."

"I promise."

"You cross your heart and hope to die?"

"Cross my heart and hope to die."

I could hear her swallowing, hesitating. "I never got to talk to a guy like you, not somebody that went to college anyways. It was nice. When I speak to you, I see what I am."

"What do you mean?"

"You got a face that can't hide things, Bill. I seen the way you looked when I left my kid locked up in the trailer. It was like you was telling me not to do it. That's what you was thinking, right?"

Pete set his plate down and eased back into a La-Z-Boy. He closed his eyes, taking it all in.

"How come you won't answer me, Bill? Is it 'cause you got a girl under the sheets there with you? A college girl from that Catholic college up the road? I bet you got a lot of college girls that want you."

I said, "I got a few."

There's a point where you give in to this sort of flattery. I might have done that, but the machine was recording everything, and Pete was sitting there listening to everything. I felt sorry for Ronny's estranged, thought of her at the end of the line in the glare of the pharmacy light, her kid out in the trailer in the cage. Maybe that boyfriend of hers didn't always just go home. There was no phone, no way to know if he was out there with the kid. And it wasn't his kid anyway.

"Hey, Mr. College Graduate, I want to ask you something. Is it true them Catholic girls up at that college wear pajamas with footies, like babies? I heard that was true."

Pete put his finger to his temple, like Ronny's estranged was crazy. He kept sitting back in the La-Z-Boy, smiling. He used the lever and extended the footrest, leaned way back.

I said, "I don't know. They don't let men up to their dorms."

"Here's another thing I was always wondering about. They got them panty raids on the girls' college. All the college guys run over there, and the college girls hang out their panties with their phone numbers on 'em. That all true, Bill?"

"Yeah, that's pretty much how it goes, all right. You see the girl you like, and you climb up her dorm drainpipes and get her panties, and then you go back to your dorm and call her."

"Anybody ever get married out of giving away their panties like that, Bill?"

"Yeah, I don't know exactly who, but I suppose there's kids that get together because of the panty raid."

"Bill?"

"Yeah?"

"How come it don't matter if a man is educated or not, he just always wants to go for the panties?"

I didn't answer her.

"Bill, you still there?"

"Yeah."

"How many panties did you get?"

"Look, I got to go. Okay?"

"Just tell me. What is the name of the girl you got with you now, under the sheets?"

I said, "Courtney."

"What's she look like, Bill? I bet she got long legs. Is she real smart? I bet you only go out with smart college girls, right?"

I heard Ronny's estranged breathe into the phone in a sort of quiver. She said, "I know who you are, Bill."

Pete got serious and stared at me. I caught my breath, almost laughed. "Who am I?"

"You live in that mansion. I asked around. You aren't just a reporter. I hear you is loaded. That right, Bill? You got so much money you don't know how to spend it."

Right then, I felt she knew something more about me than she was letting on, like there was something going on behind my back. I didn't quite get it. I could have sworn I heard somebody in the background.

Pete put his finger to his throat like I should cut the call short.

I said, "What the hell do you know about me?"

Ronny's estranged said, "It ain't a secret you got money, Bill."

I didn't say anything.

Ronny's estranged said, "Bill?"

I said, "What?"

"What the hell is it like to go to bed at night with money in the bank, to not have to worry about nothing?"

I whispered, "It's not all you think."

"That's what all the rich got to say about money, right? Money can't buy happiness. Well, maybe they just don't know where to shop."

I said nothing. I could tell Ronny's estranged was smoking, heard this soft pulling sound, the slow release of breath. I said finally, "Are you done insulting me?"

Ronny's estranged giggled into the line. She said, "What color are Courtney's eyes?"

I said, "I don't know."

"Don't lie to me, Bill. Don't lie to me."

I said again, "I don't know what color her eyes are."

"You don't look in her eyes when you're with her?"

I didn't answer.

"You know the color of my eyes. How come you know that, Bill?"

Again I didn't answer.

Ronny's estranged said, "You still there, Bill?"

"Yeah."

"You going to come see me tomorrow, Bill?"

"Sure."

She said, "I just can't get what happened to Ronny's old man out of my mind." I heard her holding something back. "I got this feeling

Ronny's old man is out there, all chopped up . . ." Ronny's estranged coughed into the phone. She was out of breath. I waited quietly. Someone spoke over the PA system, some price check.

Ronny's estranged whispered, "Bill, I don't think I really felt anything till you came out and got me thinking about it. I feel like I've lived a thousand lives, and, you know, not one of them was what I wanted. You don't know the half of what went on out there, Bill. I never told anybody, not anybody ever." She whispered, "Not anybody, Bill." Then the phone went dead in my ear. I waited a few moments, then hung up.

Pete clapped his hands together and had this huge grin on his face. "She wants to sit on your face, Bill. Hell, it's plain as day. Holy shit, you didn't tell me she was after you like this . . . I mean Christ Almighty. Who the hell needs the goddamn shears if she starts talking?"

It was going on two in the morning. I instinctively yawned, and my eyes watered. "I got another call like that tonight from her." I slumped against a chair. The moonlight fell in slats across my face. "I don't know what to make of her. I told you, she's got a kid out there she locks in a cage when she goes out to work."

"So?"

"So, she sees me in that car of mine, and she thinks what she wouldn't give for a car like that."

"I don't see the problem." Then Pete let a grin break on his face. "Oh, shit, don't tell me you're scared she's only interested in you for your money." He set his hands on his fat knees, and his fat body jiggled. "Hell, Bill, you never cease to amaze me." Pete set down the lever on the chair and got up with a grunt. His face took on a look of constipation until he got a smile going again. "You like her. Jesus, the plot thickens." He put his hand on me with a marauding familiarity. He smelled of fermented apple juice. "Bill. She's the kind of trash that can just pull everything right out from under you. Who the hell knows, she might have put her boyfriend up to killing Ronny Lawton's old man, and that's murder, Bill. Now she's scared shitless and wants out. She just might pull one over on that boyfriend of hers, stick him for the murder."

Pete began moving toward the door with me in the bulk of his arm. "Get close to the fire, Bill, but don't get burned. Hell, if she thought you were on to her, she might get her boyfriend to kill you off. You got to understand what you're dealing with here, Bill." Pete detached himself from my body, stepped back, and tapped me in the chest with his index finger. "That's right, Bill. You're dealing with trash that isn't afraid to kill. You better understand all that now, before you get mixed up in this. Any way you look at it, Bill, she's into your money in a big way."

It was the truth of it maybe, but I didn't want to believe it.

Out on the porch, moths fluttered around a globe of light. It was still warm. I heard the animals in the dark of the zoo out back of our place, the plaintive roar of beasts, like we were in some savanna. Pete turned his head and listened to the cries. He said, "That always freaked me, them animals. I don't know how the hell you live with that."

"You get used to it." But it was unnerving, something at the back of consciousness. I incorporated their cries into my dreams some nights, especially the nights of storm, when the cages trembled against the blow of wind and pelt of rain.

We lingered on the porch. Pete turned his head again and crossed his arms and stared out from the rise of our land, the man-made rise commissioned by my grandfather at some astronomical price, some vestige of that feudal mentality still with him, the need for a center to things.

Pete yawned. "Maybe you should think about getting yourself wired. I can get it arranged down at the station." He clicked his fingers. "Just like that."

I said, "Give it some time, Pete. I feel weird about this." I looked off at the gray-fingered chimneys down in the foundry yard. Despite the heat, the transients had set small fires here and there. The firelight throbbed against the dark. Pete took my hand and shook it. It was like a consolidation of a partnership. His hand was hot. We could hear cages rattling in the background. Something had upset the animals. Then the crying subsided again.

Pete lingered maybe too long. I wanted him gone, but things were going through his own head. I knew that. He was letting things sift through his head, setting himself at ease over the shears. That had to be the big thing he was silently debating. If he walked away from here, he was a conspirator. So I stayed my ground, yawned, and waited.

Pete spoke eventually. "Bill, I know this is tough on you, but maybe ninety percent of all cases are solved because someone can't keep their mouth shut. That's the name of this game, being there when people start blabbering, 'cause once they start, you pretty much get the whole story."

We were quiet for a time. Pete hiked up his shorts and burped and got going to his car.

I said, "Give my regards to Mona."

Pete was already in his car, revving the engine. I watched him leave.

A mosquito landed on my arm. I stared at it under the brilliance of the porch light. I felt that needle prick, watched the mosquito's abdomen fill with my blood, and when it had grown fat, I ended its life between my thumb and index finger. There were times when I felt I wanted that finality to things, just the oblivion of darkness and nothingness. I took in a deep breath. I could smell the animal waste from the zoo, a sour, putrid odor. It was almost an invigorating smell, something that pressed through the dark, made me aware of other things around me. I went inside. It was after two in the morning. It had been a hell of a long day, out there at River's Bend with Ed and Sam, those curious creatures of migration, longing for Florida. Some deep migratory instinct told them they had stayed too long in this place. I felt that instinct too, alienated from the woman I loved up in Chicago. The phone was ringing again. My head was sort of crazy. I felt that interrogation of Ronny's estranged, the pressing softness of her solitude and longing down at

Osco's. I didn't want to get her locked away for the rest of her life. I thought about maybe getting into my car and leaving all this behind, but the shears were still out back. I had to get them. It made the hair on my arms stand on end, the sudden anxiety of things to do, things to dispose of. I was shaking again, those tremors that got me put away once before. The phone rang again. I shouted, "Goddamn it, leave me the hell alone!" I unplugged the phone from the wall and descended into the cool of the cellar and fell into a deep sleep.

CHAPTER 10

I slept for something like fifteen hours. It was afternoon when I came up out of the basement. I called Sam down at the office. "Where the hell are you, Bill? Get your ass down here!"

I made something up, said I was sick. I showered, put on a pot of coffee, and got ready. I was way out of sync. This was the kind of thing I had to stop from happening, one of the danger signs of sickness, that relapse into a life lived in the nocturnal hours. I had unhinged myself from normality when I was going down to see Ronny Lawton at Denny's, broken routine then.

I was out of the shower when it hit me that I'd not gone out to see Ronny's estranged. Shit, that was something that could set things far back for me. I felt a sharp pain at the right side of my head. I took a long glass of cool water, drained it and poured another and drained that, then felt the pressure on my bladder and went to the toilet. I settled on the cause of all this trouble. It was the drink over the past week, all those beers and whiskey, sitting around in the heat and just sweating alcohol. I got dressed and got out the phone book. I didn't let myself know what I was doing, if you can understand that, I just started scanning for the Osco on Main Street. My heart was thumping when I heard the line ring. "No, Teri's got the night off." I put the phone down. For some reason, I didn't go right to the office. I drove out by her trailer. I stopped on the road. It was late afternoon, a whole day wasted. A huge sun set off to the west, a hallmark of our great plains, the long tendrils of evening light spreading across the sky. Dust sifted through the light out here. We were weeks without rain. Down the long corridor of corn, I saw her trailer, saw a light on inside the small window by the table. I left the car by the side of the road, went down through the cornfield. I hid in the corn amid the crickets and mosquitoes, felt their cumulative presence behind me, that mountain of sound pressing down on my back, billions of insects.

There was a beat-up old truck parked. I got close enough to read this bumper sticker on the back of the truck, "So many cats, so few recipes," a summative impression of the white trash I was dealing with.

I heard voices from inside. I knew I had better get out of there. My car was parked where anybody could see it. But I stayed long enough to see Ronny's estranged go out of the trailer to throw out a basin of water. She was wearing nothing. I mean, naked as the moment she was born. Her boyfriend said something from inside. I heard a beer can hiss. He came out and stood in the fading orange light. He was wearing a tank top and jeans and work boots. He said something to her, went out and put his arms around her waist and kissed her at the nape of the neck. She squirmed and turned and faced him, buried her face in his chest hair. I didn't catch what she was saying. He took his hands and spread them around her buttocks, and her legs rose around his waist, entwined themselves around him. I could see the parting of her buttocks.

It was such a warm night of incessant insect clicking, the fields throbbing, everything encircling them in that small trailer. Karl still held his beer in one hand. He was maybe six-two, muscular, a physical presence. He took a drink, and then she drank from the same can. His voice was deep. His hand was big enough to cover her buttocks. She sort of hiked herself up farther around his waist, rubbing the softness of herself against him. They were laughing there in the solitude of the cornfield. I didn't dare breathe. I felt the pulse of insects all around me. It was like coming upon Adam and Eve, if they lived after the Fall, the unabashed nakedness of Ronny's estranged, the long rope of her blond hair falling to the small of her back. Karl kissed her deep in the mouth. Here were maybe two murderers, a pair of lovers who had cut a man to pieces. I watched them closely, the languid desire of a big man holding the delicate frame of his woman, her long legs locked, anticipating penetration.

I hesitated, wanted to move away, but the corn was brittle, it betrayed movement like sticks breaking. I looked up. The sky was clear overhead. The last of the day's light was dying. The trailer caught the glint of fading light, burnished in a soft red. Karl disappeared with Ronny's estranged. I heard the kid's voice. The trailer started squeaking. The small light glowed in the portal of the window. I turned and got a bit away from the trailer. It was getting dark quickly. Night eclipses day in a matter of minutes out there. It was the sort of light that drained color from the corn, made everything grainy. Or maybe it was all just me. I felt the cornstalks, dry like parchment, cut against my skin as I broke into a sprint for the car.

I found it hard to breathe for some time after I got free of the cornfield. My arms were vapid, drained of any strength. My neck pained me. I went away from them through the ensuing dark, picked out the twinkle of city light, and never did I feel more alone. It was like finding the one you love with somebody else. I had to pull over and vomit a small patch of bile onto the road. I didn't even get out of the car, just opened the door. I knew this feeling was contained in just one sudden eruption. I wiped away a thread of spit, shut the door, and just got going again. I was thinking of Diane, up there in Chicago, the sense of separation. If only I had the key to a word problem, to those damn LSAT questions, if only I could have mustered the logic of abstraction, I might have been with her. The goddamn LSATs, the late twentieth century's equivalent of a medieval riddle.

I got in to the office, somehow, driving aimlessly. Ed was talking about a fire that had eaten up eight acres of corn out on Douglas Road. He had pictures already developed. Sam looked at me and said, "Goddammit, where the hell were you?"

"Sick," is all I said.

"Jesus, you look like shit."

I smelled of the vomit.

"I'm putting down some tuna melts if you want," Sam said.

I said, "Sure."

They had the story of the fire all covered. I got the grunt work, with the obituaries and legal notices. We were late at this stage. I worked for over an hour getting them ready, editing the long obituaries, tallying up the words, writing out the sums in the small ledger for the week's entries. I came up and handed over my work. Sam said to me, "It was like the biggest bowl of popcorn you're ever going to see in all your life, Bill. It just went pop, pop, pop, like it was a war zone." He showed me a shot of a field that had not been burned, but that had been close enough to absorb the furious heat. The ears of corn had flowered into small grayish brains of popped corn.

Ed said, "I like this one better though. Maybe we can use this one on page one." Ed was standing behind us. His clothes were ruined, blackened by soot. He gave the picture to Sam, who put it under the light and tipped his head in silent contemplation. "Never in all my years did I ever see anything like it, Bill," Ed said to me, touching my back with one hand as the long index finger of his other pointed at his composition. His nails were black from the soot of the fire.

I looked down at the photograph. Ed had gone into the preserved field, got a shot from a crouching position. No, I take it back. He most probably got down on the ground so he was looking up at the sky. I asked him.

Ed said, "I had to lie flat out on the ground for the angle."

He had caught a solitary stalk of corn with its ears popped. The stalk seemed to rise to the sky, well beyond its real dimension. I said, "My God, Ed, it's like a Jack and the Beanstalk fairy-tale dimension." I looked at Ed. I could see he'd cropped the stalk to suggest the limit of the camera's perspective, but also to underscore our psychological inability to understand the dimension of this land of ours. I turned and looked at him. "You did that on purpose, Ed, right? The cropping, the dimension of a stalk that exceeds our spatial and temporal understanding."

Ed gave a snort of laughter. "You got me there, Bill. Just doin' my job was all. It seemed like a good shot, I suppose."

Sam scoffed. He said, "Hell, you keep up that talk, and Ed's liable to demand a goddamn raise."

"Lord knows, I could do with the money." Ed smiled and winked.

I stared back at the picture, ostensibly all background, the vast charred blackness of ruined fields extending to a wasteland of horizon stitched to an expanse of cloudless blue sky. Ed had a gift for proportion, for giving the land its true dimension. The emptiness of space is where we lived, inhabitants of plains where once dinosaurs roamed, plains scoured by ice sheets. We were denizens of a sort of infinity. In the upper left corner, what seemed like a smudge was a blurred part of a finger, obliquely part of the composition, a hint of scale, the image of a person with their hand to their forehead, staring out across the land. From this solitary photograph, you intuited what this crop meant to the unseen population. You were looking from the vantage of the insider on the plains, and you understood the devastation, the remoteness of this place and the hidden suffering, just out of focus. You felt the burden of a people about to scream.

Ed coughed with self-consciousness. He had his hand on my back. I felt the pulse of pressure.

I said simply and honestly, "You are the Keepers of Truth."

Ed took a bow and grinned.

Sam said, "I like that." He repeated what I'd said, looked at Ed. "We are the Keepers of Truth." Sam looked at me. "Maybe you just picked my epitaph, Bill." His face folded into the soft crease of his lips. And then he got back to work.

I felt a sudden closeness as we pressed around the board. They had taken me into their world.

Sam inset the picture, used his hands like a conjurer. He worked quickly, used a ruler, measured things, got a symmetry that was too exact. He began cursing under his breath, got it nearly right. Ed softly imposed his will. He took Sam a cup of coffee. Ed eased into the light of the drawing board, and without aid of slide rules and numbers, he offset the picture to the side of the headline. Sam shouted, "Right there. We'll make the headline print larger," and they did, until it almost obscured the picture, until it was hauntingly right, until you had to study the picture's formalism. It was maybe like looking down the wrong end of a telescope, the smallness of the image containing all things. Its apparent smallness was part of its bewilderingness. Sam drank in sips from his coffee, moved his tongue over his lips, nodded like a foreman, unbegrudging, giving in to Ed, and Ed giving in to Sam, like hands on a Ouija board that somehow reveals things. It was a silent partnership of give-and-take, a pantomime of slow movements and sidesteps, never overt, just seemingly part of a natural law of motion. And why not, thirty-odd years of working together in the small confines of the office. They occupied the same vision, roamed the same escape routes from this hell, dreamed of the same woman, wanted in all things as though they were one, which they were, in a manner of speaking. The convergence of their heads in quiet talk behind my back was like a creature with two bodies and one head, some final evolutionary inevitability. Just looking at Sam there made me smile, the way he hung on Ed's shoulder, the perceptible dip in Ed's shoulder as he took on that gaze, let Sam watch with his eyes. I bowed out of their lives, left for the night without interrupting them, left my work on the counter, the trite and formal notices of our existence, the accumulation of deaths and births and marriages that had taken place among us, the notes of items for sale, the court notices.

On the porch steps lay an envelope without a postage stamp. It had evidently been left by somebody other than the mailman, since all my mail was left at a mailbox at the end of the driveway. I bent down with a strange suspicion I was being watched. I rose and averted my eyes to the dark. Had someone seen me bury the shears? That was the first thought that flitted through my head. I went inside and shut the door behind me, leaned against it and opened the envelope. Inside I smelled glue and some scent of roses, saw something constructed of newspaper lettering. I set the envelope down immediately and then withdrew the letter. Composed of newspaper lettering cut out in various sizes and styles of print, the letter formed a single sentence—*The he is ut at the torn bun at ton's old arm.*

It was illegible. The odor of roses settled around me, vaguely familiar. I breathed it in, that smell. I found a few loose letters and sorted them out on the kitchen table in a sort of Scrabble, positioned them into something meaningful over the next half hour. It eventually materialized, the grim message—*The head is out at the tornado bunker at Lawton's old farm.*

Dark globs of fear floated behind my eyes when I closed them and breathed. I got up from the horror of what I had pieced together. Could the arrangement of letters be reordered, reveal something else? I took the letters that had come undone from the glue and went at the puzzle again. It was like one of those LSAT puzzles, but each time I came up with some semblance of meaning, I had letters left over. In the end, the message materialized again and again before my eyes—*The head is out at the tornado bunker at Lawton's old farm.*

I could feel a lightness invade my body. I instinctively looked to the back porch, saw the curtain flutter in the dark, as though somebody had just vanished. The urge to get sick again filled me. I had to sit down and lean my head between my legs, take long breaths, make moaning noises. I felt like the clairvoyant who is awakened by a nightmare. My palms sweat with a coldness, a clammy horror of what was there on my kitchen table. And then the question came and settled on my brain: Who had left this message?

For the next two hours I literally did nothing about the letter. I went into avoidance mode. I played my father's old record player, sat in the sitting room in the dark and listened to the scratch and static of a Duke Ellington album, the music Ronny Lawton's mother had requested on the day she found out she was going to die. I closed my eyes and sat inert, tried to think back on what Ronny's estranged had told me about Ronny Lawton, the sadness that had turned to hatred inside him. I could envision Ronny chopping his father into pieces, a solemn task out at their country home at night, Ronny feeling the slippery bloodied tendons, cutting away the rim of cartilage of each joint, working a knife around the groin, exposing the hamstrings, sawing through the bone of each leg, all piecemeal work, a division of labor, dismantling his father, assembly-line work. If I were asked to imagine that as a juror, I could.

The A side of the record ended in a soft repeating static, like time looping in on itself. I turned it over, started into the kitchen and went and read the message. I made a pitcher of lemonade and drank it out back on the porch. By now the message had burned into my head, a mantra—*The head is out at the tornado bunker at Lawton's old farm.*

I looked into the dark gray of the zoo, listened to the night life of those beasts. I asked myself, "Why me?" then I said, "Who sent me this?" and I wondered to myself, could it be Ronny himself, leading this thing to an inevitability, trying to bring things to an end? Maybe he was tired of the publicity. He wanted it over for once and for all. I had pushed him far enough that night down at Denny's, touched at the memory of his mother. He just wanted to get things moving at his speed. And then again, maybe the letter was from Ronny's estranged. "Come on," I said out loud to myself. "She practically told me to go out to the tornado bunker." I hadn't gone to see her, hadn't followed up on what I should have done. I hadn't discovered the body. She was wondering what the hell I was playing at. Maybe that's what she wanted to tell me all along, that call last night was all part of the beginning of a confession, something she wanted to whisper in my ear about Karl. I'd been thinking maybe she hated Karl, and then things would have fallen into place. But then I thought of her out there with Karl and the simple pleasure of her nakedness. I drank the tart lemonade, felt it burn my throat. It was not dilute enough. The pulp gathered in my mouth. The glass sweated in droplets down my wrist and along my arm when I drank, trickling to the cup of my armpit. All I could settle on was it was either Ronny, or Ronny's estranged and Karl, or Karl by himself, but that was it. It was like a game of shells, moving each suspect back and forth in my head, each guilty if you looked hard enough. Maybe that was as complicated as it got, even down at the station with the fat man or the state troopers. Without forensic evidence, there was no case. I held the key piece of evidence out there in the ground, the buried shears, and now another piece of the puzzle had landed before me.

I kept looking at the electric clock on the kitchen wall, watching its big face, saw time slide by, the long red arm of the second hand clicking off the seconds mutely. Two interminable hours, and I did absolutely nothing. I had decided to do nothing. In fact, I was not going to tell anybody about this note. That came as a revelation, even to myself. Things had turned too complicated for me. I was going to burn it in the fireplace, make sure there was nothing left of it, burn each letter into ash. That was what I was going to do. I was not going to be drawn into this. I had stumbled on the shears, but this letter was part of some manipulation, some mechanism to make me do things I didn't fully understand.

I took a long shower. I even got out the goddamn LSAT book and started into a problem. My eyes watered with fatigue, but I pretended to myself, stared at a blur of text and yawned, sitting there in a towel. I was jittery as hell, my legs shaking. I thought about the old medicine I'd been taking, but decided against doing anything like that. There was no point going back into that world of induced sleep.

And then the doorbell rang. I scurried like a crab away from the kitchen light, tried to hide. I almost expected to see Ronny Lawton with a knife at the door or something.

Outside I heard Sam and Ed talking. Then Sam raised his voice. "Hey, chief, you in there?" He banged the door. I heard Ed say, "His car's here."

There was no place to hide. There are times when you do things without deliberation. Without knowing exactly what I'd do, I crawled for the bathroom, wet my head again, took a comb in my hand, and went to the door and said, "Ed, Sam," with false surprise.

Sam said, "You were in the shower," and he turned to Ed and said, "He was in the shower, Ed."

Ed said, "I see that."

"I'd live in the damn shower in this heat, if I could," Sam said. I could barely make out his face in the dim light of the hallway. "This heat is killing me." He smelled of booze. He had a box of doughnuts and a cake with him, which he gave to me, saying, "Here." He moved past me, toward the domain of static music. I followed. I had a stalk of incense burning. A gray thread of smoke rose into the air. I heard Sam sniffing the air, making a production out of it.

"It's supposed to keep flies away," I said, by way of answering an unspoken question.

Sam said, "I see." He seemed at a loss for something to say, then said, "I never took you for a Duke Ellington man, Bill." Then he began sniffing again. "God, you could do with taking out the garbage, Bill." He kept moving, even when I stopped. He went into the dim light of the front room and sat himself down.

Ed seemed to have more sense of propriety and hesitated, waited at the edge of the front room in the long hallway that smelled of aged wood and mothballs. He gave the reason for the visit. "You just up and left, Bill. We were kind of worried about you. You being sick and all."

"Come on in, Ed." The LSAT book was on the front-room table. Ed looked down at it, averted his eyes, and met mine. I didn't even begin to give an explanation, but he knew I wanted out. "Sit," is all I said, and I closed the book and went into the kitchen.

I got them lemonade, stirred the mixture and got ice and three glasses. Jesus, the note was there on the table. I braced and just went past it. We sat around in the front room and Sam said, "I don't think I've been in this house since . . ."

"The suicide," I said.

Sam made his eyes big in an apologetic way. "It was just so sudden. I mean . . ."

I looked at him directly. "I got his diaries upstairs. It wasn't sudden, Sam. He'd been planning it a long time."

Sam made his eyebrows rise on his big face. "I see."

Ed spoke. "He saw things we maybe never saw, or didn't want to believe."

I turned and looked at Ed. He was the kind of man you would want as a father, even-keeled, almost omniscient in a quiet manner, an understanding man.

"You're right, Ed. He says it all in his diaries, what he saw, how it made him feel. He scribbled notes from all them trips he took over to Southeast Asia before he died, over to countries he'd never even heard of, to begin dealings with upstart sweatshops, going around with small militias of guys in fatigues and Soviet jeeps with some businessmen in the back in suits and ties just smiling their asses off, nodding their heads like they do over there. He has it all in scribbles, the disease and sickness, cholera in fly-infested stagnant pools, the rides in trucks into goddamn jungles, stuck on washed-out roads, those little guys in cheap-ass suits talking a million miles an hour into his ear, taking him out to sheds in slashed-out parts of land, showing him how they could reduce his costs, showing him this population of small kids strapped to the backs of women, all of them working in the glare of light inside those sheds. I mean, continents of darkness just opened up for him, countries you'd never heard of, new republics. Maybe it was like when we first heard about Vietnam, some place you couldn't pick out on a map. But, in a matter of months, it was where we were going to die."

Sam said, "You're preaching to the converted, Bill."

"I'm not preaching, Sam, I'm just saying my father was better than that. He wasn't going down that road to shifting his business overseas. Sure, he saw the profits, saw the potential. He had women sent into him at night back at the shitty hotels, women who were told to do anything and everything a man wanted done to him." I was self-conscious for a moment, just sitting there before them in a towel, the slow churn of my scrotum turning compact, moving upward, recoiling. "That's how it happened, Sam, how it all came apart, how my father happened to take a gun and put it in his mouth and blow his head off. He got hooked on drugs over there. He was lost out there in the jungles, roaming around the dark continent of new labor, staring into the underbelly of foreign militias harboring harems of drugged-up whores. He got so messed up on the drugs, it was like meeting Satan in a business suit in the dark of your worst dreams."

Ed brought his hands together, and they cracked under some sullen pressure. "We sold ourselves out in the end, all of us." Ed was this stolid presence there in the dim light of the sitting room. He was the impassive figure that knew more than you could ever express in words. He seemed to stare past me to the kitchen. He'd finished the lemonade. It was almost like he had a presentiment of what was on the table. I watched his eyes, the darkness of the pupils roaming my mansion.

I said, "You know, what kills me is we were off on the goddamn Moon, exploring intergalactic space, wasting billions of dollars, when all hell began to break loose here on Earth."

Ed said, "I think the Cold War had something to do with that, Bill."

I looked at him. "I guess you're right, but you'd want to count the casualties, you'd want to number you and me and Sam here as all walking dead."

Ed looked at me. "Things just happen, Bill. Who are you going to blame for evolution?"

I let a half smile register. I didn't have an answer for that, but I knew he was right, in a way. I said, "Before my grandfather died, he just used to scream at my father, get us out with him to chop wood, kept us doing it for a day. You could see he was trying to get back to some primitive beginning. He just used to go on about how he was press-ganged over in England, waking up on a ship for South Africa. Maybe he knew there was a continent of guys like himself as a kid, over there, just waiting to work for shit wages, guys just wanting to survive. I think that's what all the wood-chopping was about, that longing for his immigrant exhaustion, the long pursuit of not thinking, just living, just going about surviving." I had my hands to my face, just letting it all come out. I looked at them. "What my father said to me a week before he killed himself was that my generation would live off the backs of women and children, on the cheap labor of places without names."

Sam coughed politely. He said slowly, "This isn't going to brighten your day, Bill, but you might as well hear it from me, Bill. I'm thinking of getting out of the paper business."

I sat still, looking over at him. "It seems like you've been saying that forever, Sam."

Ed was there, a little stooped, his head moving slightly, following Sam's words. He tipped his head in concordance. His bony fingers clawed at his knees, bunched the material of his trousers so his hairy ankles showed. I guess I just focused on that, on the two boats of his large shoes moored to the hardwood floor. They were somehow incongruous on him, white and glossy, like cheap tuxedo shoes, and the pale peach polyester trousers. He was all Darlene's creation, a creature growing into the lifestyle of a Floridian. He looked like a walking mannequin. But right then, I could tell he was anxious, dealing with a life's work coming to a close.

Sam said, "Are you listening to me, Bill?"

I snapped back and said, "How long?"

Sam breathed out a long, deep sigh. "There's an outfit over in Cass that's been knocking on my door the last few years." He trailed off.

"Six months?" I asked.

Ed opened his mouth. "I'd say more like three. Once all this Ronny Lawton stuff is over." His big feet shuffled and got still again.

"Oh," I said. "You think there's something left to say about Ronny Lawton and his old man?"

Ed turned and looked at Sam, that same conspiratorial look I'd seen down at the office. "Something has got to turn up. A man don't disappear off the face of the earth."

I said, "It happens all the time, Ed. Are you kidding me?"

Sam cut back. "I've been telling them over in Cass what the hell of a find you are, Bill. They got the stuff you wrote over at the head office. The top guy is a big fan of yours. I can't say for sure he needs someone on the paper, but if he did, you'd have a hell of a chance."

Ed seemed liked he was getting up. The letter had receded in my head, but now it came back, with all its immediacy. It was still on the table. I couldn't stop Ed. I was frozen in my chair, but I managed to get his name out of my throat. "Ed," I said, and he looked at me. "What?"

Almost miraculously, the phone rang. I didn't get it, let it ring four times before Sam said, "Ain't you getting that, Bill?"

Ed stayed standing, glared at me for a moment.

I said, "I want you to hear this, both of you." We stayed still as the phone rang and rang in the hollow of my head. I waited until the answering machine picked up.

The voice said, "Why didn't you come to see me, Bill?"

Sam said, "Who the hell's that?" but Ed said, "Shush."

"You under the sheets with Courtney, Bill?"

"Who the hell is Courtney?" Sam said.

"Jesus Christ, shut it, Sam." Ed took hold of Sam's arm.

I was going to pick up then, but waited.

"I was just trying to help you was all," Ronny's estranged said. There was loud music in the background. "I hope you come and see me tomorrow, Bill." The line was still open, the muffled scratch of someone breathing into the phone. The voice said, "I sure as hell need that house, Bill." The line went dead.

I looked at both Ed and Sam. I said, "Ronny Lawton's estranged wife has been calling me a hell of a lot."

"That sounds like a goddamn lovers' quarrel to me. What do you think, Ed?"

Ed raised his eyebrows.

"And who the hell is Courtney, Bill?"

I said, "It's a girlfriend she thinks I have, is all."

There was a humiliation and stretch of believability to my account of things, how I went out there and got speaking with her, and her telling me the story about Ronny's mother dying.

Ed shifted in his seat as I went on, took the lemonade to his lips, but it was all gone. He just held the empty glass.

I didn't say anything about the shears. I left that part out. The mounting anxiety of the letter hung behind every word I uttered. I had not called them. They had come into my domain to tell me that the paper was all washed up, and there on the table was a key piece of evidence. So I mentioned the letter. I pointed to the table, watched their eyes move along the trajectory of my arm. "I got something that might bring all this to an end."

We got up, encircled the letter. It read simply—*The head is out at the tornado bunker at Lawton's old farm.*

Sam and Ed shook their collective heads and said, "God Almighty." They were almost leaning on each other. Then their heads rose together and they just stared at me.

And was there anything more ludicrous than me in that towel? The hair on my back stood on end. I had goose bumps despite the heat. I felt naked, exposed for what I was, this half-assed intellectual who was caught up in some two-bit murder. I saw how it looked, took a step back, the unglued pieces of letters lined up. It looked like something under construction, a puzzle I was making. For a moment I thought, Jesus, they're going to think I was making this myself, like I was working with Ronny's estranged to frame Ronny . . . I could feel something pass between us right then, a momentary flux where they seemed to doubt just how I fitted into all this.

Ed had a frank uneasiness. His eyes just fixed on me and then back at the letter.

Sam was less obvious, but more vocal. "And you didn't call anybody about this, Bill? That's kind of hard to believe. I mean, just leaving it there like that." But it wasn't an accusation, just a statement.

We were all enveloped in the stalemate, afraid to touch anything. I looked at both of them. "I was scared shitless to do anything." Ed said, "Why?"

I sort of half laughed. "Ed. Don't you get it? Somebody's watching me, that's why. Somebody chose me to pick up the pieces in all this." I felt a sudden self-consciousness in the choice of words, but there was no convincing reason why I should have been chosen.

Ed pressed at me. "Why you? Why not Linda Carter?" I think he knew he'd overstepped his mark. Sam was pissed. He said, "What the hell does that mean, Ed? What the hell has Linda Carter got that Bill here doesn't have?" But I think we all got the point.

And still, it came around to why I'd got the note. The only thing in my defense, not that I needed a defense, mind you, was that there was no glue on the table, no newspaper that might have suggested I was making this note. I wanted to actually say that, but I didn't. What I said was, "Ronny Lawton followed me the other night. I think maybe he wants this done with."

"How'd that come about?" Sam said.

"I went down to Denny's and played some Duke Ellington for him. He just about lost it in the end, but maybe it did something inside his head. He followed me out around town, came up to me, seemed like he wanted it all ended."

Ed stood behind me. "You've been busy, Bill."

Sam looked at me. "What has Duke Ellington got to do with anything?"

"It was just something his mother listened to is all."

"That's good, Bill. Real smart," Ed said softly. "His estranged told you that?"

I said, "Yeah."

"She wants that house, right? She knows how to press his buttons, how to get to him. Right?"

"Yeah."

Sam kept pressing me. "Did Ronny sound like he wanted to confess?"

I said, "I don't know, Sam. I think he believes maybe his estranged had something to do with things. Maybe that was what he was telling me, but he couldn't just say to look out in the bunker, 'cause that would make it seem like he was guilty."

Sam took me by the arm. "Wait a minute here. I thought we were set on Ronny killing his father, right? Now you're saying that isn't the case?"

I just put my hands to my head. It was time to instill a moment of melodrama to get my ass out of this mess.

Sam was still talking, not to me, but to Ed. He was saying, "Who the hell do you think left this note, Ed?"

Ed didn't answer the question. He still held his glass of lemonade. He agitated the glass in a slow meditative circle, made the melting ice clink.

Sam shook his head. "Who the hell are you saying sent this, now, Ronny or his estranged wife, Bill?"

Ed said finally, "That's the million-dollar question, Sam." He cleared his throat and said, "Sam. This is a hell of a break for us. It could change the complexion of how we go about off-loading the paper, if you think about it."

A smile surfaced on Sam's face. He looked at me. "Bill, you're a goddamn genius. You've been doing your homework on this one." He slapped my back, that asshole who was going behind my back and selling us all out. But I said nothing, didn't give in to what I wanted to say. What I said was simply, "I'm just trying to be the best journalist I can be."

"And, damn it if you're not a regular Dick Tracy, Bill. I'm telling you, the measure of a reporter comes in a situation like this, how he works the principal characters, pits them one against the other. You got the instinct for the human condition, Bill, for its—"

I finished his sentence. "Its depravity."

"That's right, Bill. Human depravity . . ."

I felt a tingling sensation of pride or something. It's amazing how a guy like me can be bought and sold, even by guys like Ed and Sam. They had me truly believing I was somehow orchestrating things.

We listened to the message again. Ed picked up on the phrase "I was just trying to help you was all." Ed said, "Does she mean the letter, Bill?"

Sam rubbed his jaw. "Good point, Ed."

I shrugged my shoulders. I was still in the towel. I said, "I don't know."

Ed hit Rewind and Play again on the message player. He went too far back and got the remnants of the previous message. I looked at Ed. "You might as well listen to it all." I left them and changed into my clothes, got into a pair of shorts and a salmon-colored Izod shirt. I combed my limp hair back off my forehead, looked at myself in the mirror. We were on the verge of discovering something, and I was dressed like I was going out in a boat for a day's outing. The sheer mundanity of the way I looked was absurd. Ordinary, that's what I looked like, just plain ordinary, but maybe ordinary was far more complicated than I ever thought it could be. I heard the feet upstairs, the muted talk.

It was then that I got thinking, how the hell did they just show up like that? In all the time I'd worked for Sam, he'd never once come and seen me. At the back of my head, I was thinking there was something not exactly right. It was as if everybody was a step ahead of me. They were letting me get there first, but that's only because they'd already been and gone. It just didn't sit well with me, the way they just came out of the blue like that . . . I looked hard at myself in the mirror, saw that face of jaded fear, the apprehension I've always had when it comes to trying to bring some principle of logic to bear on a situation. This was turning out to be one of those goddamn word problems from the LSATs, the vectors of association, who knew whom, motive, opportunity, all that stuff. It just swirled in my head.

Sam looked at me when I came up out of the basement and said, "We just can't figure if she meant the letter. It doesn't say conclusively."

Ed said, "Looks like you got yourself a girlfriend, Bill."

I answered, "Maybe she's got a guilty conscience."

Ed conceded that and took a deep breath. He was still watching me. "Darlene says, 'You can't do anything without good looks these days.' And maybe she's right. Nobody could have got to her like you, Bill." It was a kind of backhanded compliment, or just a statement. I didn't respond.

Sam had that look of longing. "God, Bill. You got Ronny's old lady eating out of your hand. Chances are she wrote that. Right?

She wants you to put Ronny away so she gets the house. That seem reasonable to you, Ed?"

"If Bill here says she's living out in some trailer and is getting no support, sure. Why wouldn't she lead you to where Ronny's got the body stashed? You figure, she was with Ronny long enough to know where he had his hiding places."

Sam cut in. "Right, but she sure as hell isn't going to come out and say where she thinks Ronny hid his old man, 'cause if she comes up with the body, she looks guilty. It's not the first time a newspaper ever got an anonymous tip."

Ed joined in the complicity. "She needed a source, and that's where Bill came in."

Sam shouted. "The Source! I like that a hell of a lot. Shit, yes. The Source!"

It was strange, but I put down a pot of coffee and set the fan in the window going, took off the plastic wrap from the cake and got the doughnut box, cut open the string and set them on the table. And we just ate quietly for a good long time without talking. I felt the sweetness of the jelly centers, the warm jam heart ooze from the doughnut. You needed a taste like that every so often to cut through life, something that made you lick your fingers like a kid again. I think we all needed that right then. Sam had a big tongue that roamed the outer edges of his lips, licking things up, tearing apart the cake. Ed winked at me. "Sam, where the hell did you learn to eat?"

"Shit, don't start in on me, Ed." It was benign banter, a late-night sleepover, except we were talking about a man's head out in a tornado bunker. I was watching the last of a dying friendship, the last of small-town alliances. We were feasting on the corpse of Ronny Lawton's old man.

I said, "We might as well just go out there ourselves first and see what's there. There'd be no point getting the law involved if it's going to make us look like we were being led up the garden path. We might as well be sure, right?"

Sam had a face full of doughnut. He swallowed and wiped his

mouth. "Sure, if that's the way you want to run this. Go ahead, Bill. This is all yours, really. You did the footwork on this. Who knows, maybe Ronny's estranged is just giving us a tip of where she thinks Ronny stashed the body. It's not certain. You're right, Bill. We got to be sure about this. I don't want us looking like asses in this. Right, Ed?"

Ed said, "The less flies we have on us, the better."

Sam gave this flabbergasted look. "Ed, yes or no?"

Ed answered, "Sure, Sam, let's go see if there's a head first before we print anything."

I didn't dare say anything directly about the Linda Carter interview, other than to ask when was her interview with Ronny Lawton. It was early Thursday morning as we sat together. I knew her interview was on Sunday night. It had gained notoriety, specifically because of what Ronny Lawton was doing down at Denny's. Despite the stalemate in the investigation, his story was a spin on the general horror that was facing us as a nation. You looked at Ronny down there, and it meant something at an unconscious level.

Sam perked up and squinted his eyes, and I let him betray the delicate question, let him look from Thursday to Sunday and weigh the balance of things.

Ed stood up and creaked and flexed his long legs and arms. That's when I noticed his belt matched his tuxedo white shoes, the exact same color and gloss, plastic crap.

Sam stared after Ed. "We break this tomorrow, and Linda Carter gets to ask Ronny Lawton about the head. It'll seem like she did all the footwork."

Ed looked at Sam. "That's a hell of a long time to do nothing." Ed just shook his head. "I don't like this at all, Sam. I know what you're thinking. If it only had been Friday, we might have gotten away with it, but . . ."

Sam nodded his head.

I said, "But who the hell's got to know when we got this letter? It doesn't have a postmark or anything."

Ed turned and faced me but didn't say anything. He put his left hand to his head and kept it there, like all this was hurting the inside of his head. "I don't know."

Sam banged the table. "That's right, dammit. Bill's right, who the hell's to know when we got the tip?"

We said nothing for a long time, just looked in at the kitchen, felt the presence of the letter. Sam spoke again over his cup of coffee, holding it in his cupped hands. "I don't have the years left in me for anything big. Maybe this is all I'm ever going to get to break to the press." He swallowed and continued, "It probably don't mean a hill of beans in the end, but just getting an edge on television has got some irony, right? Look at us. We're a dying breed. This is the end of things for you and me, Ed. I want to take one thing away with me that says I wasn't too old, that I wasn't obsolete. I want to walk away with dignity, Ed." Sam quit and wiped sweat off his forehead. "Ed?"

And so it was decided in that unnerving plea in my kitchen that we would wait. The night sky flickered well off to the north, a heat lightning too distant to carry sound or bring a reprieve of rain. The curtains billowed like gray silent ghosts. The baby grand gleamed like a polished coffin in the room, catching the errant light. The small stalks of incense I had burning throbbed in the draft of flowing air. It was agreed we would meet on Saturday evening and go out and search the bunker, and if there was anything, we'd contact Pete on Sunday and get ourselves a press conference, right when Linda Carter's interview was on the air.

I got grandiose for a moment. "That Ronny Lawton's an archetypal myth of modern horror. That's what we're dealing with, really."

Sam said, "The guy's an asshole."

I said, "Yeah, that too."

Again, a moment of hesitation. Sam and Ed were looking back and forth from each other. Sam put his hand on mine. "Bill, when this hits big, I want you to tell it straight. I don't want any philosophical bullshit. Save that for the bathroom walls. What we want from you is how you got to Ronny's estranged, how you got Ronny and dug away at his conscience. Just plain simple like that, Bill. We don't need to know archetypal myths of modern horror, no theories on dismemberment. I don't want to see Nietzsche in there, Bill. I want you to swear right now to me, 'I'm not going to see Nietzsche, please, Jesus, anything but that crap . . .' " He was smiling by the time he was finished. "Despite yourself, you're going to make it big, Bill."

Ed winked, like it was a twitch. Then his face broke in a smile.

Sam was still having a go at me at my expense. I think it was the hour of night, and the knowledge that we had something up our sleeves. Sam took out his dentures. He sort of spoke in that gummy way people speak when they have no teeth. "Incorporate these into your theory of dismemberment, Bill." I mean, Sam just pounded the table with his fist, laughing like he was going to pass out.

Ed smiled. "Looks like Sam's getting slaphappy."

It ended then, as quick as it had started, and the seriousness settled. Sam put his teeth back in, made a forward motion with his jaw until the dentures set properly and his face took a sort of rigidity.

I don't know why they didn't leave after that, but they didn't.

I think we needed a few days to let it all register. It was hard to move away from the table. I caught Sam opening and closing his fists. His face just settled into blankness the more I looked at him. It felt like we were in on a conspiracy. There was nothing explicitly wrong in waiting, in trying to get the upper hand on Linda Carter, but somehow it sat wrong. The last thing they were ever going to be part of involved leaving a head out in a bunker. It smacked of human desecration.

Ed's torso and head stayed perfectly still, but his long arms reached out slowly and scanned the table for crumbs, dabbing them with his clammy fingers and placing them in his mouth. It was creepy as hell watching him do that. It made me shudder.

Again, there was that strange detachment from them. They were almost grotesque, dare I say it, two aged men with a lifetime of worry in the lines of their faces, obscure men who had done nothing of consequence in all their lives, chroniclers at a small-town paper about to go under, to get bought out. They were caricatures of survival. They saw me looking at them, felt my gaze. They had lived without aspiration to anything beyond our plains, men who had understood change, men who had written up the demise of factories, who went out and interviewed family men crying, and somehow neither had gone insane. I wanted to know their secret for surviving, know how men lived in the shell of a former life, lived amid the deflation of property values. I saw into the future of their lives, maybe two years from now, in their condominiums, out under the hot Florida sun like cold-blooded reptiles warming themselves, the wattle of their throats held to a burning blue sky, men in baggy shorts and canvas shoes, men heading off with their wives to the All-You-Can-Eat salad bars at noon, a vast herd of herbivores grazing in the pasture of retirement, popping pills, clipping coupons and taking home doggie bags, settling into the sunny, communal economy of a long journey toward death. I looked at them and even managed a smile, reached out for Ed's damp hand and then took Sam's hand, threaded myself back to them. I said, "I want to thank you for giving me a chance." My throat tightened when I said those words.

Sam said, "How about we listen to the Duke Ellington again, Bill?"

Ed was sniffing the air. He'd been doing that almost subconsciously since he'd arrived. He opened his mouth, and his nose sniffed the air. He said, "That smell, I know that smell."

I looked at him. "You mean that rose smell?"

"Yes," he whispered.

I went to the turntable. Ed got up and stared at the letters, let the scent invade his memory before he sat again.

And so Duke Ellington sang across the ages. Sam got out one of his cigars, used his clippers to cut away the old ash, that soft meditative clicking, working slowly, like a man cutting his nails if you didn't directly look at him. He took a match that flared and licked up the soft dark for a moment and brought his face into the light. The match died, and we were aware of a storm off in the distance, the pull of wind through the room. He lit another match. The cigar pulsed as he made a soft sucking sound with the intimacy of a suck- ling child. The fragrant smoke filled the room. And so, slowly, we silently emptied ourselves of words like *justice* and *morality* in the sweet smoke of what felt like a religious ceremony, went beyond *integrity* and *truth*, remorseless scavengers at the decapitated head of Ronny Lawton's old man, waiting to drag it out into the light of day. For now, the head was our collective security, rotting in the depths of a tornado bunker. "Let it wait a few more days," is what we were thinking to ourselves.

I said, "Sam." I held my hands apart and said, "We can lead with—HEAD LINE."

Maybe it was the lateness of the hour or the caffeine that made us break up laughing, or the anxiety of knowing that all this would eventually end, that things were going to play themselves out one last time for all of us before we were eclipsed by the inevitability of television.

When they were long gone, when sleep was coming down, I went over to the phone. I felt the self-consciousness of what I was about to do. I was like Ronny Lawton's estranged pleading into a phone. I thought of Diane keeping all the things I said to her on tape, playing them to her friends, all of them thinking I was sick. But it didn't stop me from whispering, "I love you," into the receiver. I said it over and over again until the line went dead in my ear, and then I slept and thought about Ronny Lawton's estranged. She was naked, like I'd seen out in the field, her body moving in the moonlight, the long shadow of her sexuality stretched across the land, falling on my obscured body, hiding, watching and wanting to go out and hold her. I woke up, and the sheets were soaked. The heat had roamed even down here into the basement, skulking in the dark.

CHAPTER 11

I awoke to a choking silt of dust that had invaded the plains overnight, a current of air from the storms to the north picking up the errant dust from fields, taking it airborne. It was a blood-red sunrise. I went downstairs and washed a cup and drank and spat up the dust. It was in my nostrils, too, that invading dust.

It was hard to believe what had transpired only hours before. I had the letter well hidden in a drawer, waiting out the two days before it enacted its part in this drama.

I phoned the office. Sam had taken on the laborious work of an article on the drought. It had rained up north last night, three hundred miles away. "That's what has the dust blown up, Bill." I knew as much.

The drought was something deep in everybody's mind. Crops were all we had now, and even their value was deflated by overproduction, but still, to have nothing produced, to have almost everything die, would lead to further crisis.

Sam told me he had a roving Indian from Nebraska who performed ritual rain dances coming by the office for an interview.

It was strange how things got eclipsed by ordinary matters once the sun rose. Sam said, "Maybe you'd want to just come on by."

I came down to the office, and it was an inferno of heat and dust. I could taste the grit in my teeth. My windshield was brown with a layer of silt, and the inside of my convertible was covered with a thin veneer of dust. I had to go back in and get a spray bottle to dampen and wipe down the seats and dash, put up the roof on the convertible. And even then, when I got going, up blew a maelstrom of dust from the vents.

My shirt was already stuck to me by the time I got down to the office. I saw the carcass of a buffalo hide on a hanger in the back of what had to be the Indian's car. It was one of those moon-buggy-looking AMC Pacers.

I leaned against the window and looked in. The monstrous buffalo head had been completely scoured. There was a long headdress of iridescent feathers in a hatbox. In the front seat was an empty McDonald's wrapper and a half-empty soda.

I walked up the stairs, and there was the Indian dressed in a gingham cowboy shirt with mother-of-pearl buttons. He had a hawk on a thick leather glove made especially for the bird's talons. The hawk swiveled its head in my direction, the obsidian eyes holding me in its vision. The Indian put his other hand to the back of the hawk's neck and stroked it gently, and the hawk settled.

"This here is Walter," Sam said by way of introduction. Sam was wearing his horn-rimmed spectacles, staring out over the bridge of his nose. He betrayed nothing of the secrecy of just a few hours before. It was like it had never happened.

The Indian had some strange resemblance to a buffalo, had a massive, dark ruddy face without a hint of neck that merged into sloping shoulders and huge torso. When he stood up to say hello, he had an almost nonexistent ass and particularly thin legs in comparison with his upper bulk.

"Good to meet you," the Indian said. His hand was rough, like leather.

I watched for a movement in the hawk. Its talons gripped the glove, the black nails half-broken and splintered as it took an awkward side step, almost a hop, to reposition itself. The Indian's cowboy boots jingled as he reset himself again on the seat.

Sam said, "I was filling Walter in about our situation here with Ronny Lawton's old man, about him being all chopped up out there."

I said, "Oh."

Sam kept his position behind his desk. "Yeah, Walter here is a diviner. Get him a rod, and he can locate you a well. That's what you do primarily, right, Walter?"

The Indian nodded his huge face. He had teeth of various creatures on a necklace hanging down across the expanse of his chest.

Sam looked at me. "Walter was telling me something real interesting, Bill."

The Indian said, "I found a white kid out in Kansas this spring."

I stood there in the heat. The sweat just beaded on my back and forehead. The dust was sort of making me want to cough, but I resisted the urge, waited.

"That's pretty impressive, isn't it, Bill?"

"Yeah, I'll say." I didn't know what was being asked of me. I looked at the Indian holding his hawk, and if I were anything other than a man of the late twentieth century, I might have fallen for this, and as a matter of fact, I didn't preclude anything just then, not with the sullen secret we had with us. We were in the domain of mutilation, of a soul unburied, left wandering on the plains. I was thinking maybe Sam was getting scared about this Indian. Maybe this Indian had already said something. Superstition and fear go hand in hand. "You think you might be able to help us?" is what I asked the Indian.

The Indian was evasive. He repeated, "I found a white kid out in Kansas . . ." Then he took whatever it was the hawk ate from a small sack tied at his waist and flicked the stuff into the air. The hawk got it clean in its yellow hooked beak, making lurching movements of his head as he bit and swallowed.

Sam wiped his forehead. "Walter was telling me just how many kids get kidnapped by their own parents. That's a real problem."

Walter looked at me. "It's a growing business, kidnapping. Divorce is the greatest tragedy facing us as a people, I should say." Walter had turquoise rings on his hand which caught the sunlight.

"A human being is about eighty-five percent water. That's what Walter just finished telling me." Sam was looking at a piece of paper on which he'd written that fact.

Walter said, "That's right. There is a secret magnetism in certain men, like myself, that lets us find things."

I had this look like Sam was out of his mind. I almost laughed in the Indian's face. I said, "You find kids with a divining rod?"

The Indian used his one free hand and slapped his knee, and the hawk seemed to shrink into itself, tighten its feathers, let its head descend into its body, its talons curled around the glove.

Sam said, "Oh, shit, I love it. You were right, Walter."

"What?" I said.

The Indian had tears in his eyes, like he thought this was the funniest thing in the world. He banged the table with his fist, and dust rose in dazzling sparkles. The hawk's eyes got really black, almost throbbed with fear. "Finding kids with a divining rod. That's funny. Oh, shit, don't they always fall for it."

Sam was still laughing. He said, "When you hear hooves, think horses, not zebras, Bill."

I still didn't get what the hell they were on about.

Sam wiped his mouth and kept grinning. "Walter here is a private eye when he isn't divining. He found that kid by tracking down the mother's social security number."

Sam was still smiling when Ed came into the office. "They got you, too?" Ed said to me. He put his hand on my back. "Walter here is a private eye, part-time."

I half smiled. "I heard."

"That's the kind of prejudice Indians are up against, though," Walter said, getting serious, leaning against Sam's desk with his free elbow. He tapped his rough index finger on the desk. Sam was writing it all down. He said, without looking up, "I see your point, Walter. It's got to be hard."

The Indian got quiet, coaxed the hawk back from its compactness, touched it down the back so the hawk spread its wings apart and flapped the hot air, made the dust rise and glitter. Walter took another piece of meat from the sack and tossed it in the air, and the hawk rose in a momentary flight, a kind of hover, and came down, wings still spread, with the hard piece of meat.

Ed had his head way back on his shoulders. I didn't understand
what he was doing until I saw him pinch his nostrils. He was stopping a nosebleed.

Sam said, "That got the better of you again, Ed?"

Ed reached into his pocket and took out a bloody handkerchief
and put it to his nose. Ed waited and finally lowered his head. "This
dust does a number on my sinuses." He stayed in the doorway. "I'll
see Walter 'bout three at the town hall. We need some shots for the
article."

Walter stood up. "Make that two-thirty. Okay? I got a television
spot at three."

Ed nodded, dabbed his nose again, and buried the handkerchief
in his pocket. "Two-thirty's fine with me." Then he said, "I got an
idea. How about we get some shots outside by the foundry? Maybe
get you up on some of the scaffolding, Walter."

Walter said, "Yeah, I could do that. I got the time I guess." The
hawk turned its head almost one hundred and eighty degrees and
preened some itch out of its feathers. It made a scratching noise
with its sharp beak. It smelled stale.

"Maybe we can get a bite to eat after the shots," Sam said.

Walter said, "You buyin', Sam?"

"Sure." Sam set the pencil he was holding behind his ear, like he
was pretty much finished with the interview.

Walter said, "Okay, but you mind if I get a drink of water before
we start shooting?" He looked like he wanted directions.

That just about made me bust a gut. I said, "Go find it with your
rod," but he didn't laugh, and neither did the others.

Sam said, "Down the hall to the left is the cooler, Walter. You
can't miss it."

The three of us waited in Sam's office, and I mean there wasn't a
hint of what had transpired between us last night, not even the eye
contact of mutual understanding, some furtive acknowledgment
that we held the secret of Ronny Lawton's old man's head. Sam
even yawned and cracked his knuckles, like he was slightly bored
by everything. He got the pencil from behind his ear again and

scratched the back of his neck. "You ever see a dust storm come up like this, Ed?"

Ed shook his head. "I hope the hell we're not heading for the Dust Bowl."

I said nothing. It was just another roasting day of August drought, when everything outside was brown and parched, when people stayed in shade as much as they could. But today, people were going to gather like in days of old and watch an Indian do a ritual dance for rain at the town hall. We still lay in the twilight of superstition out here, felt the vulnerability of a land that gave nothing without exacting a price. I turned my head to the door, could hear Walter's cowboy boots rattling with all those metal spurs. It sounded like a jailer's keys. I was wondering if he was going to arrive in his AMC Pacer, or if he'd have the presence of mind just to come walking down the street to the town hall. Though the incongruity of an Indian in a Pacer in that headdress of his had its own surrealism. It was almost futuristic.

Ed went over to a window, wiped away the dust. A shard of light cut across the floor. I was conscious just then of how gray it had been there in the room, how much the sun had been obscured.

Ed kept looking out the window, seemed to be getting ideas of how and where he was going to shoot Walter.

Walter came back up and was wiping off marbled bird droppings from his glove. He said, "I don't know if that guy you is looking for is really dead."

Sam stopped still and Ed turned from the window. Sam spoke softly, "How you figure that, Walter?"

"A piece of a finger ain't nothing really. Indian women had to cut off a piece of their smallest finger as part of a ritual of womanhood in the old days. It don't take more than a lot of booze to get up the courage to do it. You get yourself some ice and it don't hurt one bit. It don't even bleed that much, really."

Sam touched his chin in a meditative pause. We had the message about the head. I stared between Ed and Sam.

Walter shrugged his shoulders. "If you'd have told me you found a hand, or an arm, yeah, I'd say the old man was dead, but what if the father hated his son that bad? Just maybe, the father cut off part of his own finger and got everything started against his son. That ain't beyond the realm of what you might be dealing with in all this. I seen people hold out for big insurance money out of scams like this."

Sam said, "We are going to keep that in mind, Walter. Thanks."

"You stayin' for this, Bill?" Ed said to me, his face invisible as he turned to the window again.

I had been thinking about going out by Ronny's estranged, getting a bucket of Kentucky Fried Chicken for her and the kid, but I said, "I got time, I guess, for a bit anyway."

Walter said something to his bird, and we all got going outside.

I wasted another half hour, watching the time, looking at Walter all done up in war paint on his fat naked torso with the buffalo carcass over his head and draped down his back. Walter was crouched down by the Pacer's side mirror, applying more dark red paint around his eyes. The hawk was on the roof of the car, tethered to Walter by a length of string.

Walter had me go up and get a pitcher of water and then fill small balloons with the water. The balloons were like small bulbous bladders. Each balloon could be concealed in Walter's massive palm. Walter tied the balloons around his waist, hidden under the buffalo hide.

And so began a series of shots of Walter and the hawk in junked-out old cars, sitting still and stoic with his arms folded and the hawk on his shoulder, both staring out from the wreckage of machines. Walter stood in a discarded oil drum, got into the mouth of a huge drainage pipe. In each he had surreptitiously taken one of the small balloons from his waist, and he did things like take his hand to his mouth and blow a spout of water as though it had emerged from deep within him. In another series of shots, Walter had both arms extended, and a cascade of water poured from each fist, like he'd wrung the air of its humidity.

Ed took the camera away from his eye. "Maybe you could climb that turret there, Walter?"

And so Walter began an ascent of the old foundry water tower, a turret structure on thin metal legs, almost alien. His long headdress flowed down his back as he got higher up into the maze of defunct pipes and vents, the headdress colors iridescent and more brilliant against the stolid black of the water tower. Walter made a whistling sound, and his hawk emerged in flight against the sagging silos, hung perceptibly in the air listening to the secret life of rats, then made a long drawn arc, circling the blue sky. Walter whistled again and threw away into the air the remaining balloons. The hawk wheeled in the air and split them open, and Walter stood on the lip of the turret under a rainburst of pouring water.

I left as Walter began his descent, and Ed winked at me. His nose was bleeding badly again, like he'd been hit real hard.

Nothing happened fast in this heat. We had adapted an almost slow drawl to our speech, a lingering afterglow of thought and circumspection that let things unfold over time without recourse to quick movement. And so I retreated for the Y and the cool chlorine pool. I stayed under a long time, a series of long efforts underwater, swimming from one end to the other, my eyes closed, counting the swish of my legs, intuitively knowing when to turn. In the showers, I stood under a spout of freezing water, shivering, draining my internal temperature, getting myself ready for the assault of heat.

Outside, the sun had not let up all day, burning strong, the land holding the residual heat of a month's unflinching sun. I had a good mind to retreat home, to spray down my room with a mist of water and sleep. My eyes were burning from the chlorine and the grit. The sky was a dull orange-red, apocalyptic, portending that there was no relief in sight, that the great global air currents had stalled in a stalemate out on the plains of Kansas and the Dakotas. My hair dried fast in the hot air, grew in an unruly mushroom. I saw myself in the rearview mirror. I needed gel.

The National Weather Service had issued an advisory that the drought might continue through all of August. The great Pacific weather machine was producing nothing, stagnant winds with no hint of precipitation. The cold breath of the north had not come down to converge with the hot updraft of air out of the Gulf. This is where we lived, in the confluence of two massive fronts of air. It accounted for the bitterness of our winters, the blizzards and hail-storms, a February buried waist-deep in snow with plunging tem-peratures, and then the contrast of these boiling summers at one hundred degrees with drought. We lived at the cusp of what humanity could endure.

On the radio, the announcer said it was now illegal to wash your car or water your lawn. This happened every few years out on the edge of the plains. It was a tacit acknowledgment that things would continue as they were. But it was just a feature of our lives in our arid oasis of industrialism. We watched each summer as color burned from our senses, everything taking on a sepia quality, a flat-ness of perspective, a place without contrast, roads cut straight for hundreds of miles out into the corn belt. The ploughed fields revealed a stratum of minerals when it got this hot, the muddy brown and rosy pink leached by the baking heat. We knew that it would eventually rain, when everything had been ruined. The great weather machine of the north would churn and rumble, but not until our fields had been scorched and fire had raged across the plains. This was the retribution nature took against our intrusion. We had our nightmares of what had happened farther out on the plains in the thirties, in the Great Dust Bowl that had sent men like Steinbeck's Tom Joad into the arms of communist agitators, when the migratory force of destitution had sent millions of Okies in search of the orange-blossom dreams of California. You see, when things got bad out here, it reverberated through the nation. If this heartland failed, so the nation came down. We were the descen-dants of the most fanatical and fervent immigrants, the descen-dants of a people who came in covered wagons with a belief in liberty and freedom. If you lost them, then what? From us came the

consciousness of our nation, the ethic of hard labor and righteous-
ness. On Sundays, you would have found us in our churches praying for deliverance, giving thanks for past favors. We were a people
of prayer, a people who gave thanks, or we did, once upon a time,
when our ancestors tended our nation's breadbasket, sent the staple goods of wheat and corn from the heartland out in snaking rail
cars. From out of our cities by the Great Lakes, we created a newfound wealth. We hunkered down with a new dream at the edge of
the Great Lakes, built ourselves temples of steel, impervious to the
weather, came from off the land to create enclaves of industrialism,
and we got down to smelting the iron and forging the steel that
made our nation's skyscrapers, our towers of Babel, steel for rail-
ways and automobiles. You ask yourself, what other people could
have re-created themselves in such majesty and with such vision
and power? We became the overlords of industrialism. We were the
dead center of this country, geographically, spiritually, and intellec-
tually. There was enough land to humble and exalt the first settlers,
then work enough to break a man's back and make him rich in our
cities. It happened that way for the better part of this century, that
hope and resilience, that backbreaking labor in foundries and
fields, we, the creators of machines, we, the creators of prosperity.
You ask yourself, how the hell did Henry Ford just get himself born
out here in the Midwest, and the only answer is foreordained destiny, plain and simply put.

    I got a bucket of Kentucky Fried Chicken and some hair spray at
the Osco where Ronny's estranged worked. She wasn't there. I
combed my hair like I was going on a goddamn date. I felt that rush
inside me. I pulled onto the long rut of unmarked road that led
down to Ronny's estranged, saw the scarves of dust in the air, the
corn now in stalks close together like the bristles of a toothbrush. I
drove slowly. I had the bucket of Kentucky Fried Chicken, a gallon
of chocolate milk, and the cigarettes and beer she had asked me to
get. It was like I was just coming home, like this was something normal between two people. But of course it wasn't anything like that,
and just thinking things like that made me anxious, let inferiority

creep around inside me. There was this voice that kept saying, "She's playing you for a sucker!"

And then the trailer emerged as a mirage before me in the reddish light. I knew they'd be there, but somehow my mind eclipsed that with just the image of unending corn. I had trouble breaking the monotonous continuity of corn. You don't expect life out there.

But Ronny's estranged was there all right, sitting outside by a plastic kid's pool in the shape of a turtle. The kid was in a diaper, splashing about. They both turned as my car ate the dirt and spat it out.

Ronny's estranged smiled when I got out of the car. She said, "I thought maybe you'd forgotten about me."

I said, "I've been busy as hell with things." I held the paper bag of groceries. "I thought you might be hungry."

Ronny's estranged got up, took the bag. She was in faded bikini bottoms, wet from the small pool. I could see the tightness of her buttocks. I looked away, but she caught me looking and just smiled. "We was swimming," she said softly.

"That's a good idea in this heat," I said.

"So what you bring us?" she said, smiling.

"Chicken." I turned my eyes to the kid, said, "Hey, Lucas, you hungry?"

"He's always hungry, right, Lucas?"

The kid had a way of making baby noises that killed me. His little fists clenched when he made the sounds.

Ronny's estranged went into the small trailer. It emanated a fiery heat, seemed almost to shimmer in the sun, the oblong length of it rounded off at both ends. It looked like a suppository, or a silver bullet. I watched the kid. He had an alligator that spouted water through its nostrils. I said, "That alligator got a name?" but the kid just splashed the alligator into the water again. The kid looked all Ronny Lawton, the same eyes and that family chin. Even at two or three years old, he was a Lawton. I was thinking that this kid had a father who was a murderer. He had a grandfather who was chopped up into little pieces. It was something you'd have liked to have saved a kid like this from, hide him from the legacy of who and what he came from.

The kid got the alligator again, and up it came all shiny into the air, dripping and spouting water, and I just smiled.

Ronny's estranged came out with a small tray with two glasses of ice and a plastic cup with a lid for the kid. She had put on a wrap-around skirt, a modest attempt at taking away from my awkwardness. She avoided making eye contact with me, but she said, "I bet you're a breast man, right, Bill?"

I must have hesitated for just a second too long.

She said, "Bill. I was joking, jeez."

So I made sexual innuendo out of the bucket of chicken and said flatly, "I'm a leg man," even though I wanted breast. I just couldn't bring myself to say it without turning red.

Ronny's estranged focused on the kid, tearing apart the breaded meat and feeding him. The kid shone in the sunlight, brown from days of playing in the pool. Ronny's estranged was crouched, drawing her legs up under her plain shapeless skirt. She had purposely turned her back to me, waiting for me to talk. I saw the vertebrae of her spine against her thin back, saw the outline of her small breast sagging as she leaned over the kid. I wanted to talk, I really did. But I'm someone who lacks the clear ability to change the course of things between people. I linger and anguish at moments of decision, when I know something is being asked of me, and do nothing. That is how I'd lost Diane, those days of silence after she left, when I knew she was waiting for me to call, and I didn't, and now it was all silence. I tried to dredge up something to say. I said, "This is real good chicken."

She said nothing, so I said, "You think Colonel Sanders was really in the army?"

She didn't really answer, just shrugged her shoulders, said, "I guess he was."

The small generator hooked up to the trailer puttered in the silence. It made everything taste of gasoline, a kind of sweet taste, like when you pump gasoline at the station. I ate the chicken, because there was nothing else to do.

The kid was trying to stuff chicken into the alligator's nostrils. Ronny's estranged said, "Don't do that, Lucas." The kid kept doing it, though. He started splashing water at his mother and got into a racket of screaming and slapping the alligator into the pool.

All I heard was the clap of her hand on the kid's ass as he swung like an ape in midair, held by his mother as she hit the kid again hard on his soggy diapered ass. I lost my chicken in a sudden fit of mania. My legs jumped, and the chicken was ruined on the ground.

The kid was swung into the trailer, and it was bawling its head off. "Dammit, Lucas, you don't want to eat, don't eat. Asshole!" She was screaming that, "Asshole." I mean, what the hell are you supposed to do in the face of someone else's brutality?

I was standing with grease stains on my pants when Ronny's estranged came out all red-faced. She shut the inferno of the trailer. I just stood there and looked at her. She knew what I was thinking.

"This is what happens when you don't got a million dollars in a bank somewhere, Bill."

My face betrayed nothing, drained of emotion. I hate the excuse of people like her, that defiance against the world that usually gets taken out on kids in supermarkets and checkout lines. I said to myself, "Get the hell away from her," but I stayed.

Her expression quieted. "He's tired is what he is. This sun is hell on a kid."

She coaxed me into sitting again. We ate the chicken and drank the cold beer on plastic chairs. The kid got high up in his cage and looked out the window and said something in baby talk, and Ronny's estranged answered him back in their secret tongue. She passed him in a plastic plate of chewed meat and coleslaw, and the kid disappeared and ate. I heard him making cooing noises.

"You find out anything, yet?" Ronny's estranged said between bites, taking her glass to mask any expression. I saw the fixity of her eyes look at me and then close as she drained her beer.

I said simply, "I don't think Ronny killed his old man."

Ronny's estranged coughed so she spat up her drink. It spilled down her stomach, soaked her breasts. She kept up with the coughing and I took her plate and cup away from her and she kept at the coughing for what seemed like ages until I had to hit on her back. Up came this bit of chicken into her cupped hands.

"God Almighty" is all she said when the chicken was there in her hands, all wet and slick from her saliva. Her face was god-awful red, the rims of her eyes brimming with water. When she recovered, she said, "If you hadn't been here, I might have died, Bill."

I looked at her, spoke softly. "If I hadn't come, you wouldn't have had the chicken to choke on."

She knew I was pissed, maybe not the real reason behind it, the jealousy at having seen her with that Karl guy, but she knew something was up.

She got still after that, turned her toe in the hot dirt. "Why the hell do men always end up hating me, Bill?"

"I don't hate you."

"Sure you do. I can tell."

The sun poured over both of us, an insatiable throbbing heat, fire, adding to the tension again. It made me want to crawl away from conflict, to concede things to the season, to do what that fat man back in the interrogation room had said weeks ago, to hide. I watched her go at the chicken again, eat away at the special seasoned skin the Colonel had invented. "This is good chicken," is what she said. "I think I could eat chicken like this every day and not get sick of it."

I said, "He makes a hell of a mashed potato, too." I had a tub of mash which I took out of the paper bag. She extended her plate, and I scooped out the mash. She added in the chocolate milk, turned the potato brown, and spoke in that secret language to her kid, got him to stand up and take the potato from her and then disappear again.

Ronny's estranged said, "This might be a record or something. You know, Lucas has never eaten a home-cooked meal in all his life."

I looked at her. She nodded her head in this earnest way. She crossed a leg of chicken over her breast. "Cross my heart he ain't. I was just thinking that the other day."

"That's something else," is what I said and got back to sucking on the chicken bones. I called the kid "The Fast Food Kid" when his head emerged again. He wanted more mash.

Ronny's estranged had a way of shoring up time and distance. She put her arms around me when she came back from giving the kid the mash. She hugged me, said, "I bet a guy like you has a hundred million women that want to be with you?"

I can't really say how much that meant to me, to hear a woman like her want me. I mean, we had a regular picnic. Things eased up between us. She ate the chicken down to the bone. I watched her drink her beer, saw the small line of suds it left on her upper lip, and I drank, too, and wanted to get drunk, because, despite this being a murder investigation, I had other things on my mind, like wanting just to hold her, to take her out in that fancy-ass car of mine. And so, that's what I said by the next beer, which put me in a good mood. I said, "What do you say we take a spin, you, me, and the kid?"

It was like finding the key to unlock a box. Her face broke in a beautiful smile. "You mean it?" She clapped her hand like a kid, stomped her long tender legs in the hot dirt. I stared at her painted toes. I wanted to put them into my mouth. I was drunk. I just smiled at her, something filled up inside me.

We left behind that solitary trailer, left that sardine can and the small plastic pool, and we got out on the road with our booze and the kid in his small cage in the back of the convertible. It's goddamn unreal what you can find yourself doing when you should be doing something else, when you can't pass the goddamn LSATs, when you get separated from the woman you thought you just might have loved, once upon a time. So here we were, busting ass out on the road, because of all that and more. There wasn't shit out there on the road. Everything was hidden away, farmers in the cold of their cellars, animals in shade under some of the two-hundred-year-old tree groves, crowded there like they were playing a game of cards or something. I shouted, "Maybe they're talking about overthrowing the humans!" and that made Ronny Lawton's estranged put her hand to her mouth and shout back, "What the hell goes on inside a college guy's head?" She tapped my head, and I liked that, liked the way "college guy's head" sounded, the way it distinguished me from that guy she was fucking, from her animal estranged husband. I wanted to live in that intangible region. That is where she wanted to roam, in the domain of my college head. She put her hand on the inside of my thigh, and it did something to me, it made my heart race and my blood pump, and I was thinking, this is what my father must have felt like when he was with my mother way back, when he defied my grandfather and got her pregnant, when he submitted to longing. I was linked to that past, to the infinite longing of a man who found it necessary to blast his head off because he could not find love and hope and other things. I was thinking, there in the car, we are here for nothing other than to reproduce in the end, to continue our species, to fluff up our feathers and preen ourselves before the opposite sex. I had this car, this plumage of wealth, this accessory of my maleness. I made us go faster. I was smiling real big. Things were just whizzing through my head, because, hell, there are times when you would do anything for a woman. And this was one of those times. I understood right there why the sky fills with the migratory celebration of those Canada geese each year over our land, the wavering V of long-necked geese against the gray dapple of clouds, in pursuit of their mating grounds.

We went like a bat out of hell, past an intersection without slowing down. I saw Ronny's estranged catch her breath, close her eyes, squeeze my thigh, await some impact that never hit her, watched her open her eyes again and smile like she'd been reborn into a certitude that we would not die this day. There was this gathering of livestock off by a tree again, and Ronny's estranged shouted, "Say that stuff again," and so, I shouted, "What, you mean that 'maybe they're talking about overthrowing the humans?'" and her hand went up my thigh, settled itself. She mouthed, "Yeah," but I couldn't hear her, because of the speed we were going.

We were driving way too fast. I watched the needle sink into the higher numbers, go toward ninety-five on that flat line of country road. We were a tornado out there on the plains, a mass of longing heading deep into the plains, when I got some sense about me. I slowed so we could talk without screaming and, turning my head around, said, "Who wants ice cream?" to the kid, and there he was in the cage, sitting on his ass with the biggest shit-eating grin you're ever going to see on a kid. I mean, the kid was built for speed. I said, "That kid's built for flying through a world at a million miles an hour and not being stuck in some trailer in the middle of nowhere!" He was shaking with excitement, holding his bars, making his baby noises.

Ronny's estranged had such beautiful eyes. She leaned against my arm, said, "I know . . . You don't think a mother knows all these things, Bill? You don't think I've been wanting something better for him all his life?"

Her slender hand just kept at the inside of my leg. I said, "Hey, Fast Food Kid!" and Ronny's estranged said, "You got to get him a Burger King crown, Bill. That's what I want you to bring me next time, you hear me?"

I said, "You could take that kid on the road, make a whole show around him, let him eat this and that, let him rate restaurants. The kid could be an icon."

"What's an icon, Bill?"

"A star." I was staring at her green eyes.

Ronny's estranged said, "I want to know how that college head works, Bill. You drive me crazy, Bill, calling my kid the Fast Food Kid like that." Then she withdrew her hand from my leg and said softly, "You think you could ever love somebody like me, Bill? Could you?"

I've always done better in life when I don't think about it. That's maybe the only thing I really know about myself. I shouted, "We're eating ice cream!" and hit the pedal again, and the kid jerked back in his cage.

I got to this out-of-date fifties-style roller-skate diner. It had a tray that came into the car. A woman in tight shorts and a T-shirt skated up to us. She smelled of bubble gum. Her hair was all sprayed and standing up on her head like it was cotton candy, like it might taste sweet. And hell if her name tag didn't say "Candy." She was maybe the same age as Ronny's estranged, same shape, the long, delicate legs that went to the smallness of her buttocks. Candy liked the car. She said so, ran her painted pink nails along the hot metal edging. She blew this huge tumor of a bubble at the kid. She said, "That your kid?"

Ronny's estranged said abruptly, "You think we stole the kid? How about you just take our order?"

Candy ate the deflated sack of her gum and kept looking at me. That's the thing they say about having a beautiful woman with you. It attracts other good-looking women. I've heard that said, and I think just maybe it's true.

I said, "Candy," used this swaggering familiarity, "this is what we want," and we ordered a huge banana split and a little tub of ice cream coated in chocolate for the Fast Food Kid. He was behind us, rattling the bars of his cage. He wanted more speed.

I shared the banana split with Ronny's estranged, ate from the same spoon, had her feed me, felt my tongue touch where her mouth had been, taking each measure of melting ice cream into my mouth, swallowing, tasting the sweetness.

Candy came by on her skates, gliding with a tray of food for these kids who'd pulled up beside us. They were whistling and jeering at her. Candy had her ass up against our car on my side, her small ass going back and forth as she flexed and balanced on the skates, giving the kids their burgers and fries. Then she seemed to lose balance, went backward, and came in on the backseat, onto the cage with the kid inside eating his tub of ice cream. She let out this scream, and stuff just flew through the air in slow motion.

When things had settled, and she was still there on the cage, with her legs up in the air and the skate wheels still turning, I looked at Ronny's estranged and said out loud, "How about I take Candy from the baby?" and I thought that was maybe the funniest damn thing I ever said in all my life, and so did Candy and the kids in the other car, but Ronny's estranged just started shaking, crying, like she was having a fit or something.

We got away from there, and Ronny's estranged just kept crying. She was still holding the ice cream. Tears were falling into it. It was melting, but I just kept driving. I didn't know how to stop things, didn't know what to say. I was driving for maybe ten minutes when I realized where I was going. In the dark of my head I had the place in mind, the destination at the end of all this. We stopped out by the old homestead of Ronny Lawton's ancestors, where Ronny's estranged had told me to look. I pulled over in the growth of corn at the side of the road, killed the engine. She looked at me, whispered, "That bitch did that on purpose."

I said softly, "It's over." I looked at her hard, I said, "I got something that told me to come out here."

Ronny's estranged just looked at me, a blankness of expression, sniffling. She didn't get what I was asking her. "That Candy did that on purpose. I know she did," is all she said. She wiped her nose with the back of her hand and, with the other hand, began eating the ice cream again, spooning up the soft melt.

I tensed there in the car, let things slowly unfold, said, "Did you send me a letter telling me about the bunker?"

"What bunker?"

It was true. It was indistinguishable, really, on this road, no different from any other road out here. Only I knew where we were. I had followed the signs, woven us into the labyrinth of the corn-fields. "Ronny Lawton's ancestors' place, where you told me about the tornado bunker, where you told me about you and Ronny. Did you send me a letter telling me something was in there?"

Ronny's estranged betrayed nothing, if she knew anything. She was thinking about other things. She took another spoon of the ice cream before she said anything. "Bill?" she said slowly.

"What?"

"I think Lucas likes you. He really does, Bill." She leaned back, and the kid was pawing the small tub of ice cream. It was all gone. He made the word for ice cream, barely discernible. Ronny's estranged said the word for him, "Ice cream," said it slow. She looked at me. "He's a good kid, Bill. I don't hate him. I don't want you to think I hate him."

I was about to answer, but she said, "It's hard for men to love a kid that ain't their own. I understand that. My hairdresser says it ain't even men's fault. It's just something inside them." She set the ice cream aside, leaned into me. "I want you to like Lucas, Bill. I want you to teach him things. I don't want it like it is with Karl."

I held her close to me, didn't pretend anything, but I said softly, "I guess Darlene knows a lot about what men can do to women."

Ronny's estranged didn't suspect anything. She said, "What?"

I said, "You were just saying how Darlene thinks it's hard for men to love a kid that isn't theirs. I guess she's seen enough women hurt."

Ronny's estranged had her face against my arm. "I guess Darlene sort of hears all our problems. You just get talking sometimes, and it just comes out."

I said, "I was out by her place. I had supper there a while back, with her and her husband, Ed. You know, he works for the paper with me. Darlene showed me her setup, the getaway weekends, the prom dresses, the photo studio, Car Theft, the whole nine yards. She's got a real system going."

"Bill, I don't think you got it right with Darlene. She don't even always charge for what she does. You go out there, and she sees you looking down, she says, 'I know just what you need . . .' You don't have to have the money for anything but a haircut, and she'll start doing your nails or do up your face. She's just like that."

I hesitated over how to say what I wanted. I touched the soft warmth of her temple, obscured her eyes with the palm of my hand.

Ronny's estranged said, "I like that, right there, Bill. Rub me right there."

I massaged her temple. I made a leap of faith in that one instance. I said, "I guess you told Darlene all about what happened to you out at the Lawton place?"

Ronny's estranged tensed. Then she eased and kissed the palm of my hand again, kept her eyes closed. I kept my palm over her eyes.

She said quietly, "Bill, I don't want you ever thinking anything bad about me. I don't ever want that."

I whispered, "You can't tell me anything that would stop me falling in love with you."

She moved my hand aside, looked up into my face. "Darlene told you, right?"

I sort of nodded, played along with her. "I want you to tell me how it was."

She stared at me for a hell of a long time. I felt her squeeze my hand. Somehow, we were inside some cocoon of longing, some safe place, just me, her, and the kid. It was what she wanted, the solace of money and a car like this and a man who wouldn't hit her. She said softly, "Nobody was ever this nice to Lucas, Bill."

I leaned and kissed her forehead, whispered, "I want you to tell me how it was . . ."

And then she just blew everything wide open. "I don't know which of them is the father, Bill. Ronny, or his father . . ." Her voice trailed off. "I don't know . . ."

Things just spun. I saw globs of something before my eyes, closed them, and waited, breathed deep. I could feel Ronny's estranged tensing in my arms. She was speaking, but I didn't listen to what she was saying. I said, "Does Ronny know this?"

She shook her head. She said, "Bill, I don't want you to think bad of me. It wasn't what I wanted, I swear, Bill."

I felt the still hotness flush around me. "Darlene knows all this?" Ronny's estranged said, "She . . . Darlene told you." She kept looking up at me. "Bill?" She withdrew from me, realizing Darlene had said nothing. I could see the tears in her eyes. She was on the verge of crying, swallowing, then she said, "Oh, God, please don't look at me like that, Bill. I thought Darlene told you. Please, Bill."

I didn't say anything, the shock draining the blood from my face. It was hard processing things. It was like one of those LSAT questions. The facts were all jumbled up in there somewhere. I was feeling that same light-headedness I got when I couldn't quite get things all sorted in my head.

Ronny's estranged was going on about how she loved me. She was saying she thought I knew.

I interrupted her. "Ronny know about any of this?"

"I never told him anything, Bill. When Ronny came home, there was no telling him what happened, but he was shouting at me that it wasn't his kid. He had it counted up in his head, the days, and he said it sure as hell wasn't his kid. He was shouting that all the time, but I couldn't tell. I didn't know what to do. It was Darlene who told me never to tell Ronny. She said there was no putting it up to Ronny, what his father had done. She said Ronny was going to come around to thinking it was his kid, because the kid was going to look like a Lawton, and that was going to be that. Darlene said there weren't no point setting Ronny wild about things."

"You tell Karl about this, about Ronny's old man?"

She shook her head. "No, Bill. I'm only tellin' you how it was, that's all, Bill."

"And Darlene."

"Yeah, but she don't count, Bill. She don't tell secrets."

Ronny's estranged craned her head to kiss me. She whispered, "I don't ever want you to stop loving me like I love you, Bill." I felt her tongue against my lips. I gave in to her, closed my eyes.

And so there we were out on the road, small and insignificant, the sky still hot overhead, the ice cream melting in the dish,

Ronny's estranged in my arms, just hanging on to anything that would have her, the kid speaking to himself behind us, oblivious to all this shit, making a garbling noise, trying to make the words *ice cream*, shaking his cage, and not a hundred yards away, his father's—or his grandfather's—head was maybe down in a tornado bunker, rotting away.

CHAPTER 12

I wanted to confront Darlene, ask her why the hell she never mentioned anything about Ronny's estranged being raped by Ronny's father. She had goddamn circumstantial evidence about the Lawtons. It wasn't like she had to let it go beyond us at the paper. I called up Ed's house a few times but hung up. I was going to check with Darlene to see if she'd cut my hair. It was the only way I could think of getting close to asking her about Ronny's estranged.

I was nervous as hell about things. I couldn't quite reconcile why the hell Ed had been so mad when I mentioned Ronny's estranged knowing Darlene. It seemed like it had to be that Ed knew about what had happened to Ronny's estranged. That was the only way he'd have gotten so worked up. I saw Ed a few times down at the office, just passing comments as we waited out the stalemate of the note. I said nothing about Darlene.

I kept my mouth shut, for a lot of reasons. When you looked at things from Ed and Sam's point of view, they were probably still wondering why the hell I hadn't called them about the note on my table. I still had this feeling it looked to them like I was constructing the note. You give two guys like that enough time together, without me, and they were bound to be thinking there was something not right about me and that note. Or maybe that was just horseshit, and they weren't thinking that at all. But I had a lot of time on my hands. I felt the fear of having those shears out back with my prints on them. I hadn't done things right. I should have gone out and dug up the shears and thrown them away, but now I felt I was being watched since I got the note. I wanted to call Pete, to ask him what to do about the shears, but I couldn't speak to him over the phone. I mean, it got complicated as hell inside my head, keeping track of things. And so for those interminable days, I went down to the Y and hid in the deep end of the pool, thinking and waiting.

It was Saturday evening when Sam and Ed came by my house. I was pretty much a wreck. Ronny's estranged was on the phone from Osco. She was telling me the kid missed me. She said, "I swear he can say your name, Bill."

I said, "He's a good kid."

Ronny's estranged said softly into the phone, "I'm sorry for what happened to me, Bill. I don't want you to hate me."

I shouted, "I don't want you thinking that, Teri. You hear me?"

She hesitated, "I had this dream that you didn't want to see me ever."

I said, "There's someone here to see me. I got to go."

"One of your girlfriends, Bill?" And the phone went dead in my ear.

Sam and Ed had gone by the library to get a survey of the area and had picked out exactly where the bunker was located. Sam spread a rough sketch of what he'd copied on the table in the kitchen. The tension was razor-edged between them. I was breathing deep, feeling the burn of having held my breath down in the deep end of the pool. We were just staring at the outline when Sam turned and looked at me and made this sniffing noise. "Jeez, Bill, this isn't a goddamn dance. I hope you aren't planning on going out there smelling like that." It was true. I reeked of aftershave, so I excused myself and went down to the basement and washed behind my neck, and the soft skin of my wrists where I'd splashed the aftershave, but it did little good. I came up and Sam was sniffing the air again. I had this contrite look, like I had screwed up, and Ed said, "I can't hardly smell anything." And so we got back to looking at what would materialize in the coming dark that night. Sam had the rudiments of a plan. He was like a general over the map.

Ed drew his lean head back and said flatly, "I hate lying to Darlene. She's wondering what the hell has got me all worked up."

I turned to look at Ed. He burped and got that usual taste of bile. He seemed to hold it in his mouth before swallowing again. A wince invaded his face. He excused himself and went over by the sink and got down a glass. He drank from his pink bottle of Pepto-Bismol, then washed it down with the water.

We drank a beer before we left, sat in the front room and gathered some collective strength. Sam said, "There's nothing like drinking cold beer in the dark." I gathered it was something he did a lot. He made slurping sounds when he drank.

I finished my beer and opened another bottle and drank long and slow, until the bottle was nearly drained. I wanted that immediate rush of inebriation.

Ed opened another and drank like he meant business.

Sam said, "We don't want to get too messed up."

Ed slowed down.

I smiled to myself, felt the old-world intimacy between us, no radio or television to distract. We were three men stuck together in a game, two of them at the end of their lives. It was maybe that human dimension I was starved for in the wake of my father's suicide, in the absence of Diane, what I desperately wanted in Ronny Lawton's estranged, just human contact. When Sam drank, he turned his wrist, and it made a cracking noise. I watched him drink, anticipated the crack, and there it was, that slight arthritic snap. And when Ed got serious, he clenched his teeth so his breath made a slight whistling noise. It sent a shiver down my spine, that thread of camaraderie, the quiet domain of our personal lives shared. We drained the last of our cold beer as the night settled into gray, and the storm windows shuddered.

Ed said, "You mind if I call Darlene?"

Ed spoke softly, whispered things to her that weren't meant for others to hear. He had his hand cupped over the phone.

Sam and I went into the kitchen with the empty bottles, set them on the table.

"I don't want you hating me about the paper being up for sale, Bill. I've stayed with it as long as it was humanly possible."

I said, "You do what you gotta do, Sam."

Ed got off the phone, and we came back in and sat down again. Ed said simply, "You know you're in love when it pains you to lie to the woman you love."

Sam looked serious. "Every man is blessed with one thing in his life. I guess you got Darlene."

Another beer was out of the question. It was agreed we'd take my car. I felt the slight buzz of alcohol, or wanted to let myself give in to its effects to numb the prophetic sense of what lay out there beyond us. There was nothing to hide behind anymore. The dark granted us the passage through the land. Sam's wrist cracked when he rose out of the chair, Ed made his whistling noise, and just one last time we looked at the letter, at the grim message it bore. Now it seemed to possess a confessional intimacy, a secret that had been kept too long, a plea to unearth the horror of the head. Whoever had sent it must have been waiting these nights, crouched in anticipation of us doing what had been asked of us. Sam yawned, and I heard the snap of his jaws behind me.

And so we began the drive out to the Lawton ancestral property. I had the roof down. It was a night of soft warmth, the beginning of a reprieve from the exhausting heat we'd endured. Ed was up front with me, his eyes fixed on stars in the dark. Sam sat in the back of the car, sunk low into the leather seat, taking in the cosmos as well.

We were all silent witnesses to things inside us, each with his own vision of what a head would look like out there. I had somehow blanked out that image for days, but now it sifted through my head, those images from movies, the grainy effect of horror emerging from darkness. I had the radio on real low, just a faint hint of someone singing. I drove slowly through the warm land, felt the air wrap around us. A car approached with its lights on full beam. I dimmed my lights, and the car dimmed its lights, and we passed slowly out there in the land, the orbs of our collective heads turning, all of us faceless blobs, our vision obscured in the aftermath of the headlights, momentarily blinded.

At a four-way intersection I'd sped through with Ronny's

estranged and the Fast Food Kid, I stopped. The big engine pulsed. I was aware of my body absorbing its vibrations. I stepped slowly on the gas, felt the gentle pressure of my body pushed slightly back into the seat. Ed coughed and stared at me through the soft glow of instruments. His skeletal hands clawed his bony knees.

I pulled the car into the dry stalks of corn and killed the engine. In the distance behind us the lights made a pale patch on the sky. We kept up a stupefied silence, just sitting there in the dark.

Sam moved first. He got out of the car, and Ed and I followed. Sam had a flashlight to cut the dark at the edge of the ancestral farm. He illuminated the corn and moved slowly. We followed in his wake through the dry dirt. It took us a while to find what we were looking for. Sam found the stump of wood where there'd been a gate and said simply, "This is the spot." He pointed the light directly at our feet. Our eyes met in the small dome of light. The coordinates for the bunker emanated from here. Sam read them, gave us the number of feet inward. Then Sam blessed himself, and Ed made the sign of the cross on his own forehead.

We waded through the dark in single file, counting off slowly two hundred and twenty paces back from the gate until we felt the soft give of the land where we were over the bunker. Sam directed the solitary beam on the ground beneath us. It was obvious the bunker had been disturbed. The connective grass roots had been cut away. Sam focused on a thick rusted ring, like something from an old harness. Ed shifted to the side, seemed to hesitate. He had his camera with him, but he didn't go for a shot. Sam nodded at me, and I leaned forward and pulled open the door. And up from the dark confines of the bunker came this putrid odor.

Sam shone the light into the dark hole, exposing a world of beetling dark movement, the glint of insect shells, the tiny polished eyes. It was a shocking sight, the prospect of having to go down there. And that horrible smell. I took a step backward, bumped into Ed, whose large hands came down on my shoulders, holding me. I took shallow breaths.

Sam was still over the hole, illuminating it. Ed prodded me

softly. We peered into the dark, anxious, superstitious. A sense of suffocation welled in each of us. The hole threw back a weak light that washed up and illuminated the crevices of our faces, making us look ghoulish.

It was a hole maybe eight feet deep. The crypt had a dryness that made me shudder. I don't think any of us wanted to go down there in the dark. "Maybe there's evidence we might disturb," I said to the back of Sam's head. Sam turned and said, "I've been waiting my whole life for something like this." He didn't explain what "this" meant.

The moon moved through the clear black of the sky. We seemed to seek it out, a last look upward before descending into the hole.

A small ladder fixture descended into the ground. Sam said, "We'll all go down," said it very low. We went down into that dark sarcophagus, me first, then Ed, pressed up against a cold, dark wall holding our breaths, anticipating the most abhorrent of sights of that prodigy of massacre, Ronny Lawton. Sam came last, aimed the flashlight against the floor, cast away the dark, exposing the dark concrete walls creeping with insect life.

The flashlight washed over a cot without a mattress, lingered on some stale blankets, two chairs and a small table, all huddled together. Someone had been down here burning candles, the congealed stumps embedded into the table, crumpled boxes of Marlboros and discarded matches. I knew it was where Ronny had taken his wife. I felt the trembling solitude of their embrace, her and him coming to hide from the world, burrowing into the ground.

The room yielded nothing else. Sam shone the light on a hurricane lamp, the globe of glass still filled with paraffin. It smelled sweet when we got close to it. I took a match and lit the wick, tempered the flame until the room glowed with a soft shifting light, throwing our shadows on the walls. There was nothing more in the room, a small cell of darkness maybe ten feet long, a grim hole of cold insect life. We just stood there, silent, staring. It seemed we had been duped. But at the farthest corner of the room was a small doorway, the obscure darkness of yet another passage. The light found it, seeped into that dark capsular secret. Sam tipped his head toward me.

I advanced to the inevitability of what I knew it must contain. Through the dip in the short passageway I bowed in a sort of reverential atonement and entered the nightmare. There, in the small confines of the tiny room, was a stick with the dim root of what looked like a big turnip. The hurricane lamp glowed on the end of my arm. But I knew as much as I advanced, as I let my eyes adjust to the grim spectacle of the decapitated head of Ronny Lawton's father, as I looked close at the writhing mass of etiolated maggots pouring through the eye sockets. I reached for the lamp and snuffed the nightmare into blackness and retreated from the small room.

Ed hadn't even the resolve to go and photograph the head. He and Sam advanced, and Sam lit up the head from the doorway. In truth, you could not be certain it was the father's head, it was that badly affected by decay. We came up out of the ground, and each of us had to lean over and take deep breaths, each alone for a moment with the image of not only that decomposing head, but the guilt of what we had done, those days of quiet subterfuge when we had agreed to wait so we could undermine Linda Carter.

I shut the door to the bunker eventually, and we slashed our way through the corn and got to the car again. I started the car and drove us away, felt myself press into the accelerator, gaining distance on what we had uncovered in the ground and in ourselves.

Sam said, when we were well away, "I only wish I had not lived to see something like that."

Ed leaned in his seat and put his hand on Sam's hand, which came forward into the divide between the seats. Ed said, "We are leaving behind a world that bears no resemblance to the one into which we were born." He said softly, "How did that come to be?"

Sam retrieved his hand and put it to his head, like a man trying

to stop a wound. I knew he was crying, though he made no noise.
Ed turned slowly and looked into the oncoming dark. I think their
world was eclipsed in that lonely drive. I knew as much. What
would it have been like for the apostles to go to the tomb of Jesus
and find his crucified body rigid and stiff, unresurrected, lifeless, a
mutilated corpse?

In the office, I called Pete at home, asked him to come and speak
with us, intimated what we had found.

In the time it took Pete to get to us, we agreed there would be no
upstaging Linda Carter, no gloating sense of victory. The news
would break in the dead of night, roam the airwaves, be on everyone's lips tomorrow morning. The dark would open to a scene of
yellow police tape, the cordoned limit of, not a nightmare, but a
cosmology of some interior madness. And no, *madness* wasn't the
right word. There was some meaning to be extrapolated from all
this, some sense of retribution, a psychopathic sense of certitude
and ritual. We were being led through the protracted sense of ceremony, made to uncover the rotting pieces of a corpse. For what?

I put down a pot of coffee. Ed got on the phone to Darlene, told
her everything in his soft, quiet way. He was holding his side. He'd
been gulping down the Pepto-Bismol.

Sam sat smoking, obscuring himself in a haze.

I sat down at the typewriter. I found I was shaking. I tensed my
arms, closed my eyes, and just started typing. I gave a brief history
of finding the note, piecing it together in the house, then going out
to the bunker and uncovering the head. I came back with the page
for Sam. Ed was off the phone. His eyes had a glazed look. He took
his coffee to his lips and sipped. Sam looked up at me, took the
copy, and just nodded. He had his cigar between his fingers, and it
seemed like the copy was smoking. It had a macabre effect on me,
made me shiver.

Ed poured me a coffee, handed it to me. He said, "They're probably going to want to know why we went out there by ourselves and
compromised the scene."

I said, "It's in there, Ed, in what I wrote, our reasonable suspicion that it was only a hoax. I didn't say anything about waiting the few days or anything. It seems like I got the note and we just went out there."

"Send it out on the wire," Sam said. He had that vapid look of a very tired man. He yawned and stared at the window, out into the dark foundry yard.

Pete arrived and got advised of what we'd found and done. He read the wire, mouthed to himself the details, then looked up at us and said, "Why the hell am I always the last to know what the hell is going on?" He banged the table. "Jesus!" He looked at me hard in the clinical light of the office, hiked up his pants. He looked like an officious egg with a holster around its middle. He shouted, "This is all bullshit, all of this. You give me five minutes with that asshole Ronny Lawton, and I'd have him confessing everything."

Sam pinched the bridge of his nose. "You ever feel like you don't want to play their game? I mean, what if we never went out there to that bunker, what if we just let it all pass? What we're doing is creating a culture of psychopaths, plain and simple."

Pete said, "That's the first goddamn sensible thing I've heard from the press in all this bullshit. You're damn right, Sam. This bullshit is not fit for human consumption. It's something between the law and the psychopath, and that has a whole different set of rules. All this bullshit does is up the bar for the next psycho."

Ed stared out into the dark. He turned to me. "Bill, you'll be the hottest ticket in town by sunrise. You ready for that?"

Outside I stood with Pete, and he looked hard at me. "Don't yank my chain, Bill. Now, what the hell is going on? You did that note thing yourself, right? You're going after the mileage in all this. You got some sort of tip from Ronny's estranged, right?"

I shook my head. "You got it wrong, Pete."

It was maybe the first time I ever saw fear in Pete's face. He gripped my arm. "You listen to me, asshole. You got me up to my neck in all this shit. You went out there and opened up that bunker without me, fucked up a crime scene on me!"

Ed had wandered over to the window. I saw him staring from

behind a curtain. It felt strange, like he was spying. I said, "Pete, I swear to you on a stack of Bibles, I'm not in on any scam to hide the body. That note just got left on my doorstep, just the way I told you. I swear to God."

Pete took a long, slow breath. "I want you to know, I'm not planning on leaving this town. I don't have the money, like you and Sam and Ed, to start over. You hear that? I told you once, I got all that I ever wanted in this town right now. You pull anything on me again, and I'm talking. I'm going to lay out the shit you've been feeding me all along and let them make up their minds, 'cause maybe I'm just too goddamn close to you to know I'm getting screwed. But if it comes down to my ass, Bill, I'm taking you with me."

I said, "You ever go see Karl?"

Pete shook his head. "I don't see what the hell interest you have in sticking Karl with this crime, not unless you want Ronny's estranged all to yourself, that is. Is that what this is all about?"

I said, "I don't know what the hell you mean by that, Pete!"

"Think about it!"

"Think about what?" I tried to follow Pete, but he stopped and glared at me. "I got one suspect, and one suspect only. Ronny Lawton done it. I know it, you know it, and this whole damn county knows it! There are no shears, as far as I'm concerned, you hear me?"

I mouthed, "Okay."

Pete left, and I watched him turn on the siren and lights out of anger, watched him speed away into the dark. We stayed the night at the office. The story was roaming the night desks at the major newspapers. Sam had an old couch in his office, and Ed had a cot down in the darkroom. They separated and slept.

I unplugged the phone, killed the lights, curled under my desk, used a sports coat as a pillow, and felt the tide of exhaustion fill me, but I didn't sleep. The coffeepot percolated, a dark aromatic presence. I stared at the legs of a chair, the slash of moonlight pouring across the floor.

I got up, plugged the phone back in, and called Diane. A guy answered in this groggy voice. I said simply, "Are you in law school with Diane?" There was a muffled sound of voices in the background. I heard Diane's voice. The phone went dead in my ear. I called again. This time the answering machine picked up. I said quietly, "Diane, you know that case I've been following? Well, I found a man's head on a stick down in a tornado bunker this evening." Again, that never-ending silence between us. I said, "I miss you, Diane. I miss you like you wouldn't believe." Then I hung up.

I moved in the dark. There was a deal going down across the way in the shell of an abandoned building. I saw the interior light of a car go on and off, a code or something. I felt the ebb and flow of exhaustion and fear. I was going to call Ronny's estranged, but then I decided against it. This blob of tiredness, a glob of black edged in a corona of yellow, floated before me. I had to keep shaking my head to clear things. I got to my car. I looked up, and there was Ed again, silhouetted in the office window, staring after me. That felt eerie, like he knew something he was not willing to tell me. I just didn't know anymore. I was moving toward insanity, felt myself give under the pressure of the things I'd seen. How often do you stare into a hole at a decapitated head? It was all beyond my reach in the end, trying to put things in perspective.

Ed was still staring after me, but I just drove out on the dark road of the old foundry yard.

I drove around for a while before I realized where I was going. I was going down to confront Ronny at Denny's before all hell broke loose. I was trying to put words into my mouth, to give him an ultimatum or something. It was late now, so he'd be in the dying aftermath of the usual pilgrimage of high-schoolers. The numbers had fallen off over the past week. The spectacle was diminishing. The prospect of school loomed, the beginning of the fall sports schedule, guys up at six-thirty for football practice and wrestling, evening practice from three to six. Give the heat another two weeks at most, and then there would be rain. It came always at summer's end, the torrential downpours of slow-moving clouds. I had a list of kids I was supposed to get in contact with who were slated to make it big this year. If things had not gone the way they had with Ronny Lawton's old man, we might have run a midsummer section on the baseball leagues, done some specials on what the great prospects were doing over the summer, guys smiling while they flipped burgers or cut lawns, wholesome images of continuity and family and community. But everything had slowly come undone in that vacuous agitation of a murdered man that nobody really gave a shit about. It was Ronny Lawton that had been the story, his myth and physical menace had suffused some marauding sense of retribution into the landscape. He had kept us occupied. He ruined the aura of a town is what he did.

Or maybe the ugliness was there, and Ronny just showed it to us. It's what I suspected at the back of things. I drove toward the bleeding strip of neon, the solitary cars here and there, seeing the small drive-in windows, glass tombs encasing high-school dropouts, mostly young girls, some male misfits, the dim of mind, all banished to the night shift for minimum wage. It was this new destiny of strip malls and eateries that scared the shit out of me, that made me wince and understand why people kill each other. I just stared into that benign warfare of twenty-four-hour fronts, the lights that never shut off. You have to ask yourself why do they do it. What compels people to go on existing on the dark side of night? What does it do to the psyche to know this is your future, your destiny in darkness, the graveyard shift at the drive-in? This was Ronny Lawton's domain, ex-army enlistee, decommissioned into society, a monstrous figure in a white chef's hat, short-order cook with an expertise in munitions and assault rifles, trained to survive in the wilderness, scrambling eggs, making shakes, salting fries. Along these strips of neon were the killing fields of our postindustrialism, these glasshouse eateries of disaffection where people get big on greased food and baskets of fries, eating bleeding burgers, clotting up their arteries and going about dying slowly over black tar coffee. Out here at this hour you bore witness to the attenuated deaths, the casualties that go uncounted. And when the sun rises, the radio whispers of the night that has passed, it gives the grim statistics of pulverizing rapes, robberies where clerks were pistol-whipped and tied up in freezers, or shot in the face and left to bleed to death, a young woman with two children missing from a 7-Eleven, a solitary sentry, working alone of course—margins of profit dictate there can't be two clerks on duty. And it passes itself off, this violence, this madness, as nothing to do with politics. Somehow we are an apolitical nation. There are no collective actions of warfare. Everything can be dismantled to the level of the individual. Each act of violence is isolated; it forms no mood; it feeds into no general rebellion. It's maybe the greatest secret we possess as a nation, our sense of alienation from everyone else around us, our ability to have no sympathy, no empathy for others' suffering, a decentralized philosophy of individual will, a culpability that always lands back on each of us. "You can be whatever you want to be" was what my grandfather was always saying. It was the mantra of our society, the fluidity, the mobility. In the days of my father's suicide, he spoke about how men turned on each other in the unions, the sudden willingness of men to blame one another, to dissociate themselves from each other, to damn the collective of the unions as some sort of tyranny over the right of the ordinary worker.

I came to a traffic light and stopped. Outside, I noticed at these all-nighters they always flew an American flag, let it unfurl in the wind. Meanwhile, across the American plains, some masked maniac each night was taking a gun to someone's head under the American flag while the owner slept in his gated development, safely away from the people who made him rich. It's almost like, if we could keep the madness on the dark side of night shifts, maybe the dropouts would kill each other off in some evolutionary process. But I've noticed, just like in the animal kingdom of predator and prey, there is some subconscious urge to increase reproduction as numbers fall, so you get litters, not individual births. You go into any ghetto, and what you see are the offspring of the poor, or you get fertile women, like Ronny Lawton's estranged, with two children and no job living in trailers out on the plains.

The light changed again. I moved slowly. I pulled into Denny's, right beside Ronny's car. He was in there in his car. I saw his head turn, the glow of his cigarette burning. He looked at me, but his face was barely visible, just an outline. The antenna on his car was up. The controls glowed inside the car.

"We found your father's head," is what I said when I got out and stood by his car. I didn't lean into the window, said it off into the distance.

Ronny said softly, "You know, what I like about this car's radio is how you can get the Chicago stations at night."

I said again, "We found your father's head, Ronny."

Ronny hesitated. I heard him shift in the car seat. His hand squeezed the steering wheel. His voice was strained. "Why the hell does that new-car smell, smell so good?"

I waited. The cigarette traced a silent path from the steering wheel to Ronny's face. I heard Ronny sort of choke. He inhaled deeply, held things back, his head still obscured. His voice was full of spit. "I could stop the world dead right here at night and just live inside this smell, just listen to the world outside on the radio in the dark. That ain't much to ask for, is it?" Again the slow pull on the cigarette, time meted out in each deep breath. "You know, that's what me and my brother and my mother did, when it was real hot during the summer, and my old man was off on the evening shift, back when there was work to be had. We slept out in one of our junked-out cars, and we listened to life out there in Chicago. We was just kids, with our mother, just waiting on our father to come on home. We had a CB. Sometimes, my mother let us talk into it, let us speak with the truckers out there on the highway. We could just reach out in the dark and bring everything into the car." Ronny stubbed his cigarette in the ashtray and got hold of the door handle and came out into the night. He rose to an inch above me. The angular gawk of his chin and lean face searched the dark, the eyes roaming around things.

He faced me. He smelled of meat and sweat and smoke, an alchemy of sour odors, yeasty, a fermenting, sweaty fear that said he'd been waiting nervously, hiding out here, awaiting some message. That's how I felt anyway, like he'd rehearsed the things he was saying, or, if not rehearsed, then at least he had been letting the thoughts surface for the first time in ages.

He breathed on me when he spoke, pressed his finger on my chest, making me take a step back. "What I hate is when somebody looks into your life, and they don't understand what the hell it is they're seeing. It ain't the same rules with a family. We buried a kid down there in our root cellar, we got a letter about Charlie dying in Vietnam. It wasn't like we wasn't used to bad things happening to us, my old man losing his job, my mother wasting away on us. You understand what I mean just one bit? We was never lucky, that's what my mother used to say. She said some people is just born lucky, but we wasn't one of them families. She used to say there wasn't a thing you could do about it, really. When Charlie went away to Vietnam, my mother knew he wasn't coming back. I guess, so did my father. You see, we lived with that fact each day. It wasn't like he was any different. We was never lucky."

I stayed subdued but backed away slightly, to get away from the pervasive smell. He was making no real sense, just a rambling sadness.

I said, "Did you send me that note, Ronny, about your father?"

Ronny didn't answer the question. He touched the web of netting on his head, flinched slightly. His head was moving perceptibly. Then he said, "You got a note?"

"Someone told me where to find the head."

Something registered deep down inside him. He turned and looked at me.

I didn't let him infect me. "We found your father's head cut off, Ronny. Found it on a stick. Why, Ronny?"

Ronny just shook his head. He got out his pack of cigarettes and tapped the pack with the heel of his palm. His lighter flared. I saw the chiseled profile, the small, fierce eyes gleaming. Ronny dragged something from deep inside him, spat it on the ground, and scraped it with his black boot. He looked up at me. "My father used to say, 'There ain't nothing simple about simple living.' "

The parking lot smelled of oil. The radio was still going in the car. The music stopped, and over the airwaves came the late-breaking news. We stayed silent. A voice read the brief account I'd sent out on the wires, the discovery of the severed head. Then the same voice went on to the weather, told us it would burn into the nineties again today. Ronny wiped the tiredness on his face. He said nothing but looked toward Denny's.

We went across the desolate lot. The man who had weeks ago been telling the waitress how to cut away corns from her feet was in, eating a slice of yellow custard cake. He and the waitress stopped and looked askance at us, not fully turning, just stealing a look. The fluorescent light seemed to fizz and flicker. There was a small radio playing. You could tell they'd heard the news, the way they shrank from Ronny's advance, the unmistakable recoiling fear. His dominion of terror had vanished with the acknowledged savagery of the decapitated head out there in the bunker. Now that things were settled, it was all different. You could see Ronny understood that, right there and then.

Ronny got into a crescent-shaped booth. The vinyl made a flatulent sound. Ronny shouted, "I didn't goddamn fart." He shouted it so the people at the counter just shrank into their seats and didn't dare look at us. He looked at me. "If someone's going to make a goddamn seat, why the hell does it have to make that farting noise? You know what I mean?"

I said, "That's the sacrifice with vinyl. It cleans off real easy. That's what counts in the end. Efficiency. Our dignity is at the mercy of technology."

Ronny gave this bewildered look, like I should shut my mouth. It was that look that said, "Asshole, do you think I give a fuck about vinyl?" but he said nothing out loud. Ronny put his elbows on the table and just looked at me, his head moving back and forth on the thickness of his neck. The veins showed against the surface. He said, "I ain't going to say I didn't do it, 'cause you wouldn't believe me anyhow . . ."

"Did you do it?" I said softly.

Ronny looked past me, out the window to his car. He mouthed the word *no*. He showed the crooked sharpness of his teeth. He shouted, "Can we get some goddamn coffee over here? This is a goddamn restaurant, right?"

The waitress came and upturned our cups and poured the coffee to the rim. The roasted aroma steamed in each cup. The waitress said nothing, just turned and walked away. Her tips jiggled in her apron. "I get a ten percent employee discount, remember that." The waitress didn't acknowledge him.

Ronny blew over his cup. He reset himself, hunched forward like he was telling me a secret. "What I think about now is how my old man used to get my mother on the CB at night, and he'd get her to talk to the men out there in the rigs. She had a voice that made men happy. You ain't heard a woman got more ease about her, the way she could just start talking, and it seemed the world closed in, and it was only you and her. We was out there in the junked-out cars sometimes, when my old man used to just smile and feel glad for what he had. Maybe that was the closest things ever got to being normal. You could see it in my old man's face, the way he baited her, threw this line out there onto the highways, across the universe, caught the dreams of guys hauling loads across America. It was like a dream, us in the back, me and Charlie listening to the static of the CB." Ronny let his tongue come out and gather away paste on the corners of his lips. He was breathing deeply, like he was staving off things deep inside him. He lost himself in the coffee, closed his eyes, the lids coming down like two curtains. "What the hell would you say if I told you my mother used to dress us up as girls, when we was kids, I mean, when we was two and such, put us in dresses, me and Charlie. She wanted a girl real bad. That kid down in the root cellar was a girl. Maybe that's what hurt the most for my mother." Ronny shrugged his shoulders, the thick stalk of his neck a kind of suffused purple, a mat of strained veins from all the steroids. Ronny just went on talking, emptying himself of things, and I said nothing. He said, "I had a hell of a childhood. I wouldn't trade it for anything, not anything." Ronny reached for his wallet, took out a faded picture of a kid dressed in a pinafore bib with the hair tied in a bow. "What the hell do you think of that? That's me, that is. Dressed up like a girl. Can you believe it?"

There was pretty much no way of turning this conversation around. Ronny took out another, of his brother, Charlie. "We got them done down at Sears." Ronny's thick hands touched the faded colors, blanched from years of sweat, pressed against Ronny's ass. He half smiled to himself. He looked up at me. "I remember my mother brushing her hair. She used to brush her hair out every night beside me and Charlie. One hundred brushes each night is what she did. She had us keep count, me and Charlie counting to a hundred. I'd say one, and he'd say two, and I'd say three, and so on, up to a hundred. Most nights, I never got to a hundred. My eyes closed with her just brushing her hair out. That's what I think about mostly . . ." His hand came across the Formica table, gripped around my arm in a vise grip. He said in a subdued manner, bringing things to an end, "I want a running start, you hear me?"

"If you didn't do it, stay."

Ronny shook his head. "Running is all I know. I ain't giving back that car out there. It's as simple as that. It's too hard to go back to how things was. There ain't nowhere to go but down, after you've been Employee of the Month. There ain't nobody left in all my family. It's over." He looked at me. His hand reached out and gathered up the photographs. Then he stopped and pushed the picture of himself dressed as a girl toward me. "Maybe you want to use this one. Maybe you want to show that it wasn't all bad out there."

I didn't dare reach for it. Ronny pushed it toward me, like it was the last card dealt in a long game. Ronny ended things then. "Out by the bunker, right? That's where you found him?"

I nodded.

He said slowly, "There's only one other person ever knew where that bunker was." He left it at that.

Ronny looked up in the glare of fluorescent light. I saw the dark of his nostrils. His eyes closed for a moment. He set his head straight again. "I'm saying this one last time. There weren't nobody but me and her that knew that place." His head nodded for a moment, then he said again, "I want a running start . . ."

I stayed still, and Ronny got up and walked away from me. I didn't shout or anything, didn't run for the phone. Ronny didn't look back. I watched him start the roar of his Mustang, left him alone with the new-car smell, with the idling power of his V-8 engine. He threw the car into reverse, did a theatrical burnout, and disappeared onto the strip.

CHAPTER 13

There was no sign of Ronny Lawton by the time the sun rose. He was being sought for questioning. I was waiting at my house when the police came by and picked me up. I was exhausted, half-asleep by the time they knocked on the door.

I showed some detectives the note I'd received. It was taken into evidence. Ed and Sam had been questioned, corroborating the story and how we'd decided to go out and look for the head. It was just procedural bullshit.

I spent the morning out by the bunker, just waiting around. A crowd had gathered at an intersection, but they were kept back by sheriffs. The crowd had a somber look. It was a Sunday of inactivity, before football season, a dead time at summer's end. I felt like a celebrity in the back of the police car, sitting there quietly as we moved through the crowd. Linda Carter was out among the people doing the morning news. She came up to the car, and a camera focused on me. She was saying something, looking into my eyes, but I didn't lower the window, I just stared back in the camera, like a zombie. I had this somnambulant tiredness, a dream quality of slow motion.

We passed through the crowd, onto the isolated strip of road. I heard the crunch of gravel under the tires, picked out the heavy breathing of Pete up front taking us into the heart of things. He hadn't said a word to me. The car came to a slow stop. The horror of any of this murder had long passed. I had my eyes closed, leaning into the door. I opened them only occasionally. It was better to remain anonymous in all this activity. So I waited for the inevitable to unfold.

Pete went back and forth, talking and asking questions outside.

He came back and sat in the front seat, drinking coffee and talking on the CB. The car shook with his anxiousness. The mayor was pissed that I'd not contacted the authorities when I first got the note. That was the gist of what Pete told me when he decided to break the silence. Pete wanted to know where I thought Ronny might have gone. The waitress at Denny's had given a statement about our meeting. I shrugged my shoulders to Pete's questions, hid behind long exasperated breaths. I didn't tell Pete about Ronny wanting a running start. I said, "I guess he's around somewhere, Pete."

That really irked Pete. His fat face folded into a crease at his big mouth hole. He said little else to me for a bit, and then he said, "You're a loser like your father."

I didn't answer him.

"You should be locked up somewhere, you know that? It's all over town about you and Ronny's estranged. You and her out get-ting ice cream with the kid, going down and meeting her at Osco."

Again, I just stayed still and didn't answer him.

Pete just sat there with his doughnut and coffee, slurping. Pete's sidekick, Larry, that lean, spidery asshole, got in beside Pete and took his share of the doughnuts. The aroma of coffee pervaded everything. Pete said, "Don't play me for the fool, Bill."

I said, "I'm not."

The greenhouse effect inside the car made me sweat. I listened to the low murmur of voices outside. I felt the mechanism of authority working around me, felt the presence of competence, of people knowing what they were doing and doing it right.

It was a long time before things got settled. I even fell asleep for a bit. I was glad it was all coming to an end.

Pete shook me when the head was being exhumed. I sat up and yawned. Pete said, "Ed called me. He wants you back in the office soon."

I caught a look at myself in the side mirror of the police car. I was unshaven, and my hair was disheveled. I looked for all the world like a convict dragged from his bed. I got out and faced the sun, the sullen heat of another day. The morning dew was burning away fast, a sodden humidity that made your crotch and armpits moist and smelly. I stood among the ashen stalks of ruined corn, looked down the path we'd taken the previous night.

I yawned again and watched things proceed. Pete kept giving me these looks of disdain. I tried not to meet his stare.

There were dogs out sniffing the grounds. The state troopers were dressed in brown, combing the property slowly. It was strange how you become inured to all this. It was an image that was to become part of the staple footage of our news in years to come, the isolated disappearances, the vanishings, faces on milk cartons, innocent faces of kids kidnapped or murdered. You got the basic statistics: name, age, height, weight, color of the eyes. They confronted you on the most essential of our substances, on our milk. The grim reality of death greeted you as you poured milk on your cornflakes. It reminded me of that folktale of the Pied Piper of Hamelin, children stolen away.

I waited next to the car. Linda Carter moved around with her fat camera guy. You could see the crack of his ass, his trousers low on his hips, and his T-shirt riding up the girth of his big belly. Linda was moving around on high heels, a delicate walk, like someone on stilts, trying to pursue the exhumed head, her hair falling to the side of her face. She was executing this maneuver in a sherbet suit that must have cost a million bucks. I watched her with a legitimate sense of envy. She had eclipsed anything Ed or Sam or I could ever achieve, the long scissors of her legs opening and closing, the thinness of her legs, the insistent legitimacy of her concern in every shot, the candid disbelief of a woman who never quite reconciled herself to the horror of this life. She had a way of biting her lip in moments of apprehensive pause. You could see the tincture of sweat gleam under her makeup. Sometimes her nipples got hard. You wanted to say, "Linda, you're too good for all this. Don't go there! Leave that head alone!" She was the heroine of news. We lived vicariously through her beauty, that strange juxtaposition of a woman in designer clothes chasing down a severed head. I mean,

Jesus, it was like Cinderella doing an investigative report on the
Prince, on his foot fetish, or Red Riding Hood exposing the Wolf—
LIVE FOOTAGE FROM THE FOREST CARNAGE AT 10!

I was eclipsed in the new sensuality of what news meant. I felt
somehow inadequate at having received the note. If I could have
had it differently, I would have wished she had received it, maybe
concede everything to her and just vanish like those kids on the
milk cartons.

I stayed still and watched a plainclothes cop in a brown suit
move the plastic sack with the head to a van. He had weak eyes,
the loose skin around the sockets aged, two holes that had long lost
their elasticity. It took a man like this, fifties-style suit and thinning
hair, skeletal, in big shoes, former military-intelligence man, to exe-
cute this sort of grim maneuver, to exhume bodies with official
indifference, to walk toward the camera and say nothing. He had
the look of a guy who has seen the worst horrors civilians can per-
petrate on one another, an expert on psychopaths, a man who can
circumscribe a situation in one glance, label the type of mind that
has committed a murder. He was a vestige of an old world, part of
that secret society of men who took us through the Cold War, who
worked in secrecy, down in laboratories miles deep, to support the
building of bombs that could annihilate us all. Looking at him, you
intuited he would die a slow, lingering death, in retirement, the
kind of man who would regret things when disease filled his body, a
man who would look for salvation and redemption. He was the
kind of specimen I liked looking at. It's what I wanted to do most of
all, this slow character summation, the attenuated details of
human life viewed from a distance. But that wasn't a job.

You could just make out the head through the translucent plastic. It was a macabre sight that broke through the monotony and
sent a chill up my spine. Linda got in his path toward the van, but
the official had that pinched expression of absolute authority and
just brushed by Linda, leaving her in his wake. Her head was talking frantically to the camera.

The van got going, raised a cloud of dust, and disappeared. That was basically all that happened. Pete caught me yawning and just shook his head. I said, in my defense, "I haven't slept in days."

Pete stared at me frankly. "You let Ronny get away! Why? You and him have something worked out, Bill?"

I looked away from Pete. Linda had spotted me. She advanced on me, but I escaped into the back of the car and locked the door. She tapped the glass. "Is it true you were the last person to talk to Ronny Lawton?"

I just put up my hand in the sort of acknowledgment I'd seen Richard Nixon do in times of crisis, the grave but tacit acknowledgment that things were under control.

Pete got in and landed heavily in the front seat, made the car sag. He took us off the Lawton property. Up at the intersection he hit the horn and parted the crowd like a herd of animals. He was driving and looking back at me at the same time, talking through the Plexiglas partition. "You know, the way I see this, you got some stake in this that just doesn't seem right. It's a goddamn circus, all of it. What the hell are you trying to do anyway, make a name for yourself out of all this? You got together with that nut Ronny, and you're just playing this out so you can make a name for yourself. That's how I see it now. That's it, right? You're just leading that nutcase along slowly, just the way you want to. Right?"

What was the point in even answering him.

Pete was pissed. "You know, the thing is that even if you win in this rat race, you're still a rat." He turned and looked at me for a moment, then he said nothing else.

At home, I called Ed and said I was speaking to nobody. I heard Sam shouting in the background. The guy from the newspaper conglomerate was coming in later in the day to talk to Sam about the sale. They wanted me there. I said, "No!" shouted it into the phone and hung up. Then I called back and said I was sorry. Ed said the community college wanted me to give a talk on "The Role of the Media in Society." I said I'd call them.

I spent the day marooned in the confines of my basement, away from the heat. At seven o'clock *60 Minutes* came on. The small tube glowed in the dark of my basement, made me come close and listen in silence. The sound of a propeller began the segment, the chopper's instruments coming into focus, orienting viewers that we were airborne. The camera found a porthole window. It was a perfect blue sky of August heat. The lens pulled back, giving a panoramic view of land below, a flatness of fields that went on for hundreds of miles. The chopper wheeled and banked left then right, still the monotony of land, no narrative voice yet, a persistent silence, like it was hard to know how to circumscribe everything down below, the propellers droning in the background, the buffeted sound of wind way up in the sky, the gliding, shadowy mosquito of the helicopter moving across the fields like some invading creature. Then the helicopter followed the meander of our river, and finally Linda Carter's voice materialized from the drone of blades, and she spoke of how Catholic missionaries and French fur trappers had traversed the Canadian north and come down to this oxbow of river, to this great bend of the water. From this height, you could see the U, the cradle of land on which the early settlers camped in the 1800s, the dark splotch of our industrialism seen from above now. A solitary wooden cabin along the river's edge bore testimony to that first foothold on the land, then spliced footage of the cabin's interior, the camera lingering over the sparse economy, stopping to observe aged traps and leather boots, fur caps, snowshoes, a gun, a small pouch of gunpowder and fat metal shot used by the early settlers.

Then out from that dim world again for the panorama of blue sky, but now the footage was of the old foundry yards, the helicopter coming low on some reconnaissance mission, collecting data, the camera running like some Vietnam footage, jarred and immediate, taken under fire, behind enemy lines, swooping over the parking lots snared in barbed wire, dark slabs of cracked concrete like abandoned concentration camps, the yawning doors of massive furnaces ajar and dark in gutted buildings. There was a superimposed ghost of workers at machines, the din of noise, black-and-white still shots of workers. And only then, when our history had been clearly delineated, did the helicopter footage fade to gray.

What materialized in its wake was Ronny Lawton's old man's property, the ramshackle domain of broken-down cars and grass gone to seed, the hideout of a refuge from our disaster. Like in those old movies with titles and credits spinning out from a vortex, came my headlines, the abbreviated and succinct horror of what had gone on here. Then, some visible dealer dealt blanched Polaroid shots of Lawton family members to the screen, early shots of Ronny on a baby blanket lying flat on his stomach, aged one year, bare-assed and grinning, reaching with small baby hands . . . Another in a bathtub with a rubber duck, suds on his chin . . . On a tricycle in shorts . . . Pulling a puppy in a Radio Flyer wagon . . . His brother, Charlie, with a fishing rod and a string of fish on a line, looking proud and happy . . . The boys out with their father, playing base-ball in the fall . . . Ronny Lawton's mother taking a cake out of the oven . . . Charlie in military uniform . . . A shot of the letter of his death in the line of duty . . . Ronny with a tattoo of an eagle on his forearm, one of him flexing down in his gym, dark and brooding, a shot of the handwritten sign "Get Big," the American flag behind him . . . Ronny Lawton's old man in a flannel jacket with a steel lunch box in hand beside his truck in a wintry background of heavy snowfall . . . He was waving with the other hand. The camera focused on that hand, on the small finger until it was transformed into a tagged piece of evidence, the piece of finger found at the house. The question was simply put, at the end of this pictorial odyssey, "Where is Ronny Lawton's father?"

After a commercial break, Ronny was in a tank top out at his house, describing his childhood. Linda was sitting across from him in a short-sleeved cotton shirt that showed the roundness of her breasts. "I ain't goin' to say me and my ol' man were friends. We never was. He drank real heavy. He took cigarettes and used to push them into my arm. You see here, Linda." Ronny raised his arm, the bush of his armpit glistening. You could intuit its sour odor. "Right along the inside of my arm there, so nobody would see 'em." Linda leaned toward the clump of armpit hair. It was unnerving, sensual.

She took hold of Ronny's wrist, held the arm up, like he'd just won a prizefight, and just shook her head at the camera. There was a trail of dark splotches where Ronny's arm had been burned.

At Linda's request, Ronny went on and talked about the baby down in the cellar, because they had footage of that grim excavation. He explained how things like that happened out there on the plains, how secrets were just buried and not talked about. "We didn't call for no doctor. We didn't call for no minister. It never breathed. We just kept it to ourselves was all. My father baptized it, like he knew was the way. He had the words for it to settle its soul. I bet you dig up any basement round here and you're going to find some kid that didn't make it."

Linda wanted to know about his past, his time in the military. He gave a long answer, ended saying, "I'm proud to have served my country. I sort of feel maybe it's what people despise about me, Linda. I don't know why, but I feel it in my bones."

I watched the lurid ape-man, Ronny Lawton, that bulging aggressor just posturing before Linda Carter, leaning into the table when he got intense. He spoke about his brother and what he called "the Lost Days," the same thing he'd intimated to me about living in the days when his brother was dead and them not knowing. That genuinely affected him. "It's like that sunlight out there, Linda." He pointed to a window framing the blue sky. Then he stared into the camera. "They tell me that light there left the sun eight minutes ago. We are all really looking into the past. If the sun died, we wouldn't even know it, really, not for eight minutes anyways. It was like that with my brother, us just doing stuff and him dead all that time." Ronny stopped dead still and just stared into the camera. "We all put our life on the line for this country." Then he put his hand to the camera, broke down in tears, shied away, snorting, "I ain't guilty, Linda. I ain't. I ain't always been a good man, but I ain't no killer." The segment ended with a silent shot that left Ronny and went roaming to the edge of the basement darkness, suggesting unimaginable horrors.

The claustrophobia of the house was abandoned for a walk

down by the river, by the scent bed for the blind, a place nobody
went anymore because drunks and dealers lurked in the aromatic
bushes. The tall skeletal apparatus of our industrialism lurked in
the background, the prehistoric assemblage of cranes and scaffolding. Linda and a camera followed Ronny as he tried to walk away.
Something had been said that we had not been privy to. It was like
an outtake that had been salvaged from discarded footage. Whatever the premise behind this walk, it was completely lost. Linda
touched Ronny's arm. It was like they weren't aware of the camera.
Ronny stopped and shouted, "No!" He had the latent potential to
be interesting. You had to give him that much credit. The inset of
pale eyes, an intensity that suggested rough sex, a man who beat
women. He went down to the river's edge and threw stones into
the river. Linda was stumbling behind him, a moment of sudden
impact. She twisted her ankle, and you wanted to shout for her to
just stop humiliating herself.

The water level was low down where Ronny was, the banks
caked in cracked, pale brown mud. Linda got down to Ronny, she
sort of pleaded, called his name over and over again, until he
turned and glared at her.

"Did you kill your father, Ronny?"

He turned and came up the bank, shored up the distance
between them, went to her and the camera and said softly, "No,
Linda." All you could do while watching it was think, if Ronny had
her alone, he'd rape her and cut her throat. The camera contem-
plated that idea for us, showed the slit of Linda's skirt and her long
legs and then back to Ronny's muscular torso, sweating in the glare
of light. Linda and Ronny promised a latitude of sexual tension
that kept you watching. She was an innuendo made flesh. It was
her uncanny ability to put her soft body into compromising posi-
tions that set her apart from anything a man might have achieved
with Ronny Lawton. After all, we were learning nothing from any
of this, a vacuous report that gained its impetus solely in her willingness to get close to Ronny's hard body. The question was sub-
liminally there, what if he went mad and fucked her? She had

transcended the story she was covering. She was the story as much as Ronny.

At Denny's there was a segment on what the kids thought, kids jumping up and down in the glare of the light. They all loved Ronny! They had Ronny masks, grainy blowups of a newspaper photograph, the semblance of gray and white dots approximating the shape and appearance of Ronny Lawton. A carload of Ronny Lawtons pulled up in a station wagon, all in tank tops. They rallied around Linda's beauty. Their grotesqueness made her all the more beautiful, the surreal aspect of their unflinching masks bearing Ronny's military atavistic stare. Linda moved the microphone from mask to mask, like she was asking them to lick a lollipop, the damsel of the despicable, the queen of horror.

The quick juxtaposition of shots, the cumulative effect of his mania, aroused a new fear just watching it on the television. Ronny Lawton was omnipresent, a marauding force, a mood of agitation. A minister was seen out in a field with his congregation in the hotness of a Sunday afternoon, the human chain's insatiable desire to find something, to prove its collective worth, singing hymns against evil.

Back at Denny's the footage showed Ronny with the solitary sect of loners at the ungodly hour of 4 A.M. The camera lingered on the slow second hand. Then the camera found the plaque for Employees of the Month, showed the engraved carving of Ronny Lawton's name.

Then the camera found Ronny again, solemnly cutting up onions and green peppers. It silently answered his detractors, saying simply, "Yes, the man works his ass off." Ronny never even looked up at the camera, kept a candid attention to the fine chopping. The camera focused on the diced onions, then rose, and Ronny Lawton's eyes were tearing. Linda came into the picture. Ronny was crying. She put her soft hand on his hairy fist and said something into his ear. Then the camera panned back, I mean all the way back, out beyond the small porthole from where he set the orders, out the window of Denny's and across the road, where it

238   *Michael Collins*

settled on the aquarium of light that was Denny's. I just kept staring at the television.

White letters on a black screen ended everything, the printed
update that stated simply:

> Ronny Lawton's father's head was exhumed from a tornado
> bunker on the family's ancestral property this morning . . .
>
> Ronny Lawton has not been seen since the exhumation . . .

Ronny's estranged called later. She wanted to see me. She was
afraid Ronny was coming after her is what she said.

"How do you know that?" I said it abruptly.

She cried into the phone. That alarmed me, because now I was
thinking the police might have tapped my line, that they were
thinking I knew where Ronny was hiding.

I went down to Osco under cover of dark. Ronny's estranged
was working the cash register. I went over to her. She was inside
that aura of rose scent I had got from inside the envelope containing the note. I said without emotion, "You want to see me?" She
had another fifteen minutes on shift. I went outside and waited in
the lot.

Everywhere around me, I kept thinking Ronny was lurking. I
turned around and looked across the lot at empty cars. Nothing, no
sign of that Mustang.

Then Ronny's estranged came out and invaded the evening
with her smile. She got in beside me and kissed me on the side of
my face.

I staved off any reaction. "That scent you're wearing, roses,
where did you get it?"

She tried to touch me, began to smile. "You don't like it?"

I held her hand, moved it away from me. "I'm serious. Tell me!"

She retracted her hand. "Don't you start hitting me!" She raised
her voice, like she was about to scream.

I said, "Listen to me." I squeezed her arm. "Stop, do you hear me?"

She began sniffling, leaned away into the door. I said again, "Teri, listen to me. Where did you get that perfume?"

"Darlene gave me a deal on this special she has. I got her to go out and take Karl's pickup and wash it up for him. When he came home, he said he found the perfume in the car. I guess she left it there or something."

The association between Darlene and Karl just fell into place.

I said, "This is real important, now." I put my hand to her cheek, rubbed against it with my thumb. "Do you ever remember telling Darlene anything about you and Ronny out by the bunker?"

Ronny's estranged shrugged her shoulders. "I don't know, Bill. I've been going to her so long. I don't exactly remember, but maybe I did, I just don't know."

I didn't push her after that. I let her soft warmth press up against me. Time passed slowly. She smoked a cigarette, curled the hair back from her face behind her ear. "I think Ronny's going to come and get me. I know him, Bill."

I shifted and rubbed the softness of her face. "How come you think he wants to get you, if he killed his father? I don't get that."

She hesitated at that, then shrugged her shoulders, said, "'Cause he's crazy is why, Bill."

It wasn't an answer. Why hadn't he gone after her already? But I said nothing for a good while, let her settle and looked up into the dark sky. There was such solitude in these dead nights of silence. It was part of a world in which I had come to find solace, maybe like Ronny had, listening to the radio or talking on the CB when he was a kid. I told Ronny's estranged about what Ronny had told me. "You ever hear him talk about that?"

Ronny's estranged sat up and leaned against her door. "Yeah, that's what we did when we had no money. We went out far into the fields, and Ronny killed the engine, and we listened to the radio up in Chicago count down the top ten songs of the day." She stopped after that, just stared at me. She'd been sitting on her legs. Now she unfolded them and sat straight. She looked directly at me. "You don't think Ronny killed his father. I can see it in your eyes, Bill."

Michael Collins

I shook my head. "Maybe I did think he killed his father, but not after finding that head out there in the bunker. He told me only you and he knew about the bunker."

Ronny's estranged made this noise of agitation with her nails, a clicking like some insect. "So why the hell is he running now, Bill? It don't always have to add up in life. He beat me, Bill. He broke my nose, and he said he loved me the next day! I know him, Bill. I know what they done to me, Bill, Ronny and his father. I got nothing at all, Bill, nothing." She got out of the car and slammed the door, started across the lot.

I shouted to her. I got out and went over to her. She was up against the wall of Osco, crying. She leaned into me. She took my fingers and put them to her nose where it had been broken. She whispered, "He beat me bad, Bill. I don't want him coming after me. I don't . . ."

That sullen feeling of loneliness invaded me again, that impoverished need for human touch. Her face turned up toward me. She smelled of tears. It was probably what I'd wanted all along, this languid romance, coming down like this to let myself become ensnared. I leaned and kissed her, full on the lips, that same falling sensation of wanting to be held that came over me when I was with Diane. She took my hand that had felt her broken nose, and she put it on her pelvis, held it and slowly moved it lower. I crawled toward that destination, a nebulous sense of regret at the back of things, unwilling to stop. She moaned into my ear, said she wanted to be with me. I felt her bite into my neck, flinched, felt her mark me again. I felt the tenseness of her legs as they wrapped around me, concentrated on the slow invasion of longing, felt my own legs stiffen and support her weight. I moved my head back from her face, and that's when I saw her eyes were open wide, staring into the dark obscurity of my own face. And I couldn't help thinking of Ronny Lawton out there beyond us, that sullen misfit in his Mustang, out in some field, hunkered down, listening to sound coming across space.

CHAPTER 14

By the time I got home, Ronny's estranged had left a message on the machine. It said, simply, "It felt good having you inside me." There was a pause, then, "I need that house real bad, Bill." I crawled under the blankets and slept, as had become my custom now.

By morning, Sam was on the phone to me with the report that Ronny was still missing. He hadn't showed for his shift at Denny's. The days just burned away, and things had turned ominous on me. The uncovering of the head had heightened tension, made this case take on a sudden immediacy.

I got a call at the house. Two FBI guys wanted to interview me downtown. I called Sam, told him I was going in for questioning.

I was worked over down at the courthouse by the FBI guys, questioned about my association with Ronny Lawton, about my trips all along to see him at Denny's. There was a suspicion I was harboring him, which I gathered Sam and Ed had blown out of proportion, because they wanted to intimate more connection and control of this association, since it made us look more professional, like we had good contacts. It helped with the sale of the paper. What I gathered from the FBI was that Sam and Ed said I was in tight with Ronny Lawton. They told about me playing the Duke Ellington music back at my house. That seemed to lead the FBI to believe that I had vicariously attached myself to Ronny Lawton, that I had come under his sway.

It was hard under the pressure of light down there in the inter-rogation room, the same room I'd seen Ronny in way back at the beginning of all this, the base treatment of questions being rammed down your throat. "Harboring a fugitive is a crime!" is what this FBI guy shouted at me. They called it misplaced sympathy.

I tried to explain my situation, how I was just following the story the only way I knew how, but it was no good. We sat around drinking coffee, and the FBI guys took turns coming and going from the room. I stared at the glass and knew there were people staring at me. It was unnerving as hell. I shouted at the glass, "Sam, you out there? Set them straight about this shit! Sam!"

It's hard not to play the part of a psychopath when it's forced on you. I had to keep myself from shouting. I went and sat down again, took deep breaths.

The issue of the note was of primary concern. Who did I think gave it to me? I said I didn't know, but they pressed at me. The lettering had been analyzed, and according to expert analysis, it had come from our own paper. There was a flaw in the printing press that made our *h* have a splotch. I said, "There's only one goddamn newspaper in town. Why wouldn't it come from our paper?" That kind of defiance didn't sit well with the FBI guys. They had me linked up with Ronny somehow, complicit in his madness.

They had a sheet on my past medical problems, namely my breakdown. They wanted to know what I thought about my father, what I thought about my dog that got poisoned. That had been the central issue, back then in college, when things went haywire, my inability to reconcile myself to my father poisoning the dog. Then we got on to Diane. How the hell they knew I was calling her, I don't know. Maybe I had been tapped all along. I felt the fear and embarrassment of what I'd said to her, the pleading for her love, the screaming of the LSAT questions into the phone. It crippled me into humility. Had I, in any way, conspired with Ronny Lawton to make that note, to try and bring things to a resolution, to play this for my own professional end?

I shook my head. "No!" I shouted. I shouted that with all the indignation I could muster.

Again the question, who did I think sent me that note about the head?

"I don't know," is all I offered, said it in this submissive way. I conceded in the end that Ronny had probably sent it to me. I didn't exactly say it. The question was posed, and I agreed it might have been him. I wanted to tell them what Ronny's estranged had said about being raped by Ronny's old man. That was motive right there, how Ronny had his suspicions that the kid wasn't really his. Maybe it had come to a head in a fight, the old man admitting somehow what he'd done, saying it when he was drunk or something. But it just didn't seem like it was anything the old man was ever going to mention. So I said nothing, just felt the bewildering sense of fear creep over me. I was thinking of Pete and the shears, and what if he went and told the FBI I had them buried out by my house. How the hell was I going to explain any of it?

They left me alone for a bit, under the glare of light. I calmed down somewhat. Then I settled on that lingering encounter with Ronny's estranged, repeated those simple declarative words, "It felt good having you inside me." That was less than two days ago, that slow, anguishing release against the wall.

I was released from questioning. Pete was outside, sitting at a table with Ed. Pete looked up at me and then walked away.

Ed extracted his bony body from the small metal chair and came toward me. I could tell he'd watched the whole investigation unfold, a silent witness on my behalf from the newspaper. It had all been voluntary. I had submitted to the questions to clear the air.

Outside, the weather had broken into a gray movement of cloud, the slow turning of an approaching storm, something we hadn't seen all summer. It had come out of the north, across the Great Lakes, a useless rain that was coming too late.

"It's better that you cleared the air in there like you did, Bill. You've been on top of this all the time. You made the connections with Ronny and his wife. You followed this all the way. You got her to tell you about the bunker. And so, you got the idea of making up the note. Then we arrived, just out of the blue, and before you even had time to figure if you were going to go through with pretending you got the note sent to you, you felt trapped and had to just do it."

I couldn't answer that.

Ed looked at me. "Pete and me had it figured. We're not going to say anything, Bill. I said to Pete that you did this for Sam, really. You wanted to see Sam off-load the paper for a reasonable price, send him out with one last scoop . . ." Ed put his hand on my shoulder. "Nobody's going to say anything about what you did, Bill. We're all saying Ronny Lawton sent you the note, or his estranged. That's how we're playing it." Ed finished talking and said, "You see, when you start a stone rolling, it's hard to stop it. Things just got too big too fast on you."

It was strange, the way Ed dissociated himself from me in that casual manner, this humbling acknowledgment that it was my doing, all this investigation, my sense of duty, trying to rescue Sam. For a brief moment, I saw it differently. I saw the grim conspiracy of Ed and Darlene and Sam all together plotting this murder, but it was only a passing thought, something that was eclipsed in just knowing those two men, knowing what they'd been through over the past decades.

Ed put his hand on my shoulder. "I wasn't to mention this, but Pete told me they've got your phone tapped. They got Ronny's estranged speaking with you about the house, how she wants it." Ed looked at me. "You sure Ronny never called you at home?"

I said, "No." I felt stunned, the thread of implication, the long tendrils of association with each of them since all this started. I probably seemed pathetic, a plaything between Ronny and his estranged.

The late morning turned a dark green color, the sun obliterated in the clouds. The temperature just plummeted, air sodden. A downdraft swept dust in small eddying spires. It was the beginning of the late-season storms.

We made it only as far as a coffee shop across from the courthouse before all hell broke loose. We came in from the lashing rain and sat near the window and just watched the rain without speaking. The FBI guys came out and stood on the steps of the courthouse, stayed there, like they were thinking about making a dash for it. Pete was with them. He was pointing at the coffee shop where we were. All of a sudden, they were rushing down the steps, coming toward us. I gripped the ear of my cup. It was like they had uncovered something, like they were coming to get me. Ed watched them running, his eyes moving in his head. He turned his head right around when they came into the diner, soaked.

Pete saw Ed staring. Pete averted his eyes, and he and the FBI guys took a table in the back. I let out an audible sigh of relief.

It kept raining for going on half an hour more. It was awkward to think about going out into the rain, so I stayed put. "Any chance of Sam getting anything from that newspaper conglomerate?"

Ed seemed like he was off in another world. Outside sizzled in falling rain. He looked at me, said, "What's that, Bill?"

"The paper, Ed. Is Sam going to get a good deal on selling it?"

Ed looked at me. "The way Sam tells it, he's got one foot in the grave and another on a banana peel. I don't think Sam knows much of what he wants anymore. He just wants out, plain and simple. The money just isn't there. That's what this guy's been telling Sam. All the guy is really buying is the sports section. Everything else comes from a boilerplate. The guy doesn't even want to keep the name of our paper. It's really just a buyout, to make us stop putting out our paper. So you see, in the end, we're being paid off to stop doing something, paid to cease to exist."

The waitress came and refilled our cups. She had some comment about the rain coming too late. It was the kind of comment that was going to go around all day, a melancholy assessment of a ruined summer. Our breaths had fogged the window, obscured the outside world in a dull onionskin film. The diner was filled up with a din of noise, people eating BLT sandwiches, the special of the day, and cream of potato soup. Ed read down the menu but ended up ordering the special.

"You ever taste the mayonnaise here, Bill?"

"No."

I wasn't much of a conversationalist when it came to talking shit. That was one of my main failings in life. As a matter of fact, it's up there in the top three. I got that from my father, the stiff silence and pauses that made people uncomfortable around me.

Ed had always seen me for what I was, or that's how I liked to think of our relationship. He said, in midthought, "That's the thing about eating out. It tastes different somehow, from the simplest meal on upward. I think maybe we all like to be served, when it comes down to it."

I said, "Ed, I think it may be far greater than just that. You take the dissolution of churches and community, and where the hell are people supposed to gather together? Collective feeding is hardwired into us from way back in our evolution. You take Christianity, for instance. Wasn't it really conceived around the table, the Last Supper, the partaking of bread and wine? You take a business lunch, and what you have is the secularization of that first Communion."

Ed raised his eyes in what amounted to an abiding appreciation for the kind of bullshit I can spew on most subjects. Shit on it, maybe I was crazy.

Ed dug into the BLT, squeezed out the obscene mayonnaise, and just ate. Ed blew the steam off his coffee after the meal, ate a slice of mud pie, and I ordered coconut cream. I got my appetite back for something sweet.

Ed looked at me. "The best thing we can hope for now is to find Ronny hanging from a tree somewheres. That's what the FBI guys think might be the case. A guy goes as far as he can, then he cracks. He either blows his head off, or hangs himself. They got profiles of how these things turn out in the end. That's what Pete was telling me."

I ate the pie with a fork, bit into the coconut flakes on top of the cream. It tasted good. It was the kind of thing you might really miss in prison, like if your freedom was taken away from you. As you got older, you began to understand that food was sublimation for so many different things, a thing to retreat into.

Ed was eating and drinking his coffee, and so was everybody else, a quiet oblivion of easy living, hidden away from the rain, just easing into life, into a new season, anticipating the fall of leaves, the beginning of the high-school football season and the fall festivals. I leaned forward in my chair. I said quietly, "Ed, as long as I live, I'm never going to believe Ronny cut his father's head off like that. I'm just not."

Ed held a slice of mud pie on the end of his fork. He said, "Maybe you just got too close to him, Bill. It's hard for anybody who's sane to imagine what goes on inside a guy like that's head." And then he said, "And does it really matter in the end anyways? I figure, that's a whole family that was better off dead." His lips came around the fork, and he ate in silence.

By the next interminable cup of coffee, my eyes were watering with boredom. The diner had become claustrophobic, the heat from the grill an inferno. Ed had to excuse himself for his usual retreat to the toilet. He was gone ages. I got up, and there he was at the public phone. I watched his back as he nodded and spoke. I went and sat down again, felt paranoid.

Ed came back and unscrewed the cap from his bottle of Pepto-Bismol, took a long drink of that chalky pink liquid. He made a wincing face as he eased out from the table. He said, "I got a new one for you, straight from Darlene. 'Retirement: Twice as much husband, half as much money!' I'd say that pretty much says it all, right there." He got up with that and repeated what he'd just said to a waitress, who said, "That's not bad. I like that." Homegrown philosophy was like a contagion.

In the end, I was left paying the bill for both of us.

I caught a glimpse of Pete eating over in a booth with the FBI guys. He didn't see me. I heard them laughing among themselves. Everything had taken on a provincial smallness, a petty world of whispering voices, men huddled in talk, speaking under their breath. It was, of course, my own sense of things, the dull aftermath of the interrogation, if you could call it that, really. What had the FBI done, except to try to get me to clarify what the hell I'd been doing? Maybe it was just the idea of having the phone tapped that unnerved me. Then again, I had nothing to hide. Except for those goddamn shears.

It was much cooler outside the diner. The sun had emerged in the aftermath of the storm, breaking through the dark silver clouds. The air smelled fresh, like you could breathe again. The whole world shone. It was blinding, made us put our hands to our brows.

I went with Ed to the office. Sam put his arm around me in a fake patriarchal manner, a sense of overfamiliarity he had always maintained over me. I knew something was being asked of me. I felt the deflated softness of his weakened muscles float under his polyester shirt. He smelled old and of aftershave. "Where is Ronny hiding, Bill? You know, right? Let's just end this now. I know the reasons behind what you did with the note, Bill. But it's time to just end this. Where is Ronny, Bill?"

It's amazing how I was now the author of that note, how it was a foregone conclusion that I'd rigged the note based on Ronny's estranged telling me about the bunker. I mean, there was no arguing it.

I said, in a low, controlled voice, "I wish I knew, Sam. I really wish I knew." I left it at that, and Sam took his hand off my back and said, "Bill, it's over, face it. Whatever you thought you were doing to help me has gone to hell in a handbasket now. It's common news, Bill, that you and Ronny's estranged have been playing this out too long."

Ed was working a toothpick in his mouth, dislodging food, pretending to take little interest in things. But he was there all the same, there like he always was. He stopped and got something onto his tongue and held it there, inspected it, then ate it again.

My head was soaked in sweat. I wiped my face with the back of my hand.

Sam said, "Take time to sort this out, Bill. But not too long." He turned and got a pad of paper that had a list of things that needed to be taken care of, newspaper stuff. He looked at me. "We still got a paper to run here. How about you think about how the hell you want to end this while doing a little work?" Sam looked at me. "We got a special we need to get out on Cass High School and Rogers Tech. I got the coaches' names here. You think you're up to getting on this today? It'll give you time to think about things. All right? Cass has got a team picture at three o'clock this afternoon. This might be the year they go all the way to the state finals."

I looked at Sam. "That's what they say every year."

Sam stared at me across the desk. "It's about believing, Bill. That's what this business is about, more than anything else, believing in the goodness of humanity."

Ed nodded his head. "You can't live otherwise in this world. We got twenty teams out in this county, and all of them believe they're winners. That's the way it's got to be."

I sure as hell didn't know where the hell that came out of, that sudden magnanimity, putting things into focus, that veneer of philosophical understanding. But I didn't say shit. All I said was, "Yeah, sure." I took the names from his desk.

Sam said, "You got it all right, until you let Ronny walk away, Bill. There isn't anybody here doesn't think you did a hell of a job breaking Ronny. But it's like in baseball, Bill. I was watching a game the other night. The Cardinals had a pitcher who threw seven great innings. Then he started losing it, wild balls, put a runner out on third. So they sent in a relief pitcher, Bill."

Ed said, "I saw that game."

I said, "I guess you're right."

It was drizzling outside the window. I heard water falling in the drains, that lugubrious slurred sound.

Sam was cooking another of his tuna melts. Smoke was rising from the toaster. "How about one for the road, Bill." He smiled at me. "I changed my sauce slightly. I want to see if you notice."

I said, "Sure, Sam."

Sam went behind his desk, masked things in a long yawn, and then pushed a paper toward me, the preliminary details of the settlement with the newspaper guy. I knew as much. Sam looked at me. "We don't got to go into this right now, but maybe you'd want to look at what I'm proposing for you." His eyes veered to Ed, who stared back. Then Sam opened the toaster oven door, and a wave of heat poured out over us. Sam cut through the tuna melt. He got

chips and set them on a plate beside the sandwich and put everything down before me. "I think it was Napoleon that said, 'An army
marches on its belly.' "

I swallowed and said, "I think it was, Sam." I said, "I think you're
right about that."

I felt myself tense. I looked at the contract, at the part that concerned me. It was a sum of money not worth mentioning. There
was note of my dedication, but my inexperience, the length of my
employment, was underlined. It amounted to a negligible contribu-
tion against what Sam and Ed had done over the years. I was willing to concede that. There was no provision for continuing with
the new paper, not that I wanted that, but its omission struck me.
"Do I have to sign anything now?" is what I got out of my mouth.

Sam didn't answer the question. He said, "A guy like you has a
great future."

"I'll look it over, Sam, okay?"

Sam winked at me. "This is where we're at is all. I got a meeting
tomorrow morning to continue discussing what will happen. You
got any concerns, you let me know."

I said, "Sure, Sam. Don't you let the *Truth* go cheap, you hear?" I
steadied myself, tried the magnanimous tact. "You hold out for
what the *Truth* is worth, you hear me? Both of you." I could say
nothing else.

Sam said, "I love this kid, Ed."

There were a bunch of legal notices piled in the in-box, along
with material from retirement homes in Florida. Sam caught my
eye looking at them.

"How about I get on these legal notices?" and Sam said, "Sure,
but we kind of need to get that stuff ready on the football. And
Ronny Lawton, you think about how this might end, Bill. Okay?"
He reached across the desk and took my hot hand in his.

I didn't meet his stare, looked down at the desk instead, down at
a brochure. It was an image of a gray-headed guy in panama shorts
lining up a putt against a backdrop of white-sand beach and blue

sky, that ethereal bleed of colors, the dreamscape of the retiree, the hemorrhage of longing. I called that kind of blue "retirement blue," almost celestial. Florida was a launching pad to Limbo.

Sam rubbed his temples. "We got a lot of stuff to get out here, Ed. You think you can work late on this with me?"

Ed nodded.

I did the interviews out at the high school, the same monotony of another long season, guys with their heads shaved military-style as always. The cheerleaders were practicing on the track, the accordions of their skirts opening and closing with each high kick. It had turned out to be a warm day. I waited on the bleachers. Ed showed for the team photograph, and we left together. We hardly exchanged a word. All he said was, "When can we expect to see Ronny?"

I didn't answer him.

We went back to the office. Sam was working on the legal notices. Ed went down to develop his pictures. I finished the report on the team.

Ed and Sam were eating tuna melts and potato chips at the editorial desk. I looked in on them. Sam looked up and said, "I wish the hell none of this had ever happened."

I arrived out at Ed's house. There were cars parked out on the road. Darlene was busy as hell. She was pissed when I came through her parlor door, but she masked it with a smile. I said, "I hate doing this to you, Darlene, but I need a haircut bad."

The room went all quiet when I came in, like I'd invaded the last enclave of femininity. It was an intoxicating world of hair spray, perfume, bleach, nail polish, and hair coloring. Each woman had a magazine in her hands. It was like a toxic dumping ground of female inadequacy in there. The getaway destination scene of Hawaii had been pulled down, giving the illusion of travel, like everyone was crowded on a strip of a black-sand beach. It was eerie. A sticker on one of the mirrors said "The One-Hour Vacation." In the corner, I saw a small shrine of flowers, and, shit, if it wasn't Gretchen down there in a small basket, all curled up, recovering from her false miscarriage.

Darlene said, "How about I do you out in the kitchen, Bill?"

I said, "Sure."

Darlene went to make some adjustments on her clients. There were three women under those big domed dryers, all lined up with their heads invisible. It was like something out of a space-alien lab where the aliens were siphoning off the memories of the earthlings. I said that to the women, but they didn't laugh or anything. They had that look of impatience, like I was an invader.

Darlene took me out to the kitchen.

I said, "Gretchen doing all right, Darlene?" I tried to show a level of interest.

Darlene said, "She's taking it bad." It was a curt answer, a way of telling me to keep out of things. Darlene was all business. She put me in a smock, set a towel around my neck, stuffed it with tissue paper and gave me a magazine, all without so much as a word, except to ask how I wanted my hair.

I said, "Maybe you could just do what you think I need. Maybe just a trim is all."

It was hard to figure out how to get to any point of accusation, what with the physical size of Darlene circling me with a pair of scissors.

The doorbell rang. Darlene left and then came in again. "I got to get Melissa started first, Bill."

"Sure thing."

I paged through the magazine for a few tenuous minutes, and in that time, I was confronted by an array of knowledge: how to make a man want you, a recipe for pineapple upside-down cake, how to achieve multiple orgasm, how to make a home potpourri, the ten ways to know a man loves you, the three signs that a man's been cheating on you, and how to open your own business and achieve financial independence.

Shit, it was like finding the opposing team's playbook. You got a sense of the adversarial nature of sexuality. It was the kind of magazine that Diane read sometimes, with its fucked-up imperative to be both sexy and smart. You got a feeling, inside these pages, that feminist liberation was fighting it out with fairy-tale Rapunzels up in ivory towers.

Somehow, these editors had eclipsed language, not just with pictures. They had gone intuitively to our sense of smell, perfume samples on different pages, scratch-and-sniff pads, a sample swatch of lip gloss like a weeping wound that had been peeled away by a previous client.

Darlene came back in, brandishing the scissors. She turned up the radio, so it was loud. She set a kitchen timer down on the table. "I got a color going inside, Bill. I got to hurry. I don't do men like this." She took a spray bottle and wet my hair, running a comb through it.

I put the magazine down and just started right in. I said, "How come you never told us Ronny's estranged was raped by his father?"

Darlene kept spraying and combing. "Who says I knew, Bill?" I felt the teeth of the comb against my scalp. The radio was playing loud over what we said.

"Come on, Darlene. First you never mentioned that you even knew Ronny's estranged, and then I find out she's told you all the shit that's happened to her out there at the Lawtons'. She told you she was raped, and she told you about that bunker where her and Ronny went."

Darlene kept it simple. "You got anything else you want to accuse me of withholding?"

"You don't think that's a hell of a lot of stuff to say nothing about? It's not like you aren't involved in this, with Ed being at the paper. You could have helped us out, real early in this, to understand what we were dealing with. I have to ask myself why you decided to say nothing."

Darlene took a spray bottle again and made this hissing noise over my head. She kept to the business of cutting hair. Her big hand took my jaw, and she pivoted my head to the left. I waited for her to say something, but all she said was, "You want the hair above the ears, or not?"

"Don't cut it too tight. Leave it over the ears." Jesus, I shouldn't have had her cut my hair at all. Next thing, she said, "You got a cowlick, Bill, right at your crown, you know that? And I see some gray down at the roots. You got a history of premature graying in your family, Bill?"

I didn't move my head. All I said was, "It seems you know a hell of a lot about the relationship between Ronny and his estranged, and you've decided to say nothing about it. I've been counting it out in my head, who the hell knew about that bunker: you, me, Ronny and his estranged, Karl maybe, that about does it." I stopped and hesitated to threaten her, but then I said, "I'm not beyond getting you brought in for questioning in all this, Darlene. I know you had an opportunity to get with Karl, when you did that Car Theft on him."

Darlene said matter-of-factly, "God, you have no sense of the law at all. No wonder you're not going to get into any law school, with logic like that, Bill."

It was another moment of revelation that Ed must have said something about me. They were laughing at me behind my back.

Darlene set her big painted face before me, combed down the front of my hair and started cutting.

I was nervous now about things, especially my hair. There was a lot of it on the ground. "I only want a trim, Darlene. I want hair coming down on my forehead. Don't cut it too short, you hear?"

Darlene got all sweet. "Bill, it's just like this. I hear so much in this line of work, it just goes in one ear and out the other. It's a professional hazard, people telling me things. That's why I got a rule, a simple rule. I don't ever repeat what I hear, because if you lose the trust of your clients, you won't make it in this business." She stopped and said real sternly, "This is as sacred as a confessional, Bill. I'm no different than a Catholic priest, when you think about it."

I tensed up on the kitchen chair, felt things getting away from me. The kitchen timer was getting down to three minutes to go, the incessant clicking noise. It was hard to say exactly what I was thinking, the scheme I had in my head of how maybe Darlene had put it in such a way to Karl that Ronny's estranged was getting nothing of the house unless things got settled somehow . . . I just stopped dead right there. It was bullshit conjecture, unfounded, all of it.

Darlene got the hairdryer and started styling my hair, just blowing everything away in that current of hot air. I never even got to see how my hair turned out. Darlene sprinkled some talcum powder around my neck. She took the smock off me with the flourish of a bullfighter, snapping it to get the hair off. What she did say was, "You really want to tell anybody that Teri's kid is a bastard? You want the kid to know that, as he grows up, that his mother was raped by her father-in-law?"

I didn't answer her. The timer went off.

Darlene went down the hallway. I stayed to pay her. Darlene was talking up a storm down in the parlor, all uproarious fun down there.

Darlene emerged again. I think maybe she'd been doing some thinking. She looked at me. "You don't understand a damn thing about life, do you?"

I just looked back at her, a vacant stare.

"What you're doing now is using Teri, just like Ronny and Ronny's old man and Karl and all them others out there. You know, Karl has himself another woman. He wants no part of Teri and her kid. Teri got nothing out of this, nothing."

It was a weird way she looked into me, like she hated me for being a man.

Darlene pushed me toward the door. "You know what it's like to be raped, Bill, what it did to Teri? I was here for her. We all were, out here." It was maybe at that exact moment I felt the presence of the women there in the hallway, listening to what Darlene was saying. "It was common knowledge with women around here what happened to Teri, what was done to her."

I swear to God, I felt threatened by that collection of middle-aged women, the way they stared at me, there in the kitchen. Darlene was still holding the scissors. I was thinking, Jesus Christ, they might kill me. I mean, there was something deeply conspiratorial in the way they gathered there around me. Jesus Christ, killed by a goddamn beautician and her cohorts.

Darlene came toward me, the massive bulk of her body pressed against me. "It's simple, Bill, what happened out there. Ronny cut up his old man. They were always drinking and fighting. It just happened that way. What made it all complicated was you making up that note, making it seem like Ronny was creating some myth for himself. You gave Ronny the backing to go out there and stand against what he'd done. You gave him a way to be something special, to show the anger that was inside him. That's right, Bill. Ronny was something that you created." Darlene looked at me. "You say a damn thing about me to Ed, or anybody, and you'll be sorry, Bill. I swear it. You leave Ed alone, you hear me?"

I was out by the car, looking into the rearview mirror, when I saw what the hell Darlene had done to me. I mean, she'd given me this shit haircut as some sort of revenge, all chopped here and there, but at that moment, I was just glad to get the hell out of there alive.

I got home and spent the night clipping away at my hair, trying to make it look normal.

The next day, I did another special on a team over in Carlyle. Ed showed, but he said nothing about me and Darlene. He did look at my hair and make a face of bewilderment, like he thought I'd done it to myself. So, Darlene had said nothing. That sort of sealed things in my mind. There was some abiding law out there at the beauty parlor, some system of justice had been handed down.

Back at the office, Sam was drinking heavily. First thing he said was, "You come out at the wrong end of a fight with a lawn mower?" Then he burst out laughing.

I didn't answer him. I set the story on the desk.

Sam didn't even read it. He said, "Let's go with it."

Sam was all apprehensive. He drummed his nails on the counter, didn't make eye contact, then he sort of just shook his head and looked at me again. "That haircut don't do anything for your looks, Bill . . ."

I turned to go, but he said, "Bill. We got a dinner tonight with that guy from the newspaper conglomerate. I think this might be the night things get settled."

I said, "How long before it's all settled?"

"I don't know. Soon." Sam looked at me. "You did a good job here, Bill. I want you to know that. You tried something, and it . . . Well, it's . . ." He cut short whatever he was thinking of saying.

I left and began work at my desk. Ed went down and developed the print and came back up. I wrote out a strong defense of freedom of the press, citing the working over I'd got at the hands of the FBI.

I went back in to Sam and said, "You know, Darlene knew about the bunker all along, Sam. Darlene got it all from Ronny's estranged. All the women out there knew, Sam. There's something strange out there. I swear to God there is, Sam."

Sam just looked at me. "I want you to stop right now, Bill. For your own sake, don't make a fool of yourself."

Ed came in, and I didn't say anything.

Sam ended things without saying another word, just left with Ed.

I stayed behind. I resented being treated like a lunatic, the fall guy in all this.

I went at Sam's bourbon. We had a small refrigerator there in the office, one of ours, of course. I got out a sack of crushed ice and set about getting drunk fast.

I took the ice and the bourbon out to the car. The doors had cylindrical holders, top-of-the-line gadgets on this model. It was built with that American swagger of audacious power and bigness, comprised of those intangibles we had lost as a nation now. I set the drink into the holder and got out onto the road. I went out by the bunker. They had a generator going, lights infusing the air with a night-game atmosphere. A small crowd of kids were hanging around. I watched from a distance, heard them jeering and laughing. I smelled pot in the air.

I drove away, out by Ronny's estranged, poured the lights down the long trail to the trailer, burned away the dark, but nobody came

out. I was pretty much wasted. I went down there, and in the glow
of my lights, I saw the kid staring at me through the trailer window.
He was dead quiet though. It unnerved the shit out of me. I backed
away real slow.

I went by Osco, called from a pay phone. Ronny's estranged had
the night off. I hung up. I had the tumbler of booze in the other
hand. I got going again, went by the fancy restaurant where Sam
and Ed and Darlene and that newspaper guy were eating. I saw
Sam's car parked out front, found Ed's off in back. Shit, I was going
a million miles an hour. I saw them all at a table, Sam laughing his
ass off. The guy who was thinking about buying us all out was
maybe a few years older than me, dressed in a plaid coat and red
pants, hair neat, like a goddamn Realtor. That kinda got me right in
the gut, that sense of inadequacy that has always plagued me.

I went out by Ed's place, and dammit, there was a For Sale sign
planted on the lawn. Things were happening real fast, the exodus.
I got myself into Darlene's beauty parlor. I'd overheard Ed say one
time where he kept a spare key. I went into that fantasy world,
inhaled the scent of roses, and it got me thinking crazy things
again. I pulled down a relief of the Hawaiian beach, stood in that
fake aura of her dreamworld. I got in front of Ed's camera, pulled
on a cord attached to the shutter, and took a series of grimacing
Polaroids of myself on that fake beach. When I left, I didn't turn off
the lights. I left a few of the Polaroids there, for them to see it was
me who'd been there. I left a certain ambivalence behind, a calling
card that said I didn't believe all was right out here.

I was all over the town that night, in that great car of mine. I
stopped and got a chicken meal that came with a kid's toy out at
Kentucky Fried Chicken. Then I got some more bourbon and
another sack of ice, and I went again by Ronny's estranged, out by
the trailer, and still nobody was there, just the kid. His head came
up, like a small moon against the dark. I parked and took him out
and fed him, put him into the back of my car, because that's what
he remembered about me, the car.

I was hoping they'd show up, Karl and her, but they didn't. The kid was starving. I tore the chicken into strips, set them out before him on a plate which had this face of Goofy. The kid ate the chicken like it was going out of style. I had a little tub of mashed potato there for him, too. His little legs kicked in excitement, his hot little hands grabbing at me and the spoon. It was nice just to watch him eat. It was like this little gem of life existed despite all the bullshit. And yet, I was thinking, here was a kid who had it in his genes to go out and kill people one day, to hold up stores, to make life a living hell. I said to him, "You're not like that, right?" The kid made his baby noises. He wanted more food.

I poured another tall glass of bourbon, filled it with ice. The sky flickered overhead in a dim rumble of thunder. I could tell it was going to rain like all hell. I put the kid back into his small cage. I kissed the soft part of the back of his head. I gave him the toy. It was a wind-up chicken. I set it going across his crib and shut him in. I didn't quite make it home before a new rain fell out of the sky.

I awoke the next morning to Sam congratulating me on the stance I'd taken about my right to protect sources. That wasn't what I'd really said in the article, but Sam had taken some license with things, made it seem like I knew where the hell Ronny was hiding but wouldn't reveal the things I knew. I spent the day around the house doing shit.

I had my encore engagement down at Lakeview Junior College later in the evening.

I was the bloodline in the Ronny Lawton story again, or the anticipation was there that I was going to reveal the whereabouts of Ronny Lawton. That's another thing Sam put in the paper. He didn't name me by name. Instead, he called me The Source.

I went down to the Y to hide. I got so I was like a goddamn crab, crawling around the bottom of the pool. I mean, there was nothing to be gained down there at the bottom of a pool, no recollection of whatever goddamn memory of fetal bliss or whatever the hell it was I was looking for. But I stayed down, for minutes at a time, curled up and closed my eyes. Then I surfaced into the universe of air breathers, got my ass out of the pool. The caretaker was there, looking at me. "You lose something, Bill?"

"Only my mind, Tom."

He said, "Oh, is that all?"

I got to drinking heavily again before the Lakeview Junior College stint, down the street at one of those sleazy all-nighters, where they kept the lights low, and women walked around on a stage in lingerie like tired cats. It was only seven-thirty in the evening, and I was tanked. I was talking with Gloria, this woman in a G-string and tassels over her big nipples, buying her expensive drinks. She had fat legs and a paunch, and you could tell she'd had more than one kid. Her flesh was like damp dough. Her lips had that look like they were all used up, loose and useless. Still, this is what you got down here, the refuse of human existence. I was laying out my foundation for the similarity between the Red Shift Phenomenon, the theory of an expanding universe, and the current state of postindustrialism, with its emergence of niche markets. I was going on about a moral theory of relativity, not just mathematical, where anything prevails, as long as it turns a profit. I said to her, "Our enlightened age is really not born out of social conscience. No, the social liberation of women, blacks, and gays is strictly an economic expediency in the end. You see that, right?" I gripped her flabby arm. "Chaos can now be seen as serving or ratifying a political agenda. You see that, right, Gloria?"

She said she'd suck my cock for twenty dollars outside if I wanted. She had drained her drink. She wanted me to buy her more drinks. It was house policy. A black guy named Elmo in a leather coat came over and asked me to cool it. He had a purple feather in his hat and gold rings on his black fingers. I shelled out another ten dollars, and an equally bedraggled-looking specimen in fishnet stockings came and put down two brown-colored drinks on napkins. I smelled the hot liquor on Gloria's breath. A strobe light turned in the dark ceiling. I had that tragic destined feeling that I'd end up killing myself someday. My father's memory always lurked as a final slow dissolution, a way of ending things.

I got up and called Osco. A man said she hadn't showed for work. I was going to drive out by her place, but I was feeling too drunk, and I had to get down to the college and talk.

Back onstage, another middle-aged woman came out and melded with the soft thump of music and sanguine light. I sat in beside Gloria again. She wanted another drink. I ordered two drinks. I said, "Listen, this is important, Gloria." I leaned toward the warmth of her flesh, explaining, "Our ancestors came here looking for land. They were pioneers reaching out for something. They pushed forward into new frontiers. Well, you see, now, we've got no more land, so now we've turned to our own bodies, we're making them big. You've seen Rocky, right?"

Gloria whispered, "You're crazy." She tried to retract her arm. I kept hold of it.

I went at the old spiel, said, "No, I'm not, Gloria. You see, Stallone has tapped into the reality of postindustrialism, into that dimension we call 'personal growth.' He has begun to focus on the hemisphere of the self, his own personal space. He's sublimated this loss of frontier into a personal effort to make himself bigger, to achieve expansion, that new colonization of desire, journeyed to the interior of our own consciousness. You see where I'm going, right? He's scarred his own flesh, torn his pecs in raw stretch marks in an effort to outgrow his skin." I was shaking from the drink, holding the warmth of her arm. "Don't you see?"

Gloria smiled and held up her tits before me. "Like a boob job."

I said, "Exactly." It was one of those rare moments of epiphany, when I reached the common masses, made them understand. I stayed still in the ruby afterglow of light, drained my drink, then went outside into the alley and grew into the personal space of Gloria's mouth.

The next minute, I was driving down to Lakeview Junior College, still loaded out of my mind. I shuffled into the college. I had an old copy of Steinbeck's *Grapes of Wrath* with me. I began reading, "And then the dispossessed were drawn west—from Kansas, Oklahoma, Texas, New Mexico; from Nevada and Arkansas, families, tribes, dusted out, tractored out. Car-loads, caravans, homeless and hungry; twenty thousand and fifty thousand and a hundred thousand and two hundred thousand. They streamed over the mountains, hungry and restless—restless as ants, scurrying to find work to do—to lift, to push, to pull, to pick, to cut—anything, any burden to bear, for food. The kids are hungry. We got no place to live. Like ants scurrying for work, for food, and most of all for land." I looked up and shouted, "Can't you feel that epic sense of loss that Steinbeck felt, the collective solidarity of what we once were as a nation?" It was like speaking to the center of some vortex in a black hole. I resorted to my one-liners. "Our cars are getting smaller, but we're getting bigger. Ain't that fucked?" I spoke about the secularization of the sacred word *Mass*. Mass was now power, a physical force. But shit, I was losing them fast out there. I had meandered into a dead end before I'd really got going. I shouted, "This town is in deep shit, my friends. What has replaced the essential industrialism of our town is that goddamn Cabbage Patch Kid, postindustrialism's first surrogate child, who comes to us legitimized with a birth certificate. It, my friends, is not a toy. It is a spiritual placebo for a nation on the pill." I knocked over the podium at that stage, smashed a pitcher of water, and got up slowly, drenched.

I could see Dean Holton looking at me. I stared back out over the sea of heads. "Is this making any sense?" I felt my head swooning, that trapdoor feeling in my stomach. "Listen, you shit for brains, we are now moving not only within a mathematical theory of relativity, but also a social, political, and a moral theory of relativity."

I was shaking there on the stage, drunk out of my mind. I shouted, "I want to share a little something with you all about meaning and interpretation, about the death of our language." Dean Holton was offstage, trying to get me to stop. I said, "Listen to me, you shit for brains!" And so, I got going. "This scientist does an experiment on a frog," I said. "You got that? Okay, so the scientist starts with this frog and says, 'Jump, frog,' and the frog jumps four feet. Then the scientist cuts off one of the frog's legs and says, 'Jump, frog,' and the three-legged frog jumps three feet, and then the scientist cuts off another leg and says, 'Jump, frog,' and the two-legged frog jumps two feet, and on it goes until the scientist has cut all the legs off the frog. Then the scientist says, 'Jump, frog,' and the frog doesn't do anything. It just quivers. And so, the scientist has his data, and he goes and he writes up his report, and after poring over the data, he announces to the world, 'Frogs with no legs are deaf.' "

I shouted out, "You see where I'm going with this, you shit for brains? You see the irony?" I got no response, nothing! They had this blackboard behind the podium. I said, "How about this," and I scrawled a sentence.

Woman without her man is nothing

I shouted out to them. "You go ahead and punctuate that!" but of course, I didn't let those illiterates have the chance. I shouted, "Can you see this out there?" Dean Holton came out to take me offstage, but I shouted, "I want to finish this one point, dean. Indulge me!" I turned back to the blackness of the audience. I shouted, "This here is the equation of the sexes, right in this line, the embodiment of gender consciousness," which, of course, didn't mean shit to them out there, and so I got the chalk and began to punctuate the sentence, said, "This is what a man reads in that sentence."

Woman, without her man, is nothing.

"This is what a woman reads."

Woman: without her, man is nothing.

I said, "Right here is the multiplicity of interpretation that disman-
tles meaning, that makes it utterly subjective, that renders it useless. Jesus, can I make it any simpler?"

Dean Holton had me by the arm. I shouted, "Are there any
questions?"

Someone jumped up wearing a Ronny Lawton mask and
shouted, "Is it true Ronny Lawton has a ten-inch cock?"

I said, "Yes." Then I vomited into a trash can.

It was during that episode, what I like to consider my lecture on
"The Discourse of Language," that Ronny Lawton had taken it
upon himself to take his estranged wife and his kid as hostages in
his house, in a deadly last stand. Of course, nobody knew that,
until the next afternoon, during the first football game of the season, when Ronny demanded Dunkin' Donuts and coffee be delivered out by his house.

CHAPTER 15

By the time I awoke the next day, the edge of the afternoon had crossed in shadows over our town, a great gray thing like some deflating zeppelin, low and rumbling. I went up into the kitchen and drank a cold glass of water. My head was split in two. The floor was cold underfoot. I felt a shudder of booze and tiredness, of humiliation at what I'd done the previous evening. In the bathroom mirror my face had that look of green cheese, a cadaverous color of sickness. Again the bewildering shudder of discontent, of having to face another day of useless indecision. At the edge of consciousness I felt Ronny Lawton out there on this gloomy midafternoon, the peripheral figure of roving vengeance in his Mustang, doing burnouts, revving the engine, aggressive, wanting a final confrontation.

I passed the answering machine blinking, news probably from Sam about the state of the *Truth*. I went outside onto the back porch. Ancient elms swayed in the cool breeze, summer eclipsed in the convection of currents, the breath of an Ice Age up north. I remember, years ago, this was the hardest time of all for swim training, the queasy sickness, not wanting to stir, curled away in bed, my father putting a hand on my shoulder, taking me orange juice, then having to rise into the cold. My grandfather was already up, going through the *New York Times* crossword puzzle, filling in the blankness of the columns, finding meaning, deciphering facts, connecting words, building up a matrix of absolute logic, dictionary in hand, affirming the primacy of order. I went by him each morning, out into the gleam of frost on the road, the dampness invading my shoulders, sky the color of cement, low and heavy, my father's headlights burning away the morning fog, moving quietly while the world still slept. We'd hear the early-morning news, Vietnam years ago, the protesters and the war raging on, Nixon's impeachment, and just the general stuff, too, hog and grain futures out of Chicago, the late-evening baseball scores. My father didn't say much, drank his coffee, shaved with a battery-operated shaver, the tired snap of his jaw, yawning, glass-eyed from a night's drinking, the sweet after-smell of bourbon and aftershave. He drove down by our factory, the opaque lights revealing the dark geometry of metal scaffolding. There was the smell of sulfur, the din of noise, the open fire of furnaces bleeding against the gray morning air, railway boxcars shunting along the tracks, hitched and ready to move out across the land, to transport our small universe of refrigeration, our legacy, from deep in the heart of America out west and east. We were descendants of a man who walked a continent to freedom and liberty, a man who talked with conviction about the voice inside his head, the voice that told him to do this and that, the developed schizophrenia of a wandering immigrant. I often wondered how it might have sounded, that voice, that mysterious clairvoyance that made him a millionaire, the real him hidden under the hard leather of his horrible face. The eternity of morning drives filled my head, the solemn journey through history, our daily pilgrimage, this epic dream outside the car window, the vast means of production throbbing and producing things. I felt it back then, arising each morning into a regimen of training, a vigilance and austerity imposed in the form of sport, taught to put my comfort aside for team spirit, for unity, consciously practical, knowing my grandfather was at home verifying the veracity of logic and the absolute in his morning puzzle, not to mention his great fascination with Rubik's Cube, the wry smile of knowing control as his hands worked their magic and came up with the solution. His big trick was he hardly had to look at the cube. The path of logic and solution was embedded inside him. The cube's solution was the physical manifestation of a whole belief system.

I was part of a silent elite back then, those who came out from cover of sleep and accepted the challenge of this coded existence.

My father dropped me off at the side entrance and disappeared, the air permeated with the smell of chlorine, a clinical laboratory smell, the giant gills of the pool's ventilation system shuddering, showering in the communal area, naked and cold, shivering before plunging into the pool, into a daily christening of cold awareness. I longed now for that tight control, for the compunction of authority, the abiding discipline, the routine well established, "Early to bed, early to rise makes a man healthy, wealthy, and wise . . ."

I pinched the tiredness in my eyes, yawned. The zoo animals squawked down below. I focused on that. Soon they'd be taken in for the winter, locked away inside the small cement pens, abandoned for the dark of our freezing winters. It was awful to hear the shrill sadness of creatures without purpose, the hollow echoed screams of captivity through the blizzard and subzero weeks. It was strange, but there were nations like that, and we were fast becoming part of that sublimated scream, a great captivity.

I went in and sat down and closed my eyes, the myopic tiredness behind everything I did. It's hard to initiate change; the very act of thinking, of coming up with a plan, demands a certain discipline, a grunt of effort. I moved like something extricated from its shell. Inside my head the sear of darkness, the fear and sense of loss, the rambling, dissolute history, the longing for escape, the days of tedium at the office typing legal notices, the nights lost in word problems, lost in absolute logic, the calls to Diane, the pleading, the piecing together of the note at the house, Sam and Ed coming and finding me, their lugubrious need to find a small enclave of happiness at life's end, the head out there in the bunker, the escapes into Ronny's estranged, holding her, creeping away from the uncertainty of loneliness, Ronny's kid in his small cage, captive, the memory of interrogation, the real fear that I'd been implicated somehow in Ronny Lawton's father's disappearance, last night and the phantom mimicry of my father's end, out there in the alley with a prostitute, prodding the darkness. I ended up deep in the moment of my father's death, nosed around its alluring suggestion, its inevitability.

I felt that recurring memory stir, that last day, my father killing Jones downstairs, kissing Jones on the back of the head, the scratch between his floppy dog ears, assuaging guilt, telling the dog some lie, letting Jones's hot tongue lick my father's face, going back in, waiting in the kitchen, mixing bourbon and ice, checking the wall clock, going out and seeing poor Jones bleeding from his mouth and anus. It was a dark matrix of action, the camera following him. It's how I finally saw it unfold, going back upstairs, the dark prodding insistence deep inside his girlfriend's throat, the sullen acceptance, the slurping choke, the withdrawal, the melancholy release and abatement, her disappearing into the bathroom, him opening his mouth, the slow conviction, the inevitability, the burn of hot metal.

I infused his death with the spongy pith of the rubber ball I bit into when they filled my body with electricity in the mental institution, after his death, the taste of metal. It was something I craved again, the blinding erasure of jolting release, the loss of memory, the buzz of shaking silence, set out on the porch of the institution in warm light, when I should have been getting ready for exams at college. It was in that slipstream experience, moving outside the domain of ordinary life, that I found solace, hidden away from things, inert.

The wound upstairs pulsed, a vortex of discernible blackness, the center of decision, the extent of my father's life reduced to one bullet, anxiety honed down to one final conclusive end. He entered death through the eye of a needle. In my dreams, I tore open the plaster, went into this dark reel of memories. He was in there, hiding. It was those trips overseas toward the end that did him in, the constant nightmare of rapacious industry churning in steaming jungles, the long nights of indulgent living, drinking and eating and fucking, making deals with military men, cocooned inside the filth and vapid heat of a distant world, a colony of women with their legs spread open, the breeding instruments of a new army of cheap labor.

He talked about all that in the end, when he came home, spoke to me about the center of darkness, phoned me late at night at college, wanted me to understand what was out there, what he'd seen. I could do nothing but close my eyes and listen, curled up in my bunk, three roommates sleeping, saying nothing, just hearing him talk himself into exhaustion, the clink of ice in his glass, the breath of a wheezing alcoholic, then the inevitable hang-up, abrupt, but sometimes a dead silence, him passed out, the thread of communication still open, the dull static of his sonorous breath. In those moments I cradled the phone to my chest, drew my legs up into my torso, and held the phone like a precious bone, something sacred, my father breathing into my chest. It was maybe the closest I ever got to him.

He said to me one night, when he was real drunk, "Many men stumble across the truth, but most manage to pick themselves up and continue, as if nothing had happened. I'm not one of those men, Bill." He was quoting famous people, reading and underlining paragraphs in books. I found that out later, when I went through his things. I found one such passage he'd said to me toward the end, underlined, from Dostoyevsky: "Every man has some reminiscences which he would not tell to everyone, but only to his friends. He has others which he would not reveal even to his friends, but only to himself, and that in secret. But finally there are still others which a man is even afraid to tell himself, and every decent man has a considerable number of things stored away." In the end, to stop the accumulation of facts and memories, he could do nothing else but blow apart the lattice of consciousness and surrender to darkness.

The phone had been ringing for God knows how long. It was Ronny Lawton. He said bluntly, "I killed Karl Rogers dead out by his trailer, dead."

I said nothing.

Ronny said, "I thought maybe you might just want to know about Karl and all. You might as well get the story first."

In the background, I heard Duke Ellington music playing. I said, "You know they got this line bugged, Ronny?"

There was a long pause. Ronny shouted, "Motherfucker!" at the top of his voice. I had to take my ear away from the phone. He shouted it again and again. Ronny's kid started crying. Ronny shouted something to the kid. The kid's voice got louder. I had the phone a good six inches away from my ear, and I heard every word coming out of his mouth, and then it was all just heavy breathing, spent anger. Ronny said, "You still there?"

"You finished screaming?"

I felt him collect himself.

"What are you planning on doing, Ronny?"

"Guess I'm following some instinct that brought me back home. I figure it might just be time to end things for good."

I didn't say anything, just waited for him to say something else. He did finally. It was addressed to the cops listening in. "I got the place booby-trapped real good. I don't want nobody coming near the house unless they want to die. I'm in a killing mood."

The line went dead in my ear. I hung up, and then the phone rang again. It was Ronny. He said, "Oh, yeah, I about forgot, the kid wants some chicken." I heard Teri in the background trying to hush the kid. Ronny said, "The kind you got him before, and a toy like you got him, too. He don't got the toy with him here. He wants the toy, the windup chicken you got him. He wants that."

Ronny shouted, "Teri! Shut it, *now!*" Ronny spoke to me again. "And you think you could see your way to bringing us out some Pall Malls, maybe a carton?"

I said, "Sure, Ronny."

Ronny hung up, and then it was the FBI ringing. They wanted my full cooperation in matters. I was to meet them downtown. The guy didn't identify himself, but I knew it was the FBI guy who'd interrogated me. I felt a twinge of anger. I said, "Fuck you!" and hung up and waited for the phone to ring again, but it didn't.

I got dressed. I brewed strong coffee. I turned on the radio, felt a certain clairvoyance in knowing something the general public didn't know, about Karl out there at the trailer, about Ronny out there with his wife and kid. It sort of infused me with satisfaction, a juvenile smugness. I sat at the table and watched the clouds pass overhead, low and gray, the patches of blue sky breaking through slowly. On the radio, I got the score from the local game. We were getting our asses kicked. It was late in the fourth quarter.

The complicity of seasonal cold, the rot of vegetation, the wind-blown rainclouds, the fall of leaves, the migration of Canada geese, it all came in the final stages of Ronny Lawton's destiny, the swirl of wind through the emptiness of our machinery and lives, the demise of our football team. You could say a showdown was in the air. I went by KFC, gave my order at the drive-through, and pulled up. I saw Pete's car waiting for me. He got out and came over. "You planning a picnic, Bill?"

"What if I am?"

I could see Larry sitting in another cop car. He was talking into a radio.

"FBI guy says, you go out there, and Ronny's likely to put a bullet through you. They got profiles of how these things turn out."

I looked at him blankly. "I'll take my chances."

I moved toward the drive-through window. Pete walked beside the car. "Bill?"

Inside I saw a guy in a suit with the chicken guy. I looked at Pete. "What the hell is this, Pete?" It was one of the FBI guys.

Pete leaned into the passenger door. "FBI figures we can slip something into the chicken, drug old Ronny. He ain't going to suspect you. He trusts you."

"You want me to go out there and poison Ronny?"

"It's not poison, just something to knock him out cold."

I said, "You're out of your goddamn mind! I'm not doing it!"

Pete had a swollen face, flushed almost purple around the neck. "Bill, you'd best go along with what the FBI want."

The manager was a guy I knew from high school, Clifford Fry. He put his head through the drive-through. He was dressed in a white shirt and a tie laced like the Colonel. He said, "Hey, Bill. You want Extra Crispy or Original?"

I said, "Clifford. What the hell are you doing? This isn't the kind

of product placement you ideally want, is it? You want KFC associated with a poisoning?"

That pretty much ended the poisoning suggestion. I heard Clifford Fry shout, "Shit, no! The Colonel worked too damn hard to
have his name tied up in all this."

I shouted, "Call the main office, Clifford. Get the Colonel on
the line! See how he likes being associated with a family massacre!"
I waited there in the drive-through, and the FBI guys came out and
got into a black car. They were heading out ahead of me like a gang
of morticians.

Pete said, "Let them handle it, Bill. Best thing you can do is butt
out."

I didn't answer him. I got the chicken and the toy and some
mashed potato. It smelled real good inside the car. I think I was
smiling. There was some end in sight.

It was a day of brilliant sunshine, almost too bright, kind of hard
to reconcile this brilliance with what was unfolding around me.
The world had an insubstantial feel, almost two-dimensional. I was
driving through a cardboard flatness. Along Main Street, the windows were all decorated for the game in the red and black of the
school colors. Pete followed behind me, and Larry was right in back
of him. We moved real slow, toward our destination. I turned on
the radio. We had lost bad. The coach was making up some lame
excuse. The crowd was roaring in the background. I heard the
interview cut short. The first news flash about Ronny Lawton and
his hostages was delivered by Linda Carter. I turned off the radio,
kept moving toward the inevitable.

I was thinking, life is lived, for the most part, in between feeling
and fact, in the murk of premonition, in that realm of intuition and
unseen energy we let pass between us. Maybe I had known it was
going to end like this. I'd seen it on the television, the shoot-out,
the hostage situation. That was the way it was these days. You look
back at the sixties, and it was all assassinations, knocking people
off, putting a bullet into their heads, JFK, MLK, RFK. Shots ring
out, a man falls down dead. But now, maybe we want something

more. We don't want to be some faceless triggerman, we want to get on the evening news, we want that fifteen minutes of fame.

On the last mile out to Ronny's, I ran into the caravan of the curious, the masses from the game now pouring out toward the hostage scene. The story had broken across the land. Pete came up behind me and got his lights flashing and siren going, and he pressed down a dirt embankment and disappeared into dust. It took me twenty minutes to get near the property. When I got out to the Lawton place, Ronny had his estranged tied to a chair behind a lace curtain in a front room on the first floor facing the long driveway. She was blindfolded. Ronny said he had the perimeter of the house booby-trapped. He shouted, "I ain't exactly had a good night's sleep, so let's do this my way!"

I arrived at the same time the doughnut guy arrived. He was maybe sixteen years old. He came with a dozen doughnuts, a gallon of cold milk, and two steaming coffees, dressed in his striped brown uniform and paper hat. Ronny insisted the kid bring the doughnuts up to the house. He was cursing up a storm inside. He didn't want cops coming near the house.

The roving mass from the football game was still arriving, cars lining the country road. The late-afternoon light was strong, but cool in the shadows. The horde had that dissatisfaction of a bad defeat. They wanted blood spilt. The guys from the football team were wearing their letterman jackets. They had a gloomy look, like they just wanted to start fighting, right then and there. They hung around in a tight circle, self-conscious and acting tough. Pete was already working to keep them back.

The doughnut guy was like a celebrity, getting prepped by the FBI. He was smiling, like he wanted in on this scene. His face was broken out in acne, red bumps and oily skin, a guy that didn't play sports or anything, working a Saturday-morning shift, and then, bang, Ronny Lawton called up looking for doughnuts. You could pretty much live off that story for a long time. That's how the kid had it figured, anyway. Linda Carter tried to interview him, but an FBI guy kept her back. She roamed the edge of the property, the fat-assed assistant following her. It was like a carnival by the time the cheerleaders arrived in station wagons, honking the horns.

Ronny set the tone. "I ain't afraid to die!" is what he shouted to any request from the FBI. They wanted Ronny's kid in exchange for the doughnuts. Ronny went crazy and put a gun in his estranged's mouth. She had her mouth open wide. "I ain't afraid to die!" is all he said, and that pushed matters along. His estranged was choking on the end of the barrel.

The doughnut guy went on up the yard, moving slowly. He looked back from time to time, touched his paper hat, pushed it back on his head. He went through stalks of corn like Moses parting the sea. There were guns trained on the window. The window swung open slowly, curtains sucked outward in the breeze. The house was in shadow. Ronny orchestrated things from behind the barrel of a gun, hunkered down behind his estranged. You could hear Ronny's kid crying in the background with the window open, a cry that cut through the sudden stillness. The crowd kept their mouths shut. The doughnut guy was communing with death, close to making the exchange. The SWAT guys didn't breathe, their guns aimed right for Ronny. Ronny never materialized. He just shouted, "I got this room soaked in gasoline, you hear me out there?" Ronny had the doughnut guy open the box and eat a doughnut and drink from both coffees. The guy ate slowly, in small bites. The crowd pressed along the edge of the yellow-lined perimeter. The doughnut guy looked back up the long driveway, and it seemed a hell of a long time Ronny kept the guy just standing there. Ronny shouted out, "How much I owe you?" and the doughnut guy looked back, like he didn't know what the hell to do.

An FBI guy got on the bullhorn. "How about we settle all accounts when you come out?"

"Who says I'm coming out?" Ronny shouted, a flat elemental statement of fact.

The doughnut guy had a look of fear as he moved his head back and forth between the volley of words. He was still standing, which was all Ronny had been interested in, really. Ronny seemed satisfied the doughnut guy wasn't going to fall over dead, so he had the guy lean in through the window and hand over the box of doughnuts and coffee. Ronny set some bills on the windowsill. The window closed, and the doughnut guy backed away, turned, and in a sudden relief, thrust his hands into the air and started running like he'd scored a touchdown. The crowd just lost it, whistling and cheering the doughnut guy, who ran back into the arms of the FBI.

I followed next in the procession of gifts brought to the manger, came forth with the chicken. Jesus, it was Ronny's room they were holed up in, the kaleidoscope of color and images swirling inside, the dismembered images of models and rock stars pasted on all the walls. I saw Ronny in there, just another image moving amid the color, almost camouflaged, part of the iconography of his age, the disparate anger, the madman who puts a bullet into his wife's head. Ronny had found his way back into that density of space he'd created, the essence of desire, a burrow of sanctuary. Ronny just shrugged his shoulders, hiding behind his weight bench when I got up to the window. He said, "I can't figure a way out of this." He had the barrel of his gun trained on me.

I looked at him. "You have to decide how this ends."

Ronny's estranged stared up at me, her eyes wild with fear. The chair she was tied to shifted slightly. The ropes had cut against her skin around her arms and ankles.

I said, "You want to talk about things?"

Ronny shook his head, wiped the back of his mouth, and said, "Not now. Maybe later."

I passed the chicken into the room. I saw the kid in his small cage. His big eyes were looking at me. He made the word for chicken. Ronny said, "Chicken, that's right, chicken." The kid made a sound again. Ronny looked at me. "You think every parent thinks his kid is a genius?" A slight smile surfaced around his lips.

I said, "I think the kid is something real special, Ronny. You know, maybe we aren't the sum total of all our parts. You ever hear of Beethoven? Well, his mother was a prostitute. They never even knew who was the father."

Ronny looked into my eyes. "I hear Elvis's daddy pumped gas was all. It don't always figure what two people can create." His eyes drifted to the kid again.

Ronny's estranged had tears in her eyes.

I left it at that. Ronny set the box of chicken into the kid's cage.

I smelled the gasoline, the redolent odor that told me Ronny really was thinking about ending things. Ronny had brought up his weights out of the basement and set them against the door.

I was about to turn when Ronny leaned forward, touched my hand for a brief moment. He said softly, "There ain't no going back for me."

Ronny's estranged was making this animal whine. Ronny turned the gun on her. "Quit it."

Ronny looked up at me. "Watch they don't come at me." He moved on his hands and knees to the weight bench and got pumping the bar. He had his gun on his stomach. I heard the jiggle of weights, the grunt of effort. Ronny's estranged was crying without sound. Her eyes just filled with tears.

I felt the pressure of a thousand eyes fixed on me, the guns trained right on me. The light had turned a mackerel color, dark and mottled.

Ronny got done on the bench. His face was this outcrop of pain, a darkish purple color with veins showing, eyes bulging. It was like he might die of a heart attack or something. You could tell he'd been doing steroids. He was big, I mean that bigness where the skin shines over the muscles, it was that taut. He was breathing deep, like he was testing new lungs, in and out. I said quietly, "I don't believe you did it, Ronny."

He pointed the gun at me, like he wanted me gone.

I just walked away.

It settled down after that, into a long evening of encroaching chill. A generator throbbed and illuminated beams of light around a small encampment of tents. Shadows moved against the canvas, the murmur of discussion. An odor of coffee filled the air. A Baptist choir sang in the background, until Ronny opened the window and said he'd kill his kid if the Baptists didn't shut their goddamn mouths. I was with Ronny all the way on that one. Goddamn Baptists. I watched them dissipate like phantoms in their white gowns, steered off the property into the dark.

I sat in among the FBI, listened to them calculate a head shot, about how to take Ronny out. They had a microphone planted on the roof, picking up everything that was being said. It was a distant sound, the old conversation, like something outside of reality. The guy looked up at me and said, "He's on the edge. Real close." He drew his index finger under his throat real slow.

The whole focus was how to kill Ronny Lawton. A pellet might be used to take him out. There was no chance of a spark using a heavy pellet. They had experience in this sort of operation, a psychological profile, a timeline of when Ronny was likely to snap. The gist of it all was simple. The longer Ronny stayed in there, the more he was going to feel there was no turning back. Chances were, he was going to kill himself and his wife and kid. The more he thought about what he did to Karl, the more he was going to know he would get the death penalty. That was the hand he'd forced. We were just witnesses to an appointed execution was all. Once the stakes were set that way, it was easy to talk about killing Ronny Lawton, taking him out before he got a chance to off his wife and kid. The FBI had a big sheet of paper spread out on a table, a group of men leaning over a provisional map of the room where Ronny was holed up.

I had a report to get out, so I left by night. They let me put a call into Ronny before I left. I said, "Ronny, I got to go now, but you want me to come back in the morning?"

Ronny said something away from the phone. I could see the hunch of his back moving at the window. He was not fifty yards from me. I was expecting a shot to drop him, but he was hunkered down too low. Ronny got back on the line. "The kid likes that Big Breakfast from McDonald's. You bring out three of them breakfasts tomorrow. And hash browns." I thought he was gone, but he said, "I want you to bring me the receipt for all of it, the chicken, the breakfasts, you hear? I want receipts for everything."

I said, "Sure, Ronny. You got it."

"I ain't above paying my way in this world. I always did. I want you to put that in your paper. We never owed anybody a red cent out here. That's the God's honest truth. I got a brother who lay down his goddamn life for this country."

I said, "I'll tell them that, Ronny."

It must have done something deep inside Ronny, that statement, because next thing there was this picture set in the window. I didn't get to see that. I was out on the road going toward the police station. It wasn't until I watched the news later that night that I saw it, a small grotto of regret, a plaintive statement. Ronny had taken down the drapes and put up an American flag. In the window was Charlie Lawton's military photograph, along with the letter of condolence on his death in Vietnam, and there along with those things was the Employee of the Month plaque from Denny's.

CHAPTER 16

I never did go out by the trailer to see Karl's head for myself, because Karl was small potatoes in all this, just a guy in a corn-field with his head blown open. Back at the police station, Pete was heading up things. I came in on his brief to the press. Karl was unrecognizable, by all accounts. Karl's face was a black mess of gore, singed meat. That's what Pete told us, anyway. There were a hell of a lot of reporters from the big cities standing around taking notes.

At some deep, satisfying level, Pete communed with firearms and what they can do to the human body. He was describing the wound. It was that lawman's presiding belief that all things can be controlled with a show of force, with enough gunpower, never mind that this death was carried out by the enemy, Ronny Lawton. The end effect, the gaping wound, had this resolute and final truth. It ended things for good. For the foot soldiers like Pete, law was about life and death at its heart. Pete had the measurement of the wound to the millimeter. I didn't take down the measurement, but you could have driven a truck through Karl's face, it was that damn big, according to Pete.

Pete explained how Karl must have staggered around outside the trailer, because there were bits of his brains all over the outside. Karl was found out in his car, like he'd made a futile attempt, after having his face shot, to try and drive away. He'd gotten from inside the trailer, where he'd been shot, all the way out to his car. Pete told that to lots of people, the same level of detail to anybody who was willing to listen, even after his briefing to individual reporters, how Karl must have been staring out into a world of blood just trying to get away from Ronny Lawton. Karl was probably blind by all accounts, wandering around like that, but you had to think about what was going through his mind, the fear, just trying to escape like that. You had to think of Ronny Lawton just standing there watching it all, probably laughing, saying, "Hey, Karl, over here!" and Karl moving around like a zombie in one of those Saturday matinee movies. Pete said Karl had a long time to think about death in those last minutes, roaming around in the evening with his face blown off his head. It was something Pete liked thinking about, you could tell that. He walked the blind path Karl took, staggered there in the office, put his own hand to his face, wandered around the spectacle of death inside his own head, trying to shape it.

There were shots of the scene back at the office, a distant shot of the trailer set amid the corn, the car, and Karl's body slumped against the steering wheel. The shots were there for me, like they had materialized out of thin air. Ed wasn't anywhere in sight. Neither was Sam. I checked my answering machine. Nothing. I went down to Ed's darkroom. I touched his red light, felt it for heat. Dead cold. Nobody had been here for hours, maybe not all day, except to drop off the shots.

The office was steeped in darkness, slats of light falling across the floor from the streetlights outside. I stood in that dark, immersed, like in the pool, silent. I put down coffee, went at the report, found my head wandering. I got up and stretched, checked the coffee, poured it strong, no milk or sugar, felt its bitterness, felt the heat of the cup invade my fingers, warm me. Still no call from either Sam or Ed. The old domestic smell of burnt food prevailed, Sam and his tuna melts and potato chips ingrained forever into the wood. I had a feeling things had all but died on me.

I watched the hostage situation on mute all through the time I was writing the report, borrowed from its aura, took details that had escaped me, the Mustang off to the side of the house, burnt out. That, more than anything else, made me realize Ronny Lawton was never coming out of the house alive. I didn't put that in the paper. It was something that registered deep inside me, a premonition of gunfire, or a body mutilated in the front room, Ronny's estranged with a bullet in her temple, the kid facedown in a pool of blood in his cage. Call it "Ronny Lawton's Last Stand!" Think of it as the obliteration of a genetic heritage, the final end to a dream of some long-dead European ancestor who left behind oppression, escaped for America, crossed deep into its heart. And now, this sad end to it all, amid dead fields of corn.

I watched Karl's father on the television, a giant with carrot-colored hair, all wild, sprouting from under a baseball cap. It was strange to see a man like that cry. His face condensed under the brim of his hat around his pale blue eyes. He was stupefied at the notion of his son's death, his big, gnarled hands, crescents of dirt under the nails, pulling at his wife's sweater. She was holding a picture of Karl, his high-school photo. As always, it began and ended with the high-school photo. Cows wandered into the shot behind Karl's parents. You could see the distended pink sacks of udders. It looked like it was North Dakota where they lived, rural and barren and flat, a different century.

I checked my answering machine again. One message from Sam. A laconic few words: "Bill, never look back, somebody might be gaining on you!"

I tried Sam at home, no answer.

I checked my messages again, half an hour later. A call from Diane. It said simply, "Bill, I want to come down and see you." Then a moment of hesitation before her voice again. "All right, you want the truth? I need the extra credit, Bill. I'm getting killed in criminal law. I need to interview you about the case. Please, Bill. It's not like I haven't missed you." Again the silence. Then, "I dream about you at night sometimes."

I called her back, heard her voice on the other end, but I said nothing. I heard her say, "Bill! Goddamn it. It's you, isn't it? You're sick! You hear me, *sick!*" I read her a word problem over her shouting, one about filling a swimming pool that had sprung a leak. She was screaming "*asshole!*" over everything I was saying. She had hung up before I told her all the details.

I went at the article again, but I was freezing cold inside. Maybe

I was coming down with something. I drank more coffee. I called my answering machine again; no call. It ended that way, in rebuke and everlasting silence. It's maybe not real hard to see how men take guns to their girlfriends' heads, and then to their own. It was distance that assuaged those feelings in me. It was too much of an effort to go find her. I called one last time. Nothing. I replayed Sam's message, felt the words burn into my brain, "Never look back, somebody might be gaining on you." It was a saying from Satchel Paige, the black baseball player from the old Negro leagues. It felt sad, and yet defiant.

It was much later, at Sam's desk, that I saw a sheet of paper in the typewriter. It said simply, "The truth is dead the truth is dead the truth is dead . . ." It repeated that phrase over and over again, down almost three-quarters of the page, without punctuation or anything, a dribbling incantation. I stared at the words. My eyes burnt inside the sockets.

It was dark and lonely in the office through that night. I felt the coldness wrap itself around me. I sat at my small black cherrywood desk pressed into a corner of the room, banging away at the obituaries, chronicling a limbo world of dark accountancy, one of the Keepers of Death, etching the scroll of the dead, an underling to the shadows of the Apocalypse.

I called Sam on the old-fashioned heavy phone. No answer. I let it ring. I shouted, "Sam!" No answering machine or anything. I slept at his desk into the early morning. The phone woke me. It was the guy who'd bid on the paper. He wanted to speak to Sam. I said Sam wasn't around. The guy was all chummy. He called me chief. He said, "Nuts!" when I said Sam wasn't around. He was pulling this fifties-lingo bullshit with me, this soft-shoe approach. In the background, I was watching the quietude of Ronny Lawton's home on the television, the gray dark of early morning. A solitary light glowed in the room that held Ronny and his hostages.

The newspaper guy was speaking into my ear. I got back to listening to him for a moment. He said he'd seen my articles. Did I want to give him an exclusive? He'd work things for me, pull strings. He wanted an account of my dealings with Ronny. He said I was a "swell" reporter. I said, "I don't need any of your beeswax." I could give it as good as I got it. He asked me how I liked covering sports, said he had a slot, just maybe, if I wanted to come by his office. He said, "Sports is the new religion." I wasn't rude or anything, just declined at the present time. The guy didn't even wait for an explanation. He said, "Okay, kiddo!"

I said, "Okay, slick!" The phone went dead in my ear.

I went down by McDonald's and got Ronny's order and the receipt. It was maybe six in the morning about then. It was cold outside and empty of life. The sun peeked slowly on the horizon. I went out of the city, toward the house, turned on the radio. The hostage situation resurrected itself on the airwaves, filled the inside of my car. The madness found its way into houses all over America, that strange clairvoyance of the spoken word and images projected in time and space. You felt the world shore up, become real small. It was like people all over the country knew Ronny Lawton. He was right there in their bedrooms and kitchens, speaking to them through their radios as they awoke to the new day.

People were sitting up in their beds talking casually about Ronny Lawton, like he lived next door, saying things like, "You can't blame it all on Ronny. You see what they did to his brother over there in Vietnam? You want to begin somewhere, you begin with what this country did to its veterans! And you see what his wife did to him?" You got the rebuttal, right there in the warmth of the bed. "Hogwash is what that is! A man's got to see beyond the barrel of a gun. Nobody has a right to kill a man the way Ronny killed that Karl Rogers. You mean to tell me, if I left, you might just shoot me? Is that what you're getting at?" I mean, there were people not on speaking terms over what they felt about Ronny Lawton. It wasn't exactly clear who the hell had killed Ronny Lawton's old man, and maybe it was that latitude of uncertainty that made Ronny Lawton the kind of guy who represented so many things to so many different people.

Out along the road, you could see the orange tumors of pumpkins growing. You were looking toward Halloween and Thanksgiving when you saw that, the way the world turned that orange-brown, the flare of autumn foliage. My head was wandering. It was a dream really, all of it, driving out there to a guy like Ronny Lawton and his estranged.

I got out by Ronny's house, and shit, it was a circus, the errant voices even at this early hour. The occasional shout: "Ronny!" The masked faces were sitting on flatbed trucks, masks on their heads, the real faces revealed, eating breakfast, drinking steaming coffee. The major networks had sent down their top guys. They had trailers with generators and spotlights. A TV guy was getting makeup put on him. He was about to go before America with an update. All the morning talk shows were doing specials on the situation. I saw Linda Carter getting her hair sprayed inside one of the trailers. The trailer had her name on it. She turned and saw me coming with the McDonald's bag of breakfasts. She came out and got her guy with the camera to follow me. She thrust a camera in my face. She wanted me to open the bag. She wanted to know what Ronny was having for breakfast.

I said, "His family!"

She said, "Cut!" to her camera guy, then she said right to my face, "Asshole! This is way beyond you."

I said calmly, "I know it is."

I was let through only because of my association with Ronny. I had his breakfast order. It was getting cold fast. You don't piss off a guy like Ronny. And that's how I advanced down the gravel driveway, with impunity, outside of the law really. I felt this sudden power, a heightened awareness that I might be going to die. My last words before walking away from the cops were, "You want to send somebody out to my boss's house and check on things?" Pete looked at me, but I was finished with anything we ever had in the past.

It was a glorious morning of cold sunlight, like so many days we get at this time of year, cold, crisp autumnal light.

I got to the window, and Ronny said, "Get your ass in the window." There was genuine fear in his voice. Things had sifted into an image of bloodshed. Even for a guy like Ronny, dispossessed of everything, I guess there is something that makes him want to live at the back of it all. But it wasn't going to be that way. That was the fatalism Ronny was staring into. I could have dived to the side, made an attempt to escape. You figure, Ronny goes wild, stands up to shoot me, and the SWAT team takes him out. It could have gone that way, but there was nothing for me outside anymore. You see, I'd been out by Sam's house.

Sam had so many goddamn brochures on Florida it wasn't funny in that house of his. He had nothing else in the house, just a toaster oven. It was like the house was built to hold just the toaster oven and the brochures. His presence was just an afterthought. That's all the guy ever ate, toasted this and toasted that. Him and his god-damn special sauce and his tuna melts and cold beer and whiskey, the occasional cigar out at the bars. There wasn't a light on in the house. I went into the house, door not even locked or anything. You had to see that hallway, no decor, nothing, just a gray space with walls, cold. Sam saved every goddamn penny he ever made, then lost it over the last years keeping the paper going, sinking his own money when we had nobody placing advertising. I never heard that proper about him, but I figure that's where the money went, a guy with no kids or nothing, wearing the same shirts and pants, the same car from 1963. You could tell the house was just some place to sleep, nothing else, a lawn without flowers, the siding coming off in long sheets, the driveway cracked and worn, not a single affecta-tion, not one ornament, nothing, a sort of indifferent depravity. Mental illness is what you might have called it. In the kitchen, I saw the tabernacle of the gleaming toaster oven, a loaf of Wonder Bread and peanut butter set on the countertop. Maybe it's because I knew what was next that I just wanted Sam to say, one more time, "I'm taking orders here, Bill!"

Sam was in bed, at the end of a long hallway, a box of enclosed dark invaded by the smell of mothballs. It was night outside, maybe

two o'clock. The curtains were drawn. I heard cars going by, a television in some house, that topography of urban sound. The toilet
bowl gurgled, squat in the shadows.

   You get a feeling in a dead man's room, something like serenity
laced with sadness. It was like the breath had been taken out of the
room, a long exhalation. It was hard to breathe. I stood at the
threshold of the doorway, said his name softly, said it maybe a few
times, then I blessed myself. It smelled of cold damp linen too long
unwashed, the odor of socks. There was no point checking his
pulse. There was nothing I could do. I saw the bottle of pills, empty.
A suitcase beside the bed, forlorn. I got close enough to see his
hands crossed. His eyes were open, staring into the dark. His hands
were stiff and cold, like a saint's, maybe, in some church. He was
holding that picture of him out at Ed's place, standing before a
backdrop of beach. He had that tropical drink with an umbrella. I
guess he died staring into that picture. I like to think of him in
Florida, just maybe he got himself there in the end . . . I went downstairs, sat in his kitchen, cold and numb.

   I was crying without tears. What that man upstairs had been was
a storyteller, maybe that's what's lost today, lost on guys like me.
There was this story he told us once, back in the office, about how
he was covering one of those riots in the late sixties, when people
didn't know what the hell to make of this country. He got with this
girl who was saying her mother didn't understand her, that she and
her mother spoke a different language. So Sam said, how about if
he went along and covered an interview of the girl asking her
mother to understand her. And so it happened, according to Sam,
just like that. They met face-to-face and got to the problem in the
end, with the girl saying, "You're not a liberated woman, Mother!"
That's basically what the girl kept saying, "You're not a liberated
woman, Mother!" over and over again, until the mother said, "I
don't know what that means, 'liberated woman.' What does that
mean?" And the mother looked at Sam, and looked at the girl, who
was lost for words, and then the girl shouted, "You don't say *shit* or
fuck!" and the mother said softly, "That's true," and she waited just

a moment so she could maybe understand something, and then her head sort of nodded, and she said real soft, "No, I don't *say* them words, but I've *done* both." I mean, you knew it didn't happen like that, but what it did was make you understand something about the people out there. He brought them together in his own mind, gave you a key to understanding that we are basically the same. We just change our hairstyles and such things, but we can't escape that we are all the same.

I got on the phone in the kitchen. I spoke to an answering machine at Ed's place. I said, "Ed! There's something that always gave me the chills in all this. I know you smelled it, Ed. That smell of roses. You ever think about asking that woman you're with what the hell she said to Karl? You ask her what deal she made with the devil?" I knew they were there, listening.

Darlene picked up. She said very calmly, "I think we've all had enough of what you've done, Bill. We were speaking with Pete. He told us everything, Bill. All the things you told him." She left it that vague. "I want you out of our lives forever."

Ed got on the phone. His voice was shaky, like he'd been drinking. He said, "Bill, why did you break into our house? I think you need help, Bill."

I said simply, "Sam is dead, Ed."

There was no response, just a heavy sigh. Then Ed told Darlene Sam was dead, and the phone went dead in my ear.

Back home, I went outside and saw that someone had dug up the shears. I almost expected the cops to be right there, to take me on account of my prints on the shears . . .

You should have heard the cops and the FBI screaming at me to stay put as I started climbing into the window. Of course, they were just doing that because that was their job. But I'd decided to walk into this death trap. I was too much of a coward to just kill myself. Time had unhinged itself for me. I looked back into a sea of heads all wearing the visage of Ronny Lawton, the masked faces, effigies of madness. They were like a sect, the identical specter of horror and revulsion, pumping their fists, the incantation, "Ronny! Ronny! Ronny!" They were acting up for the camera. But I ignored them. I called out to Ronny, and the American flag came down, as did the picture of Charlie Lawton, and I disappeared into the room, went in to be with the remnants of the Lawton family, into the shrapnel of a new world, into the spliced images of bikini-clad women, movie stars, and rock musicians, into that cave of desire, into a moment transpiring on television.

I saw the real face of Ronny Lawton, staring at me, crouched down. He had the gun on me. Ronny had a small television. It lagged maybe twenty seconds behind. I saw myself getting in through the window, right there on TV. It was weird as hell, seeing that. It was like an out-of-body experience, totally disorienting. I handed the McDonald's breakfast as an offering, the penitent before the deity, Ronny Lawton. I sort of wished I'd bought myself a breakfast just then. I felt a sudden hunger rage inside me as Ronny uncocked the gun and took the breakfasts.

CHAPTER 17

Ronny pumped weights for going on an hour after breakfast. He tied my legs and hands when he worked out. He had the gun on his torso. He kept adding weight to the bar after every ten reps. There was a point when it seemed like he wasn't going to get that bar off his chest, just this one time when his face went purple, when the whole bench shook, and Ronny was trembling like it was all over. The gun fell off his torso. I thought about making a move, crawling wormlike toward the gun, but didn't. Ronny's estranged was looking between me and Ronny. I shook my head slowly. The gun was halfway between me and Ronny. Ronny's face was invisible, staring at the ceiling, at a galaxy of naked women, but you knew it was all contortion. He was suffocating, it seemed like, this hiss of breath, and then, from somewhere deep inside him, he found the strength, and up came the bar, real slowly, and Ronny got it onto the supports. He gave this grunt of effort. His feet stomped the floor. It was like looking at a guy who had literally lifted the weight of the world off his shoulders. He was huge in the aftermath of that lift, engorged by blood, a veneer of sweat on his bulging muscles. The veins in his forehead throbbed. His legs were like sticks next to the massive growth of his naked torso when he stood up. He looked at his kid. He made each pec move independently. The kid was squeezing the cold egg from the breakfast in his small hands. He had jelly all over his face. I mean, the kid didn't know anything. Ronny bent down, and the kid made this cooing noise. His small hand touched Ronny. It was nice just looking at the kid. Ronny turned and did the same thing to his estranged, moved his nipple and just smiled, then he did the same for me, the twitch of the dark small nipple in his plate of armor. He looked at me real serious. He said, "You ever see anything like it?"

I said honestly, "No, I haven't."

The morning somehow passed into midday. Ronny untied me, untied his estranged. The kid had gone in his diaper. It smelled real bad. Ronny's estranged got the diaper off the kid, and Ronny took it and pitched it out the window. An FBI sniper shot the diaper in midair. Maybe he thought it was a bomb or something. We saw it on television. I mean, it got us laughing our asses off. Even the kid was laughing, even though he didn't understand what the hell was going on. Fear and laughter is like a contagion, when you get wound up like this. The whole place was a riot of sound and shouting outside. In the end, Ronny had me say what it was to the cops. I said, "It's nothing but the kid's shit!" Still, it was just left there for a hell of a long time.

What I said pissed off the FBI guy in charge. He denied a request for hamburgers. That's when Ronny took me to the window, and he put a gun under my chin and said he was going to kill me.

We ordered Burger King. Ronny requested a crown from Burger King.

I wrote on a piece of paper that we were being recorded. Ronny nodded. He shouted, "You come near me, and they all die! You hear me?"

There was no response.

The burgers came, and out I went through the window. Ronny had the gun trained on me. The diaper was still there in the yard. Pete came forward, and we made the exchange. I liked humiliating him like that. I put on the Burger King hat, just for the hell of it. Maybe it was some sort of euphoria. I don't really know, but it got the cult of Ronnys going wild. Pete was left holding the diaper of shit. I mean, it's not every day you get to give someone a bag of shit. Pete was pissed. He said, "I guess this is what you wanted all along."

I said, "How do you mean?"

"Like father, like son. You want Ronny to pull the trigger on you. You want to end it, like your old man." Pete turned his fat cinched ass and walked away from me.

Inside, Ronny set the crown on his own head. The kid started tightening his fists in a contraction of laughter. Ronny was prancing around the room, hopping from one leg to another.

Ronny's estranged said, "Shit never changes, does it?" It was the first thing I'd heard her say all day.

Ronny said, "No, it don't. You're still the same bitch you always was."

That stopped Ronny's antics. But he kept the crown on his head. I think he basically forgot he had it on.

Food has a way of making you tired. We ate and began a long silence, save for the flow of music coming from the small cassette player turned down real low. Ronny seemed to drift but caught himself. He shouted, "I ain't asleep!" in defiance to the microphone listening in on us. "I ain't asleep!" He set himself with me and his estranged shielding him, put us in the line of fire. I was facing Ronny, his estranged was facing outward. He got her tied up again, her hands tied and connected to her ankles. She sort of bent forward, resting her head on her knee. Her long hair fell in a wall down over her shins. From time to time she said, "Ronny, put my hair behind my ear like you used to." And Ronny did it, swept her hair off to the side of her head. Sometimes she was crying without sound, her eyes all wet, and her knees wet as well. It was hard looking into her eyes. There was something primitive and sad about her. It was like she had accepted that, just maybe, she was going to die here today. When she caught me staring at her, she closed her eyes, like she wanted me to disappear.

Ronny spoke close to my ear, like I was hearing confession, on account of the microphone outside. Out of the blue, he said, "I had a dog called Lucky once. She can tell you, that's the God's honest truth."

Ronny was speaking and smoking, and the smoke was coming out of his mouth while he talked. He had the kid cradled against his chest. "That was the dumbest-ass name to put on a dog. You tempt fate with a name like that. That dog had the worst of it with luck. Shit, it got caught up in a thresher once, lost a leg, then it died under the wheel of a car, not a year later." Ronny leaned forward and whispered, "That dog was anything but lucky!" He shook his head slow, the crown still on his head, the kid with his eyes closed. And then Ronny shouted, "I ain't asleep!" and the kid jerked alive and started screaming, and Ronny had to quiet him again. He said, not in a scream, but loud enough for the microphone to catch it, "I got a kid here that needs to sleep. I ain't going to keep telling you I'm not sleeping, because I ain't sleeping now, and I ain't going to be doing any sleeping, so don't get any ideas."

The room fell into a shade of gray, the light outside defining our enclosure. The mumble of the crowd lay at the edge of consciousness, right there after the voice of Duke Ellington singing to us from the cassette player. Ronny was near exhaustion. The yawns came closer and closer together, the tired snap of his jaw, his eyes watering.

His estranged said softly, "I gotta go real bad, Ronny."

The door to the hallway was barricaded with a dresser. Ronny seemed to look around for something she could go in, but there was nothing, until he said, "What about the McDonald's bag?" His estranged said calmly, "I don't mind you got me here, Ronny, but I ain't going in any goddamn bag. You'll have to kill me first."

Ronny said, "If you want to make the choice for me, that makes it all the easier." But he didn't kill her.

I got the job of talking to them. I spoke to the ubiquitous microphone recording us, and then the phone rang in the room, and it was the first time we were really speaking with the FBI guy. It was agreed Ronny's estranged could go down the hallway and come back. Ronny said he'd kill the kid or her if anything happened. And so, Ronny got the dresser moved, untied his estranged like he was undoing a present, and she walked out the door into the dark hallway. And we waited. For a while I thought she wasn't coming back. Ronny had the gun up against the kid's face. Ronny was still wearing the crown. The kid was staring up at Ronny, his small hands around the gun, his mouth trying to suckle the barrel. Ronny's whole arm was shaking, like he just might do it, if something went wrong. It seemed like forever before we heard the distant rumble of the toilet flush, the knock of old pipes. And there she was again, right back with us. She had brushed her hair and washed her face. She smelled of soap. Ronny looked at her.

The dresser went back against the door, and we resumed the evening with our demand for food from Burger King again.

I went out the window when the food arrived. An FBI guy said, "The food's drugged."

Ronny shouted, "I want a receipt. They got a receipt, Bill?"

They didn't have a receipt, and Ronny blew a gasket.

I got back in through the window and told Ronny the food was drugged anyway, whispered it into his ear. Ronny was pissed. He tied me up again. He threw the food out the window, said nothing. But he kept the crowns. By night, we were all kings and queens in the fiefdom of Ronny Lawton's insane asylum.

The kid was back in his small cage, and Ronny went at the weights again. He was whining like an animal.

I lay tied up on the floor, but I managed to turn myself and look at Ronny's estranged. She said simply, "There was no face left on Karl." Her eyes were filled with tears. It was one of the few things she got to say.

Ronny shouted, "Goddamn it, shut it, Teri!" Ronny finished and crawled back behind us, curled up with his kid.

You got a feeling things were coming to an end.

The phone rang. The FBI guy wanted Ronny to release the kid. Ronny shouted, "You want me to just kill them all right now? Do you? Maybe you haven't got it yet, shit for brains. I got the kid in here. I'm calling the shots, you hear me? Do you?" He just hung up the phone. The sense of hysteria smelled inside the room, the stench of fear. Ronny looked like shit. His shoulders hunched forward, the thick stalk of his neck huge and swollen. The phone rang again. Ronny shouted again, "How much goddamn money does it cost to kill me? How come I could never get my hands on that type of money when I needed it? How much goddamn money you spending on trying to kill me now?"

The FBI was saying something on their end of the phone.

"How much goddamn money you spending on trying to kill me? I asked you a goddamn question, asshole!" Ronny just burst into tears. He started talking about Charlie, about his mother, and what it did to her to have her elder son killed like that.

I said to Ronny, I said it a few times before I got his attention, "You stay there, and they'll line a shot up and blow your head off."

Ronny just hung up the line and got down low and came back behind me and his estranged. The kid was crying softly, like it needed to eat.

Ronny was still whining, shaking from the affliction of knowing he was going to die. I think it got harder to reconcile himself to that the longer he stayed alive. That's what the experts outside knew. The euphoria of killing and trying to escape was getting drained, leaving just the cold fact that Ronny was going to die. You could see Ronny was thinking he wanted to live, that awful look of pain in his face.

Ronny untied me, and I got up, and light outside showed only cops. I told him that, said the people had been cleared back.

Again, the intense solitude. Ronny was trembling. He smelled ripe, the odor of armpits and fatigue. He had his hands crossed on his knees, the enigmatic NOWHERE showing. He was searching for some way out. But his mind was just rambling. He leaned forward to me, whispered, "Right here in this house, I seen a man walk on the moon on the television." His estranged sort of leaned back into Ronny. She was still tied up. Ronny gave in to her that much, touched her forehead, pushed the hair off her face. She had her eyes closed. She said, "That was before Charlie went off to Vietnam, right? You were watching TV here with your ma and Charlie?"

Ronny said real soft, "Don't get ahead of me, Teri."

Ronny looked at me through the slate dark. He had the kid in the cage right beside us. The kid's eyes were wide open, but it didn't say anything for a bit, stayed quiet.

Ronny got to talking. "That's right, here in this house, we watched men walk on the moon, and, I tell you honestly, it didn't mean shit to me or my folks seeing a man up there on the moon. We went to bed that night, and it was like an empty feeling inside. I was with my mother and Charlie, and we had us coffee and cake in the kitchen after seeing the television, and my mother said, 'There's things that ain't worth knowing. Maybe that's what people got to learn in this life.' It was right before Charlie went off to Vietnam."

Ronny's estranged said, "See, I told you so."

Ronny rolled his eyes. "You mind if I tell it my way, Teri?" His hand lay softly on his estranged's shoulder. She said, "No, I don't mind, Ronny."

"You see, we had us a *National Geographic* on the kitchen table that my mother looked at each night, showing me where Charlie was going. We was looking between Vietnam and the moon in the window that night. It was like the longest journey your mind could take. We looked out the window before going on up to bed, and there was the moon, all big and round, but there weren't no mystery about it, there weren't no cow jumping over the moon, or no Man in the Moon. It weren't made of cheese. It was like every story you heard about the moon was all dead." He laced his hands together.

Ronny's estranged was staring at Ronny. At some stage, you knew she had loved him. He had something sad inside him, something that attracts women.

The kid made a cooing noise as Ronny talked.

Ronny's face was dark. He caught up with the train of his thoughts again. "It was like we had lost a sense of what it is to live inside . . . inside what's around us, to stay near home and work. It wasn't long ago there was people round these parts that went nowheres, stayed put where they was and lived by and by. But you can't no more." He put his lips on his estranged's shoulder, crying inside of himself.

I saw her eyes open and look at me.

Ronny was moving slowly toward some destination. "You tell me what my brother Charlie died for? I never did hear anybody explain it right. There was kids that said he deserved what he got. They was saying at school that he killed babies over there, and raped women. But I can swear on any Bible here that Charlie wasn't like that!" He stopped and drew his breath.

Ronny's estranged said, "Charlie was going to work with his father at the car plant, but he got drafted, and he didn't run off and hide or nothing. He showed up and went over there to Vietnam. Ain't that right, Ronny?"

Ronny said quietly, "He believed in this country." He looked at me. "Was anything ever settled over there?" He shook his head vigorously, his arm extended toward the wall, toward the glow of light outside, to the small shrine of the American flag and picture of Charlie. Ronny stopped talking, and then he said abruptly, "Tell me what you think is on the other side of life?" He had the gun by his side.

I didn't get to answer.

Ronny's estranged said softly, "You're talking crazy, Ronny."

Ronny said, "No, I'm not." He looked at me. "You think my mother and my brother and my father is going to be over there, sitting down to supper like we did out here? You think my baby sister is going to be on the other side?" Ronny said, "You got to wonder what age they are all going to be. I never quite figured how we might all look, now that it comes right down to it."

I said, "Maybe we see them as we want to see them."

"Maybe . . ." That held Ronny's attention for a moment. His face squinted. It was like being inside the labyrinth of Ronny's mind, that dark closure of the room spliced and cut in a collage of memory, the shrapnel of some imploding reality, the large tits of women hanging from posters, the bombshells of sexuality and desire. Ronny turned and felt the vague hint of an exterior reality in the soft glow of lights outside the window, the static hiss of a CB in a car, the FBI closing in around him, military maneuvers. Ronny breathed deep and long, the picture of Charlie back in the window, that small grotto of patriotism.

Ronny looked at me with a frank exhaustion, like he was settling things. He said flatly, "I figure, she don't deserve the house."

Ronny's estranged twitched slightly, still leaning against Ronny. I averted my eyes, hoped she'd keep her mouth shut. Ronny was wandering around a way of killing her and the kid, trying to get the courage to do that. You could see that taking shape. He stood up, and his body creaked. He took his chin in his palm and turned his head until it made a snap, then he turned his head the other way and did the same. The crown on his head tipped, and he repositioned it again. He half smiled. It eased the tension for half a second.

Ronny went and looked down on his kid. I think Ronny was crying inside. He said, "You had to see how she had him out there in that trailer. I got there, and the kid was locked up. They were out most of the night, came back all tanked up. I seen Karl get out of the car. I followed him into the trailer. He was so shit-faced drunk, he didn't flinch or nothing when he saw me. I went right up to his face. He opened his mouth, like he had something real important to say, but I said it for him. You had to see the way he just walked around, stumbling back outside like he was too drunk to die. I just waited. She was screaming her ass off. I heard him still walking around. I thought I was going to have to go out there and maybe finish things, but it ended just like that. He got to the car and just died."

I stared into the lax darkness of fatigue in Ronny's face. He took the kid into his arms, pressed the kid against his big chest. Ronny touched the Burger King crown. We all were wearing the crowns, for that matter. That's what made it all the more pathetic and sad. Ronny kept talking, in a sort of whine. "That Karl wasn't worth pissing on. I swear to God! You think I'm going to let a kid of mine grow up like that, with her treating him like an animal?" Ronny had the gun cocked. He took the gun to the kid's head, kept saying, "What the hell am I going to do with my kid?" Everything exploded just like that.

Ronny's estranged was crying, still tied up. She said, "Don't, Ronny."

"Don't, Ronny, what? I got to do this. It ain't the kid. There's nothing for it!" His voice was full of tears.

I shouted, "You want to give me that kid?"

Ronny was panting. The kid was holding the barrel of the gun.

"I got the money, Ronny."

It stopped Ronny for a moment. He was panting between his breaths, the kid holding the barrel of the gun.

I said, "You ever hear of King Solomon?"

Ronny didn't answer, just looked at me. He went down on his haunches. The phone rang. It rang for going on a minute. "You speak to them!" Ronny shouted. "You tell them I'm not far off killing everybody if it comes to it." He put his hand to his forehead. "No, you tell them I want a Ford Mustang. I want out of here!" The phone was ringing all the time he was talking.

I picked it up, and the FBI guy knew it was me, because Ronny was still talking in the background. The FBI guy said, "Get him near the window. Tell him we might be able to get him a car. But we have to speak with him."

I said, "Fuck you!" and hung up.

Ronny looked at me. "What the hell was that?"

"They want to kill you."

Ronny just nodded his head and got real still. He had the gun to the kid's head.

I said, "Ronny, I was telling you about this King Solomon."

Ronny seemed distracted, looked at the window. He had me come and get with his estranged, and we encircled him.

In the tight intimacy of sweat and fear, I whispered, "You see, way back in Old Testament times, there was this King Solomon, who was known as the wisest king that ever lived. He was always fixing things between people. Well, one day, two women came to him saying they both owned this baby. They each gave their account of how it was their baby. But the king sat there, and he couldn't decide who really owned the kid, so he said, 'I just can't figure things, so I'll have to cut the baby in half, and you each get a half. That's the only fair thing to do.' But one of the women started crying and said, 'No, give her the baby. Don't kill my baby like that, please! Give her my baby.' And, of course, the king, who was the

wisest of kings, knew right then who really owned the baby. You
don't let your own kid get cut in two. The mother knew, it was better that the kid live and the mother never see it again . . ."

Ronny had his hand on the kid's small head. Ronny put his lips
to the kid's head. He stayed down, closed up into himself with the
kid.

"You got to choose, Ronny." We were like a dark wreath, pressed
into the corner of the room. Outside, you could hear noise.

He looked up with glazed eyes, mumbling something. "You serious about keeping the kid?"

I nodded.

Ronny was still not buying it all the way. His head was moving
perceptibly. He took shallow breaths. He reached and touched me
with the gun, put it under my chin. "I hope the hell this isn't just
about her, 'cause she'd leave you in a second. I been there with her,
and she got a mind of her own when it comes to men. I ain't even
saying it's her fault. It's just something deep inside her."

I felt myself flinch, like this was the only way I could get to
Ronny's estranged. I was conscious of the microphone picking up
everything, the sound of my voice low and shaky. They had to
know what I did outside, how I called my girlfriend the way I did,
shouting out those questions to her. But I put that aside. I said,
"This isn't about her, Ronny. It's about what we talked about, about
men like Elvis's father and mother getting together to make something special. Maybe that kid doesn't have to die out here, Ronny."

"Maybe." He looked at his estranged, the smallness of her figure
curled up. He was shaking his head. "How 'bout I take her with me,
save you the trouble she could bring you?"

I said, "How 'bout you let her live?"

Ronny said, "I'd be doing you a favor, really I would." Ronny had
this horrible fatalistic look, the words just dribbling out of his
mouth. "How come everybody else knows what's best for us, except
ourselves. I'm telling you, she's going to get under your skin. You're
going to be thinking, 'I should have let old Ronny kill her when he
offered.' I just know I'd be doing you a favor."

I didn't say anything.

Ronny's estranged was moving like a grub on the floor. I think Ronny got some pleasure in taking the gun to the back of her neck. He pushed the hair aside, obscured her face, and pressed the gun into the nape of her neck. "It really isn't any trouble at all, if you change your mind. Maybe I could arrange for you to go see Karl? You want a one-way ticket to see him, Teri?"

It was all being recorded out there. I felt an attack was imminent. But things got quiet. I shouted, "We need some more time in here!"

It was the last words we spoke for a while. The kid seemed to find his own destiny. His small head went down on Ronny's chest and found Ronny's mannish nipple. It was something to see the sudden look in Ronny's face. The kid stayed that way a long time. I shut my eyes and curled up on the floor, feeling cold.

In the end, Ronny leaned down and whispered into my ear that there was a way out. He pulled back the carpet from a corner by the door, and there it was, a square trapdoor. Ronny put a finger to his lips. His eyebrows arched. We were still tied up, me and Ronny's estranged.

Ronny came and sat beside me, whispered again into my ear that there was a passage down there that led out to a barn out back of the property. He did something real creepy, put his arm around me. I felt the hot meat of his arm, the stench of his armpit. It was like something sad was passing between us. Maybe we all need that in the end, the sense of touch. I knew I was with a dead man.

"Ain't like any of us Lawton men ever got to consecrated ground. We sort of just disappeared." He said it soft in my ear, the heavy hotness of fear, almost confessional. "I guess we find our way in the end."

In the final moments of his existence, Ronny held his son in his arms, rocked the kid gently. Ronny had the crown on his head, the benevolent king of losers decreeing our freedom. He untied me. I stood up and stretched. I mean, it was surreal. Ronny's estranged uncurled herself and stood up and said nothing. She was looking at the dark hole that led to our freedom.

Ronny was all business in the end. He said softly, "I got a ten-speed I want to will the kid. And I want him to get my plaque. I want him to know I wasn't afraid of work." He had me transcribe the items he was leaving to his kid on a piece of the Burger King bag, and he signed it, and I signed it. "It's out by the barn. Just make sure he gets it sometime. It's been hardly ridden. All you got to do is oil it now and then. But you got to oil it."

Everything was orchestrated in silence after that, except Ronny couldn't resist saying just one more time, "I could just as easy blow her head off for you." But his estranged was the first down into the dark, beginning her long escape. She went down without the kid.

I looked at Ronny one last time. I said softly, "Where's your old man, Ronny?"

He never did answer. He just brought the hands together again, the enigmatic NOWHERE showing. He closed the trapdoor and submerged us wholly into dark. The kid began to cry, stiff in my arms. That's all you heard was the crying, the fervor of terror in the kid's voice. I was going "Shoo, shoo" to the kid, but we were down deep enough that sound was trapped.

It was a rudimentary passageway. It took us ages to move through the passage, groping forward, Ronny's estranged holding my belt, edging through the dark. And so, we began our resurrection, through the dark tunnel of this obscure world. We came up in the end, into an abandoned barn, ramshackle. In the distance, the house was aflame, a great bonfire lighting up the night. Ronny's estranged said, "Goddammit," under her breath. She looked at me, "You think I'm entitled to Karl's trailer?"

I didn't answer her. We walked out of the dead cornfields to the edge of the road. I went back, and in the commotion of dark and flame, I got my car, turned it away from the flames, and in the obscurity of the night, we disappeared.

CHAPTER 18

I went for the solitude of the north with them, along a narrow dirt road that led way back into the woods and ended at my family's small cottage. It was a place my father took me as a kid to fish.

It smelled of tar and moss, a crisp fragrance of cold dew up this far north. Winter was here, a coat of snow on the hills. There was nothing out here at the cottage save the woods, no people, a town thirty miles back. It was just the open coldness of the north, the still blue of our lake, immense and flat with its secret passageways, small tributaries, and backwoods pools as yet unnamed, lapping black waters. We hardly said anything at all in those first days of hibernation, those days of reclaiming our lives. Ronny's estranged had me sleep with her and the kid in my father's bed. She had the kid pressed against herself, and she sort of leaned back into me, set her back and small buttocks against me, received the warmth of my flesh against her. We were fitting together, a dark, secret warmth, the jigsaw of our anatomy lined up and made to fit together. In the background, we had the radio on real low. I awoke at times to the enigma of our own deaths, the voice of Linda Carter explaining how we had all been burned to death.

I had dreams those first nights, images of flames, a pyre of smoke, the ritualistic flame of Ronny Lawton's self-cremation out at his house. I saw him staring from the window, with the flames licking the walls. It was like seeing clips of those bald monks during the Vietnam War who set themselves on fire, the profound sacrifice.

It was my father's old garden that occupied my time over the first days. I pulled away at the dark web of matted roots in the overgrown garden, felt the cold, hard tumors of potatoes and parsnips, the bulbs of small onions, things that go on seeding and existing long after a gardener has gone. I felt the legacy of my father's work. He was out here still in a way, in the growth of things planted, the quiet longing for solitude that had so escaped him all his life. I worked slowly and methodically. I wanted it that way.

My body smoked in the coldness of the dying evening light as I kept digging. I felt the bite of the shovel upturning the roots, felt the pressure of my spine. I sought out stillness and solitude as much as the cold roots, felt the beat of my pulse in my temples. It was a simple satisfaction that any man who has ever planted must feel, the abiding metronome of seasonal change, ticked off in silence, the sacred contract of simple living, knowing things will take their natural course, that there are laws governing all things. It is how I remembered my father, out here in fall and winter, letting a beard take shape on his face, the dark growth of sprouting hair, the emergence of the dormant simplicity, the lack of language, of words that were so lacking in him all his life. I watched the transformation, the abatement of sound for a simple nodding contentment, the movement of his fingers fixing a fishing line, threading a hook. He was all hands at his essence, the crescent of dirt at the fingertips, the blunted roundness of his hands inherited from some distant lineage. You could see the peasant face emerge against the shift of light, a man wanting little in life, just stillness and the essential food to sustain life.

That was the horror my grandfather endured, the sight of his own son incapable of continuing what the father had begun, retreating into what my grandfather had escaped. In the dark interlude of those long-gone years, my father hunkered down during my childhood for long weeks here at the cabin, took me with him, usually in deep winter, us frozen off from the world, the fracturing sound of ice breaking tree limbs, my father dressing in furs, leaving me alone while he went off hunting deer out in the woods. He left me alone for days sometimes, emerging again with a dead deer, which he skinned in the cabin, curing the meat, smoking it on hooks, feeding me the soft warmth of animal innards with salt and onions and fried potatoes along with potato soup by candlelight, while, hundreds of miles away, our factory rang out twenty-four hours a day with the clang of metal and grunt of sweating men.

It was that essential incongruity between my grandfather and father which crippled me, the extremes, the quiet times of hibernation alongside my father, the distant look he had of staring back to some primeval existence, poking the fire, eating sizzling meat smoked and blackened, the slurping sound of taking tea so boiling hot it burned the tongue. I ate those meals in my father's company. I used to watch his twitching anxiety of wanting all this to sustain him out here, that blurred primordial vision experienced for brief moments against reality, the confines of the cabin a time capsule, my father slowly enumerating the things that were essential for mere existence, the things he had procured against the coldness of the season, the chopped wood, the jars of preserves, the wax sheets of honeycomb, the salted jerky deer meat, dried sockeye, the cold bunker of potatoes and onions and garlic. In the face of my grandfather's rebuke, when he came and found us hiding, my father answered simply, "I have heard Albert Einstein say World War Four will be fought with sticks and stones. I am just preparing for the inevitable."

At night, Ronny's estranged paged through a catalogue by the fire. To let her bathe, I boiled a cauldron of water, used a bellows under the fire, got the flames glowing. She took off her robe and let the light burnish her nakedness. She put her hair up in a bun. Outside, I could see the constellation of sparks from the chimney rising into the inky darkness. Way up here in the north, we existed in a fold in history, a wrinkle in time where evolution had not yet created mankind.

When she emerged, she was glazed against the fire, the softness of her flesh there before me. She let me put a towel around her. I remember the soft sucking sound of her feet against the floor as she went and stood before the fireplace, the way she shuddered and wanted me to hold her. She liked me looking at her body. You could see that.

I lit a hurricane lamp against the outside dark, tempered the flame so it assuaged the dark, but just barely, in a soft yellowish tongue. I rubbed the wounds of her captivity, the raw marks from the rope burns around her ankles and wrists. Then we played backgammon at night, for nickels, and for things in the catalogue, which she marked as things she wanted. She wanted so many things. But I wanted it that way.

On the fifth day, it was known we had survived the fire, that we had escaped through the tunnel. We had maybe a day before we were discovered. I stopped for the first time in all of this and realized that what everybody had wanted all along was for Ronny Lawton to die. He had killed his old man, it was as simple as that. I spent a day reconciling that in my head and couldn't make myself believe it. I tried to put it out of my head, all of it. It was all finished. And yet there was some fatalism Ronny showed out at the house before he died, like he had been pushed to sacrifice himself in the end, like he was fulfilling a prophecy of the damned.

But there's an old saying, the killer is the last one standing. When you looked at it that way, you were left looking at Darlene. I won't say she killed Ronny Lawton's old man. I don't see that, but somehow, she set things in motion, put the word in Karl's ear about how Ronny's estranged wasn't getting the house until the two Lawtons were out of the picture. I could see Darlene laying out the facts, pushing Karl toward the inevitable.

It hurt my head just thinking of how it might have transpired, the thread of deception, pitting men against one another. You had to think, who had the vision, the brains, to pull off a plot like that, where all the principal men implicated with Ronny's estranged would kill one another in a domino effect of fate?

Somehow there was a complicity out there with the women at Darlene's beauty parlor, some synod of moral reckoning, women meeting in a garage, painting themselves in ritualistic ceremony, a

cult, those other Keepers of Truth, with their roll call of the dispossessed and injured, the abused, the raped, the litany of wrongs
committed against women. When you looked into that parlor, you
were looking into the apparatus of the female psyche, the under-
ground resistance, the triage of longing, women rescued from the
hell of abuse.

Ronny's estranged had been raped and abandoned and beaten
by those men, and all the women knew it, and yet they said nothing
to those outside their sex, kept the secret within the dominion of
women, understood that to say anything would stigmatize Ronny's
estranged as a soiled woman, make her undesirable to men, and
make the kid a bastard.

You only had to look at the name of Darlene's beauty parlor,
Curl Up and Dye, to see the subliminal meaning that this was far
more than a place to get a haircut. That's where I wanted to go, to
the semantics of language, to the irony of meaning, to unlock the
code. I was a man of interpretation, the last of the Keepers of Truth.
Or just maybe I was full of shit.

I had to keep myself from going on like that, rescue myself from
the psychosis of logic that has shaped my destiny these past years.
Out there in the cold, I split a cord of wood, withdrew to a more
primitive language of grunting effort, feeling the hot sweat on my
back. I said to myself, "You must stop yourself from looking into
things. You can only survive at the surface of meaning. There is a
woman in there, and a kid that needs you." I needed that jolt of
reality, or responsibility, to rescue me.

Over those nights of playing backgammon, Ronny's estranged
had a lot of stuff she wanted from the catalogue. She kept a list of
what I had to buy her. She made me swear I'd send away for all of
the stuff. And I swore I would get her all the things she deserved.

We went down and baptized the kid on that fifth day, the day we
had been resurrected from anonymity. A fog was descending,
invading the water, making it smoke, a white, shapeless sun on the
horizon. It was snowing without sound, a tranquillity without language. A loon took flight, the splash of water somewhere deep in

the fog. I took the kid out into the smoking water, pinched his nose, and took him under. He came up screaming across the water, a sound that wandered into the fog and was lost forever.

We had agreed to move away, to rename the kid, to tell him nothing of his past. It was almost a small experiment, reclaiming this child, this small consumer of fast food.

Ronny's estranged had the catalogue in her hands. She'd seen something that she "had to have." The catalogue had taken on the aura of a sacred text. I called it *The Book of Wants,* but she looked at me the way maybe religious fanatics look at you for refuting the existence of God.

I said simply, "Can I read you something?"

She looked at me, said, "What?" with such an air of disaffection. She wanted me to go to the nearest town and place her orders. She got herself into a state and cried and got the kid and said she knew I hated her really.

I said, "You know that's not true."

After a time, I read a passage from my father's worn copy of Thoreau. I said softly, "An honest man has hardly need to count more than his ten fingers, or in extreme cases he may add his ten toes, and lump the rest. Simplicity, simplicity, simplicity! I say, let your affairs be as two or three, and not a hundred or a thousand . . . keep your accounts on your thumb nail."

She just blurted out, "They got a toll-free number to call. It won't cost you a dime, Bill."

I said, "We'll call."

"You swear on it, Bill?"

"I swear on it."

We got the car packed again, set out before anybody showed up, headed farther north, to a place more remote, a road that funneled into a stark scar deep in the forest, way up to a cabin at the top of the Great Lakes. It was a place where the sky takes its mood from the general gloom of forests that merge into forests that merge into a general wilderness. Up there were the still lakes, huge spheres of still obsidian that stare into the heavens, the eyes of our continent that contemplate the cosmos above. I wanted that stillness before humanity, that place from which storms came, that dark continent of vegetation and wilderness, that last breath of an Ice Age. It was a place to disappear into for a time, to keep hiding until I figured something out.

In a small diner, we ate hotcakes with glazed apples and real cream. It was good, that taste. I filled up on coffee for the journey. It was a long drive. Ronny's estranged wanted fudge. It said the fudge here was world famous. That was enough for Ronny's estranged. She had to have it. I gave her the money and she went off.

It was over, all of it. I kept telling myself that. But then I got thinking about those shears Pete had, with my prints. It was the one loose end, the thing that tied me to Old Man Lawton's murder, something Pete and Ed and Darlene had over me. That scared the hell out of me, them having the upper hand on me like that.

I couldn't stop myself from calling Pete. I had the kid in one arm and the phone against my ear. Pete shouted, "What the hell are you doing?"

I said simply, "We don't want anything but to be left alone, Pete. It's over."

Pete said, "Don't call me anymore, ever."

I said, "What about those shears, Pete?"

Pete said simply, "There were no shears. Ronny Lawton killed his old man, and that's all there ever was to this case. End of story! You hear me, Bill? But if you want to make something of it, then just maybe them shears will show up again. You understand me?"

I didn't get to answer. I heard the phone go dead in my ear. I stayed holding the receiver, but that was it. Things had folded in on themselves. Things had been preordained way back at the beginning of all this. Ronny Lawton killed his old man. That was the lore that would be passed on, the truth that all abided by in the end.

I stood there, and my eyes found another one of those Employee of the Month plaques on the wall near the phone. It made me smile for a moment, remembering Ronny, how it touched something inside him, how he said, unaware of the irony, there wasn't anyplace to go but down after you got to be Employee of the Month. It was getting to be like that all over, this new currency of appreciation, where you didn't get a raise. What you got were accolades, awards, and certificates of merit, your name up on a neon sign or on a plaque. It was weird as hell, how it meant so goddamn much to them, how money was eclipsed by a need for respect, an insatiable need to be honored. People were being robbed of a decent living, but they didn't even seem to understand that. Managers and trainee managers were presenting so many goddamn certificates and plaques, it was just plain hard to complain. People were being appreciated and honored every time they opened their mouths. I could see right there that we were moving toward some other destiny, that revolution was never coming. Or maybe it was happening right under our noses, a silent revolution from within. As in days of old, we bestowed titles upon ourselves. The revolution of semantics, of language, had already won the war. Our Orwellian nightmare had arrived, the newsspeak of postindustrialism. Who among us was equipped to understand that serf and prole were now manager, or trainee manager, in this world?

I sat back down again and set the kid in his baby chair. I felt that giddy sensation of dissociation, like I was outside things. It's hard to stare into the essence of things the way I do.

And then I felt this euphoria of freedom, just knowing things were over, that I was escaping for a time, fill my head. I think I might even have been laughing, because the waitress looked over at me. Yeah, I was laughing out loud. I had to stop myself. I drank more coffee and felt what it's like to be free of all burdens for the first time in ages, to feel the pressure inside my head ease. I put my hands to my face, and there were tears in my eyes. I couldn't stop things for a time, then wiped my eyes and took a few deep breaths. It was all over. The kid pawed at me, making his unintelligible sounds. He thought I was playing peekaboo, hiding my face like that. It was nice having him there with me like that, so I played with him like he was my own kid.

In the far corner of the diner, I watched a man playing some new game. The machine was making all sorts of noise. The kid kept looking over there. He wanted to see what was going on. And so we went over there, the kid in my arms. The guy was working a lever control, giving the illusion of a man working machinery. I got up close and stared into the screen, stared into the future is more like it, felt this strange clairvoyance in the glass. I mean, right there before me was this voracious head opening and closing its mouth, this consumer of all things, racing around a maze, frantically eating everything. The guy was working the controls real fast. He was oblivious to my presence, totally engrossed. The kid dug his nails into my arms. The noise was driving him wild. He wanted a turn. And so we waited a long time, until the guy left.

I mean, you've never seen a kid take to a game so quickly. He seemed to understand the fundamental concept of consumption. Ronny's estranged got in on the act. She pushed me aside, gave me the world-famous fudge to hold, so it was just her and the kid working the controls.

I went and had more coffee, and I watched Ronny's estranged and the kid. It was maybe the first time she had really held the kid in all the days since we'd disappeared. I was just shaking my head, the prophetic destiny of our future encoded in a game, the distillation of capitalism in the demigod they called Pac-Man.

The flat-footed waitress came and set the check down before me. I could see she half-recognized me from the television. She kept looking at me and Ronny's estranged and the kid. Things were settling for her that we were the missing people. Our eyes locked for a moment, and then she knew.

I left some bills on the table and got Ronny's estranged away from the machine, and we drove off.

At the last town before the end of civilization, at the request of my beloved, I pulled up by a roadside phone, and I recited from *The Book of Wants*. She was holding my arm like she adored me. I think she really did. She put her tongue in my ear. It felt wet and hot, full of desire. She had her hand on my thigh. And just maybe it was enough for me. I hadn't fully decided yet.

EPILOGUE

The corpse of Ronny Lawton's father was never found, his death remains a mystery, unsolved. He is surely out there, because we do not entirely disappear. It is a mathematical law. Mass is neither created nor destroyed. But where is he?

When is the moment of death, of extinction? Isn't that the ethereal nature of history, of epochs, of evolution, of transformation and mutation, the mystery of how we crawled as single-celled organisms from some primordial sea to build cars and refrigerators? But still, you persist. Who killed Ronny Lawton's father? You might as well ask what one event closed our factories, what one event killed our town? How did we one day abandon our assembly lines, stop bending metal into the shapes of cars and appliances? Why did we walk away from the means of production, stop doing things with our hands? There are numerous factors, numerous suspects, but there are no convictions likely.

About the Author

Michael Collins was born in Limerick, Ireland, and now lives in Seattle, Washington. His first book, *The Man Who Dreamt of Lobsters*, was a *New York Times* Notable Book of the Year in 1993. Michael Collins received his Ph.D. from the University of Illinois in Chicago.